HEYWOOD HERBALIST COZY MYSTERIES: BOOKS 4-6

A CONTEMPORARY SMALL TOWN COZY MYSTERY

HEYWOOD HERBALIST COZY MYSTERIES

CARLY WINTER

WESTWARD PUBLISHING / CARLY FALL, LLC

ABOUT THE BOOK

In books 4-6 of this cozy mystery box set, disgraced soap opera star and amateur sleuth, Samantha Rathbone, continues to navigate her new life in a small town and solve the pesky murders that keep happening with the help of her quirky friends... and one cute cop.

Mistletoe and Mayhem: Deck the Halls... with a dead body?

When Mrs. Claus is found murdered days before the Annual Heywood Christmas Festival, Sheriff Mallory Richards cancels the beloved event.

As the flu takes out the whole sheriff's department—except for Deputy Jordan Branson—he begs Sam to help him find the killer.

She and Annabelle set out to catch the murderer but land themselves in a tangled web of deception and danger.

Will they be able to find the killer and save the Christmas Festival, or will Sam and Annabelle get too close to the truth and end up silenced?

Thyme and Trouble: Her past has caught up with her... will a killer do the same?

When Mrs. Mason, the owner of Knit Wit, finds her husband

murdered, Sam Jones steps in to console her despite her own troubled life filled with uncertainty and loneliness.

As their friendship blossoms, Sam confronts her past and the mistakes she's made. But will it be enough for the local deputy, Jordan Branson, to forgive her?

While the police hunt for clues as to who the killer is, Sam also worries for her own life. Will the murderer be revealed before Sam becomes the next victim?

Chamomile and Chaos

When the town doctor dies at the Farmers Market, it is quickly discovered he was poisoned.

The gossip vine turns its sights on Sam because she was one of the last people to see the man alive, and if anyone wanted him dead, it was her.

As Sam fights to maintain her reputation as well as find the real killer, she discovers that once again, her future is going to be deeply affected by her past.

Will Sam find the murderer before her life is left in tatters?

HAVE YOU DOWNLOADED YOUR FREE BOOK?

To find out the full story of Samantha's life before Heywood, please download Dandelions and Deception!

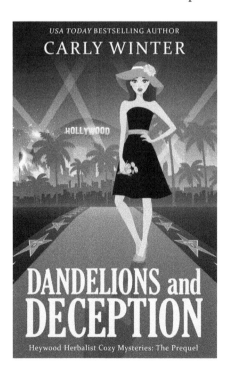

MISTLETOE AND MAYHEM

A CHRISTMAS COZY MYSTERY

PREVIOUSLY IN THE HEYWOOD HERBALIST COZY MYSTERIES...

Previously in the Heywood Herbalist Cozy Mysteries...

In *Herbs and Homicide*, daytime soap opera star Samantha Rathbone flees Hollywood, leaving her life literally on fire, and she ends up in Heywood, Arizona. Adjusting to the small-town life isn't easy, but she finds the locals welcoming despite her worries that her true identity will be discovered. She takes a job at Sage Advice, the local apothecary, and tries to settle into a life of anonymity.

When Sam finds her boss, Bonnie, dead, she quickly becomes the main suspect. Surprisingly, Bonnie has left Sage Advice to her and Sam has the most to gain by her death. As Sam struggles to catch the real killer, she also finds herself in a position where she can't trust anyone. Is the killer Bonnie's daughter? Annabelle, Sam's co-worker? Doctor Garrett Butte, the physician who hates Bonnie? Or maybe Doug, the local homeless man who lives under the bridge? He was there that morning...

Meanwhile, in *Lavender and Lies*, Deputy Jordan Branson continues to remind Sam of George Clooney—except when she's mad at him, which is quite frequently. She also discovers her employee and friend, Annabelle, enjoys exacting revenge on those who wrong her and the people she cares about. When their friend, Gina, the dog rescuer /

nail salon owner / writer is accused of murdering the most hated man in town, who also happens to be her ex-husband, Sam finds herself once again embroiled in a murder investigation. Heywood is an old town with many secrets, and Sam slowly begins to uncover some of them. This leads to her being able to prove Gina wasn't the killer, yet when the real murderer is revealed, Sam feels terrible about exposing them.

In *Mint and Murder*, Deputy Jordan Branson is accused of killing a woman in order to cover up a departmental investigation into his alleged wrongdoings. When he is relieved of his job, he asks Sam to help find the real killer.

The problem?

She's not sure he's innocent as all clues lead back to him. Then there's that horrible story in his past that mirrors the current charges...

The investigation leads Sam and Gina to sign up for dance lessons at Groove and Go Dance where they both discover they're really terrible at dancing, but it's also where they find the real killer.

And now on to *Mistletoe and Mayhem*...

MISTLETOE AND MAYHEM

Deck the Halls... with a dead body?

When Mrs. Claus is found murdered days before the Annual Heywood Christmas Festival, Sheriff Mallory Richards cancels the beloved event.

As the flu takes out the whole sheriff's department—except for Deputy Jordan Branson—he begs Sam to help him find the killer.

She and Annabelle set out to catch the murderer but land themselves in a tangled web of deception and danger.

Will they be able to find the killer and save the Christmas Festival, or will Sam and Annabelle get too close to the truth and end up silenced?

CHAPTER 1

CHRISTMAS. My favorite time of the year. I loved everything about the holiday: the decorations, the food, and... the Christmas songs were wonderful—until they weren't.

You know that song, "Last Christmas I Gave You My Heart," by Wham!? The beautiful pop-like ballad oozing so much emotion, tears may spring to your eyes while listening to it?

Yes, it's one of my favorites. Well, it was until my friend and employee, Annabelle, decided to play it on loop.

"Can we listen to something else?" I asked after the fourth time of listening to her belt out the song off tune.

"Don't be such a Scrooge," she said. "Who doesn't love this song?"

I knew quite a few people who couldn't stand the tune, but I'd let that one slide. "There are a million other Christmas songs so let's go for some variety, okay?"

She ran a hand over her crimped blonde hair as I returned to my task of tying bows on the gift baskets of products made from my store, Sage Advice. With Christmas only a week away, we'd been working overtime to fulfill the online orders, as well as those from the locals of Heywood, Arizona, where we lived. But these particular baskets were for the Christmas festival being held in a few short days.

Finally, Bing Crosby's smooth voice filled the air singing "White Christmas." I loved George Michael, but not enough to listen to his song on repeat. Annabelle, however, had a dedication to the 80s I'd never seen in anyone before... and it wasn't just the music. Her hair, the way she dressed, her vintage t-shirts... Sometimes, I wondered if it could be a little unhealthy and she should leave the past where it was.

"Did you ever meet him?" she asked.

"Who? Bing Crosby? I'm not that old, Annabelle." I shook my head and rolled my eyes.

"No, silly! George Michael! Did you ever meet him?"

As a former Hollywood starlet, I'd had the opportunity to meet a lot of famous people. "Yes," I said.

She squealed and clapped her hands together. Although she was in her fifties, she sometimes acted childish, which I appreciated because it made me feel younger as well. "Tell me everything! Was he as sweet as he seemed in interviews?"

I nodded and set down my scissors. "I'd been invited to a dinner party at a producer's house. There were about twenty of us. He was very kind and soft-spoken. Quite funny. I really enjoyed that evening."

"Oh, my gosh," Annabelle said. "I envy your former life so much!"

Smiling, I returned to my task. My former life had been great in some respects, like meeting George Michael, having rabid fans for my soap opera, *As The Years Turn*, and being quite wealthy. But there were downsides as well. Hollywood could be a cruel place and I'd suffered greatly at its hands when my husband had been murdered. All in all, I preferred my anonymous life in Heywood, running my herbal store.

"We just need to finish the bows on these, then they're ready to go," I said. "Next, we better make some more sage soap. Those seem to be flying off the shelves."

"Agreed," Annabelle said. "We should also put out more Elderberry tinctures. Everyone's trying to stay healthy for Christmas."

With the flu going around Heywood, people were getting sick faster than I could keep track.

"We should also get set up at the Christmas Festival," Annabelle said. "Hopefully they gave us a prime table to show our gift baskets. We have to be there by six."

I hadn't been sure about participating in the festival, but Annabelle had convinced me it would be a great idea for the business. I glanced at the clock. Gosh. Where had the day gone? It was just after five, and although I'd been working since seven this morning, I'd been so busy, time had flown by. I'd even skipped lunch. "You're right. We better get moving."

After loading the gift baskets in the back of Annabelle's car, saying goodbye to my cat, Catnip, and locking up the store, we drove a few blocks to the community center. Normally, I would've walked the short distance, but we'd received even more snow and the roads were slippery.

"There's supposed to be a dress rehearsal tonight," Annabelle said. "The choir is going to work out their placement on the stage, Santa and Mrs. Claus are going to practice their entrance, and the cheer team from the high school will also be going through their performance. I love watching it all come together before the big night."

The big night, as she called it, consisted of the whole town gathering to watch the show, kids getting their pictures taken with Santa and Mrs. Claus, a Christmas pie and cookie bakeoff, and singing carols. Not to mention people being able to complete their last-minute shopping from local vendors. Annabelle had told me stories of fists flying when one baker felt slighted in the judging portion of the night. I couldn't imagine getting upset over someone liking another person's cookies more than mine, but I also couldn't bake worth a darn.

As we drove, I stared out the passenger window at the transformation of Heywood. Lights decorated every store. Most had wreaths hanging from their doors and Christmas offerings showcased in their display windows. Small Christmas flags and garland decorations hung from the streetlights while Christmas music played from speakers around town I hadn't even known existed. The place looked like something out of a Hallmark Christmas movie, and I was still in awe of its beauty. It had all begun the day after Thanksgiving and it seemed like all the merchants were working in coordination to get it done a few days later.

How different this holiday was from my Hollywood years.

First, I never decorated. My housekeeper and I came up with a theme sometime around Halloween, and then she contacted a professional decorator. I literally arrived home from work one evening and found my house transformed into a wonderland of beautiful, sparkly baubles. Every year, my husband, Gerald, and I held a catered Christmas party. All our so-called friends would come to the outdoor gathering where our backyard was also transformed into a winter wonderland, even though we lived in Los Angeles. Ice sculptures and piles of fake snow were placed strategically around our yard while Santa and a live reindeer or two were available for pictures. A first-class buffet was tended to by servers in bowties, bringing around trays of champagne from the open bar.

This Christmas, I was headed to the Heywood Community Center to set out my handmade gift baskets with the hope people would buy them. And I was worried about how I would afford Christmas gifts for Annabelle and my friend—who might have been my boyfriend if I dated—Deputy Jordan Branson, as well as my other friend, Gina, the dog rescuer, ghost writer, and owner of a local nail salon.

Once we arrived at the Community Center, I exited the car and glanced upward as snow began to fall once again, the flakes hitting my cheeks.

"I wonder where everyone is?" Annabelle asked, opening the trunk to her car. "I thought more store owners would be here to set up their tables."

Glancing around the parking lot, I realized we were the only ones there, but the footprints in the snow indicated some people had been in and out. "Looks like they were here earlier," I said, pointing at the ground.

I grabbed as many baskets as I could carry and carefully treaded through the calf-high snow. Unfortunately, the town snowplow had some mechanical issues and hadn't been able to clear the roads and parking lots in two days. As the gentle flakes continued their beautiful descent, cold silence engulfed us. A chill ran down my spine and I felt as if we were the only two people left in Heywood... or in the middle of a horror movie.

Lights blazed from the building ahead, and when we got closer, I heard "Silent Night" playing from within. Hopefully, setup would be quick and easy as I was longing to curl up on my couch with Catnip and have a glass of wine or two. My shoulders slumped with exhaustion, and I realized the holidays were a lot of work when I couldn't pass the duties to someone else.

Annabelle balanced her baskets on her leg and pulled open the door. Once inside, we stamped our boots on the large red welcome rug to remove the snow.

"The wood floor gets a little slick when it's wet, so watch your step," Annabelle said.

Great. Just what I needed—another fall. I'd already had three since the snow started about two months ago, and my distaste for winter grew with each day. I loved looking at the snow, I just didn't like trying to live my life in it.

We walked through the foyer, hung a right, and headed for the big gymnasium. A strange odor of pine needles, cinnamon, and sweaty shoes engulfed us the closer we got, causing me to grimace. It was my understanding that the boys' basketball teams often practiced here, which explained the sweaty shoe smell.

When we entered the huge space, I gasped, forgetting the odor. Never would I have imagined a gym could look so pretty.

A large Christmas tree twinkled in the middle of the basketball court while thousands of tiny lights had been strung across the ceiling and along the walls, all glittering and giving off enough illumination the harsh, fluorescent lights weren't necessary. In a corner sat two high-back red velvet chairs with silver legs and gold and silver intricacies woven into the fabric, placed on a red and green rug. "That's for Santa and his wife," Annabelle said, pointing at them. "Last year they had elves as well. I don't know if they'll do that this year, though."

"Why's that?"

"Well, Santa, like, has a bit of a drinking problem and him and one of the elves he'd been boozing with got into a fistfight."

"Oh, my."

"Yes. They were rolling on the floor with fists swinging, cursing at each other. It wasn't one of Heywood's finest moments."

"Why don't they get a new Santa?" I asked.

"Wait until you see him," she said. "You couldn't find a more perfect

Santa. He's been playing the role for fifteen years now and loves it. He plans for it all year long."

Along the walls sat empty tables. I noted a few had been decorated with tablecloths and had goods arranged on them. "See? I told you we weren't the first ones here," I said, pointing at them.

"Apparently not," Annabelle, replied. "Let's find our table. Hopefully we've got a good one close to the door."

We found our spot along with a couple fold-out metal chairs labeled Sage Advice, fourth in from the door, in between Jemisphere, the local jewelry shop, and Locked and Loaded, the gun store.

"This is great!" Annabelle said as we set down our baskets and purses, then I stripped out of my coat as a hot flash hit while Annabelle kept hers on.

"Who's going to buy someone a gun for Christmas?" I asked, pointing at the Locked and Loaded table.

"Your California mentality is showing," Annabelle muttered, rolling her eyes. "I love getting guns and gear to go with them for Christmas."

Huh. Well, at least I knew what to put under the tree for her.

As Annabelle danced around to "Rockin' Around the Christmas Tree" coming through the gymnasium speakers, we set out our own tablecloth—green with red and silver trim bearing the store's name—to cover the old, worn table.

Our gift baskets were tied with red or green bows, a sneaky idea we'd come up with while preparing them. A red bow meant one price, a green bow meant another. That way we'd know on sight how much to charge the customer. Genius, if you asked me.

We arranged the display, adding a few embellishments like the candy dish full of candy canes and a few bows we pinned on the front of the tablecloth surrounding the store's name, as well as a string of small white lights to go around the table. We then placed our inventory underneath and stepped back to admire our work.

"That looks fantastic," Annabelle said. Glancing around at the other tables, she leaned in and whispered, "Much better than the other ones that have been set up."

I nodded in agreement. "Let's go take a closer look."

We walked around, stopping at Knit Wit's table to check out her offerings. Since the physical store sat next to mine out on Comfort Road, I knew the owner, Mrs. Mason, well. She was offering knitted dolls and discounts on knitting classes.

"Gina's going to try to adopt out some of her rescues," I said, pointing at a sign that read Heywood Hounds, the name of Gina's rescue business.

The next table took us to the other side of the gym where we found Too Hot To Handle, a hot sauce joint.

"I wonder how hot that Devil's Juice is," Annabelle said, pointing to the jar. "I imagine it would fry off your eyebrows."

"Probably." I turned to glance at the tree and a scream stuck in my throat as I grabbed Annabelle's arm.

"What?" she asked.

I pointed at the tree, still unable to speak.

"Oh my gosh!" she yelled. We ran over to find a woman dressed in a Santa suit staring up at the ceiling with milky, dead eyes, a small pool of blood surrounding her head. Annabelle fell to her knees and felt for a pulse, but I already knew the answer.

She turned and looked up at me, tears brimming in her eyes. "Who in the world would kill Mrs. Claus?"

CHAPTER 2

"We aren't certain if someone killed her," I said, immediately doubting my own words.

"How can you say that! Look at the blood!"

"I'll call Jordan," I said, backing away while Annabelle jumped to her feet. I pulled out my phone while she began to pace, cursing fiercely under her breath.

"Did she, like, trip over?" Annabelle said, her voice loud and pitched with panic. "And what did she hit her head on? The floor? Can banging her head against the floor make this mess?"

Thankfully, Jordan had been reinstated as a deputy after being arrested for murder. Threatening to sue Sheriff Mallory Richards had guaranteed he'd keep his job, but he still held ill-will towards his boss, which was completely understandable. He answered on the third ring. "Hey, Sam. What's up?"

With his exhaustion evident in his voice, I hated to break the news to him. "I think you need to come down to the Community Center," I said, turning away from the body. "Mrs. Claus is dead."

A long silence stretched between us, then he said, "You're a laugh a minute, you know that? Is Christmas now canceled?"

"I wish I were kidding, Jordan. Annabelle and I came down to put our baskets on display for the festival and Mrs. Claus... we found Mrs. Claus lying by the tree."

He swore as well, just not as colorfully as Annabelle. "Are you kidding me?"

"No." Then I realized I didn't even know the dead woman's real name. "I'm sorry, I've never met her. She's dressed in an outfit that resembles Santa, so we're assuming she's the one who is playing Mrs. Claus. According to Annabelle, Mr. and Mrs. Claus were supposed to have a dress rehearsal tonight."

"It's going to take some time for me to get there," he replied, sighing. "I'm out of town a ways, but I'll call for an ambulance and be there as fast as I can."

Glancing over at the dead woman, I said, "Jordan, she either slipped and fell, then hit her head, or she was killed."

"How do you know that?"

"There's blood around her head."

"Well, let's hope she took a fall," he muttered. I didn't have the heart to tell him I didn't think that was the case. "But I need you two to do me a favor. Does Annabelle have her piece on her?"

Piece? Piece of what? "I'm sorry?"

"Her gun. Does Annabelle have her gun on her?"

Right. The piece. One would think I knew that term by now. I turned to my friend. "Do you have your gun?"

She nodded and pulled her coat open to reveal the holster and weapon. "I never go anywhere without it."

Would I ever get used to the gun culture in this town? "She has it."

"Okay. Listen carefully. I'd like you two just to walk around the center and make sure no one else is hurt."

"Can you send someone else?"

"No."

"Why is that?"

"It's a long story. I'm the only one on the payroll tonight. Just do a quick search of the building, and also stay away from Mrs. Claus. Don't go near the body."

"Well, we already did. Annabelle checked if there was a pulse."

More cursing ensued. "Don't touch her again. Stay ten feet away from her and take a quick look around the building."

"Okay."

"And Sam? Be very careful. If she was murdered, we have a killer on the loose. I don't want to see you or Annabelle injured."

Great. Perfect. I hung up and turned to Annabelle again. "We have to search the building and make sure no one else is hurt." And hopefully not run into the killer.

"Why do I need my gun?" Annabelle asked.

I sighed, wishing we'd never come to the Community Center. "Jordan said he wants us to have it while we search to see if anyone else is hurt in case this is a murder."

"So I can shoot the killer?" she asked. "That would sure save him time investigation-wise."

"I guess so." Goodness, I hoped we didn't run into anyone.

"Well, this evening turned out far more exciting than I could've imagined," Annabelle said, her gaze scanning the room. "I kind of feel like those two guys from *Miami Vice*."

As we left the main room and followed the hallway down to another area, I stayed a couple steps behind Annabelle. She walked with the gun at her side, her trigger finger hovering on the side of the weapon. I knew she had decades of experience with guns, but it didn't make me feel any safer. Hopefully, if Mrs. Claus had been killed, the murderer had fled long ago.

She held up her hand and we came to a halt. "Do you hear that?" she asked.

Furrowing my brow, I listened intently. The wind had picked up outside and a whistling sound moved creepily through the building, causing my heart to race. But I had a feeling that wasn't what she meant. "No."

"Must be my imagination," she muttered. "I thought I heard a door close. Let's check out these rooms."

When we entered the first one, Annabelle flipped on the lights and raised her gun in front of her, sweeping the room, while a shudder of fear went through me. Obviously, she'd watched a lot of cop shows.

Chairs sat in a circle, the brick walls bare except a few posters touting the benefits of sobriety.

"This is where AA meets," Annabelle whispered.

I hadn't even known there was an Alcoholic Anonymous in Heywood. I imagined there was one in every town, but I just hadn't given it any thought. After glancing around quickly, I said, "I don't see anyone." There wasn't anywhere to hide.

"Let's check the next room." We left, switching off the lights behind us.

As we entered the second space and hit the light switch, it was much different. Kids' drawings and the ABCs covered the walls, a brightly covered carpet lay on the floor, and little chairs and tables had been lined up in a classroom style. "After school care?" I asked.

Annabelle nodded. "A few years ago, I did a -soap-making presentation for them. It was a disaster."

"What happened?"

"Two of them tried to eat it. I had to pull it out of one kid's mouth. Thankfully, the second spit it out."

I turned off the lights. I'd have loved to hear more of the story and imagined I'd laugh until I cried, but all I could manage with my current state of anxiety was a small snicker.

We went to the next room where we found collapsed tables and chairs lined up against the wall—storage. And that wrapped up our search.

"There's two more places to check," Annabelle whispered. "The kitchen area and the bathrooms."

Dang it. And I thought we'd been in the clear.

I followed her as she headed back down the hall, past the main entrance and into another passage. Down this way, the carpets were a different color than in the other hallway—more worn and I noticed some lights out. If this were a movie or television show, the killer would definitely be hiding in this area and we'd be dead within minutes. I wiped my sweaty palms on my jeans and prayed real life didn't follow the predictable horror flick script.

Annabelle seemed less afraid than me, which made me feel foolish and wimpy. As she pushed open the men's bathroom door, she hummed, "Last Christmas," not seeming to have a care in the world. That quickly ended when the smell of urine assaulted our senses.

"Why can't they ever hit the bowl?" Annabelle muttered as I covered my nose. "And who's supposed to clean this place?"

Upon inspection, it looked clean, but the odor told us otherwise.

"No one in here," I said, happy to be exiting. "Let's check the women's then head down to the kitchen. Hopefully Jordan will be here by then."

We found the women's restroom empty as well and I sighed with relief.

"On to the kitchen!" Annabelle instructed, holstering her gun. "I'm pretty sure, like, no one else is here. I mean, if Mrs. Claus was killed, I doubt the murderer is going to stick around and make coffee or anything. But when Jordan gets here, we'll at least be able to tell him we did what he asked."

"Agreed. He sounded pretty frazzled."

"Did he say why?"

I shook my head as we strode down the hallway. "Just that he was out of town a ways and he was heading in after he called the ambulance."

As we entered the kitchen, we glanced around. The coffee machine had been left on and the smell of brewing beans filled the room, along with the scent of bleach. Maybe the killer had needed a cup of coffee after his or her deed, and cleaned their hands?

Two warming ovens sat empty, the stainless-steel tables clean and sparkling under the fluorescent lights.

"I wonder who started the coffee?" Annabelle said. "Do you think it was the killer? Or Mrs. Claus before she died?"

"Who knows?" I replied, shrugging. "But it makes sense. If tonight was a rehearsal, then they'd want to have coffee for everyone who wanted some." I refused to believe a murderer would want caffeine after killing someone.

Annabelle strode over to the stainless-steel double-doored refrigerator and yanked it open. "They have cupcakes, too. And some cookies. Rehearsal was going to be one heck of a good time."

"Not anymore," I said, crossing my arms over my chest as my

stomach growled. The mention of cake and cookies reminded me that I hadn't eaten since lunch. "I think we're in the clear."

Just as we were about to leave, both of us stopped in our tracks, a noise catching our attention. For a moment it almost sounded like some type of motor. I turned and looked around the kitchen again, trying to figure out where it was coming from.

"A mixer?" Annabelle whispered. "Or is it a motorcycle outside?"

"I have no idea."

We stood for a long moment, listening.

"Over there," I hissed, pointing at a door I hadn't noticed before-hand. "It sounds like it's coming from in there."

"Isn't that the pantry?"

"I have no idea," I replied, rolling my eyes. "I've never been in here before."

We slowly approached the door and I amended my previous thought: if there was a killer, behind the door would be exactly where he'd be hiding. And of course, Annabelle and I were stupid enough to investigate the weird sound, and therefore, stupid enough to die, according to the slasher movies. I grabbed her arm and put my mouth right next to her ear. "Maybe we should wait for Jordan."

She shook her head and pulled her gun out of the holster again, holding it in front of her.

What was in there? It sounded like a bear.

"Maybe it's a coyote," Annabelle muttered.

But how would a bear or coyote get into a Community Center pantry?

"Open it!" she mouthed, her brow furrowed in concentration.

After taking a deep breath, I flung open the door and turned my back toward her. Crouching down and wrapping my arms around my head, I waited for the shots to be fired.

For a few seconds, all was quiet except for the sounds form the pantry. As I glanced over my shoulder, I noted Annabelle lowering her gun, her eyes wide.

Slowly, I stood and joined her.

As I processed the sight before me, I realized I'd have been less surprised if it had been a coyote. Or a bear. Or a coyote having tea with a bear.

Instead, we found Santa slouched in a chair in the corner of the pantry, passed out and snoring with a silver flask in his lap, the air reeking of whisky.

CHAPTER 3

ANNABELLE SEEMED JUST as shocked as I was. Why was Santa in the pantry?

I hurried in, placed my hand on his shoulder and gave him a good shake. He slowly woke, his eyes blinking as he tried to focus on me.

"What... is it time for rehearsal?" he mumbled. "I must've overslept."

"Mrs. Claus is dead!" Annabelle shouted. "Get up! The police are going to be here soon!" She walked out of the pantry and came back moments later with a cup of coffee. "Drink this."

He took the mug, his brow furrowed in confusion. "What do you mean Mrs. Claus is dead?"

"She's dead! She doesn't, like, exist any longer!"

"What happened? Did she have a heart attack or something?"

"We aren't sure," I said. "The police are on their way. What in the world are you doing sleeping inside the pantry?"

With a groan, he stood and we all exited. Santa placed the cup of coffee on the counter, untouched. "Joyce—that's Mrs. Claus' real name —was fighting with her sister. The two of them were screaming and yelling... it was awful. I kept telling them to take it outside or put a sock in it, but they wouldn't listen. So, I found the one place in the building where I could sit in peace and quiet and have a little drinky-poo until rehearsal."

For the first time, I really studied the older man. Standing at about six feet, his thick gray hair fell in soft waves down to his earlobes while his matching beard was perfectly trimmed. With his rosy cheeks, twinkling eyes, and large belly, I could see why everyone wanted him to play Santa. The only costume required was the red suit.

"What were they arguing about?" I asked.

"Something about an inheritance."

Annabelle and I exchanged glances. Money was always a great motivator for murder. A second later, Sheriff Mallory Richards entered the kitchen and I stifled a groan. I'd tried so hard to like the short, muscular woman, but failed at every attempt. I found her rude, condescending and frankly, a terrible leader.

"Well, what do we have here?" she said, glancing at all three of us with red-rimmed eyes, her hands propped on her gun belt under her open parka. When our gazes met, she rolled her eyes. "Why am I not surprised to find you here, Ms. Jones?"

"Just my lucky day," I said, shrugging. "Annabelle and I will be leaving now that you've arrived."

"No, you won't," Mallory said, then coughed into her hand. "You'll come out to the gym, sit down where I tell you to, and answer all my questions thoroughly and truthfully." She pointed at the three of us. "Everyone follow me."

Annabelle handed me a zinc lozenge. "Suck on this," she whispered. "It sounds like the sheriff is sick."

With a sigh, I bit my lip then popped the cherry flavored lozenge in my mouth, falling in line behind Annabelle with Santa bringing up the rear. Annabelle and I had made the cherry-flavored zinc prophylactic and I had to admit, they were very good.

Santa tapped me on the shoulder. When I glanced behind me, he held up his flask.

"Do you want a little nip?" he whispered.

"No, thanks." If it had been wine, I may have considered it.

When we entered the gym, the sheriff turned on the overhead fluorescent lights, then pointed at three collapsed, metal chairs leaning against the wall and coughed again. "Each of you take one and sit right there."

I sat in between Annabelle and Santa, hoping Mallory's germs had traveled away from me.

My friend leaned over, whispering, "She's definitely sick. She shouldn't be out spreading all her cooties around."

I nodded, noting Mallory wasn't moving too quickly, as though it hurt to walk or the basic function required a great deal of energy. She strode around to the other side of the Christmas tree where Joyce lay. Every now and then, she'd step into our line of sight as she studied the crime scene and snap photos with her phone.

When the front door opened, I glanced over to see Jordan strolling in, looking haggard, but giving off a George Clooney vibe as he raked his hand through his salt and pepper hair. Funny how his resemblance to the actor depended on my mood. When I was upset with him, there was no likeness to the actor at all, but when we were on good terms, the similarities abounded. I smiled when our gazes met, and he gave me a quick nod as he hurried over to his horrible boss.

They stood, speaking in low tones, but not loud enough for us to hear what was being said. Mallory coughed, then fished out a handkerchief from her pocket and blew her nose. Jordan stepped away from her, and I didn't blame him. No one wanted to be sick so close to Christmas and it seemed our esteemed sheriff had caught the dreaded flu going around.

After a few minutes of Mallory pointing and gesturing around the building, Jordan returned to us. "Looks like I'm taking your statements," he said. "Let's start with you, Santa. What's your real name?"

"Paul Lance," he said, taking a swig of his flask.

"Are you seriously drinking right now?" Jordan asked, grabbing a chair and sitting down.

"Yep. Now is as good a time as any."

"Can you stop while I take your statement?" Jordan asked, rubbing his thumb on his forehead, obviously irritated with Paul's imbibing.

"Sorry about that. I guess I'm a bit nervous." He screwed the lid back on the flask and set it down beside him. "Mind if I take off this coat as well? It's a little warm."

"Help yourself," Jordan replied while he removed his own parka and pulled out a pen and paper from one of its pockets. "Can you tell me what happened here tonight, Paul?"

"Sure thing, boss," he said, then cleared his throat. "Joyce and I have been playing the Clauses for three years. My prior partner, Carol, it's my understanding she went on vacation in the Virgin Islands and found herself a nice young man to support, so she never came back. Joyce stepped in to help me out."

We all stared at Paul, waiting for him to continue. His gaze fell on the Christmas tree and I assumed he was thinking of the body on the other side of it. Finally, he shook his head and continued. "Now, Joyce and I had our differences. She was what the younger folk call a 'Karen.' Sticking her nose in everyone's business all the time, things were done her way or the highway, if you get my drift."

"So you two argued a lot?" Jordan asked, making notes.

"Yes, sir, we did."

"Can you give me an example?"

"Well, for instance, last year she said I wasn't fat enough, so she made me eat some beans. Then she got mad when they gave me gas. This year, my beard was too long, the Christmas tree wasn't properly centered in the gym, and her chair over there isn't very comfortable. Oh, and she hated me nipping at my flask."

"What did you say to all that?"

"Well, I told her that this wasn't a Broadway production, the tree looked fine, she only had to sit in the chair for a little while, and to mind her own dang business for once."

"Did you fight about all that today?" Jordan asked.

"Yes. Except the beans. That was last year. Can't remember if I clarified that or not."

Jordan smiled and nodded. "Of course. What happened then?"

"I was just about to ask her not to talk to me until the rehearsal began, then this other woman came in, screaming at Joyce like a banshee. I figured they were related just by looking at them and their general disposition, but then Joyce told the other woman she was the worst sister anyone could have."

"And what did you do at that point?" Jordan asked.

"I asked them to stop yelling. I'm a peaceful man and I hate fights. That's why I live alone. I told the other woman, Mary, to leave. Neither listened to me."

"You didn't think to call the police?"

"Nah. I figured it was a family squabble and it would work itself out." He glanced back over at the tree. "Guess I was wrong."

"So, what happened after you told them to quiet down?"

"Well, they didn't, so I found my way into the pantry and shut the door where I could at least hear myself think. I must have fallen asleep in there because the next thing I knew, these two were shaking me awake, and here we are."

"Do you have anything to add?" Jordan asked, glancing at me and then at Annabelle.

We shook our heads. "Like I told you on the phone, we came here to set up our table for the festival and walked into this mess," I replied.

Jordan nodded and sat back in his chair, his focus once again on Paul. "Were Joyce and her sister arguing enough that they might have come to blows?"

"It wouldn't surprise me," he said, reaching for his flask. Not bothering to ask Jordan's permission, he took a small sip.

Our attention was turned to the door when a gurney was rolled in by two male EMTs.

"We'll need an autopsy to reveal the cause of death," Jordan said.

"What's your initial guess?" I asked.

He shrugged and shook his head. "I can't officially comment on an ongoing investigation, Sam."

Annabelle snorted while I rolled my eyes. "Then comment unofficially," I said. "Do you think this is a murder?"

Jordan glanced over at Paul, then back at me, and I realized he didn't want to say anything while Santa was within earshot. Fair enough.

"Can we go now?" Annabelle asked. "I may starve to death if I sit here any longer."

"Let me run it by the sheriff and see what she has to say," Jordan replied, standing. As he walked away, the three of us sat quietly, watching the commotion on the other side of the Christmas tree the best we could.

"I hope they let me go home, too," Paul said. "There's a football game on tonight I want to see."

"The Cardinals?" Annabelle asked.

Paul nodded. "I had high hopes for them this year, but I think they're going to let me down again."

"They do every year," Annabelle said, sighing.

"We have to have faith," Paul said.

"I lost faith in them long ago," Annabelle muttered. The statement was so odd, I turned to look at her. She was usually so upbeat, I found her lack of enthusiasm troubling.

"Are you okay?" I asked.

She nodded. "Just hungry. I get angry when I'm hungry."

"They call that hangry," Santa said. "When you're hungry and you get angry, it's called hangry."

"Okay, Santa," Annabelle said. "Thanks for the lesson."

"Just trying to be helpful," Paul muttered. "No need to be rude."

We sat in silence for a moment, then Jordan returned to us and said Annabelle and I could leave. "The sheriff says she has a few more questions for you, though, Paul. Are you okay sticking around for a bit?"

The gurney carrying the black body bag was pushed out from behind the Christmas tree by the two EMTs, headed toward the front door.

"Sure. That's fine," Paul said, watching it. "Poor thing. Even if she was a Karen and drove me crazy, I don't want her dead."

"I'm heading to the office to meet her sister there," Jordan said. "Mallory found her number in the deceased's phone and called. She's definitely broken up about it."

"Can't really blame her," I said, standing. "Even if they were fighting."

"You're right. I'll come by the store tomorrow," Jordan said, giving my arm a squeeze and me a tired smile.

Annabelle and I walked over to our table where we'd left our coats and purses. Once we were wrapped up to face the cold outside, I turned to her. "Ready?"

She nodded and we took a couple of steps until we heard someone yelling outside.

"That's my sister in there!" a woman screamed. "Get out of the way and let me in!"

We exchanged glances as Jordan and Mallory rushed toward the double doors and the two men pushing the gurney stopped, unsure of what to do.

"Let me in there! Joyce! Oh... please, no! Is she really dead? Joyce!"

Annabelle arched an eyebrow. "I think we should stick around for this."

"Most definitely," I said, removing my coat.

CHAPTER 4

"IF WE STAY RIGHT HERE, I bet no one notices us," I whispered. After quietly opening the two folding chairs lying against the wall behind our table, we sat down while Joyce's sister continued to yell.

"I asked you to meet me at the sheriff's department," Jordan said calmly. "Not here."

The woman finally pushed through and came into the room. As she stared at the black bag on top of the gurney, I studied her and noticed the resemblance immediately. Maybe in her sixties, she had a thin and athletic build and platinum blonde hair, just like her sister. She sank to her knees by the gurney and sobbed while we all looked on.

After a moment, Mallory walked over and helped Mary to her feet. "Ma'am, why in the world would you come here?"

"I had to see for myself," she said, pulling away. "I knew he was nothing but trouble."

"Who?" Jordan and the sheriff asked in unison.

Mary glanced around, her gaze landing on Paul. "Him!" she shouted. "He was so rude to both of us earlier! I never should have left Joyce alone with him!"

"Wait a gosh darn second here," Paul said, standing. "What the heck are you talking about?"

"When I left, I knew you were so angry that you'd hurt her!"

"I went into the dang pantry to get away from you two bickering!" Paul yelled.

Leaning over to Annabelle, I whispered, "Someone's lying. And no one ever said Joyce had been hurt. They're still trying to figure out if it was a slip and fall or a murder."

She nodded and we turned our attention back to the argument.

"You did no such thing!" Mary yelled. "When I left, you were right in here, telling Joyce to put a sock in it and that you didn't want to listen to us argue!"

Paul narrowed his gaze, placing his hands on his thick hips. "I did say all those things. But when I went into the pantry to find a little peace and quiet, you two were still going at it like alley cats! If anyone hurt Joyce, it was you!"

"How dare you," Mary hissed. "My sister and I had our disagreements, but I'd never hurt her."

"Right. You think I'm just some stupid old man who doesn't like a bunch of noise? Wrong. I hear everything, I pay attention to what's being said. You two were arguing about your father's passing. You said you wanted more of the inheritance because you took care of him while she accused you of elder abuse." His face reddened as he pointed at Jordan. "So put *that* in your pipe and smoke it. Sounds like a perfect reason to murder your sister, lady. *Money.*"

"We don't know if it was murder," Jordan reminded them. Based on the tone of his voice, he was losing patience.

"Oh, this is getting interesting," Annabelle murmured. "Jordan looks like he's about to blow his top."

"How dare you even make such a suggestion?" Mary yelled, sobbing once again. Because of my years in Hollywood, I could cry on the drop of a dime. However, most of the "normal" population couldn't. It required placing oneself in an unpleasant headspace and accessing the emotions associated with that bad experience. If asked, I'd simply remember my childhood, or when my husband was murdered and my life was burnt to the ground, both figuratively and literally. Some actors really had to work to get to that space. I could access it in seconds.

Squinting, I tried to see if real tears were present on Mary's cheeks, but I couldn't tell from where I sat. I either needed to clean my glasses or a new prescription was in order. My guess was the latter. I took them off and rubbed the lenses on the hem of my shirt.

She placed her head in her hands, the anguish rolling off her in waves. Or was it? Was this all an act? Something felt off. Her performance lacked authenticity.

"Mary, I'm sorry for your loss," Mallory said. "I want to take you down to the station and get your statement about what happened tonight. Will you please come with me?"

"I've just told you everything!" Mary yelled. "Didn't you hear a word I said? If my sister was killed, he did it!"

"We can discuss all this at the department," Mallory said again, then sneezed four consecutive times, her face now as pale as an egg white.

"What's going to happen to my sister?" Mary asked. The way the light hit her cheeks revealed dryness. If tears had been present, her skin should've appeared somewhat shiny.

Interesting.

Jordan glanced over at Annabelle and me, then did a double-take, as if surprised to find us sitting on the sidelines watching the drama. Annabelle smiled and waved, and he shook his head.

"Come with me," Mallory said, taking Mary's hand. "Let's go down to the station and allow everyone else to find out what happened to your sister."

After they left, the EMTs waited a few moments, then rolled out the body as other cops wearing different uniforms than our sheriff's department came in. They hurried over to the crime scene as Jordan approached us. "I thought you two were gone."

"We didn't want to miss anything," Annabelle said, standing. "We'll leave now, though."

Jordan chuckled and rubbed his face.

"What's wrong?" I asked.

Sighing, he placed his hands on his hips. "My whole department has the flu. Mallory says she's fine, but I don't believe her, especially the way she's coughing and sneezing everywhere." He hitched a thumb over his shoulder. "Those guys working the crime scene? We had to call them in from out of town. We literally have no one to assist me on this, especially if it is a murder."

I wish I knew how to help. What I could do was put together some herbal remedies to prevent him from getting sick. "Come by the store after you're done," I said. "I'll give you some stuff to make sure you don't catch the flu. Or if you do, it will be mild enough for you to function and it will pass quickly."

"Thanks, I appreciate that, Sam. I'll be by later."

WHEN I HAD MENTIONED to Jordan to stop by the store, I'd imagined he'd be around in an hour or two. How wrong I'd been, and it showed how little I knew about policework. The banging that woke me in the early morning hours scared me and my cat, Catnip, half to death. Both of us jumped from the couch where we'd dozed off and hurried downstairs to find Jordan at the front door of the store. I quickly unlocked the door.

"I had no idea you'd be this late," I said, a chilly wind nearly freezing me in place while Jordan hurried inside. After quickly turning the lock, I faced him and pulled my sweater tighter around my torso.

"Me neither. Mallory finally went down for the count with the flu, so it's just little old me trying to pick up all the pieces."

"I'm sorry to hear that."

He sounded quite defeated, which I found odd for a cop from Chicago who landed in the little town of Heywood. Perhaps when the flu went around Chicago, there were enough staff to cover those out sick. Heywood operated at bare bones on all municipal fronts, hence the reason the streets hadn't been plowed. Apparently, they couldn't locate a mechanic to work on the machine. Word on the street was they were trying to gather enough volunteers to move the snow, but I'd stay far away from that.

"So what did you have for me?" Jordan asked.

Right. Herbal remedies to keep him healthy. I walked to the counter and pulled out a bag from under the register. "This is your Elderberry tincture," I said. "Start this right away along with a teaspoon of fire cider." I set the second bottle down in front of him. "These zinc lozenges will help keep the germs at bay, as will this nasal wash. Use it multiple times. If you've already been infected, then it will lower the viral load. I wrote out notes here for you so you don't have to remember everything."

He smiled and met my gaze. "Wow, Sam. Thanks a lot. I really appreciate this."

"You're welcome."

As I packed everything back into the bag, he asked, "Aren't you curious what happened with Mrs. Claus?"

"Of course I am." I glanced up at the clock. Dawn would be upon us soon. But did I want to hear about the drama, or try to get back to sleep? Ha! Easy choice. "Why don't you come upstairs and tell me about it? I'll make some Echinacea tea to help boost both our immune systems."

He followed me up the stairs to my apartment where Catnip sat in the living room waiting for us, his black tail swishing back and forth as he studied the intruder through hooded green eyes. "You remember Jordan," I said. "Be nice, please."

"Hey Catnip," Jordan said, sinking into the sofa. "It's nice to see you, buddy."

My cat sniffed his shoes, then his hand, and finally curled up on his lap.

"I don't even like cats," Jordan said a few minutes later as I handed him the hot cup of tea.

"That's probably why he's sitting on you. He senses your dislike and is determined to be the biggest pain in the butt you've had today."

Jordan laughed, then took a sip. "If this is your idea of being a pain in the butt, Catnip, you need to up your game."

I sat down on the other side of the couch and took a sip of tea.

"I'm afraid I'm going to get you sick," Jordan said. "Frankly, I'm surprised I'm not out of it. With everyone having the flu in my department, I figure it's just a matter of time before it hits me."

"Well, it is what it is," I said. "Mallory was coughing all over tonight, so we'll see what happens."

He nodded and drank more tea. "Tonight was interesting. I found out more about Joyce Taylor, or Mrs. Claus, as she was known, than I could've ever imagined."

"Like what?"

"That woman has more drama in her life than a daytime soap opera."

My breath caught in my throat while my heart skipped a beat. I'd never shared my past life as a daytime starlet with Jordan, and that was the way I wanted it. I lived in Heywood under a different name, and without the help of Botox, fillers, professional makeup artists and kind lighting, I didn't look like the same woman—maybe a distant ghost of Samantha Rathbone, Emmy winning star. Sometimes, people thought I, Sam Jones, resembled Andie MacDowell with my long, curly hair and thin frame, but my true identity hadn't been discovered by the masses quite yet. Hopefully, I'd be able to live the rest of my days in sweet anonymity in Heywood, keeping my deep grudges and hatred of Hollywood and my dead husband to myself. Because of all this, Jordan's comment about daytime soap operas caught me off guard.

I took a long sip of tea to calm my nerves. "Oh, really?"

"Yes. It's crazy."

"Tell me all about it."

CHAPTER 5

"Well, the first thing we did was ask Mary that if someone did kill Joyce, who did she think it would be?"

"Let me guess," I replied. "Anyone but her?"

"Pretty much. She had a list of people. First up was Joyce's stalker."

"Her stalker?" I asked, now thoroughly intrigued. I'd once been the lucky owner of one, but studio security had assigned a couple of men to watch over me until he'd been caught. They'd also provided me with classes on what to do if I was kidnapped or held for ransom. I hadn't felt safe in the least bit, even though I'd been completely insulated both at work and at home. What did someone without those resources do?

"Yes. She's apparently a very active Conservative on social media, and she's picked up a stalker who goes by Kill All Konservatives, or KAK, for short."

"That sounds violent. And unoriginal."

"She's reported them many times, both to the social media platform and the police, but according to Mary, no one's done squat about it. They need to know the person's real name so they can serve a restraining order and apparently, no one's been able to track that down."

"I would think it wouldn't be that hard," I said. "Police have all sorts of technology at their fingertips."

"It's not. My guess is that nothing's been done. These small-town cops are used to road accidents and helping people contain their loose cows. Cybercrime is a little above their abilities."

That made sense to me, especially with my experience of past interactions with Sherriff Mallory Richards. In my book, she was completely unqualified to herd cows, let alone investigate cyber-stalking.

"What does the stalker say?" I asked.

"Oh, you know. The usual. That he wants to burn her house down, she should be careful when driving because he'll get her when she least expects it... some other pretty gruesome stuff about her animals."

I grimaced and glanced at Catnip, still sleeping soundly in Jordan's lap. I'd become quite fond of my little adopted friend and couldn't imagine how I'd feel if someone did something awful to him. "You don't have to tell me the details."

"Probably best I don't. It's hard to stomach."

"So, if the department doesn't have the means to find the online stalker, what do you do? Do you think he lives in the area?"

"I'm not sure of his whereabouts, but I have a friend in Chicago who works in the cyberstalking unit. I texted him last night and he's going to look into it today and get back to me on all the details."

I took a sip of tea. "It doesn't make any sense, though. How would Kill All Konservatives know where she was earlier tonight?"

With a long sigh, Jordan rubbed his face. "Joyce was one of those people who makes the mistake of living her life online. She posted on a host of subjects and was quite opinionated. Everything she did, or was going to do, was documented on her timeline. She was a completely open book and had zero security set on who could see her account and who couldn't. She made a post a few days ago about the dress rehearsal at the Community Center. She even gave the time and address. Anyone who looked at her profile was aware of exactly where she was going to be and when."

While in Hollywood, I'd hated social media. It seemed silly to me to post pictures of me eating dinner in a bikini as my bosses had wanted, and I wasn't comfortable sharing my personal life with the fans. I gave them my work, and I felt that should've been enough. What I did on my own time wasn't anyone's business, and the fans didn't have a right to know it. I still felt this way. Thankfully, Annabelle and a kid at the college handled all our social media for Sage Advice. I wanted nothing to do with any platform, although I did find TikTok somewhat amusing at times when Annabelle showed me videos.

"KAK sounds promising," I said. "Who else?"

"What murder investigation wouldn't be complete without the ex-husband?"

I rolled my eyes. Of course there was an ex-husband. "Oh, this should be good."

"Joyce filed for divorce about six months ago. It wasn't contested by the ex. According to Mary, Joyce felt they'd grown apart."

"Any kids?"

"No."

"How did they grow apart?" I asked.

"Again, according to Mary... Joyce had recently become almost manic about volunteering for conservative causes. She felt it was her calling. But George—that's the ex—had no interest. He shared the same values as Joyce, but he didn't want to donate his time to the causes. He said he gave enough time to his work before retirement and now he wanted to spend his energies doing things he liked to do."

"And what was that, if not activism?"

"Fishing. Some golf. He joined a pinochle group at the Senior Center and played every day at noon. He also wanted to travel with Joyce, return to the countries of their ancestors, as Mary put it, but Joyce was having none of it. Said there was important work to do here at home instead of traipsing around Europe. According to Mary, Joyce viewed herself as an American patriot and was determined to save our country."

"I thought it was already pretty good," I said.

"Well, Joyce had other ideas."

"And she divorced him over all this?"

Jordan nodded. "It devastated George."

"According to Mary."

"Right."

I sighed and rubbed my forehead. "I don't understand how a divorce leads to murder."

"Because George said that if he couldn't have Joyce, no one could."

"What does that mean?" I asked, furrowing my brow. "It seems to me she wasn't looking for another man. She was dedicated to her causes."

"But she *did* meet another man," Jordan said, wiggling his eyebrows. "One who was as committed as Joyce was. One who didn't want to play golf, travel Europe, and spend his nights playing pinochle. He wanted to knock on doors for candidates, volunteer on voting day, and spread the word through social media. His name is Terry Warner."

"Oh, my." I set my now-empty mug down on the coffee table. "When do you talk to George?"

"Tomorrow."

While he yawned and stretched his arms over his head, I asked, "Was there anyone else who wanted Joyce dead?"

"Believe it or not, there's a possibility."

"My gosh, you're right. This woman has more drama than a daytime soap." It truly sounded like a plotline written for my character, Cassie, on *As the Years Turn*. Except I couldn't imagine her being involved in politics. "Who's the next suspect?"

"Well, there's a woman in George's pinochle group who has the hots for him, but she understands he can't get over Joyce. Mary's theory is that the woman killed Joyce to help George find his way past his ex-wife. If Joyce is gone, maybe she'll have a chance."

"That seems a little thin."

"I agree, but I'll have to look into it."

"What's that woman's name?"

"Sarah. Mary didn't have a last name, so it looks like I'm going to a pinochle game at some point."

"Sounds like a great time," I said with just a hint of sarcasm. I'd never played, so I really had no idea. However, I wasn't really a game or card person. I enjoyed some of the older games, like *Clue*, every now and then, but I'd rather sit down with a book or watch a movie for my entertainment.

"But then we come back to our friend, Santa," Jordan said. "There was an obvious discrepancy regarding what happened between his story and Mary's. One of them is either lying or confused."

"Do you really think Santa—or Paul—could've killed her, then went and sat in the pantry?" I asked. "It seems a little strange."

"But it also makes him look less guilty. Who sticks around after killing someone, drinking in the pantry? It could've been a cold, calculated move. How was he when you found him?"

"He was asleep," I replied, shrugging. "Snoring so loud, I thought an animal had somehow been trapped in there. When I shook him awake, he was disoriented for a moment."

Jordan bit his lip, furrowing his brow. "It's hard to imagine someone killing another person then shutting themselves off in the pantry to take a nap. Are you sure he was asleep?"

"Positive."

"That would be a whole new level of deception," Jordan muttered, then took a sip of tea. "But something I need to think about."

"And what about Mary?" I asked. "The fact she was there and her story doesn't match with Paul's, not to mention she's got a list of suspects all ready for you... to me, that makes her look pretty guilty."

"I agree. It's like she's throwing names against the wall to see which one sticks for the investigation. The problem is, she's got one of the best motives."

"Tell me about that."

"Well, she was taking care of their elderly father in his home. They aren't wealthy by any means, but they didn't have any financial worries. The father passed a couple of months ago from dementia. Mary said in the end, he had no idea who she was.

"According to her, the will specifically spells out that everything was to be divided fifty-fifty. But Mary thinks she should get more—maybe divide it sixty-forty, since she was the one who took care of him."

I nodded, recalling the fight between Mary and Paul at the Community Center, and what he'd overheard the two sisters yelling about. "And Joyce said no and accused Mary of elder abuse."

"Exactly."

"With Joyce gone, too, Mary gets everything she thinks she deserves, plus some," I said.

"Yes. I'm going to be digging into Mary's financial situation as well. If she's in trouble, that's another arrow pointing to her as the killer."

"You sure have a lot of work ahead of you," I said.

"I do. And that's why I need some help."

"Well, maybe someone in your department will get over the flu soon enough."

"I don't think so," Jordan said. "I was hoping you'd be able to lend me a hand."

Well, this conversation had certainly taken an unexpected turn. "Me? What in the world can I do?"

"Talk to the suspects. Just poke around a little, ask a few questions, then report back to me."

"Jordan, I'm not a cop."

"It's never stopped you before," he said. "People talk to you, and you'd be helping me out. What's that saying? 'A friend in need is a friend, indeed.' I'm drowning here, Sam. I'm not ashamed to admit it. The department is held together with bungy cords and duct tape, and right now, I'm on a sinking ship."

It wasn't like I didn't have any experience solving murders—I'd done it before. My husband had been killed and so had my boss, Bonnie, who once owned Sage Advice. I'd found both their killers because I'd had skin in the game. People were accusing me of murdering Bonnie, and I was trying to clear my name from my husband's illegal deeds. There'd been a few other dead bodies along the way, and I'd found those killers because my friends had been in the crosshairs.

Then there was Sheriff Mallory Richards. I didn't want to tangle with her. We had a mutual dislike of one another and she was the sheriff, whether I liked it or not. While out and about in town, I actively avoided her and now, if I decided to help Jordan, I'd be stepping directly into her domain.

Did I really want to get involved in this mess?

I stared at my friend who was fighting to keep his eyes open. It wouldn't hurt for me to ask a few questions here and there. Maybe I'd unearth something that would help him put a killer behind bars.

Besides, it was almost Christmas and I was feeling charitable.

"All right, Jordan," I said with a sigh, regretting my decision almost immediately. "I'm in. I guess I'll have to take a crash course on how to play pinochle."

CHAPTER 6

AFTER JORDAN FELL asleep on my couch with Catnip, I fished out a blanket from the closet. I gently removed the protesting feline from his lap, then covered him up and placed the cat back. I waved at Catnip as I left the apartment and went downstairs to start a pot of coffee in the back workroom. Considering the sun wasn't even up, it was going to be a long day for me.

While the coffee brewed, I stared out at the white flakes falling in front of the streetlight. As I admired their beauty, I also decided I hated winter with a passion. Maybe things would be different if the town's snowplow could be kept functioning, and if I could adjust to the cold. It had settled into my bones during the first snowfall in October and I often wondered if I'd ever be warm again. According to Annabelle, I'd be complaining about the summer heat in a few months as well, which was probably true. I didn't really like being hot, either, but while the furnace groaned to warm the space, I'd gladly take a blast of oppressive summer heat.

Except when it started fires.

After my husband had swindled millions and died for it, then I'd been blacklisted from Hollywood and our house had burned to the ground. I hadn't really liked the home, so it wasn't that big of a loss for me. Gerald had designed it and the sleek white lines had never really suited me because I prefer a cozy décor. And because it was his baby, I didn't mind it burning to the ground because he'd done the same to my life—figuratively, of course. As I drove away from the flames engulfing my house, I'd considered the fire a good thing. It provided me cover to get out of town unnoticed and start my life again away from the cameras and trappings of Hollywood. A phoenix rising from the ashes.

A shiver traveled through me as the coffee pot hissed at me and I went to pour a cup. I added a little cream and greedily sipped the hot liquid, feeling the caffeine take hold of all my internal systems, giving them a jolt of energy.

After mopping the floor, dusting the display tables, checking the online store orders and comparing them to the inventory we had, the sun had risen and it was time to unlock the front door.

I flipped the sign to open and peeked at the main street, Comfort Road. A few people milled about, but the snow was keeping most inside. "Another slow day," I muttered. Although, with the way the flu was going around, we'd certainly have some people in looking for relief.

After returning to the counter, I took a seat on the stool and waited. I hated being idle. It gave me a chance to ruminate on things that were better left in my past. I disliked the bitterness that emerged when I did give my dead husband and his embezzlement some thought. Honestly, I kept hoping it would simply fade into a bad memory instead of the traumatic event it had been.

Just as I was about to mop the floor again to have something to do, Annabelle sauntered in wearing her calf-length neon-pink parka with a black scarf wrapping her face, leaving only her eyes visible. "Good morning!" she chirped as she stamped her feet on the welcome mat.

"Good morning." Today she had red and green ribbons braided within her hair. No one could accuse her of a lack of Christmas spirit.

I'd hoped Jordan would be up and out the door before Annabelle arrived. She desperately wanted us to become a couple, but it simply wasn't going to happen. When Jordan emerged, she'd have a lot to say and I wasn't sure I possessed the patience to deal with it.

"That was crazy last night, wasn't it?" she asked, shaking her head as she peeled off her coat. "I can't believe Mrs. Claus is dead. I mean, it's terrible that someone died, but it seems doubly evil that someone might have killed Mrs. Claus just days before Christmas. It's like they want to ruin the holiday for the whole town or something."

"I don't think her dying had anything to do with her playing the character," I said. "Most likely someone in her personal life was responsible, if she was killed."

She narrowed her gaze on me as she hung her coat. "You sound like you know something."

"Jordan came by last night and we talked about who could be responsible if it was ruled a homicide."

"Does he think it could be anything else? Like a slip and fall?"

"It doesn't sound like it."

A small smile turned her lips. "He was here *last night*? So, does that mean you two are dating?"

I shook my head and sighed. "Of course not. I don't date, Annabelle. Jordan and I are friends. That's it."

She rubbed her hands together and blew on her fingers. "It's just that you spend so much time with him. I don't know why you don't consider it dating."

Just as I was about to answer, footsteps sounded down the back stairs. Annabelle's eyes widened as she glanced around the corner, then to me. "He spent the night here?" she hissed. "You are, like, *definitely* dating!"

"Good morning," Jordan said, coming into the front of the store, carrying his parka and gloves. As he yawned, he ran his free hand through his salt and pepper hair.

"How are you feeling?" I asked.

"Tired, but I don't think I'm getting sick... yet."

Annabelle's gaze jumped from him to me, then back again. Finally, I said, "He showed up last night so I could give him some preventative care for the flu, then he fell asleep on my couch. That's it, Annabelle."

Jordan nodded. "Yeah, I'm sorry about that, Sam. I shouldn't have inconvenienced you like that."

"It's not a problem," I replied. "Besides, Catnip loved it."

"He was protesting when I had to move him to get up," Jordan said, chuckling. "I thought he might scratch my eyes out there for a minute."

I smiled, not doubting his fear. My cat didn't like to be moved when he'd found comfort. "I'm glad you were able to rest for a few hours," I said. "There's coffee in back if want a cup before you go."

I shot Annabelle a glare as he turned and walked into the back room, hoping to convey the conversation about me dating the deputy was over. He returned a moment later with a steaming mug.

After taking a sip, he said, "I received a call—that's what woke me. Joyce was murdered."

Annabelle and I both gasped, even though the news shouldn't have come as a surprise.

"Blunt force trauma," Jordan continued. "Which is a nice way of saying someone beat her on the back of the head with something."

"Oh, my goodness," Annabelle whispered.

"Do they know what the weapon was?" I asked.

"Something metal. I'm going back over to the Community Center to try to locate anything that fits that description. We did a preliminary search, but now I know what I'm looking for so I have to go over the place again."

"Maybe you'll get lucky and it will have fingerprints on it," Annabelle said.

"Wouldn't that be nice?" Jordan chuckled. "I could have this whole mess wrapped up before Christmas."

"And the town could have the Christmas Festival!" Annabelle said. "You need to solve the case of Who Killed Mrs. Claus, Jordan."

He glanced over at me, then grinned. "I'm hoping to get a little help. You still up for some pinochle?"

"What does that mean?" Annabelle asked.

"Jordan wants me to ask around, talk to some people, and see if I can help him solve the murder," I replied.

"I've got to head out," Jordan said, setting down his cup on the counter. "I hope to hear from you soon, Sam."

Annabelle waited until he'd exited before turning to me. "Tell me what's going on here."

"Last night, Jordan interviewed Joyce's sister, Mary. She gave him a list of people who she thought could've killed her sister. Everyone at the sheriff's office has the flu, so Jordan asked me to talk to those people and report back to him on anything I may learn about the murder."

"Oh! So you're, like, looking for clues?"

"Exactly."

"Can I come?" she asked.

"I was hoping you'd ask," I said. Even though Annabelle was ditzy at times, she did carry a firearm everywhere she went and had decades of training on using it. If I was going to poke around and ask people about a murder, I definitely wanted some protection.

"Oh, this is exciting," Annabelle said, rubbing her hands together. "Where do we start?"

I gave her a quick rundown of all the names Mary had thrown out to Jordan the previous night and their motivation for wanting Joyce dead.

"Well, we can't confront Kill All Konservatives since we don't know where he or she is," Annabelle said. "They're off the list."

"And it may be best to let Jordan handle that one," I said. "That stalker is pretty creepy."

"You're right," Annabelle said.

"I was thinking we should leave Mary alone for a few days," I replied. "If she *didn't* kill her sister, I want to give her space. If she is the killer, then maybe her story will change with a little time in between the murder and us speaking with her."

"Great idea. I think we should start with the husband. Or ex-husband, I should say."

"Jordan said he was going to talk to George today. Do you think we should visit the boyfriend, Terry Warner?"

"Is he even a suspect?"

"Not really, but maybe he can give us some insight into Joyce's life."

Annabelle nodded. "That would be a good place to start. We can get an idea of what Joyce's life is like now, and then we can also talk to George and find out what she was like when they were together."

"Great point," I said. "We should be able to find Terry's address pretty easily."

Annabelle picked up her phone and typed away for a minute or two. "Here it is," she said. "Public records have his address on Blue Ridge

Road, just out of town." I peeked over her shoulder and memorized the address. "What time do you think we should go?"

I glanced out the front of the store. No one had even walked by this morning and the snow was still falling. People were hunkered inside.

Which meant we'd probably find Terry at home as well.

"Let's go now," I replied. "Maybe when we get back, the snow will have stopped and the plow will have come by."

"Sounds good!" Annabelle said, reaching for her coat. "Let's go catch ourselves a murderer!"

CHAPTER 7

ANNABELLE DROVE SLOWLY, the snow crunching under her tires and the windshield wipers swishing back and forth. I glanced at the heating control, noting it was turned up all the way. When in the world would I feel the warmth? Wrapping my parka tighter around me, I shivered while my teeth chattered.

"Next winter will be easier for you," she said, keeping her eyes on the road. "You get used to it."

As we came to a stop sign, Annabelle stepped on the brakes, but we kept going and skidded through the intersection. I closed my eyes and gripped the seatbelt, my memories taking me back to shortly after my arrival in Heywood, when I'd wrapped my car around a tree while trying to avoid a deer. I hadn't been hurt then, but my car had been totaled. I hoped nothing similar happened with my current situation.

Thankfully, the roads were fairly empty and we sailed through without kissing anyone else's fenders.

As we rounded the corner, the backend of the car fishtailed, but she was able to get it quickly under control. Soon enough, we arrived at Terry's, my nerves so frayed I considered walking home—until I stepped out of the car into shin-deep snow. Winter was awful.

"Okay, let's make this a quick conversation or we're going to have to dig the car out," Annabelle said as we approached the porch. Blue paint was flaking from the house and the rusted gutters needed replacement.

After ringing the doorbell, I realized it didn't work so I knocked, hoping Terry would answer soon. And that he kept his house extra warm.

A spry man in his seventies answered with a bright white smile. "Well, isn't this a pleasant surprise. What can I do for you two beautiful young ladies?"

Thick gray hair, twinkling brown eyes and physically fit, Terry was a man who took care of himself and was obviously a player into his old age.

"Terry Warner?" I asked as he met my gaze. No doubt about it, he had been a lady-killer in his younger days.

"That's me."

"We were wondering if we could talk to you about Joyce Mercer."

"What about her?" he asked, furrowing his brow.

Annabelle and I exchanged glances. Was he going to be difficult, or would he help us out by answering our questions? "We understood that she was your girlfriend?"

He chuckled and waved his hand in front of my face. "Heck, no, she wasn't my girlfriend."

As Annabelle cleared her throat and I studied the man who stared at my chest, I was left speechless. Had I misheard the story details Jordan had shared in the early morning hours?

"So you didn't know her?" Annabelle asked.

"I was intimately acquainted with Joyce," he said. "But I wouldn't call her my girlfriend."

"Were you aware she's dead?" I asked.

He nodded, then stepped aside and waved us in. "Come where it's warm. I'll explain everything."

Thank goodness. Even if I found the gentleman a little creepy, I'd sit with Ted Bundy himself for a little while to warm up a bit.

As I followed Annabelle inside, a shiver traveled over me, giving me goosebumps. Was it the cold or Terry's incessant stare?

He led us through the entryway into a living room with worn black leather couches, which I stared at with distaste. My dead husband had been a fan of the same and if he were alive, I'd probably kill him. My heart skipped a beat as my blood pressure rose. Who knew I could have such a visceral reaction to a piece of furniture?

Annabelle and I sat on the sofa while Terry took the lounger across from us and turned off the news blaring from the television. A Christmas tree about three feet tall sat in the corner, bare and looking quite pathetic. Why hadn't he decorated it?

"You don't seem too concerned about Joyce," Annabelle said, removing her gloves and setting them on the glass coffee table.

"Oh, sure I am," Terry said. "But when you get to be my age, people start dropping dead. After a while it loses it shock value."

"She didn't just drop dead," I replied. "She was murdered."

His eyes widened and he sat back in the chair. "Well, that's something I didn't know. Wow. Who did it? How?"

As I narrowed my gaze, searching for any indication that his surprise was manufactured, Annabelle said, "Someone hit her in the head from behind."

"Did they catch the killer?" he asked.

"No," I said. "We were hoping you could give us some information on Joyce's life."

"I didn't catch your name," Terry said. "Are you with the police?"

"My name's Sam and that's Annabelle," I said. "We're doing some legwork for the sheriff's department."

I sounded official, without giving important titles civilians liked to hear. Ambiguity for the win.

Terry nodded and clasped his hands in his lap, his smile fading. "What can I tell you?" Terry asked.

"We'd been told that you and Joyce were an item," I said. "Based on your reaction here, I'm guessing that's not the case... at least, not for you."

He shook his head, sighed and stared at the floor. "When men my age lose their wives, as I did, most marry right away. I have no interest in serious relationships. I did like Joyce. I liked spending time with her, and we had a lot in common. But no, I wouldn't consider her my girlfriend, my significant other... anything that describes us as an item," he explained after a moment.

"It's our understanding she left her husband for you," I said.

"I don't know who told you that, but Joyce made it clear her husband bored her to tears. She was looking for more excitement than he could provide." He chuckled and leaned forward. "Let's be honest. Pinochle? Fishing? Could there be anyone more boring?"

Even though I agreed, I asked, "What do you consider exciting activities?"

"I love politics," he replied, rubbing his hand together. "Leading up to the election it's like watching the football playoffs, then election night is like the Super Bowl for me. I love cheering my candidate and if they win, I like to think I had something to do with it."

"Because you do a lot of campaigning for candidates you support?" I asked.

He nodded. "I'll walk door-to-door for someone I believe in. But I'm also not above a good online scuffle." Grinning, he held up his fist and boxed the air in front of him. "I actually enjoy getting on social media and scrapping it out with the other side."

In my opinion, that was the problem with the nation. There was this side and that side. It seemed like the middle had disappeared, which is where I personally resided. It was a lonely place without a lot of company.

"How many times a week did you see Joyce?" I asked, still confused on their relationship status.

"Oh, probably four or five. She enjoyed cooking for me so she often brought over meals. Every now and then, we'd go for a walk or something, when there wasn't a bunch of snow on the ground. Like I said we were friendly, but we weren't dating."

Still perplexed, I asked, "Did she know that?"

"Yeah," Annabelle chimed in. "Dinner multiple times a week? Nice walks? It all sounds a lot like you two were a couple... kind of like someone else I know."

I glanced over at her and she smirked, then turned her attention back to Terry.

He pursed his lips and shrugged. "I thought I'd made it clear to Joyce that we were friends. I guess the younger generation would call us "friends with benefits," but I wasn't looking for a commitment. I enjoy the company of a few ladies, and I'm not ready to settle down."

Why did I feel like I was talking to a twenty-something man instead of a seventy-something one? It was my understanding that men his age were on the hunt for a new companion before their spouse had gone cold after death. Not Terry, though. He preferred to play the field—the whole dang thing, from one end to the other. Either his middle-aged years had been stifled and unfulfilling or he'd never fully grown up.

"You said you were married before Joyce came into the picture?" I asked.

He nodded. "Almost forty-five years. My beautiful Irene succumbed to cancer. After that, I decided my heart belonged to her, but I do like companionship."

As a headache formed behind my eyes, I rubbed my temples. "Did you know Mary? Joyce's sister?"

"Yes. We were introduced."

"Did you two get along?" I asked, sitting back against the cushions.

"I thought so," Terry replied. "She was nice enough. Not quite the looker like her sister, Joyce, but I didn't have a problem with her."

"Did you ever hear the two of them fight?" Annabelle asked.

Terry shrugged. "About what?"

"Anything," Annabelle replied. "Politics? Life? The color of their nails?"

At first, Terry shook his head. Then, he snapped his fingers. "I did. Over their father. He passed a few months ago and Mary was moving in on the inheritance, claiming that because she took care of the man, she deserved more than fifty percent of the will."

"What did Joyce say to that?" I asked, finally feeling as if we were moving into seemingly familiar territory, or at least a place that didn't contradict everything I'd been told beforehand.

"She said they'd keep at fifty-fifty because Mary had been a horrible caretaker who didn't do much caretaking. In fact, she mentioned elder abuse a time or two, but I steered away from that conversation. It's too dark a topic for me."

Apparently, this guy could accept meals from Joyce, take walks with her, and I assumed sleep in her bed, but discussing her sister's actions and her father's death was too heavy of a subject? Okay, then. I was dealing with an old man-child.

"If Joyce suspected elder abuse, why didn't she do anything about it?" Annabelle asked. "Why didn't she take over the care?"

"You'd have to ask her," Terry said.

"Well, I'd like to, but she's, like, dead," Annabelle shot back.

Okay, not exactly the most agreeable answer, but hopefully we could work past it.

"I think it's time for you two to leave," Terry muttered.

No, not quite.

"May I use your restroom?" I asked, springing to my feet. Something was off with Terry, and I wanted to look around.

"Sure. Right down the hallway. First door on the right."

I shot Annabelle a glare, hoping she'd tone down her line of questioning and keep Terry occupied while I illegally invaded his space.

"So tell me about canvasing for a political candidate," Annabelle said as I walked down the hall. "Like, how many hours do you put in? And how do you know they're telling the truth while trying to get elected, then not become the status quo once in office?"

Good question, and one I wished I could listen in on, but there was a murder to solve.

I crept past the bathroom down to the bedrooms and counted three of them. Two guestrooms and the master. A quick glance at the guestrooms indicated they hadn't been used in a while. The master, also done in sleek black like the living room, housed an unmade king-sized bed, some clothing thrown over a chair, a treadmill and dresser. As I entered, I scanned the area for something that would make all of Mary's and Terry's contradictions make sense. One thought he was seriously dating her sister, the other thought they were bed buddies without commitment. Where did the truth lie?

Unfortunately, I found nothing out of the ordinary upon my first inspection. I hurried out of the room and into the hallway bathroom, where I used the facilities. After washing my hands, I opened the cabinet to study its contents.

"What have we here?" I whispered, pulling out a prescription bottle apparently belonging to Mary, Joyce's sister. "Why in the world would she have her pills here?"

I recognized the prescription as one used for arthritis. After taking a picture of the label, I set it back into the cabinet, my thoughts spinning. Was Two-Timing Terry having an affair with Mary? Or was it something as simple as Joyce borrowing her pills and leaving them at Terry's house? Could the sisters have shared arthritis pain medication?

Even if I claimed serious gastronomical distress, I'd overstayed my unsupervised time in Terry's home. I hurried to the front of the house and beamed at them.

Annabelle glared at me, while Terry stared as if he wondered if I'd clogged his plumbing.

"Thanks for answering our questions," I said, reaching for my scarf and gloves. "We appreciate your time."

"I'm sorry I couldn't be more help," Terry said, standing. "Like I said, I knew Joyce, I liked her, but we weren't that close."

After saying our goodbyes, Annabelle and I waved and smiled as we carefully made our way down the snowy walkway. When we were both inside the car, Annabelle turned to me. "What were you doing back there?"

"Just looking around." I glanced back at the house to see Terry standing at the window with his arms crossed over his chest, staring at us. "Let's go. He's watching."

Annabelle pulled away and I told her about the drug bottle belonging to Mary.

"What does it, like, mean, though?" she asked. "Why are Mary's drugs in Terry's house?"

"I figure it's either an affair or Joyce borrowed them. It was arthritis pain medication."

Annabelle drove slowly, her forehead furrowed as she watched the street. "That man's a player, Sam. I wouldn't be a bit surprised if he was sleeping with both Mary and Joyce."

I nodded. "Me neither."

And if that were the case, the question became: did he kill Joyce to be with Mary?

CHAPTER 8

OH, how I wanted to speak with Mary and find out why her prescription was in Terry's bathroom vanity, but I decided to hold off. Instead, I set my sites on George, Joyce's ex-husband.

Yes, Jordan had said he was going to interview him, but he'd been right about one thing—people talked to me and I'd probably get more out of the man than the cops would.

I phoned Jordan when we returned to the store and asked if he'd had a chance to interview George.

"Not yet," he said. "I was planning to go by later this afternoon, but if you want to take a stab at him, please do."

"Okay, I'll let you know. Do you have his address?"

As I jotted it down on a piece of paper, I felt Annabelle's stare. "See you later, Jordan."

I set my phone on the counter and turned to my friend. "I think we need to speak to George. Do you want to go with me?"

"Yes, I do, but I think it may be best to keep the store open the rest of the day. My neighbor texted me and said the plow is up and running, so we may have some customers once it clears the streets."

"Customers are good," I said. With all the snow, our sales had dipped. Thankfully, the online store was chugging right along, but we also needed to get the orders out as soon as possible. With only a few days until Christmas, we were cutting things pretty close.

"Listen, I'll stay here and take care of everything," Annabelle said. "You go see George. Text me when you get there and then when you leave." She turned and rummaged through her bag, pulling out a set of keys. "Take my car. Just don't crash it."

Without making any promises, I swiped the keys from her grasp then grabbed my own bag. Just as I exited the building, the plow drove by, leaving the roads clear but wet. I could handle damp, and my chances of not totaling her car rose substantially.

I recognized the street George lived on because I had a customer who resided a few doors down from him and I often delivered her herbal remedies when she requested it. Finding George's house was a breeze, and his street was plowed. Things were looking up!

After I parked and slid out of the car, I made my way up the shoveled path. George was on top of his winter game, and I appreciated it. What would make my day was if he offered me hot chocolate and led me into his living room where a fire danced in the fireplace once I introduced myself, but I didn't get my hopes up.

I rang the bell and waited. A man in his seventies answered, but he didn't have Terry's vitality. Hunched at the shoulders, bald with Bassett hound eyes, he smiled sadly. "Can I help you?" he asked.

Frankly, if I dated, I'd rather have stepped out with George than Terry. But thankfully, I didn't date. "My name's Sam, George. I was wondering if I could talk to you for a minute about Joyce."

"My ex?"

I nodded.

"She's dead, you know."

"Yes. I was one of the people who found her body."

His eyes widened and he stepped aside. "Come in, please. I'd love to speak with you."

With a smile, I walked inside. The front door led directly to the living room / dining room combination. The dining room table hadn't been used to feed anyone in a long time. Instead, it served as a desk, complete with stacks of papers, a computer, and a few books. I also noted shelving that housed pictures of George and Joyce throughout the years.

"I had those put away until last night," he said. "Decided to take them out again since she's gone for good now."

As I sank into the comfortable blue couch, George lowered himself into a side chair.

"What do you want to know about Joyce?" he asked.

While glancing over at the pictures, I suddenly became exceedingly uncomfortable. I'd imagined a bitter man who hated his ex for leaving him but instead, I'd found a shrine of sorts dedicated to her.

"I'm sorry for your loss," I said.

He nodded and looked around. "Well, she left me, you know. Said she was on to new, exciting things in her life... things I couldn't give her."

"I understand that you wanted to travel with her. That sounds quite nice." *Such a sap.* Here I was trying to make a potential killer feel better.

"Yes, I did. See, Joyce and I had a traditional marriage. I worked, she kept the house. We weren't able to have children, and although I didn't realize it at the time, she was lonely throughout most of our years together."

"Why didn't she do something about it?" I asked. "She could've gotten a job or volunteered at different organizations."

"I recall her bringing up those things over the years, and like I said, I didn't realize what she was going through. I should have encouraged her to get out more, but I didn't. I was selfish and wanted her home."

"What about playing Mrs. Claus?" I asked. "I understand she's been doing it for a while."

"I didn't even know she had taken on the role until the Christmas Festival a few years back. She disappeared from my side while we were there looking at all the offerings from the town stores, then the next thing I knew, she was walking in on the arm of Santa—or Paul Lance, I believe is his real name. Watching her that first time, the way she beamed with joy... she was so good at the job, who was I to say she couldn't volunteer for it? I mean, besides the rehearsals, it was only for one night."

"So, what happened then? Why the divorce?"

"Once I retired and we started spending time together again, she decided she didn't like me anymore."

"How did that make you feel?"

"Well, at first, I was furious. I'd busted my butt for decades giving her a beautiful home, saving for retirement, and we had a couple of nice vacations, as well. I thought that was enough."

"During your marriage or after your divorce, did you ever threaten her?"

He shrugged. "During the marriage, never. I naively thought we had a perfect relationship. After she left me, possibly. I felt like I was out of my mind with grief, like she'd died. If I ever said anything derogatory about Joyce, it came from a place of pain. I'd never hurt her, though."

Once again, I felt sorrow for the man sitting across from me. Based on what he'd told me, if he murdered his wife, I'd be shocked.

"I loved her with every fiber of my being and honestly thought the years after my retirement would be the best we'd have," he continued. "I wanted to travel back to Europe and see our homelands. I'm of Irish descent, and her ancestors came from Germany. I imagined us going to the Senior Center and having cocktails or playing cards with other couples. I'd worked so hard my whole life and wanted to enjoy my remaining years with Joyce. But I ruined it." He glanced over at the pictures. "All that time I thought I was taking care of her, I was really suffocating her."

His sadness was almost palpable. But I also understood Joyce's choices. If her misery was something they'd discussed and George had brushed it off, I'd be bitter, too, in her shoes. So much so that I'd divorce him as well simply because I'd have to be around him all the time after he'd retired.

"When you found out she was spending time with Terry, did that upset you?"

George chuckled and shook his head. "Ah, yes. Terry. A real Lothario. The guy thinks he's Casanova himself. Kind of a leery fellow, if you ask me. The way he stares at women... I find it disrespectful."

Having been on the receiving end, I nodded in agreement.

"Anyway, I knew she was making a mistake by hanging around him. Figured he'd use her and spit her out just as he's done every other woman since his wife died. That's all the ladies down at the Senior Center talk about... how he's dedicated to the memory of his wife, but that doesn't mean he won't have the ladies cook for him and share his bed. All of that comes with a strict clause: no commitment from him."

At least Terry was honest and didn't lead anyone on, though. Everyone seemed to know right up front where they stood with him.

"What about Joyce's sister, Mary?" I asked. "Were you two close?"

He sighed again and glanced back at the pictures. After a few long moments, he said, "During my whole marriage, I tried to like Mary, but I never quite got there. I'm sure she'd say the same about me. I think the best description of our relationship is that we tolerated each other."

"Did you ever argue?"

"Not that I recall. We were pleasant to each other, the way people who don't really like each other are so they don't cause trouble at family functions." He sighed and rubbed a hand over his bald head. "I should call her to give my condolences."

He obviously hadn't realized that Mary had served him up as a possibility of being Joyce's killer.

"George, did you ever say something to the effect of if you couldn't have Joyce, then no one could?"

"Who told you I said that?" he asked, his forehead wrinkling in confusion.

Should I tell him it was his sister-in-law? If George was indeed the killer, that would put Mary in his sights if he found out she'd been mentioning his name to the police. "It's just something I heard through the gossip vine."

He shook his head. "I can't imagine I'd say something like that. It's a little dramatic. And I can't imagine any conversation where that would be appropriate."

I nodded and stood, unable to think of any further lines of questioning. "Thank you for your time today. I appreciate it."

"Of course," he said, also getting to his feet. "It was nice to meet you, Sam. I know you're a little young for the Senior Center, but maybe you should come by sometime and play pinochle. We're old, but we have fun."

"Thank you," I said as we walked to the front door. "I've never played before. Is that going to be a problem?"

He smiled. "We play to win, but we'd take it easy on you for a while until you get the hang of things."

"I appreciate the offer. Maybe I'll take you up on it."

"Look forward to seeing you soon, Sam," he said, opening the door. A blast of cold hit me square in the face. "Take care."

As I hurried to Annabelle's car, I considered the conversation. George had no reason to murder Joyce, except his broken heart. Therefore, the killing would be considered a crime of passion.

However, after spending a little time with the man, I didn't see a spark of passion in him. Not even a little flicker. And then there was his age. He wasn't as robust as Terry, even though they were both in their seventies. People grew old at different rates. Did George have the physical strength to hit Joyce hard enough to kill her?

And more importantly, did he have the heart?

CHAPTER 9

ON THE WAY back to Sage Advice, I stopped at Locked and Loaded, the gun shop, to purchase a Christmas gift for Annabelle. After deciding on a pink gun holster, I had them gift wrap it and shoved it into my big bag, thankful I'd chosen to bring it instead of one of the other little purses I owned. In fact, donating them would be a smart move because I hardly ever used them. I needed the large tote for deliveries.

I parked in front of the store and found the walkway had been cleared. Upon entering, I found Annabelle packing up the last of the online orders.

"Who cleared the sidewalk?" I asked, shucking my parka and hanging it up.

"Some kids came by looking to make some extra cash, so I gave them twenty to do it."

"Where have they been all season?" I asked, thinking of all the times I'd done the shoveling myself. "I'd gladly pay for that service."

"I told them to come back after it snows again. Hopefully, they will."

As I stared at all the boxes ready to be shipped, a huge wave of gratitude washed over me. What in the world would I do without

Annabelle? "Thanks so much for taking care of all this," I said. "I'd be lost without you."

With a grin, she placed the label on the last box, then gave me a hug. "You're welcome," she said. "I just love working here, and I love you like a sister. Thank you for everything, Sam."

Tears welled in my eyes as I gave her a good squeeze, then let go.

"Tell me about George," she said, sitting on her stool at the workbench where she made her tinctures and capsules. "Do you think he killed Joyce?"

After recapping the conversation, I replied, "I'm not sure. I don't know if he's got the physical ability to hit her hard enough to kill her."

"Doesn't sound like he's mad enough about their breakup, either."

"I agree, but who knows?" I shrugged and sat down next to her. "I have to report back to Jordan and see what he says. He's got the final call on all this."

My long day suddenly took its toll and exhaustion ripped through me and settled in my bones, making it a battle to keep my eyes open as my shoulders slumped.

"Jeez, Sam," Annabelle said. "You look like you're about ready to go to sleep."

"I am. I just became really tired. I've been up for too many hours."

Suddenly, *Ho! Ho! Ho! Merry Christmas!* sounded through the store. Jumping to my feet, I glanced around, trying to figure out where it was coming from while Annabelle burst into peals of laughter.

"I programmed that while you were gone," she said.

"How?"

"Through the alarm system. It indicates someone just came through the front door."

"Why didn't I hear it when I came in?" I asked.

"Because it only sounds in the workroom. Who's here, Sam?"

I glanced around the corner to see Jordan strolling in, removing his gloves. As our gazes met, he grinned and waved.

"Who is it?" Annabelle asked again.

"Jordan."

"Okay, I'm going to take these packages to the post office, then head home. I'll see you in the morning."

I hurried into the main store. "Did you catch Mrs. Claus' killer?"

Jordan glanced over his shoulder, then pointed his thumb at his chest, his eyes wide. "Who? Me?"

"You *are* the police," I said, biting back a smile. "That *is* your job."

"I thought I tasked that to you."

"Ha, ha, deputy. I'm just along for the ride."

With a chuckle, he shook his head. "No, I haven't pinned the killing on anyone, but I wanted to hear what you learned today."

I sighed and glanced at the clock. Almost dinnertime. What I really wanted was to go upstairs, kick off my boots, and curl up with Catnip. "Can I give you the information tomorrow?"

"Nope," he said. "I can see you're almost as tired as me. Grab your coat, herb lady."

Did I really want to go out? No. Was I curious about what Jordan had to say? Yes. "Where are we going?"

"It's a secret, and I promise you'll feel much better afterward. Also, you'll most likely have the best sleep of your life."

The best sleep of my life? Well, wouldn't that be something, as I barely remembered what sleep felt like with the menopausal hot flashes crashing through me multiple times a night.

"Do what the deputy says!" Annabelle yelled from the back. "I'll lock up!"

Without further argument and seeing I was completely outnumbered, I grabbed my parka and bundled up with my scarf and gloves, then followed Jordan out to his truck.

He held the passenger door open for me, then shut it once I was settled in. As he slid into the drivers' seat, my teeth began to chatter.

"You really aren't cut out for winter, are you?" he asked, firing up the engine.

"N-no."

He pulled away from the curb and turned the heat to high. Within seconds, the warmth engulfed me and I leaned my head against the seat.

"Don't you fall asleep on me, Sam," he said. "Sleep is for the weak."

Ignoring him, I rested my eyes as we drove down Comfort Road. A short time later when we parked, I opened them to find us at On The River, a lovely little restaurant resembling a log cabin inside that served wonderful sandwiches and soups in the winter, and beautiful salads during the warmer months.

"How is food going to make me sleep better?" I asked.

"Trust me on this," he said, exiting the car.

I followed him into the restaurant and studied the pictures on the wall while waiting for the hostess to come seat us. One photo always caught my eye—a bear walking the shoreline of the river right below the restaurant with two cubs trailing behind her on a bright, sunny day. I tried to imagine what had happened. Had everyone eating on the deck, enjoying the sunshine, run inside, or had they stayed to watch? Where had the bear gone after? Had she been upset to be seen by so many humans?

"Jordan! Sam! What can we do for you?" I glanced over to see the owner, Sally, rushing toward us. Bottom heavy with a beak-like nose, wide eyes and long brown hair, she reminded me a bit of an ostrich.

"Hey, Sally," he said. "I was hoping Sam and I could get your special."

She placed her hands on her hips and narrowed her gaze. "Jordan, I'd move the sun and stars for you. Come on in."

As she led us to a table near the front of the building instead of by the windows overlooking the river, I admired the huge Christmas tree in the middle of the restaurant, the lights strung from the rafters and the little holiday knick-knacks throughout. Heywood and its citizens really got into the Christmas spirit, and my fatigue lifted just a little bit to witness the cheer.

When we sat down, I was grateful to not be near the windows. I knew from experience those seats could be quite drafty and cold during the winter months.

Sally pointed at me as I shucked my parka. "This is a secret between me and Jordan, so please don't go around telling people about it. It's *not* on the menu this time of day, okay?"

I nodded, now more intrigued than ever. After she left, I asked, "What are we eating?"

"You'll see," he said. "Tell me about your day before the food comes out."

I quickly gave him the rundown of my chats with Terry and George, only stopping when Sally placed two hot chocolates piled high with whipped cream on our table.

"How's all this sugar going to help me sleep better?" I asked, eyeing the delicacy. In my Hollywood years, I'd never have touched such a waist-expander. As I considered it now, my mouth salivated. The heck with it. I wasn't in Hollywood now, and I never would be again. If I gained a few pounds, no one was going to care or berate me for it.

I took a long sip, whipped cream dotting my nose. Jordan swiped at it with his finger before I could pick up my napkin. "This is really good," I said. "It doesn't taste like normal hot chocolate, though."

"Sally's secret recipe," he whispered. "After dinner, ask her about it. But tell me your thoughts on George. Could Joyce's death be a crime of passion?"

I shook my head. "I don't think so. He doesn't seem to have a cruel bone in his body. I believe he's more broken than angry over the split. What about the murder weapon? Did you find it?"

"No." Jordan sighed. "I scoured that Community Center but didn't find anything that matches the dimensions the coroner gave me. The killer must have taken it with them."

"So does that rule out Paul, then?" I asked. "Or did he dump the weapon somewhere then go into the pantry to take a nap?"

"I'm not ruling anyone out at this time. No one's giving me any reason to do so."

When Sally set my bowl in front of me, I glanced at Jordan, thoroughly confused. "Is this dinner?"

Smiling, he picked up his spoon. "Yup. Breakfast for dinner is the best."

The oatmeal was sprinkled with blueberries, cinnamon, and what looked like brown sugar. I picked up my spoon and took a bite. Delicious.

"What would you do if I say I hated oatmeal?" I asked.

"I'd encourage you to try Sally's. It's special, and healthy. Except for the brown sugar, of course, but you can always get it without that."

After having another bite, I realized it wasn't the typical oatmeal I'd grown up on. It tasted similar, but it was definitely different.

We ate in silence as I inhaled my breakfast-for-dinner and finished my cocoa. When I was done, I sat back and smiled, completely satiated.

"Good stuff, right?"

I nodded as a yawn fought its way and I covered my mouth.

When Sally came over to take the plates, I asked her about the food and hot chocolate.

"It's a low carb oatmeal, consisting of seeds, some collagen, and coconut milk. Did you like it?"

"Very much," I said, feeling more relaxed than I had in ages.

"The hot chocolate is actually my own recipe. It includes some mushrooms called Lion's Mane and Reishi. They're very good for you."

I recalled my studies on Reishi. After all, I did own an herbal apothecary, so my livelihood, as well as the health of my customers, was on the line if I wasn't familiar with our products. "Reishi calms the nervous system," I said. "Lessens anxiety, on top of a host of other things."

"Correct!" Sally said, placing her finger on her nose. "Right on the button! I've been playing around with recipes using it, and this was a winner."

An idea suddenly came to me. "Sally, could I make an appointment with you to talk about us carrying your hot chocolate?"

She stared at me a long moment, then exclaimed, "Sure! Why not! Wow... funny how life is. I never expected something like this to happen tonight."

Me neither.

Jordan paid and I decided to use the restroom before having him drive me back to the store. As I walked through the restaurant, I hummed along with "Silver Bells" coming through the speakers. Maybe we could add little packages of the hot chocolate to our baskets for the Christmas Festival? Or, if the event didn't take place—which seemed likely, considering it was a murder scene—we could carry it seasonally, during the winter months. I passed the front door, making a mental list of what I could put in the brand-new, post-holiday comfort winter baskets. What could get people through the rest of the winter months, relaxed and happy? What were the trends after the holidays? Losing weight, for sure. Surviving the rest of dark winter and—

Something caught my eye outside in the parking lot.

A fight?

I hurried to the side window next to the door and cupped my hands to block the glare from the restaurant lights.

Yes, definitely a fight.

Two men scuffled under the streetlight, then fell to the ground. I realized I knew both. What the heck was going on?

My need to use the facilities forgotten, I hurried back to the table and grabbed my coat. "Hurry, Jordan! Santa Claus and George are engaged in a fistfight outside!"

CHAPTER 10

WE BOLTED from the restaurant into the parking lot and discovered the wet pavement had now turned to ice. Jordan steadied me as I attempted to keep my balance. My arms pinwheeled while we approached the two elderly men rolling around throwing punches.

"Knock it off!" Jordan growled as he pulled George off Santa. Or I should say Paul. Even though the man was the spitting image of the fictional character, I should use his real name.

"He just hit me with a crowbar!" Paul yelled, holding the back of his shoulder.

"Get up," Jordan demanded, pulling him to his feet. As he stood between the men, his gaze darted from one to the other. "Now, can I trust you two to act like adults, or do I need to cuff you both until this is sorted out?"

"No need to cuff me," George said, his breath sawing in little puffs of white condensation. "But I'm not a killer, either."

"I didn't kill anyone!" Paul yelled. "You watch your mouth, George, or I'm going to make you eat my fist!"

"Okay, cuffs it is," Jordan muttered as he snapped them on Paul.

However, George put up a bit of a fight. "I'll have no problem taking you down to the station and letting you sit a night in jail, George," Jordan muttered. "Don't test me."

The man finally acquiesced and allowed Jordan to slide the silver bracelets on and lock them.

I stood with my teeth chattering, trying to understand why George would be convinced Paul had killed his ex-wife.

"Now that you two are subdued, Paul, tell me what happened," Jordan said as he pulled out his notebook from his jacket pocket.

"I'd just finished eating at the restaurant here and was on my way out to my car. Next thing I knew, I was attacked from behind. Someone hit me with something. I turned around and George was standing there all crazy-eyed, holding a tire iron above his head!"

"You said he hit you with it?" Jordan asked.

"Yes, sir. But, he's either weak or my parka is so thick, it protected me. There's no damage."

"I'd like to get you some medical attention," Jordan said, pulling out his phone.

"That's not necessary," Paul said. "I haven't seen a doctor in fifteen years. No sense in starting now."

"When was the last time you were hit with a crowbar?" I asked. When he didn't answer, I said, "That's what I thought. Probably best to get yourself checked out."

As he huffed his indignation, I smelled the alcohol on his breath.

"George, do you really think Paul killed Joyce?" Jordan asked.

"Yes, I do," he said, straightening his shoulders and staring daggers at his foe.

"Why is that?" I asked.

"Because he was there," George spat. "Joyce and Paul hated each other. I'd seen them fight in prior years before and during the Christmas Festival. Joyce was always trying to make things better, and Paul fought her every step of the way."

"She wasn't trying to make anything better!" Paul yelled. "She was trying to henpeck me to death!"

"Joyce never henpecked anyone in her whole life!" George shouted.

Paul simply shook his head and pursed his lips. There was something he wasn't sharing.

"George, you can't go around beating people with crowbars," Jordan chided. "I understand you're angry and you've suffered a great loss, but you can't assault people you think may be guilty of the crime."

He nodded and stared at the pavement.

"Where is it?" Jordan asked, glancing around. "Where's the crowbar?"

"Under that car," Paul said, nodding toward a Jeep. "I got it away from him and threw it over that way."

Jordan strolled over, not slipping once. When would I master the finer points of surviving winter, like making it across an icy parking lot without falling? He bent over and pulled out the weapon, then returned to us.

"I'm going to hold on to this," he said. "Paul, do you want to press charges?"

He stared at George for a long while, then finally shook his head. "Nah. I know he's upset about Joyce's passing. I just wish he wouldn't have taken it out on me. I had nothing to do with it, George. Joyce drove me nuts, but I'd never kill her."

George did meet his gaze, but I noticed his shoulders slumped a bit. Relief he wasn't going to prison? Shame for what he'd done?

"Okay, then," Jordan said. "The less paperwork I have to do, the happier I am. George, if Paul's not going to press charges, then I'm going to let you go with the condition that you stay away from Paul. I don't want you looking at him, talking to him, or breathing on him. Do you understand me?"

George nodded and remained quiet.

"Paul, let's get you out of these cuffs first," Jordan said. "Are you sure I can't call you an ambulance?"

"Yes. I'll go to the clinic in the morning if there's something wrong."

"Do you know the signs of concussion, Paul?" Jordan asked, removing the handcuffs.

"My brains oozing from my ears?" Paul replied, rubbing his wrists.

"Nothing quite that dramatic," Jordan said. "If you experience a bad headache, pressure in your head, or blurry vision, call an ambulance."

As Jordan listed more symptoms, Paul nodded, but I could tell he wasn't listening. Yikes. The man should be seen by a medical professional immediately. I had my suspicions that he was mentioning a visit to the clinic in the morning to placate Jordan.

"Let me take a look at you," Jordan said. After pulling out the flashlight, he studied the back of Paul's head, fingering his way through the thick gray hair. I looked as well, seeing nothing out of the ordinary.

"I think your parka took the brunt of the hit," Jordan said. "Do you want me to look at your back and shoulders?"

"No," Paul growled. "I want to go home and watch M.A.S.H. reruns."

"I'd prefer if you got checked out," Jordan said. "But I can't drag you to the hospital."

"I'm going home," Paul insisted. "And George, if I see you again anywhere near me, I won't be unprepared next time. Do you understand me?"

The two had a brief stare down and I wondered if they were going to come to blows once again. Finally, Paul said, "I'll wait until he's gone before I head home. I don't want to be ambushed."

Jordan turned to George and unlocked his handcuffs. "If I catch you assaulting people with any weapon, you're going to jail next time. I don't care how much paperwork I have to complete. Do you understand?"

The man nodded and shoved his hands in his pockets. Without another word, he turned and walked to his car parked at the far end of the lot. After a moment, the car lights came on and he drove away.

"Can I give you a lift home, Paul?" Jordan asked. "Or better yet, to the hospital?"

"Thanks, Deputy, but I'm fine."

"Are you sure?"

He nodded, still rubbing his wrists. "You had those on a little tight."

"Sorry about that."

"You know, I've got a theory on Joyce and George," Paul said. "Would you like to hear it?"

"I'm all ears," Jordan said. "Fire away."

"Joyce and I have been playing Mr. and Mrs. Santa for a few years now, so I've seen her interact with George many times. He's not a bad man, but I noticed him ignoring her, or dismissing her, more than once. It's like she was there, but she didn't really exist for him. Does that make sense?"

Based on what George had shared earlier in the day, it did. "What's your theory?" I asked.

"Well, I've been thinking about this a lot since she died, and I wonder if she was so dang bossy with me, always nitpicking about everything, because I heard her. I may have argued with her, but at least I listened."

As I stared at Santa, I understood what he was saying. People needed to be heard, and George had made it very clear he hadn't been the best listener. He fully admitted it had cost him his marriage. Maybe Paul was right—Joyce had felt so out of control in her own life, she'd desperately tried to rule over her small part of the Christmas Festival, including Paul.

"I wonder if there will even be a festival this year," Paul mused. "Joyce drove me nuts, but I can't imagine it without her. Every Santa needs his Mrs. Claus."

A wave a sadness broke through my bitter coldness and settled in my heart. Even though I'd never participated in the Heywood Christmas Festival, I knew it was important to everyone in town. It was a time of coming together and celebrating the holidays. From what Annabelle had told me, the night was truly magical.

"It's going to happen," I said as Jordan arched an eyebrow in my direction. "We're going to make sure of it."

Paul nodded and smiled. "I hope you're right." His gaze darted between Jordan and me. "If there's nothing else, I'd like to get home to my M.A.S.H. reruns."

"Sure," Jordan said. "Have a good one. Don't slip on the ice."

We watched until he was out of the parking lot and down the street.

"That's a pretty bold promise there, Sam," Jordan said.

Taking my elbow, he escorted me to the car. Hopefully I wouldn't freeze to death before we made it inside, and I was grateful chivalry wasn't quite dead yet.

"I k-know, b-but we need to catch this killer," I stuttered from the cold. "T-the festival has to happen. It's t-too important."

Once Jordan had tossed the tire iron in the back truck bed, we entered the cab and he turned up the heat again. "I won't disagree with you, but I can't let the crime scene go quite yet. I can't get past the feeling that the murder weapon is there."

"Understandable," I said. Placing my hands in front of the vents, I gave silent thanks to the warm air. "But if we catch the killer and he or she confesses, then we can have the festival because you'll have all the evidence you need."

"True."

"What do you think about George?" he asked. "I thought you said he didn't have a mean bone in his body."

"Well, obviously I was wrong about that," I said. "But what's interesting is that he didn't injure Paul, so it must not have been a very hard hit. But if he had killed Joyce, could he have struck her hard enough to kill her? Had Paul's coat really stopped the impact, or was George just not that strong?"

"Good points," Jordan said, pulling out of the parking lot. "But I do find it noteworthy that he chose a crowbar to attack Paul with. The coroner said the weapon used on Joyce would have been something similar, but wider."

"It might just be a coincidence," I said.

"I usually don't believe in coincidences," Jordan muttered.

We rode up Comfort Road in silence. When he parked in front of Sage Advice, I unbuckled my seatbelt and turned to him. "That's what we need to do."

"What?"

"Find the killer so the festival can go on this year," I said, my resolve stronger than ever.

"In three days' time?"

"Yes."

No pressure or anything.

CHAPTER 11

Jordan had been right—I'd slept better than I had in ages, and I knew it was the hot chocolate. With all its herbal goodness, I vowed to carry it in my store and hoped Sally and I could come to a mutually beneficial agreement. We could include little pouches in our bath baskets, put together baskets specifically for sleep and / or anxiety, sell it separately... the possibilities excited me.

After showering, doing some light yoga, drinking my coffee and feeding Catnip, I hurried downstairs to find a couple of customers at the front door, waiting to come in.

Once I unlocked the door, two women walked in, but I didn't get the sense they were together. One—a little younger than me—coughed and blew her nose while the elderly one gave her dirty looks.

"I need something for the flu," the sick woman said. I pointed her to our table of antivirals, then turned to my second customer and smiled.

"You shouldn't allow people that sick in your store," she hissed. "And *she* shouldn't be out in public!"

I glanced over my shoulder. What was the woman to do if she lived alone? Suffer at home, with no relief? I wasn't going to argue. "What can I help you with?"

"Anxiety," she said. "And probably the flu after being in the same space as snotty nose over there."

Figures. As I studied her lined face, I could practically feel the worry and sadness coming off her. With her gray hair piled on top of her head in a messy bun and her thick glasses enhancing the bags under her eyes, she did look like she wasn't getting enough sleep, if any. And she reminded me of a Sphynx cat—the bald, wrinkly ones. Her lack of sleep made her my kindred spirit, but I didn't appreciate her nasty attitude.

"Let's head over to this table," I said, shuffling her over the anxiety tinctures and capsules. After asking her a few questions, I decided the Passionflower and Valerian mixture would most likely work best for her. "I'm sorry you're so stressed out," I said, leading her up to the cash register. "The holidays can do that to some people. I'm sure this will help, though. Just take it as directed."

Unfortunately, the sick woman found what she needed and stood behind my anxiety-ridden customer waiting to purchase her goods... and began sneezing.

The cat-like woman whipped around and pushed the cold sufferer so hard, she fell into one of the glass display tables with a loud yelp. "Stay away from me, you germ-infested pig!"

Time seemed to slow. Products went flying and glass crashed to the floor. I gasped in horror as my customer lay in the middle of it all covered in oils and pieces of bottles. What in the world had just happened? Was a sneeze a reason to become violent? Stunned, I simply stood behind the register and tried to comprehend the scene that reminded me of something that would have happened in *As The Years Turn.* Except, this was real glass, and as my gaze locked with the sick woman's, she burst into real tears. They spurned me into action.

"Get out," I yelled to the older customer, finally able to move. "Get out of my store, and don't come back!"

"She shouldn't be out in public!" she shouted. "What has this world come to where people go out with a cold or the flu and spread it to everyone?"

"You need more than an anxiety tincture," I hissed as I hurried around her to help my customer. Glass crunched under my sneakers as I carefully walked through the wreckage.

I grabbed the woman's hand and squatted next to her. "Are you okay? Do you think you can stand?"

Wait. *Should* she stand?

"I think I'm fine," she whispered. "I just needed something to help me feel better."

As I assisted her to her feet, I shot the older woman a glare. "I changed my mind. Don't you move a muscle."

I led the sick woman behind the counter so she could sit down on a stool. Once she was settled, I turned to her attacker. "What's your name?" I asked.

She lifted her chin defiantly and I was tempted to give it a good smack.

"Tell me your name," I hissed, grabbing her purse out of her hand.

"Hey!" she yelled. "You can't do that!"

"I don't care," I said. "I'm taking down your name and your address, and then I'm going to make sure you pay for all the repairs."

Yanking open her purse, I found her wallet. Sarah Billings. After jotting down her address with a shaky hand, I handed it back to her. "You will pay for the damage you've caused, and if this lady wants to press charges against you, I'll testify to what I saw." I glanced over at the sick woman. "Do you want me to call the police?"

She shook her head. "I really want my medicine and to go back to bed."

I nodded, but pulled my phone out of my pocket anyway, then dialed Jordan while continuing to shake with anger. If this had happened on my soap opera, *As The Years Turn*, my character, Cassie, would unleash a verbal tirade and probably make plans to kill Sarah. I held my tongue and reminded myself those pesky, little things called laws prevented me from plotting a murder. But one could daydream, right?

After Jordan answered and I had explained what happened, he sighed.

"I can't get there right now," he said. "I'm at an accident on the highway. Take down everyone's name and phone number, snap some pictures, then I'll deal with it later."

"When are you going to get some help?" I asked.

74

"I don't know. The sheriff has a temperature of a hundred-and-four. Another deputy can't leave his bathroom. Everyone's still down for the count."

"Are you feeling okay?"

"So far so good. Gotta go."

I placed my phone on the counter and met Sarah's gaze. "You will leave my store, and you are persona non grata here. I never want to see you again. And as an herbalist, I'm going to suggest you see a doctor. Maybe even a psychiatrist, because your actions here today have been so far out of line, I believe you should be in jail, or a psych ward."

Sarah showed absolutely no regret for her activities. "I'm not the problem here. She is. Everyone knows they should stay home when sick instead of being out in public and spreading germs. She's probably just ruined my Christmas, and yours."

"Leave," I said, pointing at the door. "Now."

As she walked toward the front door, glass crunched under her shoes. She looked over her shoulder, smiled, and said, "I'd clean this up if I were you. "Someone's going to get glass in their foot."

While she broke out into laughter, Annabelle entered. Sarah pushed past her out the door, but Annabelle didn't even flinch while taking in the disaster.

"What in the world happened?" she asked, bringing her hand to her mouth. Tears sprung to her eyes as our gazes met.

"Hang on," I said. "Let me help this customer." I grabbed a fresh batch of tincture for her, then placed it in a bag along with our business card. After handing it to her, I said, "If you want to press charges, let me know. My number's in the sack."

"Thank you," she said. "Let me pay for this, though."

I shook my head. "Go home and feel better soon."

She smiled and slowly made her way through the carnage. Then I focused on Annabelle who was hanging up her coat. After explaining the whole debacle, I said, "Sarah Billings is to never step foot in this store again."

Annabelle nodded, then sprayed the room with a lemon-scented disinfectant she'd formulated. "That girl was really sick and her cooties

75

are floating around everywhere," she muttered. "I get why Sarah was upset, but dang, talk about an overreaction."

I took the pictures as Jordan had suggested while Annabelle went into the back room to fetch the broom and dustpan. Then, we both carefully gathered the larger pieces of glass and set them into the garbage can.

Clean up took longer and was more difficult than I imagined. The oils had begun to settle into the hardwood floors. The glass was slippery. Annabelle cut her finger and the blood pooled with the oils. After a while, both of us had taken to swearing.

"Okay, I think we're good," she said over an hour later. "I have a feeling there's going to be a stain on the floor though."

I sat cross-legged on the hardwood and nodded. "Maybe we should move some of the other tables... reconfigure the whole store so this spot is covered." Then I remembered my exciting discovery the previous night. "Yes! We'll have to do that because I found us a new product!"

As I told Annabelle about the hot chocolate, her enthusiasm levels reached mine. "Oh, my gosh! I can't wait to try it! I didn't know she had that on the menu!"

"She doesn't. It's a special recipe she's been perfecting. It was so tasty, and my sleep was amazing."

"When are we going to carry it?"

"I have to make an appointment to meet with her to discuss it, but she seemed as motivated as me about the arrangement."

Ho! Ho! Ho! Merry Christmas! Sounded from the back room.

Annabelle and I glanced at the front door to find a gentleman staring at us. Of course he would be—we were sitting on the floor and the whole store smelled overwhelmingly of essential oils and herbs due to the debacle earlier.

As we scrambled to our feet, I took the garbage can to the back room while Annabelle assisted him in finding a gift for his teenaged daughter.

I looked at the clock on the wall. Almost noon. Should I go to the Senior Center today or skip it? It could very well lead me to clues on who the murderer was, so I decided to head over.

After donning my boots and parka I kept by the rear door, I went to the front of the store to share my plans with Annabelle. I found the gentleman customer leaving with not one, but two big gift baskets.

"One for his wife, too," Annabelle whispered as she waved at him. "I told him she'd be jealous if she didn't get one as well."

"I'm sure you're right," I replied. "You probably just saved him from an embarrassing scene on Christmas morning."

Annabelle glanced at me from head-to-toe. "Where are you off to?"

"The Senior Center. After that I thought I'd stop by On The River and talk with Sally about carrying the hot chocolate."

"I'll hold down the fort here, Captain!" she said, giving a salute. "If you can, bring me a sample of Sally's offerings. I could use a little hot cocoa right now!"

As I strode out the door, I gave her a quick wave over my shoulder.

"And don't you worry about Sarah Billings," Annabelle called. "I'll make sure she gets hers!"

I paused for a moment, unsure if I wanted to know what revenge Annabelle had in store. The last time someone had crossed her, she'd hid a dead fish in his car. Before that, she'd stolen a bunch of money that was due to Gina and given it to her. Did I really want to be let in on what she planned next? Maybe? But honestly, I had enough to worry about, so I pushed through the door. Since the sun was shining above and the pavement was clear but wet, I decided to walk.

When I arrived at the overly-decorated Senior Center, I took a moment to take in the Christmas embellishments. Twinkling lights and red and green streamers hung from the ceiling. A large Christmas tree stood at the front door, its branches heavy with ornaments. No place was safe from Christmas in Heywood, and I loved it.

I asked the elderly receptionist where the pinochle game was being held, and she pointed me to a room at the end of a corridor.

As I walked down the hall, I glanced at the pictures of the Senior Center members at their events—lectures, parties, and of course, pinochle games. I noted a coat rack outside the door and hung up my own parka. Running a hand over the front of my shirt, I hoped I looked okay and none of these people would trounce me too badly. I had to make an effort to learn the game, even though I really wanted to meet the woman who had a crush on George.

Stepping into the room, I noted the table with cookies and coffee to my right. I found George and he smiled and waved, his antics from the previous night forgotten. Thank goodness he wasn't going to make things awkward.

My grin faded when I saw the woman standing next to him. No, George wasn't going to make this afternoon awkward, but chances were good Sarah Billings would.

The Sarah who had pushed the customer in my store and the one who had a crush on George were one and the same.

CHAPTER 12

ANGER HAD CLOUDED my thought processes at the store and I hadn't put the two together. Jordan had shared the woman who had a crush on George was named Sarah. Of course, there could very well be more than one woman with that name in town. As my luck would have it, that wasn't the case in this scenario.

While she spoke to George, she batted her eyelashes, which I found ridiculous for a woman her age. Heck, the gesture looked silly on any woman. I also noticed she'd unbuttoned her blouse a couple slots from when she was at Sage Advice, revealing some cleavage. There was no mistaking she was trying to garner George's attention, and he seemed to be completely oblivious to it. In fact, if she undressed and stood before him naked, he probably wouldn't notice. He smiled and nodded politely, completely immune to her caress of his shoulder.

He waved again and excused himself to Sarah. As he approached me, I watched her. When she noticed where he was going, her eyes widened in surprise, then narrowed, as if she were trying to figure out a way to get rid of me in the most violent way possible.

"Hey, Sam," he said. "I'm so glad you could make it."

I shook his offered palm and smiled, keeping an eye on Sarah. "Thanks again for the invite. How are you feeling today?" My basic manners prevented me from saying what I wanted, which was, *how are you feeling after trying to club Santa to death?*

"I'm fine," he muttered, glancing around to make sure no one overheard us. "I shouldn't have done what I did last night, and I have to admit, I'm ashamed of my actions. It helps me to be around my group of people here. Helps keep my sanity."

"Your grief got the best of you," I replied. Hopefully it didn't sound like I was forgiving or excusing him. "I know it's hard, but you've got to try to deal with it in ways that aren't going to hurt others."

He stared at me a long moment before he said, "I feel like that's coming from a place of deep knowledge. You're familiar with the pain of losing a loved one."

I nodded but held my tongue. To this day, the only person I'd wanted to kill was my husband, who was already dead. His murderer had gotten his dues and would rot in prison for the rest of his miserable life. My husband, on the other hand, had not atoned to me for ruining my life, and I'd never get that satisfaction or much needed closure.

A string of curses sat on the tip of my tongue, but I smiled and tried to ignore the sudden hot flash railing through me like a freight train. "I did lose someone in a violent way. The need for revenge is overwhelming at times." No reason to tell him I wanted to off the dead guy.

"I'd like to hear about that sometime," he said. As I met his gaze, I realized he considered our shared emotions a bonding moment. I had no intention of bonding with anyone here. I just wanted to collect information.

"Perhaps," I said. "It's a painful story I don't like to remember very often."

"I understand, Sam. Come and meet the rest of the crew, then we'll give you a quick lesson before we get down to business."

As he led me around the room introducing me to people, I smiled and nodded, shook hands and kept Sarah in my sights. Her hateful glare followed me, making me nervous, yet she kept her distance.

"You look familiar," a woman said after we'd been introduced. Elderly like everyone in the room, she wore her gray hair short and spiky. As she narrowed her gaze and pursed her heavily lined lips, she reminded me of a bird. For the life of me, I couldn't remember her name, even though she'd just told me. My attention was focused on making sure Sarah didn't stab me in the back or hit me over the head with a chair.

"Sam Jones," I said. "I own Sage Advice. Perhaps you've been in the store and seen me there?"

"Oh, no, I don't go in there. My doctor forbids it."

Ah, yes. "Would that be Doctor Butte?" I asked.

She nodded. "He says you peddle weeds and witchcraft."

Of course he did.

Garrett Butte was what my former boss, Bonnie, called a drug dealer with a license. She believed he didn't like curing his patients but keep them just sick enough so they continued to come back to him for more drugs. They'd had many arguments about herbs versus pharmaceuticals and the role of an herbalist versus the role of a doctor, and they'd always dissolved into name-calling, screaming matches. If Butte had his way, Sage Advice would close its doors.

"Well, I don't think that's quite accurate," I said, smiling. "We do help people with natural remedies provided by Mother Nature. There's nothing wrong with it, and our products do work."

I heard a snicker from the other side of the room and glanced over to find Sarah smiling. I should've amended my statement. *Our products work as long as customers don't shove other customers into tables and ruin the products.*

"Well, I'm perfectly happy with the prescription Doctor Butte has me on," the woman continued. "My blood pressure medication is working wonderfully, as do my acid reflux pills."

"That's great," I said, fighting the urge to tell her that both could be controlled through herbal remedies. I wasn't here to fight anyone about medication.

"I know! You look like that actress, Andie MacDowell!" the woman said.

After hearing the comparison often and for years, I simply smiled. "Thank you. I'll take that as a compliment."

"Well, I have no idea who that is," George said, chuckling. "But let me introduce you to my friend, Sarah."

Wonderful. Absolutely wonderful.

Taking a deep breath, I allowed him to lead me over to her. Our stares locked and her gaze brought back an unpleasant memory. One day during the spring, I'd been strolling along the Riverwalk. The birds had been singing, the leaves on the trees sprouting, and the fresh scent of renewal filled the air. It had been a perfect day until I came across an unleashed dog. He stared at me, and I at him. He growled and bared his teeth, and I'd been terrified I was going to be attacked. The same feeling came over me as I stood in front of Sarah. Her gaze softened as she looked at George.

"Sarah, this is Sam," George said. "She's going to be joining us for the game today."

"We've met," she said.

"Oh! I didn't know you two were acquainted!" George exclaimed.

"It was a brief encounter," I replied. Although spilling the whole story of Sarah and her incredibly offensive behavior in my store sat on the tip of my tongue, I held it in place. If she wanted to share it with George, she could do so herself, but I had a feeling she wouldn't. How would she justify pushing a stranger into a glass table?

Sarah placed her hand on George's shoulder. "We're still going to be partners today, correct?"

I noted the tone of her voice was much softer and sweeter when she spoke to George than when she'd been at Sage Advice. Then, she might as well have been possessed by Satan himself.

"Not today," George said. "I figured I'd partner with Sam and help her learn the game."

A blush crawled from Sarah's forehead, down her cheeks and neck and into her shirt. As her hands fisted at her sides and her mouth drew into a fine line, a jolt of fear pierced my heart. After her hateful glare and what I'd seen her do at my store, I wondered if I could be staring at a murderer. If she was this upset about George trying to teach me a game, her fury would be off the charts at him being unable to get over his ex-wife.

And I didn't want to be in the same room as her.

"George, I think it's best if I go," I said. "I had an incident at Sage Advice today and I'm needed there."

"That's too bad," he said, furrowing his brow. "I was looking forward to playing with you and getting to know you better."

"Yes, well, I wanted to drop in and say hello because I said I would, but I really can't stay."

"I can walk you out," Sarah said. As she placed her hand on my forearm, her fingers dug into my skin just enough to convey that I didn't have an option.

Gosh, she was really starting to make me uncomfortable. "I can see myself out," I said, yanking my arm away. "Thanks, though."

I hurried from the room, grabbed my coat from the rack, and headed down the hall. When I heard footsteps behind me, I turned to see Sarah following.

What was wrong with this psychopath? What was she going to do? Attack me in the corridor?

Pushing my curls from my face, I rushed to the front desk, hoping to find safety with the elderly woman who had been there when I walked in, although I wasn't quite sure what she could've done.

It was empty.

Sarah was now jogging down the hallway and would be on top of me in seconds.

I ran from the building to the parking lot, thankful it wasn't a sheet of ice. Cars drove up and down Comfort Road, so I hoped she'd leave me alone.

How wrong I'd been.

A hand landed on my shoulder and I spun around. "What?!" I yelled. "What do you want?"

She smiled and said, "Someone's a little skittish today."

Cassie, my character from *As The Years Turn* surfaced, and I straightened my shoulders. "You showed up in my store, pushed a woman for sneezing, ruined a display table and a bunch of my product, and if you weren't acting like a psychopath then, you most certainly are now. Leave me alone or you'll regret it, Sarah."

"Is that a threat?" she asked, arching a brow. "Because if it is, I don't take kindly to threats."

"I don't threaten people. I make promises." That had been an actual line from a script. In the show, I'd pulled out a gun and shot the woman after reciting it. Too bad laws prevented me from doing that now. Well, that and the fact I didn't own a gun. Details matter.

"You listen to me," she hissed, her finger an inch away from my face. "I don't know who you think you are moving in on George like that. He's off-limits to you."

Wait a minute. She thought I wanted to start dating George?

I burst out laughing and slapped her finger to the side. "You want George? He's yours," I said. "I have no interest in him."

Confusion flickered across her face. "Then what are you doing here with him?"

"I told him I'd stop by, so I did," I replied. "And just for the record... I think you're wasting your time. His heart belonged to Joyce, and I have a feeling it always will." Besides, who wanted to date someone who resembled a bald cat?

"Joyce is dead," she said, shrugging.

Once again, I wondered if I had discovered the murderer. She obviously had no sympathy for Joyce's passing, and when a small smile curled her lips, I couldn't stand to be in her presence any longer. As Annabelle would've said, Sarah had really bad juju.

"I feel sorry for you," I said. "It must be hard going through life with such disdain in your heart."

"What does that mean?" she asked.

"I can see you aren't the least bit upset over Joyce's death. In fact, if I had to assign an emotion to your feelings on it, I would say you're happy. Do you think it clears the way for you and George to be together?"

Her cheeks reddened and she didn't answer.

"That's what I thought. Have a good day, Sarah, and don't forget to stay the heck away from me."

I hurried down the street toward Sage Advice, glancing over my shoulder once or twice to make sure she stayed where she was.

Too upset to stop in and see Sally, I headed toward the store, pulled my phone out of my parka pocket, and dialed Jordan.

"What's up, Sam?"

"I need to see you," I said. "I think I may have just found the killer... and if she isn't the murderer, she's a danger to society."

CHAPTER 13

I HUNG UP MY PHONE, shoved it in my parka pocket, then flung open the door of my store to find Annabelle with a customer. Both turned to me and my heart sank when I saw who it was.

Mary, Joyce's sister.

Suppressing a groan, I shucked my coat and smiled. Yes, I may be able to talk tough, but my encounter with Sarah had shaken me to my core, and my hands trembled from my frayed nerves.

And now I had to deal with Mary.

"Hi, Sam!" Annabelle said. "You remember Mary, Joyce's sister?"

I nodded and shook the woman's hand. "Sam Jones," I said. "I'm terribly sorry for your loss."

"You found my sister, correct?" Mary asked as she pushed a lock of platinum blonde hair behind her ear, her blue eyes brimming with tears.

"We did."

"I was wondering if you could walk me through what happened that evening?" she asked. "I want the police to find the killer so badly, and I'm hoping I can give them more information."

"Of course," I said, trading glances with Annabelle. "Would you like some coffee or something?"

She shook her head.

I smiled and laid my hand on her forearm. "Let me grab another stool from the back room and the three of us can chat for a bit."

I walked into the workroom and dumped my parka on the counter. Placing my palms on the surface, I closed my eyes and took a few deep breaths to calm myself. When visiting the Senior Center, I had expected sweet old people, not a woman who resembled a bald cat with a derangement syndrome. As anger overtook my fear, I whispered a curse. Sarah had gotten under my skin and now I was furious I'd allowed her to do so. I never should've run from her or shown any other sign of weakness. She seemed to be the type to thrive on it.

Glancing at the doorway to the main store, I sighed. I was happy to talk with Mary. I just wished I'd had time to recuperate from Sarah first.

After a moment I felt slightly better, and grabbed a stool. Annabelle was already perched on one behind the cash register, another one at her side. I brought it out to Mary and then sat next to Annabelle.

"Thanks so much for speaking with me," she said.

"Of course. What can we tell you?"

"Just... just how your whole evening went. What were you doing there? How did you find Paul? What are your thoughts?"

"Well, we want the killer caught just as much as you do," Annabelle said. "It was, like, terrible what happened to Joyce."

"Thank you. I've given the police a few ideas of who did it so they could look into them, but I'm hoping to provide them with more details."

"We've talked to them, too," I said. "We've already told them everything that happened that night."

"And I appreciate that," Mary said, smiling. "I'd just like to hear it for myself."

"We went there because we were setting up our table for the Christmas Festival," Annabelle said. "Our table was close to the main door. Once we were done, we walked around to see who else was offering their products."

"The Christmas tree was in the middle of the gym, so our view was blocked," I said. When we got to the other side of the tree, that's when we found Joyce."

"Then you called the police?" Mary asked.

"Yes, of course."

"How did you stumble on Paul? You found him in the pantry, right?"

Annabelle nodded. "When we called the police, they asked us to take a look around and see if there was anyone else injured. Then we found Paul because he was, like, snoring so loudly in the pantry."

"We actually thought an animal had been trapped in there," I said, smiling. "He was *loud*."

Mary grinned but narrowed her gaze. "So no one else was there?"

Annabelle and I exchanged glances, both of us shaking our heads. "It was just us."

"Do you think Paul was faking his sleeping?" she asked.

"I don't," I said. "He was pretty out of it when we woke him, just like he'd been deep in dreamland."

"And you didn't find anyone else in the building?"

"No, we didn't," I said, having a bad feeling the conversation was leading somewhere I didn't want it to go.

"So, you two could've easily have been the killers," Mary stated.

Thick silence fell over us. Annabelle stared at her slack-jawed, while I froze in place.

After a long moment, I asked, "Are you accusing us of killing your sister?"

Mary shrugged. "I'm saying it's a definite possibility."

"And what would our motive be?"

"I have no idea. Joyce could be difficult at times. For all I know, you three could've had some type of argument and you lost your tempers, killed her, then claimed to find the body."

"You're, like, out of your mind," Annabelle said, shaking her head. "Neither of us knew Joyce."

"Well, who do you think killed her?" Mary asked.

"There are quite a few suspects," I said, without mentioning she was one of them. "We'll have to let the police sift through all their clues and give them a chance to figure it out." Then, I remembered a question I needed answered. "Can you tell me what your prescription bottle was doing in Terry Warner's house?"

She furrowed her brow in confusion. "What are you talking about?"

"I was at Terry's speaking with him the other day. I found a prescription bottle for arthritis pain killer with your name on it in his medicine chest."

"What were you doing looking in there?" Mary asked.

"I had a cut on my finger that was bothering me and decided to see if he had a Band-Aid while I was using the restroom," I lied.

She shook her head. "Joyce was always forgetting to fill her pain meds, so she often took mine. Drove me nuts."

I pursed my lips in disappointment, but it was just as I'd expected.

"Have they questioned you?" Mary asked, her voice holding an accusing tone.

"As a matter of fact, they have," I said. "Very thoroughly. We don't appreciate you coming in here and blaming us for your sister's death."

"I'm trying to find out who murdered her," Mary said.

"I understand that, but you can't go around blaming people like this," I said. "I think it may be time for you to leave."

We stared at each other for a long moment. "You know, defensiveness only makes you look guilty," she finally said.

I'd worked my tail off trying to find out who killed her sister, but she didn't know that. It may have been something I'd share with her, except, between my confrontation with Sarah and now Mary, anger railed through me and I fisted my hands at my sides. I didn't have the patience to explain myself. Instead, I needed some peace and quiet, and not another woman in my face blaming me for something I didn't do. "Like I said, I think you better leave."

"Cassie's in the house," Annabelle muttered, referring to my character on *As The Years Turn*. Funny how I could adopt her persona when I felt threatened.

"I'll be speaking to the police about you," Mary said, standing.

Movement at the front door caught my eye. Jordan strode up the walkway. "You won't have to go far," I said. "Help yourself."

As he entered, everyone stared at him. After wiping his boots on the welcome mat, he glanced up and smiled. The grin quickly faded as the tense vibe hit him.

"What's going on here?" he asked.

"Mary's accusing us of murdering her sister," Annabelle said, her voice dripping with sarcasm. "Isn't that sweet?"

Jordan rolled his eyes and unzipped his coat as he strode over to us. "You've got to be kidding. Mary, I've asked you to allow me to handle this investigation, remember?"

"Yes, I do, and the killer still hasn't been caught!" she yelled. "I want justice for my sister!"

"Everyone does," Jordan said gently. He placed a hand on her shoulder. "But you can't go around accusing people of murder like this."

"Then do your job," she hissed at Jordan. Turning, she strode to the front door, then glared at all three of us before leaving.

"Well, wasn't that something else," Annabelle said. "What a witch!"

"She's been calling me multiple times a day to check if I've caught the murderer yet," Jordan said, running his hand over his beard. Obviously, he hadn't bothered to shave in a few days and the facial hair was growing in more white than black. Another couple of days, and he'd be able to play Santa in the Christmas Festival... if the town had one this year. "I've been ignoring her."

"How's the investigation going?" I asked.

"Okay. But first, tell me about Sarah."

He sat where Mary had been, and I began my tale. Now that some time had passed, I was able to look at the encounter with a little less emotion. "She was trying to intimidate me," I said. "There's no doubt about it in my mind."

"Did you feel unsafe?" Jordan asked. "Do you think she could hurt someone?"

"I do. She's got the disposition for it, and she certainly has the physical strength. She proved that this morning when she pushed the woman through a glass table and to the floor."

"That could've been very messy," he said, wincing. "I'm glad no one was seriously hurt."

Annabelle raised her hand, showing him her bandage. "The cleaning crew took the brunt of it," she said.

"Ouch. Do you need stitches, Annabelle?" Jordan asked.

She shook her head. "It's deep, but I think it'll be okay. I'm using some of my herbal salves to promote healing. If I decide I need stitches, I'll go to the clinic."

"Is that other customer going to press charges?" Jordan asked.

"She said she wasn't," I replied. "But we shall see. I've banned Sarah from the store, though."

"Smart move." Jordan sighed. "Are *you* going to press charges against her?"

"I haven't made my up mind yet." The vengeful part of me wanted to sic my lawyer on her, but another part didn't want to deal with any of it.

"You've had quite the day." Jordan reached across the counter and squeezed my fingers.

The gesture comforted me and I smiled. "Tell me about it. I've been blamed for a murder and also accused of trying to steal George from Sarah. Both are absurd allegations."

"So, George isn't your type?" Annabelle asked.

I shook my head.

She stared at Jordan, wiggling her eyebrows. "Well I wonder what your type would be?"

I glared at her, hoping to convey that Jordan and I were friends, and we would remain that way.

Jordan's gaze wandered around the store, oblivious to Annabelle's hints. "You know, if she's making threats like that to you, I don't see any reason why she wouldn't kill Joyce so that hopefully George would focus on her."

"I agree," I said. "Sarah was very territorial over him. I think she needs to be investigated further."

"It all fits," he muttered. "She's not getting the attention she wants from George and knows he's pining over his ex-wife, who has moved past their marriage. In her mind, she gets rid of Joyce and George would be all hers. A crime of passion."

"Sounds like you've got it all figured out," Annabelle said. "Go arrest the conniving vixen!"

"I wish it were that simple," Jordan said. "I need proof. Maybe a search warrant of her house will give me the murder weapon."

"You still can't find it?" I asked.

He shook his head. "Without a huge stroke of luck, I don't think we will. It's been too long, unless the killer is keeping it under wraps."

"Or maybe as a souvenir," Annabelle said, nodding. "Which is totally sick and twisted, just like Sarah."

We sat in silence for a brief moment, each of us lost in our own thoughts. But then I remember Jordan was going to give us updates on the investigation, hopefully something we didn't already know. "Do you have any new news on your end?" I asked.

He nodded. "Yes. I almost forgot to tell you... we found out who the online stalker is."

Annabelle gasped. "What was his name again? KAK?"

"Yes. Short for Kill All Konservatives," Jordan replied.

"Well, don't keep us in suspense," I said. "Who is it? Who is crazy KAK?"

CHAPTER 14

"Is KAK in town?" I asked, holding my breath.

"Yes. My guy from Chicago called this morning. The computer signal was pinged all around the world and he was finally able to track to Heywood."

"Isn't that incredible?" Annabelle asked. "Technology is, like, so amazing."

"Who is it?" I asked, tapping the counter. "Don't keep us in suspense!"

"It's George," Jordan said. "The signal was pinpointed to his house."

Stunned, I sat in silence and Annabelle gasped. "George?!" she yelled. "George as in Joyce's husband? He was hassling his own wife online?"

Jordan nodded. "Don't forget the "ex" there, Annabelle. She'd left him and they were divorced, but yes. I haven't talked to him about it, but it's been formally traced back to his house. George is the person behind Kill All Konservatives."

I recalled the dining room table being used as a desk... the papers and computer littering the surface.

"Do you think he killed her?" I asked. "If he threatened to online, would he actually go through with it in real life?"

"I don't know," Jordan said. "He's got the motivation and the opportunity."

"He knew exactly where she was going to be," I said. "She'd posted it online."

"Yes, he did. And, as he said, if he couldn't have her, no one else could."

My heart thundered as I stared at him. "Do you think you've caught him?"

"Maybe."

Annabelle pulled out her phone and began typing. A moment later, she had the screen face toward us. "He's on there right now, arguing with Terry about immigration and taxes."

Shouldn't George be at pinocle? I glanced at the clock. Over an hour had passed since I'd been at the Senior Center. Where had the time gone?

Squinting, I read the exchange.

KILL ALL CONSERVATIVES: *You idiots are so dumb, you couldn't find your hand if it was in front of your face. Don't you know that we are all people of this planet, that there aren't any borders?*

Terry Warner: *And you libtards are idiots for thinking that way. Of course there are borders, and the people flooding them are sucking our resources dry, forcing all of us to pay more taxes!*

THE FIGHT CONTINUED, but I didn't want to read anymore. I hated politics.

I imagined George hunched over his computer in the dining room, typing away, maybe laughing at the argument. But why hassle his ex-wife the way he had? It just made no sense to me.

"Well, we know George isn't as harmless as he looks by the way he took a swing at Paul," Jordan said, rubbing his forehead. "And maybe, he's going after Terry, studying his online habits and getting ready to kill him as well."

A point I hadn't considered.

Jordan stood and stretched his hands over his head, then yawned. "I think I better head over there and make an arrest for cyberstalking. At least that will get him offline. Then, I can focus on questioning him about the murder."

"I want to go with you," I said.

"Civilians aren't allowed to accompany officers on an arrest," Jordan replied.

I rolled my eyes. "I think all rules are out the window at this point. You sort of deputized me when you asked me to talk to the suspects."

Jordan sighed. "I knew that was a mistake, but I was between a rock and a hard place."

I shrugged and went into the back room to fetch my coat.

When I returned, Jordan said, "George could turn dangerous if he feels threatened, Sam. I'm not going to put you in harm's way."

"He's not going to hurt me," I replied. "In fact, I think he probably wants to date me."

Annabelle snorted, then burst out laughing while Jordan's nostrils flared.

"Did you tell him you don't date?" Jordan asked. "I mean, that's what you told me, remember?"

"No, I didn't specifically say that to him, but I have no intention of getting together with George. He's practically old enough to be my father."

Annabelle wiped the tears tracking down her cheeks. "Oh, my goodness. This is too funny."

"Let's head out, Jordan," I said, ignoring her. "I'm going with you."

His shoulder sagged in defeat, and he finally nodded. We walked out the door in silence, entered his truck and drove to George's house.

"I'm glad the snow has stayed away," Jordan said. "But look over the mountain there. I think we're going to get hit yet again."

The white peaks were shrouded in thick, heavy clouds. "Maybe it will bypass us," I said. The thought of more snow made me want to cry and scream all at once.

When we arrived at George's, Jordan turned to me. "I wish you'd stay in the car."

I smiled, then opened the door. "Sorry, I'm not a genie. I can't make all your wishes come true."

He cursed under his breath and we headed up the walkway.

After knocking, Jordan stepped in front of me, acting as a shield between me and the old man who answered. I hit him in the back as he completely blocked my view.

"Officer!" George exclaimed. "What can I do for you? Did you find Joyce's killer?"

"Possibly," Jordan said. "Can we come in?"

I peeked around the deputy's shoulder and waved. "Hi, George."

"Sam! What a lovely surprise. I didn't see you back there. Yes! Please! Everyone come in!"

We entered the house and followed George to the living room. I eyed the computer as we sat down.

"What can I do for you two?" George asked.

"Well, first, I want you to sign off from your computer, George," Jordan said. "I know you're responsible for the Kill All Konservatives persona."

The color drained from his wrinkled face. "How... how did you find out? I've been so careful!"

"You have," Jordan said. "And frankly, I'm impressed. Most seniors I know can barely turn on a computer, let alone reroute an IP through a few different countries."

George pursed his lips and nodded. "So, what now?"

"Please go turn off the computer as I asked," Jordan commanded, pointing at the device.

George walked over to the dining room table and pressed a few buttons. With a sigh, he returned to the living room and sat down, staring at Jordan expectantly.

"I see you've been harassing Terry Warner, as well," Jordan said.

"Just a little fun and games for the jerk," George said. "He thinks he's quite smart, but he can't form an argument to save his life."

"Why did you choose Kill All Konservatives as your online name?" I asked.

"Because I'm as conservative as they come," George said, winking. "I figure no one would ever think it was me. And, I thought I'd been careful enough to hide my identity."

"It took a Chicago cybersecurity cop to dismantle all your misdirection," Jordan said. "Like I mentioned before, I'm impressed, but you still broke the law."

George clasped his hands in his lap and furrowed his brow. "I didn't mean any harm. I'm just a lonely old man looking to stir the pot a little with Terry the Turd."

"That may be the case, George, but you still broke the law," Jordan said as I coughed in my hand to hide a snicker. "I'm going to need to arrest you for the online harassment of Terry Warner, and we need to have an honest conversation on Joyce's death."

"What about it?" George asked.

"You threatened to kill her online multiple times," Jordan said. "Did that bleed over into real life?"

George's eyes widened. "No! I didn't hurt Joyce! How dare you even consider such a thing!"

As I studied him, I tried to decipher if he was truly mortified or if it was all an act. Honestly, I couldn't tell. I wanted this case to be over so the Christmas Festival could move forward and I wouldn't have to think about killers anymore.

"Then what about the threats to Joyce?" I asked. "Why bully her and tell her you were going to kill her?"

He sighed and slumped in the chair. "I was hoping that if she saw how scary the world could be, she'd come back to me."

The room quieted for a few seconds as I tried to wrap my mind around George's thinking processes. "Let me get this straight," I said, pushing my glasses up my nose. "First, Joyce left you and you weren't happy about it, correct?"

"No, I wasn't happy about it at all."

"And then, she got into politics, where she met Terry, which also didn't make you happy."

"That's correct," George replied. "She should be spending her twilight years traveling and socializing, not bothering with politics."

"Well, that's what *you'd* like to see her do," I reminded him. "So, in order for her to bend to your wishes, you thought it would be a good idea to create an online persona and scare the heck out of her?"

He lowered his head and wouldn't meet my gaze. "Well, I can see how that sounds now."

"You were online, threatening to kill your ex-wife!" I said. "So that she'd come back to you?"

The room went quiet again and I shook my head. "Seriously, George. What kind of mental gymnastics did you go through to come to the conclusion that was a good idea?"

"At the time, I thought it was a crazy plan that may work," he said. "Now, I can see that I was out of my mind with grief over the loss of my marriage."

"George, you told me you took responsibility for the end of it," I said. "You admitted you were the problem."

"And I still believe that," he said.

"But you didn't kill her?" I asked.

He shook his head. "I'd never do anything to hurt Joyce."

But he had no issues making death threats to scare her. Moving from threats to carrying them out wasn't that big of a jump.

Jordan sighed. "Let's head down to the station, George."

"Do you really need to arrest me?" he asked. "I didn't hurt anyone."

"I still haven't determined that," Jordan said.

"But I just told you!" George replied, shooting to his feet.

Jordan also stood and placed his hands on his gun belt. "You made threats against your wife, as well as Terry Warner, and you actually tried to beat Paul over the head with a crowbar. What you say right now isn't that convincing with the evidence piling up against you, George."

The two men stared at each other, the elderly man's hands fisted at his sides.

"We can do this the hard way, or the easy way," Jordan said. "I'd personally prefer the easy way. I'm feeling a bit tired and lazy today."

Finally, George nodded and Jordan led him out of the house. I trailed behind, feeling a little sorry for the old man. He'd admitted to being an online stalker and jerk, but had denied killing Joyce.

Had we found the killer, or was he or she still out there?

CHAPTER 15

THE NEXT MORNING, I woke early and wrapped Annabelle's gun holster, still unsure what to get Jordan or Gina. I'd have to ask Annabelle for some ideas when she came in. In my Hollywood days, Gerald and I hadn't exchanged gifts. What did you get someone who had everything they wanted and if they didn't have it, could buy it at any time? In my Hollywood life, I found my Christmas joy by writing out checks to different charities I supported. Despite the murder, this year was different. My soul felt unlike any other time in my life—full of happiness and love—and I had none of the blessings, or maybe I should say trappings, of wealth that I'd had before.

In fact, I would say our money had gotten in the way of the true meaning of Christmas. My Hollywood life during the holidays had been about big parties and dressing in the most elegant gowns I could find, not about spending quality time with friends and family. This year, I had worried and was quite depressed about being alone on Christmas Day, but Annabelle had assured me that wouldn't be the case. What that entailed, I had no idea. She definitely had something up her sleeve, and I'd go along for the ride without question, happy to be included in her plans.

Once I finished wrapping the holster, I set it under my little tree, which only stood about two feet high. I regretted not getting a larger one, refraining because I was afraid Catnip would tear it down. For the same reason, I also hadn't bought any other decorations for my small apartment, but next year would be different. Surprisingly, Catnip had left everything alone. Either he wasn't interested, or things weren't flashy enough for him to put the effort in to destroy. Next year, I'd put as much energy into decorating my personal space as I had the store. The lights and baubles warmed me from the inside out.

"No! Gosh dang it!"

The yelling downstairs caught me by surprise, but I wasn't concerned because I recognized the voice as Annabelle's. I opened the apartment door and called, "Everything okay?"

"It's fine," she said, her sigh loud enough for me to hear. It indicated things weren't fine as she suggested.

I hurried down the stairs.

"What's up?" I asked, finding her in the back room. Today she wore a knitted red and green sweater featuring Billy Idol's face and famous sneer wearing a Santa hat, a pair of jeans, and black boots. Where in the world had she found that sweater?

"I just got a text from a friend, and they said the Christmas Festival is canceled."

"Oh, no," I said, furrowing my brow. "Why? Is it because of the murder?"

"There's that, but then Santa showed up at the Emergency Clinic in town last night. He's got something wrong with his head. They took him in an ambulance to the hospital in Sedona. We can't have the Christmas Festival without Santa."

So Paul had been hit in the head when George took a tire iron to him in the parking lot. The fact George had hurt him placed the man a few slots up on my list of potential murderers. Maybe he wasn't as physically or mentally weak as I'd originally thought. If I hadn't seen the commotion between the two in the On The River parking lot, perhaps he would have been successful in bashing in Paul's skull.

Then there was the fact he'd created an online persona for the sole purpose of hassling his ex-wife in the hopes of scaring her so much, she'd go back to him. A few screws loose, perhaps? Most definitely, in my book.

"Well, I'm sure they would've canceled it anyway because a murder had taken place at the Community Center," I said. "We should see if we can get in there and retrieve the gift baskets we left." Glancing around the store, I chewed my lip. "There isn't a lot of time to move them before Christmas, but maybe we can discount them."

"The sheriff's office put out a statement that they were going to allow the festival to go on. It was in yesterday's paper, Sam."

"But now you think the organizers will cancel it?"

She nodded. "I *know* they are. My friend works on the festival's committee. They put it to a vote and it's over. What's a Christmas Festival without a Santa? Mrs. Santa only made it better, but we *need* a Santa."

"Can't they find someone else?" I asked. "Won't someone else volunteer?"

Ho! Ho! Ho! Merry Christmas!

Annabelle and I both glanced around the corner into the store to see Jordan strolling in looking worse for wear. His beard had grown out even more while deep purple circles hung under his eyes. "I hope he isn't sick," I muttered.

"If he is, are you going to throw him through a glass table?" Annabelle replied, snickering.

I still needed to decide if I was going to press charges against Sarah. Part of me wanted to figuratively nail her to the wall, but at the same time, she frightened me. Did I really want to be on her bad side even more than I was? And did I need an enemy in a town as small as Heywood? Well, one more enemy. Doctor Butte and I had a mutual hatred of each other, so I always considered him enemy number one. I didn't really care to have an enemy number two.

"How are you feeling?" I asked, stepping into the store as Jordan weaved through the display tables.

"Doing okay," he replied. "Just tired."

Annabelle stood next to me, her arms crossed over her chest as she stared at Jordan.

"Did you find your killer yet?" I asked.

He shook his head. "I was hoping you'd take care of that for me."

"No, I haven't. I thought you were coming here to tell me that George had confessed and everything was wrapped up."

"Unfortunately, no," he replied. "He admits to being KAK, admits to knocking Paul with a tire iron, but says he didn't kill Joyce."

"Did you know Paul's in the hospital?" Annabelle asked.

Jordan's gaze widened. "No, I hadn't heard that. What happened?"

"I don't know all the details, but, like, he's got something wrong with his head."

"Getting clobbered by a tire iron will do that," Jordan muttered.

"They're canceling the Christmas Festival because they don't have a Santa," Annabelle said. She was obviously much more upset about the festival not happening than Paul's potential brain damage.

"That's too bad. I think they should have it regardless," Jordan replied, scratching his beard.

"But what do we tell the kids?" Annabelle asked. "That Santa decided he didn't want to visit Heywood this year?" Tears welled in her eyes. "It's better to cancel the whole event unless we can come up with a new Santa."

"Aw, Annabelle, please don't cry," Jordan begged. "Please."

"It's just so unfair," she sniffed. "It's the best day of the year and it's ruined." Her gaze darted between Jordan and me. "Unless..."

"Unless what?" I asked, my heart anxiously skipping a beat. I didn't like the way she was looking at us.

"You two could play Mr. and Mrs. Claus."

A long beat of silence engulfed us, then Jordan and I both responded in unison. "No."

"Oh, come on!" Annabelle shouted, throwing her hands in the air. "You're perfect! Jordan, you've already got the beard. Granted, it's a little shorter than the preferred Santa length, but we can make it work!"

"My beard isn't white," Jordan said, running his hands over the black and gray strands.

"Sorry to break it to you, but there's way more gray than black there," she replied, then turned to me. "And Sam... you'd be a perfect Mrs. Claus. We can use some non-permanent coloring on both of you so you're all white."

No way was I pretending to be Mrs. Claus. No way at all. "Annabelle, I—"

"We need the festival to go on so we can sell those baskets!" she said. "You put everything you had saved into building the deck out back during the summer. I know things are tight and moving the baskets would help a lot."

Okay, she had a point there, and obviously meant to hit me where it would hurt a lot. My wallet.

"While you get your jolly on, I can sell the baskets," Annabelle said. "It's a win for everyone!"

Jordan and I exchanged glances. "We don't have costumes," he said.

"The festival organizers will have some extras. We can figure out how to make you fat, Jordan. Maybe they have some padding or something."

I had no idea how to play the Mrs. Claus character since I really didn't have a maternal bone in my body that I was aware of. I could play a psycho killer with a soft heart with ease, but Mrs. Claus? I was lost on where to start.

"Please?" Annabelle begged. "The kids. Think of the kids!" When neither of us answered, she continued, "And your wallet, Sam. Think about your wallet! Selling those baskets would ease the strain!"

I sighed and closed my eyes for a moment, then glanced over at Jordan.

"What do you think?" he asked. "It could be fun."

Arching an eyebrow at him, I said, "Are you serious?"

He nodded. "I miss being around kids that aren't spray painting or toilet papering something... kids I have to speak with about bad choices and what happens when they do bad stuff after they turn eighteen."

Annabelle stared at me, hope gleaming in her eyes as she pressed her hands together in a prayer position, silently begging me to agree to this ludicrous plan.

"Okay," I grumbled. "I'll do it."

Annabelle squealed in delight as Jordan smiled. Nerves tickled my belly and my hands began to sweat. What had I done?

"I'll call you later," Jordan said, tapping the glass counter with a finger.

"Stop by City Hall," Annabelle said. "I'm texting my friend to tell her Heywood has its Santa!"

As she pulled out her phone and began typing away, I wondered what excuse I could use to get out of the debacle. The flu seemed to be a solid one.

"And you..." she said, pointing at me as she put away her phone. "You and I are going down to City Hall together so I make sure you don't back out."

She knew me too well.

"I've got a meeting with Sally over at On The River about carrying her hot chocolate in the store."

"That's okay. I'll, like, go with you and we can stop by on the way back."

"What about the store?" I asked. "Who's going to watch it?"

Annabelle glanced around then shrugged. "We better hurry so we aren't, like, closed too long."

CHAPTER 16

"Sam! Good to see you!"

As Sally approached us at On The River, I smiled. "Nice to see you as well. Will you have time to speak with us about your hot chocolate?"

"Of course. Why don't you grab a seat? I'll take care of a few things in back and then bring you out a sample and we can talk."

"Perfect." I gestured to my co-worker. "Do you know Annabelle?"

"Sure do," she said. "You won the dance contest in the spring, if I remember correctly."

Annabelle nodded and grinned. "That's me!"

"Quite the performance," Sally said. "Let's get you two settled in." She led us over to a table. "Give me about ten minutes."

"Where in the world did you find that sweater?" I asked as we removed our coats and slid into the booth while Sally raced off.

Annabelle glanced down at her Billy Idol Santa sweater. "Mrs. Mason over at Knit Wit made it for me a couple of years ago."

"I'm surprised she knew who Billy Idol is."

"She may be older, but she loves *Rebel Yell* as much as the next person with any taste."

Sally had sat us by the big windows overlooking the deck and the river beyond. The cool air came through the glass, but I never tired of the view. As the river rolled lazily along, the tree branches lining the far side hung heavy with snow.

"That water looks cold," Annabelle said.

I nodded in agreement. "Probably wouldn't last too long if you fell in."

We sat in silence for a few minutes taking in the scenery until Sally came by and set three white mugs on the table, then scooted in next to Annabelle.

"I'm glad you finally got the chance to come by," she said.

"Me, too," I replied. "I wanted to stop by yesterday, but I've been crazy busy."

She didn't need to know I was trying to find Mrs. Claus' murderer.

"The holidays will do that," Sally said. "Just when I think I have everything under control, I remember a bunch of stuff I need to do."

Which reminded me I still hadn't picked up anything for Jordan or Gina, nor did I have a clue on what to get them. Time was running out, so I made a mental note to get that mess sorted immediately after my meeting with Sally and my fitting at City Hall.

Ugh. Why had I said yes to Annabelle's crazy plan?

"Is this the hot chocolate Sam was telling me about?" Annabelle asked as she wrapped her hands around the cup and sniffed.

"Yes, it is. I hope you like it, Annabelle," Sally replied, taking a sip. "It's my favorite go-to in times of stress."

"Like I said, I had the best sleep after drinking this." I blew on my hot chocolate, looking forward to it being cool enough for me to taste. Finally, I was able to take a sip and my taste buds tingled as I sighed.

"Oh, I like this," Annabelle said, setting down her mug. "Not too sweet, but very comforting. And, like, super delish!"

"I'm so glad," Sally said, then shifted her gaze to me. "What kind of deal did you have in mind for carrying it in your store?"

"Well, let's talk about production," I said. "How much do you think you can produce a week? How long does it keep?"

As Sally talked about her production schedule, the ingredients, and we tossed around ideas for packaging, the time flew by. When I finally disengaged from our conversation, I realized the sun had almost fully sunk behind the trees lining the river and our hot chocolate was long gone.

"I think this is a great collaboration," Annabelle said. "If you have the product made now, we should get a few packets and put them in the baskets for the Christmas Festival, and also add it to the store as fast as we can."

I nodded in agreement. "I only wish we'd thought of all this a few months ago. We could've had a big push on it as a comfort food item that relaxes during the holidays."

"Well, now we can market it as the comfort item that melts away the stress left over from the holidays," Annabelle said. "We can push it through the winter months."

"I'll leave you two to discuss marketing strategies, and I'll go package some up for you," Sally said. With a wink, she grabbed our empty mugs and hurried back to the kitchen.

"We better go," Annabelle said, pulling out her phone. "City Hall is going to close soon and we still need to get you a costume."

I sighed and crossed my arms over my chest, regretting my decision to be Mrs. Claus with every fiber in my being. "Annabelle, I—"

"No!" she said, holding her hand out between us. "The conversation is over. You promised me you'd do it. And you, Sam Jones, aren't the type of person who backs out of a promise. You're a good human who honors her agreements."

What an expert manipulator. I didn't know whether to be angry or impressed.

"Here you go," Sally said as she set down a plastic bag full of hot chocolate pouches. I glanced in to find plain brown wrapping. Not exactly festive, but we could dress them up with a fancy label.

"Thanks, Sally." I stood from the table and gave her a quick hug. "Can you send over the invoice via email?"

"Of course. I still have your business card, so I'll take care of that tomorrow."

"Wonderful."

"You two sit and stay as long as you need," she said. "We aren't too busy, so you don't have to leave."

Annabelle also stood and said her goodbyes to Sally. Just as I was about to suggest we head out to get my stupid Mrs. Claus fitting over with, two people in a far booth caught my eye—George and Sarah.

I grabbed Annabelle's arm and motioned for her to sit down, then asked Sally for another hot chocolate. She hurried to the kitchen to oblige.

"We have to get you fitted!" Annabelle hissed. "They're at City Hall waiting for you!"

"What are those two doing here?" I whispered, gesturing over to the table. "I thought George was in jail?"

Annabelle turned to gander a glance, then shrugged. "Maybe Jordan let him out? Or the sheriff is back on duty and she did?"

Sarah reached across the table and squeezed George's arm. I strained to read their lips as they spoke.

"What are they saying?" I mumbled as Sally walked over to them and blocked my view.

"They're probably discussing how Sarah is now receiving hundreds of emails a day for services and contests she never signed up for."

What? For a moment, I had no idea what Annabelle could possibly be talking about, but then it hit me.

I stared at my friend for a long beat. "You didn't."

"Yes, I did. I took her email address and spent two hours the other night signing her up for all sorts of things she doesn't want. Information on cruises, every department store I could think of, and loads of contests. Her inbox is a mess, just like she left our store."

I groaned and placed my elbows on the table, my head in my hands. "You took her email out of our database, right?"

"Yep."

"That's illegal, Annabelle."

"Who cares?" she hissed. "We need to go!"

Right. Back to the issue at hand. I had a fitting to attend, but I also desperately wanted to know what George and Sarah were discussing. "Just a minute. We'll get there. Text your friend and tell her we'll be there in ten more minutes."

Annabelle swore under her breath as she pulled out her phone. Sally left George's table and then hurried to the kitchen, only to return to our table moments later with our hot chocolates.

I hated dragging someone else into a murder investigation, but I did feel Sally and I had become friends. If not friends, then really affable business partners. "Sally, what were those two over there talking about when you walked up to their table?"

She glanced over her shoulder, then turned back to me and lowered her voice while placing the mugs in front of us. "That's George and his friend, Sarah. Apparently, George just found out his wife never took his name off a very large joint savings account that was supposed to be hers in the divorce. He's getting it now." After giving me a wink, she whispered, "But you didn't get that from me. Running this place in such a small town, I have to keep the conversations I overhear to myself."

Annabelle gasped as I nodded absently, my gaze once again wandering over to George and Sarah.

Sally left to go seat another couple waiting by the door and I wondered how many steps she got in each day. It had to be way over the recommended ten thousand.

"What if he knew that before she died?" Annabelle whispered.

I nodded, then took another sip of hot chocolate. Yes, indeed. What if he had known his name hadn't been taken off the savings account?

WE ARRIVED at City Hall to find Jordan also being fitted for his costume. His smile indicated he was far more excited about this than I was.

"You ready for this?" Jordan asked.

I wanted to ask him about George's release and tell him about the savings account, but I didn't feel comfortable with the other people in the room. "As ready as I'll ever be."

Maybe it was because Santa was such an easy character to play. But what did Mrs. Claus do? Sit around and smile? Bake cookies? I wasn't up on my Christmas movies, so maybe I'd have to sit down and watch a few. If I recalled, Goldie Hawn and Kurt Russell had made a couple where she played Mrs. Claus. That would be a good place to start, and it would be nice to see some old friends again on the screen.

While Annabelle and the woman I assumed was her contact at the

Christmas Festival ushered me into another room and helped me don the heavy, red coat, all the while prattling on about how I'd have to wear a white turtleneck, black leggings and matching boots, I only half-listened, despite the hot flash railing through me. The coat wasn't any help.

I tried to piece together the plotline of George being the murderer. Done with her husband's controlling and demeaning ways, Joyce divorced him. When he couldn't win her back, he tried to scare her to return to him by hassling her online as someone named Kill All Konservatives. Originally, I had considered him a suspect for a crime of passion, but what if it all came down to money?

"How much?" I wondered out loud.

"How much what?" Annabelle asked.

I shook my head. "Nothing. Sorry." A trickle of sweat made its way down my face. I'd never survive playing Mrs. Claus unless the temperature in the Community Center hovered around North Pole numbers.

"Take a look," Annabelle said, turning me toward the mirror. "See? I'll color your hair fully gray, and maybe we can pull it up so it knots at your neck." She gently palmed my curls and wrapped them in a bun at the nape of my neck. "A little blush and your glasses... you're going to be a perfect Mrs. Claus."

"Ho, ho ho." I turned to find Jordan in the doorway, also fully dressed and smiling. "Looking good there, wifey."

I snorted as he joined me in front of the mirror. As I stared at our reflection, I tried to imagine his beard and my hair fully white, and suddenly, I couldn't wait for our act to begin.

"We're going to kill this," I said, turning to him. Without thinking, I threw my arms around his neck. He stiffened for a brief moment, but then wrapped his arms around my waist.

"Yes, ma'am. We are."

As we disentangled and discussed our entrance into the Christmas Festival, for the first time in a long while, I wasn't thinking about murderers.

It didn't last long, though.

CHAPTER 17

THE DAY of the Christmas Festival had arrived. Despite there being a murderer on the loose, the air in Heywood crackled with excitement. Annabelle and I remained busy throughout the day and almost every customer mentioned the festival and how much they looked forward to it.

I found the whole day quite fascinating as the town rallied around another event. First, it had been the Annual Dance Contest, and now the Christmas Festival. It was like nothing I'd ever seen before, and I found my heart beating a little faster as I became caught up in the enthusiasm.

None of them knew I was going to play Mrs. Claus, which gave me a little bit of the nervous jitters on top of the anticipation. All day I felt overcaffeinated, and I wasn't sure why. I was an Emmy winning actress. I needed to smile

To my utter delight, Sally's hot cocoa sold out except for the packages we'd kept behind the counter to add to the baskets at the Christmas Festival. After an evening of watching the *Christmas Chronicles* with Kurt Russell and Goldie Hawn, I'd come down early to prepare the fancy labels and display table for the batch of hot chocolate. I'd created a small flyer about the benefits of the mushrooms used to make it, prepared some samples, and it had been gone before noon.

The movie had warmed my heart, and I wasn't sure if the tears in my eyes were from the film, or because I missed my two dear friends. I considered calling them, but was afraid they'd cast me aside as the rest of Hollywood had. But I knew exactly how I was going to play Mrs. Claus —I'd mirror Goldie Hawn's character with my own added flair. If only my smile was as bright and warm as hers.

After Annabelle rang up the last hot chocolate packet, I put a "sold out" sign on its display table and a sign-up sheet to be emailed when the product came back in. Then I texted Sally and told her we needed more, and she said she'd get right on it.

"Well, are you set to go, Mrs. Claus?" Annabelle asked. "We should head over to the Community Center so we can get you ready. That hair dye may take longer to work into your hair than I originally thought."

"Sure," I said, hoping my nervous butterflies didn't show in my voice. I was once again back to wondering why I'd volunteered myself for the role.

And that's what I had to remember. It was simply another character to play. I had to smile and be nice to kids, which shouldn't be too hard. I may not have a lot of experience with children, but most seemed quite decent. Except that one kid in Hollywood... I couldn't remember who he belonged to, but I'd met him when I'd accompanied a friend to a party. Somewhere around five years old, he'd spent the night screaming at his parents while the nanny tried to corral him upstairs. I'd felt a little bad for him because his mother and father basically ignored him, as if he didn't exist. Had that been typical throughout his young life, or was it because his parents were entertaining Hollywood's elite that night?

Once we'd locked up the store, Annabelle drove us over to the Community Center. The bitter night air sniped at my cheeks as we entered.

"I was told we were going to be getting ready in the after-school daycare room," Annabelle said, nudging me down that hallway.

We opened the door, turned on the light, then stepped inside. Annabelle locked it while I tried to locate a couple of adult-sized chairs. I doubted the little ones the kids used would hold my weight.

"Okay, let's get started," she said. I found a couple of chairs and pulled them out into the middle of the colorful ABC's carpet.

As Annabelle stood behind me and worked the dye into my curls, I marveled at the silence. It didn't seem like this building would burst with the joy and frivolity of the season Annabelle described.

"It's the calm before the storm," Annabelle said, reading my mind. "It's a little creepy, especially since we just found a dead person here a couple of days ago and the killer hasn't been caught."

I nodded in agreement as my phone buzzed. Leaning over, I fished it out of my bag. Jordan had texted me.

ON MY WAY, *Mrs. Claus. Or should I just call you wifey?*

I ROLLED my eyes and shoved it back into my purse. If he called me wifey one more time, I may never speak to him again.

Once the color was in, Annabelle took a hairdryer to me and straightened my curls. A couple of curses fell from her lips, and I could only nod in agreement. My hair fought straightening—always had.

"Okay, you're already dressed, except for the coat. Let's add just a touch of makeup."

I closed my eyes as Annabelle worked and worried she'd overdo it and I'd resemble Boy George when she was through. Thankfully, a couple minutes later she announced she was finished and shoved a mirror in front of my face.

Solid gray hair gathered at the nape of my neck in a loose bun while a few stray curls framed my face. My cheeks held just a tint of pink, which matched the coloring on my lips. I slid on my glasses and turned my head from side to side. "You did a fantastic job, Annabelle."

She nodded. "I know. Now we just have to wait for Jordan."

On cue, the door swung open and in walked the man himself. "Sorry I'm a bit late," he said, his gaze never leaving me. "You look really pretty, Sam. The gray hair suits you."

A slow blush crawled up my neck. Annabelle pointed at her chair and ordered, "Sit down, buddy. You can admire her later. We need to get your beard whitened, and I'm running out of time. They're going to open up the gym for the vendor sale soon and I've got to run the Sage Advice table."

"Yes, ma'am," he said, shucking his coat and hurrying over to the chair.

We chatted as Annabelle painted the dye into his hair, then onto his beard. It had grown in thick but wasn't as long as Santa's. However, it would have to do.

The sound of voices rang down the hall just as Annabelle finished. "Okay, I have to go," she said. "It sounds like they've opened the doors. Your coats are over there and someone will be by to grab you when it's time for you to make your grand entrance."

"Thanks for everything," I said, giving my friend a hug. She waved and hurried out the door. "I hope she sells all those baskets."

"I'm sure she will," Jordan replied. "She's a heck of a salesperson. I mean, she sold us on this crazy idea, right?"

"Absolutely," I said, smiling. "Not sure how we got roped into this, but here we are."

A knock sounded at the door and a woman I didn't know rushed in carrying two plastic cups. Short and round with cropped brown hair, the bags under her eyes and her thin, tight mouth indicated she was a bit haggard. "I'm one of the organizers," she said breathlessly. "We thought you'd appreciate a little red wine before you go out."

"Oh, well, thank you," I said, taking the cup. Did Mrs. Claus drink alcohol? I took a sip. Well, my version of her did.

"You'll come out in about ten minutes. I'll be back to get you." She left as fast as she'd come in.

"Cheers, Mrs. C.," Jordan said, tapping my cup.

"Cheers," I muttered, taking another sip.

Just as I finished my wine, the coordinator rushed in, this time without knocking. "Get your coats on! Get your coats on! Hurry!"

Jordan and I sprang into action, donning our red coats with white trim. We took a quick look in the mirror.

Old. We looked like a happy old couple who had been together many years... like we belonged side-by-side. The thought caught me by surprise.

"She did a really good job," Jordan said, running a hand over his grayed hair. "I think we can pass."

Pushing my ruminations aside, I nodded and grinned. "Heck yeah, we can. We look great."

"Let's go, let's go!" the organizer said as she burst from the room. We hurried down the hall after her.

She led us to an area with a curtain and held up her hand in a sign for us to stop. On the other side of the drapery, I could hear the hustle and bustle of the townspeople above the sound of Christmas music coming through the speakers.

Taking a few deep breaths, I reminded myself it was simply a live performance. I didn't even have any lines to remember. All I needed to do was smile, say hello, and be nice to kids.

"Ladies and gentlemen," the man with the microphone announced. "If everyone could please gather around, we have a special surprise for the kiddos."

Jordan grabbed my hand. "That's you and me. Are you ready?"

I nodded and squeezed his fingers.

The presenter continued. "Everyone, all the way from the North Pole, please welcome Santa and Mrs. Claus!"

The curtain rose and everyone cheered. The energy in the room rushed toward us like a gust of wind, causing me to take a small step back. Jordan and I waved and smiled as the children screamed. In the audience, I found Annabelle applauding and jumping up and down just as excited as the kids.

Everywhere I looked I found a familiar face. Doctor Butte smiled and clapped until he realized who I was, then he shook his head and sneered. Sarah also tossed a glare my way. Mary crossed her arms over her chest, her expression unreadable. Was she thinking about Joyce as she stared at me?

She stood next to Terry, who for the love of everything holy, was still staring at my chest, smirking. I glanced down to see if the red jacket was straining across my bust, but I couldn't really tell. I shot him a glare, but he never received it.

Gina and her whole family were there. Her brother, Vic, wiggled his eyebrows at me while her father waved. I glanced over to another part of the gym to find Mrs. Pugh and her son, Bobby. Both seemed to be enjoying themselves, and I hoped Bobby had the strength to remain sober in order to help his mom with the farm. I'd sent his father to prison for murder.

I locked gazes with Charlie Tupper. Even though I'd discovered his wife had killed my old boss Bonnie, he grinned and waved. The man had the most forgiving heart.

Jordan turned to me, leaned down, and planted a kiss on my lips. Stunned, I could only stare. "Don't look so surprised," he whispered. "We are standing under the mistletoe, and Santa would kiss his wife, right?"

Glancing upward, I noted the green and red plant, unable to speak as electric sparks coursed through me from head-to-toe. Was that someone in the audience cat-calling? If I had to guess, it was Annabelle.

"I'm sure I hated that almost as much as you," he said, winking.

While I tried to find my grip on reality and my smile, we were led over to the high-back red velvet chairs while volunteers lined up the kids. Forget the kiss, at least for now. It hadn't meant anything. Had he really hated it, though? Because I wasn't sure I had.

As we sat down on the chairs, I found my smile again as my chair tipped slightly, as if the legs weren't on quite right. The kids in line jumped up and down, their faces beaming bright with excitement.

One of the organizers brought up the first kid in line to sit on Santa's lap, a shy boy of about four with blond hair and the bluest eyes I'd ever seen. He approached slowly, unsure of the man in the red suit.

"Ho, ho, ho!" Jordan bellowed, reaching for the boy with his white-gloved hand. "Come here, son. Tell Santa what you want for Christmas."

"His name's Chris," the volunteer whispered with her back to the boy. "His parents own a farm on the south side of town."

Jordan nodded slightly and motioned Chris again. "Come tell me about your farm, Chris. What horse is your favorite?"

That seemed to earn the boy's trust. He jumped on Jordan's lap and told him about the pony named Stomper and how much he wanted a set of dirt-digging trucks for Christmas.

Jordan smiled from ear-to-ear as he listened, and my heart ached for him. He must've been a wonderful father, and it was obvious he missed having a child. Losing his daughter had almost destroyed him.

Child after child came up and sat on Santa's lap. Parents snapped pictures. All the while I listened intently to the kids' wishes, grinned, and acted surprised when they shared their secret hopes of what they'd find under the tree.

All the while, my chair kept teetering. When I leaned a certain way, it felt like I may tip over. Visions of the time I fell at the Emmys played in my mind. If the same happened at the festival, at least I wore leggings and wouldn't flash the audience my thong, but it would still be embarrassing.

After about an hour, I stood and kneeled next to the chair. Maybe I could tuck something under the unstable leg? I grabbed the leg and gasped, then slowly pulled my hand away.

Standing, I stared down at the chair, my heart thundering. On the side of the metal leg that wasn't visible to the audience, blood had crusted. And... was that a hair?

Jordan had a brother and sister on his lap. The three smiled and posed for the parents taking pictures. He radiated joy and I didn't want to burst his bubble, but darn it... I was pretty certain I'd just discovered the murder weapon.

I turned around and sat down, careful not to rock the chair too much. Glancing around the crowd, I placed a smile on my face. I studied everyone, searching for my suspects.

George had arrived, or I hadn't seen him earlier. Sarah had attached herself to him, linking her arm with his. They chatted with a few men and women I recognized from the Senior Center.

Why did I feel as if I were being watched?

"Smile, Mrs. Claus!" one of the parents called.

Turning to the camera, I flashed my best grin. The children stepped down and a mother brought up a baby. Obviously, the little one couldn't vocalize their Christmas desires, but mom wanted a picture.

The infant didn't.

Howling ensued while I took stock of the audience again.

There.

Terry stared at me, our gazes locked. After a long moment, he turned and hurried toward the exit.

I shot to my feet, my pretty chair toppling backward. "Stop him!" I yelled, not sure if anyone would hear me over the din.

CHAPTER 18

"Grab him!" I yelled, hurling myself off the small stage and into the crowd. As I shoved through, people did move but just not fast enough. Some received elbows from me, others I outright pushed. With my heart thundering, I continued to yell for someone to stop Terry, but I was met with confused stares.

I finally reached the tables by the door.

"What are you doing?" Annabelle shouted, grabbing my arm.

"Terry! We have to stop him!"

"Why?"

Why, indeed? He hadn't done a darn thing to make me want to chase him, except try to leave. "B-because he's running!"

It didn't mean he was guilty, but the fact I'd found the blood on the leg of the chair and he watched me do so, then tried to leave the building had me feeling as if he were hiding something... like a murder confession.

Annabelle's jaw worked as she stared at me, probably deciding if I'd finally lost all my marbles. After a quick moment, she ran ahead of me toward the door.

I took a quick peek at our table and silently appreciated the fact all our gift baskets had sold, then followed Annabelle.

Terry moved fast for an old guy, and I respected his dedication to taking care of his body for all these years. The fact he was outrunning both Annabelle and me upset me, and I vowed to get more exercise in case there ever came a time where I had to chase a senior citizen again in the future.

He sprinted down the hallway toward the kitchen where we'd found Paul. Why hadn't he gone out the front door? It was much closer.

"Terry!" I shouted. "You can't get away from us! We know it was you!"

Well, I had no idea, but circumstances seemed to indicate it as so.

Just as we burst into the kitchen, we found him at the back door trying to push it open. Cakes and cookies lined the steel tables, each labeled with the name of the person who had made them. As Terry shoved on the door one last time, I heard commotion behind me. My mad exit hadn't gone unnoticed.

My suspect turned, his gaze darting all around like a madman. As my breath sawed from my mad sprint, I approached him slowly. "Terry, let's discuss this like adults. Tell me what happened."

He grimaced, picked up a cake, and threw it at me. It landed on the wall to my right, splattering bits of an absolutely delicious chocolate lava cake on my hair, face, and Mrs. Claus suit. What a waste.

"Don't do that!" Annabelle yelled. "You're going to ruin the baking contest!" She received a pie to the chest for her efforts.

"Stop it!" I yelled. "Please! Terry, tell me what happened that night with Joyce."

"I don't know!" he replied, trying the door again. "I wasn't here!"

"Then why are you running?" I asked as I wiped away bits of cake and a trickle of sweat from my face.

After one last shove, his shoulder slumped. "I didn't kill Joyce," he said. "I swear to you, I didn't. My car's parked out back. Just please let me leave."

With a sigh, I crossed my arms over my chest, ignoring the chunk of cake stuck to the center of my jacket. "No, Terry. You aren't going anywhere, not until you tell me why you're running."

"Don't try to deny anything," Annabelle hissed, her hands fisted at her sides. "Only an absolute monster would ruin the entries in the baking contest! You killed Mrs. Claus!"

How she went from throwing a cake to murder was beyond me, but if the leap got Terry talking, I was happy she'd made it.

"No, I didn't!" he screamed. As his face turned a shade of red I'd never seen, I worried he may have a stroke.

"Then who did?" I asked.

He glanced past me to the doorway. There I found Mary glaring at him, her hands on her hips.

Had it been Mary? It made sense. She was the one who had been saying she deserved more of their father's inheritance since she was the one who took care of him. Paul had told us they were fighting so loudly, he'd had to leave. Or, he was guilty as sin and trying to pin the killing on someone else.

"Mary?" Terry said. "It's over."

"I don't know what you're talking about," she replied, shaking her head. "What have you done?" Tears welled in her eyes as she pursed her lips. "Was it you, Terry? Did you kill my sister?"

"Absolutely not!" he shouted. "You know what happened that night, Mary!"

"I know my sister was brutally killed," she whispered, the tears now falling freely. "I never imagined you could've done it."

"I didn't!"

The blame game continued and I became more confused with every passing moment. "Wait a minute," I interjected. "Let's take a step back here. Terry, tell me everything."

His gaze never left Mary as his breath heaved. Finally, he spoke. "I was sleeping with both sisters. Mary and Joyce. Only Mary was aware of this. She knew I was low on money. Weeks ago, she came to me with a plan. I was to convince Joyce that Mary deserved more of the inheritance because she'd taken care of their father."

I recalled his run-down home that desperately needed a paint job and new gutters. "But Joyce said no," I urged. "She thought Mary was guilty of elder abuse."

He nodded as Mary grimaced, pain lancing across her face as if she'd been slapped.

"And Mary didn't like that," Terry continued. "She wanted it all. Felt she deserved it, especially since Joyce was out living her new life without George while Mary was caregiving."

"You're a sick, sick man," Mary whispered. "How dare you say such things?"

"You came here that night with the intention of convincing Joyce you deserved more of the inheritance. You told me that, Mary. Then you asked me to clean up your mess."

I recalled the evening we'd found Joyce. Annabelle had thought she'd heard a door close. Had we walked in on Terry trying to do something with the body? "What time were you here?" I asked.

Terry shook his head. "I don't remember the exact time. It was about an hour or so after Mary came to me and told me what she'd done."

"And were you... interrupted?" I asked.

Terry nodded. "I'd tried to wipe down the chair leg and put it back together, but I heard someone coming in, so I ran and headed out one of the back doors."

"Why are you doing this?" she asked, taking a step toward him. "Why are you trying to convince these people that I murdered my beloved sister?"

"Because you told me you did," he spat.

"Can you tell us exactly what she said when she came to you?" I asked, noting a flash of red out of the corner of my eye. I glanced over to find Jordan in the doorway. I held up a hand, hoping to stop him right there. We were on a roll and I didn't want him to interrupt Terry's train of thought.

"She showed up at my door that night, very upset," he said. "She'd come down here to the Community Center in hopes of talking some sense into Joyce and make her understand that she deserved more of the inheritance for taking care of her father. Paul was here, and they were putting together the Mr. and Mrs. Claus chairs, getting ready for the dress rehearsal. Joyce and Mary began fighting and Paul got angry, then left the gym. Mary said she'd thought he'd gone home. She picked up one of the chair legs, then, in a fit of rage, she bashed Joyce's head."

He glanced over at the killer. She stood stone-faced, not an emotion to be found. I recalled how upset she'd been when she'd arrived just as they were wheeling out her sister's body. Had it been an act, or was there real remorse for what she'd done?

"After she killed Joyce, I guess she freaked out and came to me to fix everything," Terry continued. "She wanted me to get rid of the body and clean up the mess."

"Why didn't you, like, just go to the police?" Annabelle asked.

His cheeks flushed and he lowered his gaze to the shiny countertop before him.

"Because everyone knows that Terry's low on cash," Mary spat. "He's the big player with a string of women ready to cook for him, warm his bed, and slide him some money every now and then after they fall for his charms."

"Is that what happened with you?" I asked, recalling her prescription bottle in his bathroom. "Did you fall for his charms, Mary?"

She didn't answer but based on the way her face was tinged pink, I took that as a yes.

"I told her to go to the police," Terry said, his voice barely a whisper. "But she said we could share the inheritance that was now fully hers."

A moment of silence filled the room as the air crackled with anxiety. I'd expected everyone to settle down now that the confession was out in the open, but how wrong I'd been.

With a primal scream, Mary lunged at Terry. She grabbed a knife as she flew around the table with the weapon raised above her head.

Without thinking, I hurried to Terry and wrapped my arms around him, trying to pull him out of the way. Jordan raced at Mary, sliding over the steel table and landing in between her and Terry. Unfortunately, he also took out a plate of chocolate chip cookies. As they crashed to the floor, he grabbed Mary's raised hands and wrenched the knife away. He tossed the weapon to the ground, then pinned her face down on the steel table. Sobs wracked her body as he placed his elbow in the middle of her back.

"I... I didn't mean to kill her," Mary cried. "I honestly didn't. I lost control of my temper for a minute and went out of my mind. I'd never hurt my sister!"

It was then I realized a crowd had gathered at the doorway and the reporter, Barry, from the *Heywood Sentinel*, stood front and center, jotting down notes in a notebook.

Loosening my grip on Terry, I stepped away and grabbed the knife Jordan had dropped. All weapons should be cleared from the room until someone with a pair of handcuffs arrived for Mary. Glancing around, I realized that would be impossible since it was a kitchen. It would take us hours to find and remove them all.

"Sam, fish my phone out of my pocket, please," Jordan ordered, and I quickly did as he asked.

As he leaned on Mary's back, he phoned the department, reported the incident, and hung up. "See if you can find something to tie her hands," he asked. "Maybe there's something in the pantry?"

"Where are your handcuffs?" I asked.

"Santa doesn't carry handcuffs. I'm off duty."

Annabelle joined me in my search. "It's weird to think just a few of days ago we thought there was a wolf or something in here," she whispered as we rifled through the shelf contents. "And it was a snoring Santa."

"I know," I replied. "I hate that the Christmas Festival has been interrupted like this. Maybe I should've waited to confront Terry. I feel like I've ruined everything."

"Well, you did, but it is what it is," Annabelle said, winking.

"Do you think we can put everything back on track?"

"I don't know. We can try. But that stupid sheriff better hurry up and get here because I don't see anything to tie someone up with. Is plastic wrap strong enough?"

CHAPTER 19

Christmas Eve

JORDAN HAD BROUGHT A LARGE, portable fire pit over and we'd placed it on the deck. Flames crackled, danced, and warmed us as Annabelle, Jordan, Gina and I sat around them. Annabelle had made some hot toddies she swore had some great herbs in them, though I quickly decided that the amount of alcohol she'd used canceled any herbal benefits. But as the smell of cinnamon and spices wafted up from my warm mug, I didn't care.

In the distance, a coyote howled. We'd strung white Christmas lights along the deck railing, which cast a warm glow around the area. The bitter cold of the night gnawed at my cheeks, but I couldn't remember a time when I'd been so happy, especially on Christmas Eve. In my former life, the night had been about extravagant parties, expensive gowns, and spending time in the hair and makeup chair. As I sat in my parka and snow boots with my hair tucked into my ski cap, I smiled. I'd take my new life over my old one any day.

Jordan was telling a story of a drunk driver he'd pulled over earlier in the day who'd fallen face-first into a snowbank and passed out.

Although I hated anyone who got behind the wheel after consuming alcohol, I couldn't help but giggle while Jordan shared the tale.

"He'll be off the streets for a day or two," he said. "And, he's going to be sorry once he wakes up. Man, he was plastered."

Gina told us about her trip to visit her friend in Phoenix and how much fun they'd had. "It was so nice being warm," she grumbled as she sipped from her mug. "I think I want a house down there for winter, then spend the summers up here."

I didn't blame her. The one-hundred-and-fifteen-degree heat of the Phoenix area summer, day after day, would be a tough one to take.

As Gina spoke, my mind returned to the kiss Jordan had given me at the Christmas Festival, which to everyone's disappointment, closed up once the sheriff arrived and arrested Mary. The murder weapon had to be processed, which everyone understood, but I'd been looking forward to the caroling around the tree. Next year, hopefully, no one would murder anyone and mess it up for the rest of us. Crass, yes, but I'd make no apologies.

But the kiss... wow. My toes had curled. I glanced over at him as he laughed. He'd washed the gray from his beard, and I could've sworn I was sitting next to George Clooney in the firelight.

Maybe I should start dating him. Unofficially, we spent a lot of time together. We had coffee together almost every morning, and the same with dinner. I *liked* him. We had fun and he made me laugh. But maybe our relationship should become official.

Just the thought turned my stomach. I hated my trust issues with a passion. Yet, the only way I could see to get past them was to actually put my heart out on the line and hope he didn't stomp on it.

He glanced over at me and smiled, then grabbed my hand. As I stared at our gloves, I wondered how to approach him with my past and true identity. Over coffee? In private? Either way, I had to come clean. In order to move forward, I had to clear my conscience with him—and probably Gina, too. It would be one of the most difficult things I'd ever done and the longer I took in not sharing this very important part of my identity, the harder it became to hide it. Sometimes, hiding the truth was just as bad as an outward lie.

"Merry Christmas!"

I glanced over at Knit Wit to find the owner, Mrs. Mason, waving from her own deck.

"Mrs. Mason!" I called, standing. "Merry Christmas! Come over and join us!"

"Oh, I'd love that! Just give me a minute to get my coat."

"If she starts trying to get me into a knitting class, I'm leaving," Gina muttered. "I hate knitting."

"Oh, stop it," I said. "She's a sweet old lady."

"Hello, everyone!" Mrs. Mason said as she arrived, wearing a red coat and a plate in hand. Short, round, and in her seventies, she always had a smile for everyone. "Thanks so much for the invitation!"

"Where's your husband?" Annabelle asked as Jordan fetched her a chair from the workroom, then set it on the other side of the fire from me.

"He's at the house," Mrs. Mason replied, sitting down. "I had a few things to finish up at the store, but I'll head home in a little bit." She stretched out her arms, offering the plate. "Everyone, take a cookie! Chocolate, chocolate chip with marshmallows."

"Now that's a cookie," Gina said as she reached for them. "Mind if I grab two?"

"Of course not, dear."

I walked around the fire and took one. "This is so good," I said, my mouth full. "You make one heck of a cookie, Mrs. Mason."

The others nodded in agreement.

"Can I get you a hot toddy?" Annabelle asked.

"No, thank you. I have to drive home. I live too far to walk and Russell won't be happy if he has to come get me."

I assumed Russell was her husband, although I'd rarely laid eyes on him and we'd never been introduced. The store seemed to be Mrs. Mason's domain.

"Oh! By the way, I wanted to bring you this," she said, reaching into her jacket. When she pulled out a newspaper, Jordan and I groaned while Annabelle exploded into a fit of giggles. "You're famous!"

"We've seen it," Jordan said, glancing at me and grinning.

Barry from the *Heywood Sentinel* had snapped a picture of the melee in the Community Center kitchen and it had graced the front page.

He'd caught the moment when Mary lunged at Terry and Jordan and I stepped in to break it up. Terry had his hands up, his head turned away from Mary and my arms wrapped around his waist. My mouth hung open in an O, my eyes wide in surprise, my glasses skewed and bits of cake smattered across my face and Mrs. Claus outfit. Jordan had grabbed Mary's hands while she held the knife, his brow furrowed in concentration while Mary screamed like her world was ending. In a way, it had been.

"Oh, you've seen the *L.A. Times*?" Mrs. Mason asked. "I didn't think anyone but me got regular papers any longer, especially from other cities."

I shot to my feet. The *L.A. Times* had somehow picked up the picture from the *Heywood Sentinel*? "What?!" Rounding the fire, I grabbed the paper out of her hand. Sure enough, there I was on the front of the *Los Angeles Times* Lifestyle page. Bile rose in my throat as I read the headline: *Santa and Mrs. Claus Deliver a Blow to Crime.*

Quickly, I scanned the article looking for my name. For a brief second, relief swept through me when I didn't find any mention of it. I studied the picture again, this time with a neutral eye. Would anyone from my former life recognize me with the fully gray hair and Mrs. Claus suit?

If they didn't, I'd be surprised.

Swallowing past my tears, I handed the paper back to Mrs. Mason and glanced at Annabelle. She stared at me, her eyes wide. As the only one in attendance who knew my true identity, she realized the implications of my face being plastered across the *Los Angeles Times.*

If I didn't tell my friends now, they'd find out if the Los Angeles Police showed up. I had left the whole investigation into my husband's fraud literally up in flames. They probably had a few questions for me. If they didn't, someone from my past may decide to pay me visit and rub in my fall from Hollywood grace, even though leaving Hollywood was the best thing I'd ever done for myself. Everyone in Hollywood liked to rub salt in another's wound when they could.

"Sam, are you okay?" Jordan asked. "You look a little sick."

I nodded, unsure of what to do. Should I ruin everyone else's evening by confessing my sins? Or carry on as if nothing was wrong and hope to at least get past the holidays without being outed?

"Sam, it's okay," Annabelle said. I glanced at her and she nodded. Leave it to her to understand my dilemma without me uttering a word.

I slowly returned to my chair. Jordan placed his hand over mine again, his brow furrowed in concern.

"T-there's something I need to tell everyone," I began.

"What's going on?" Jordan asked, squeezing my fingers. I kept my gaze firmly on the fire.

"I'm... I'm not who I said I was," I replied. The words felt like cement blocks as I forced them out. "My name isn't Sam Jones."

Gina snorted and laughed. "Then what is it? George Orwell?"

If only. "No. My name's Samantha Rathbone. I came from Hollywood where I was a daytime television soap opera star."

"Don't be so modest," Annabelle exclaimed. "She's, like, an Emmy winner!"

My other friends remained silent. Was anyone having trouble breathing besides me? Or was I in cardiac arrest? My chest certainly hurt bad enough for me to consider it.

"What is this?" Gina asked. "Some type of early April Fool's joke?"

"Why didn't you tell us who you were?" Jordan asked. "Why lie to us all this time?"

I shut my eyes. What wonderful questions. "When I left Hollywood, my house was on fire, I'd been dismissed from my job, and my husband had been murdered."

"Murdered!" Gina yelled. "Are you kidding me?"

Shaking my head, I pressed on. "Apparently, he'd also run one of the biggest Ponzi schemes since Bernie Madoff. I didn't know anything about it. In fact, I didn't believe the accusations at all until I found my husbands' secret office in our house where he confessed to everything and kept the ledgers. He stole millions."

"That still doesn't answer my question," Jordan growled. "Why have you lied to us all this time?"

"Because I wanted to start a fresh life," I said. "I came here almost penniless. I didn't want to be known. I wanted time to heal, to work through the... the way my Hollywood life had ended." My tears now cascaded down my cheeks. "I didn't trust anyone."

"Except Annabelle," Gina muttered.

I shook my head. "No. Unbeknownst to me, Annabelle was a fan of the show. She recognized me right away but didn't say anything until after I figured out who killed Bonnie."

"That's true," Annabelle said. "She looks different with her hair curly and no makeup, but I loved her character on the show. I watched it all the time."

Silence engulfed us, the only sound the crackling of the fire. Even the coyotes had gone quiet.

"Well, this is quite the exciting news," Mrs. Mason said. "Although, I get the feeling that you sharing this with us was quite challenging. I can see the pain in your eyes, Sam."

I nodded, relieved someone seemed to understand. Turning to Jordan, my heart sank as he stared at me, his mouth pursed in a thin line of anger.

"You know, everything makes sense now," he muttered. "Everything."

As he stood and walked toward the path on the side of the building leading to the front, I reached for him. "Jordan, please. Wait."

"Not now, Sam," he said, waving over his shoulder. "Not now."

I remembered all the times he'd tried to get to know me and how I'd blown him off, deflected, or changed the subject.

Oh, heck. What had I done?

"You know, there's a very small difference between outright lying to someone and hiding the truth," Gina said. "And sometimes, I'm not sure which is worse."

"I'm sorry, Gina," I replied, my nose now running. "I was so hurt and confused from my husband's betrayal. Then, the longer I didn't say anything, the harder it was to come forward."

She nodded. "I get it. We all have our secrets, Sam. But it doesn't make it any easier to know you aren't the person I thought you were."

Mrs. Mason stood. "Well, I for one am thrilled to know a celebrity. Does anyone want another cookie before I go?"

"No," I said, shaking my head and feeling sick to my stomach.

"Thank you, though." I glanced over at where Jordan had disappeared into the darkness.

"Men sometimes need time," Mrs. Mason said as she rounded the fire and placed her hand on my shoulder. "Give him some space, dear. And if you want to talk, you know where to find me. I can see how difficult this has been for you, and I'm sorry I ruined your evening."

I squeezed her fingers, so grateful she'd forgiven me. However, I wasn't close to Mrs. Mason like I was to Gina and Jordan.

My remaining friends were quiet as Mrs. Mason made her way back to her store.

"I'm sorry, Gina," I whispered. "I should've told you sooner."

She pursed her lips. "I wish you would have, but I have no right to be upset. You did what you thought was best, Sam. Or should I say Samantha? Ms. Rathbone? I'm not sure what to call you."

"Sam is fine," I said. "I'm still the same person, Gina." After swiping my coat sleeve across my face, I asked, "What do you guys think about Jordan? Do you think he'll ever speak to me again?"

Neither answered.

But the coyote gave a long, sad howl into the cold night as the snow began to fall, and I'd never felt so alone.

EPILOGUE

New Year's Day

EVEN THOUGH WE were closed on New Year's Day, I worked in the store doing various tasks to take my mind off my sadness. Tears pricked my eyes. The stress of my situation weighed heavy on my heart, and if I were perfectly honest, I fiercely missed Jordan. I'd called and even stopped by his house in the past week, but he'd said he needed time to come to terms with my deception.

And, when I wasn't thinking about Jordan, I was consumed with the fear of when my past would come knocking and I'd have to face the mess I'd left behind in Hollywood.

I turned when I heard the lock on the front door click. Annabelle strode in carrying two coffees from Cup of Go. "Good morning!" she chirped as she approached.

"Good morning," I replied. "What are you doing here? We aren't open today."

Her thick, sparkly blue eyeliner outlined her eyes while her crimped hair cascaded around her face.

"Oh, I know," she said, shucking her floor-length pink parka. "I just figured you'd, like, want some company."

I sighed with relief that I wasn't alone any longer, but at the same time, I was pretty deep in my own pity party and wanted to be left alone to continue.

"So what did you end up doing last night?" Annabelle asked, her dozens of bracelets clinking up and down her arm as she handed me my latte. "Anything exciting?"

I shook my head and took the cup from her. I wouldn't admit I'd had too much wine and shed a few tears. "Thank you for this," I said, taking a long sip. So good. "What about you? Did you end up going out?"

"Oh, heck yes," she replied, shucking her coat. "Gina and I hit the party at On The River. Sally really knows how to throw a fiesta!"

"Tell me about it." Anything to take my mind off my own problems for a bit.

"Well, we had a couple tequila shots, ate some food, danced, and then I sang karaoke."

"Gina didn't join you?" I asked, then took a sip of my latte to hide my smile.

"No. She's, like, a total chicken. I mean, I'd carry us. She just had to be backup."

"What song?"

"You Give Love a Bad Name by Bon Jovi."

Recalling the song and knowing Annabelle, I couldn't hide my grin any longer. She took her eighties music quite seriously.

"Do you want to see it?" she asked, pulling her phone from her pocket. "Someone filmed it and put it on TikTok. I have over two thousand views so far."

I stayed far away from social media except for the odd video or post Annabelle shared with me. "Sure. Let's take a look at your performance."

After she pulled up the video, she turned on the sound. I was witnessing a female Bon Jovi singing her heart out, in tune. "You're really good," I said at the end. To my horror, the next video served up showed my face.

"I-I did well," Annabelle stuttered, quickly pulling the phone from my view. Her cheeks reddened and she wouldn't meet my gaze.

"What was that?" I asked. Did I really want to know?

"Oh, nothing."

"That wasn't nothing, Annabelle. Let me see the video."

She rolled her eyes and sighed. "Sam, it's probably better if you don't."

The sickening dread that had consumed me all week only grew. Perhaps she was right. Maybe I shouldn't watch the video. Yet, if I didn't, I'd worry about it and only make my anxiety worse.

"Is it bad?" I asked.

She nodded and wouldn't meet my gaze.

"Did... did you put it up there?"

"Oh, my gosh!" she shouted, stepping away while her brow furrowed in anger. "Of course not!"

"Let me see it," I said, waving her back. "Please."

She groaned, but held up her phone. A few taps later, my face appeared again.

The picture was from a few years ago. I stood on stage at the Emmy's wearing a stunning purple sequined gown. As I held up the trophy, I beamed with pride, my smile wide, my eyes glistening with tears. Along the bottom, writing appeared. *This is...*

The second photo was from my fall at the Emmy's where I'd toppled backward and flashed everyone my red thong. I cringed as I recalled the horror of that night and how thrilled I'd been when I learned my hideous moment hadn't been televised. Now, it was out on TikTok for everyone to see—and it included the red thong and my butt cheeks.

How to...

The final picture flashed—Jordan and me dressed in Santa suits trying to prevent Mary from killing her lover, Terry, that had been plastered on the front of the L.A. Times.

Fail at life. Don't be like Samantha Rathbone!

Laugh emojis ran across the screen.

I'd forgotten about social media. People didn't even need to show up at my door to mock and ridicule me. A larger reach could be found on the internet.

Annabelle shoved the phone back in her pocket. "I'm sorry you had to see that."

"Who put it up?" I asked, trying to steel my spine so the video didn't cut too close.

"Your former co-star, Bradley Bass."

Ah, yes. Good old Bradley—the highly functioning drunk I used to work with who always smelled of whisky. It didn't surprise me he'd stoop so low.

I sighed and twisted a curl around my finger, determined not to let all this get to me. There was nothing I could do about a stupid video placed on social media by a stupid man who only wanted to demean me. I had my life directly in front of me that needed my attention.

"Thanks for showing that to me," I said.

"He's just a big idiot," Annabelle said. "You shouldn't think about it."

I nodded and wished I could do that, but unfortunately, that video would eat away at me until I became exhausted and could no longer give the energy to care anymore. That was the way I handled most embarrassing events.

"Anyway," Annabelle continued, "I was wondering if you wanted to go to On The River and get something to eat?"

"Is Sally open today? Even after the party last night?"

"Oh, yeah. She's got a huge buffet going."

"Sure. That sounds good. I'd like to get—"

"Did you just hear that?" Annabelle interrupted.

Both of us remained quiet, then a scream sounded from outside. Annabelle's eyes widened, then we rushed out onto the deck just as Mrs. Mason came stumbling out her back door. She cried out again.

"Mrs. Mason!" I yelled, hurrying over to her, Annabelle right behind me. "What's wrong?"

She pointed to her store as she covered her hand with her mouth. Slowly, Annabelle and I walked inside. The back room was lined with shelves stocked with yarn. The front of the store had display tables showcasing some sweaters, mittens and blankets.

"I don't see anything," Annabelle whispered.

My gaze darted all around. "Do you think she saw a mouse or something?"

"In the small alcove off the back room!" Mrs. Mason yelled.

We retraced our steps and rounded the corner to find a man in a pool of blood.

"Who is this?" I asked.

"I'm pretty sure that's Russell Mason," Annabelle whispered.

With a gasp, I placed my hand over my mouth. Who in the world would kill Mrs. Mason's husband?

THYME AND TROUBLE

A SMALL TOWN CONTEMPORARY COZY MYSTERY

ABOUT THE BOOK

Her past has caught up with her... will a killer do the same?

When Mrs. Mason, the owner of Knit Wit, finds her husband murdered, Sam Jones steps in to console her despite her own troubled life filled with uncertainty and loneliness.

As their friendship blossoms, Sam confronts her past and the mistakes she's made. But will it be enough for the local deputy, Jordan Branson, to forgive her?

While the police hunt for clues as to who the killer is, Sam also worries for her own life. Will the murderer be revealed before Sam becomes the next victim?

CHAPTER 1

New Year's Day

Although the New Year was supposed to be a time of renewal, a heavy weight sat on my shoulders, threatening to suffocate me. Standing outside in the bitter cold morning air drinking coffee on the deck that had once given me such joy, my chest clenched with dread. I hadn't spoken to Deputy Jordan Branson since that fateful Christmas Eve when he'd found out my secret— a secret I never should have kept from those close to me: my true identity and the fraud my dead husband had committed which had led me to Heywood.

I'd called a few times and even stopped by his house, but he'd claimed he needed time to think things through and he wasn't sure he trusted me. I reminded him that I had believed in him when he'd been accused of a crime he didn't commit, but according to him, my situation was different. I wasn't sure how, but I finally stopped chasing him. If he wanted to be my friend—and possibly more—then he could come around when he was ready. Only then would I give him another thought... or so I told myself.

Since that fateful night when I'd seen my face plastered across the

Los Angeles Times, I'd been looking over my shoulder, waiting for the inevitable. Either the L.A.P.D. or one of my so-called friends from my former life would travel to Heywood.

The L.A.P.D. most likely had some more questions for me about my husband's dealings. Why had I left town? Was there something I was hiding? Did I have information I hadn't previously shared?

I could see a couple of the "friends" I'd had making the trip to rub my face in my dismissal from Hollywood and chastise me for the simple life I'd built. *You don't have a housekeeper? You really need to hit those lines around your eyes with a couple shots of Botox. You live in this tiny apartment and run this silly business?*

Nothing was below them.

The time would come when I would have to confront what I'd left behind—I felt it in my bones. I just didn't know where or when.

"Good morning, Sam!" I glanced at the walkway between my store, Sage Advice, and the one next to mine, Knit Wit. Mrs. Mason waved as she walked up the path from the Riverwalk. In her seventies, she was short and round, but I freely admitted she seemed to have more energy than me.

"Good morning, Mrs. Mason!" I called, hoping my attempt at sounding cheerful worked. "How are things today?"

"Fine. Just took a quick walk before opening the store." She climbed to the top of the hill, her chest heaving. Pulling off her purple knit cap that matched her gloves, she flashed a smile on her pale, doughy face. "It feels good to get the old blood pumping."

I nodded and chastised myself for not even taking a walk in the past month. The cold seemed to have paralyzed me, making it impossible to get warm. The last thing I wanted to do was be out in it, yet here I stood, staring at the river below. My worries had distracted me, my loneliness overwhelming. I hurried over to the path.

"Are you going to be busy today?" I asked. "I'm surprised you're open on New Year's Day."

"I could say the same about you," she replied, her smile fading. "You look so sad, Sam. Have you heard from Jordan?"

Mrs. Mason had been there Christmas Eve and witnessed Jordan's reaction when I shared my past. She'd watched him walk away. "No. Well, not really. He says he needs time to process what I told him."

Clucking her tongue, she rolled her eyes. "Men. Even on their best days they're more difficult than children. I would think he'd be thrilled to be in the company of someone so exciting."

'Exciting' wasn't really a word I'd use to describe myself, but I supposed to those who had never lived in Hollywood, I may be that. And for many years, I'd considered my life very full. It wasn't until I was out of the spotlight that I realized just how empty I'd felt. "Well, I guess he prefers boring."

"Nonsense. He just needs some time. He'll be back. I saw the way he looks at you. Trust me on this one." She reached out and patted my parka-clad arm with her glove. "I best get into the store. The knitting club is meeting today and I have to get the coffee on."

"On New Year's Day?"

Mrs. Mason nodded. "We set our goals for the year, talk about what happened over the holidays, and complain about relatives who came to visit and have now returned home. It's a great time."

With a smile, I said my goodbyes and went inside my own store. My teeth chattered as I pulled off my gloves and switched on the space heater. Despite the furnace running, it didn't provide enough warmth for me, especially since I'd become lost in thought standing out in the freezing cold.

Once I could feel my fingers and toes, I pulled out the inventory clipboard. My cat, Catnip, meowed hello as he descended the stairs leading up to our apartment, then stretched out in front of the space heater. Closing his eyes, he purred loudly.

"Glad you like it, buddy," I said, then walked to the front of the store to see what products needed replenishing. Definitely more cold and flu remedies as we weren't out of that season quite yet. We were also running low on Sally's special hot chocolate made from mushrooms. I knew the item would sell well, but I'd had no idea just how fast it would fly off the shelf. Thankfully, Sally had no interest in selling it in her own store beyond making it for special customers. She'd told me she had too many other things to worry about.

Annabelle and I also needed to plan our themes for spring so I could get the items ordered and give her time to work her magic with the tinctures. I had no intention of opening on New Year's Day, but I had to keep myself busy so my thoughts weren't consumed with my current reality.

As I worked, tears pricked my eyes. No matter how hard I tried to concentrate on my business, all I could think about was when my past would come knocking at my front door. And I wouldn't have Jordan by my side to help me weather the storm.

I turned when the lock on the front door clicked. Annabelle strode in carrying two cups from Cup of Go. "Good morning!" she chirped as she headed for the cash register.

"Good morning," I replied. "What are you doing here? We aren't open today."

Her thick, sparkly blue eyeliner outlined her eyes while her crimped hair cascaded around her face. She set the coffee down on the counter.

"Oh, I know," she said, shucking her pink calf-length parka. "I just figured you'd, like, want some company."

I sighed with relief that I wasn't alone any longer, but at the same time, I was pretty deep in my own pity party and wanted to be left to continue.

"So what did you end up doing last night?" Annabelle asked, her dozens of bracelets clinking up and down her arm as she hung her coat. "Anything exciting?"

I shook my head and grabbed the vanilla latte. "Thank you for this," I said, taking a long sip. So good. "What about you? Did you end up going out?"

"Oh, heck yes," she replied. "Gina and I hit the party at On The River. Sally really knows how to throw a fiesta!"

"Tell me about it." Anything to take my mind off my own problems for a bit.

"Well, we had a couple tequila shots, ate some food, danced, and then I sang karaoke."

"Gina didn't join you?" I asked, then took a sip of my coffee to hide my smile.

"No. She's, like, a chicken. I mean, I'd totally carry us. She just had to be backup."

"What song?"

"You Give Love a Bad Name by Bon Jovi."

Recalling the song and knowing Annabelle, I couldn't hide my grin any longer. She took her eighties music quite seriously.

"Do you want to see it?" she asked, pulling her phone from her pocket. "Someone filmed it and put it on TikTok. I have over five-thousand views so far."

I stayed far away from social media except for the odd video or post Annabelle shared with me. "Sure. Let's see your performance."

After she pulled up the video, she turned on the sound and I witnessed a female Bon Jovi singing her heart out, in tune. "You're really good," I said at the end. To my horror, the next video served up showed my face.

"I-I did well," Annabelle said, pulling the phone from my view. Her cheeks reddened and she wouldn't meet my gaze.

"What was that?" I asked. Did I really want to know?

"Oh, nothing."

"That wasn't nothing, Annabelle. Let me see the video."

She rolled her eyes and sighed. "Sam, it's probably better if you don't."

The sickening dread that had consumed me all week only grew. Perhaps she was right. Maybe I shouldn't watch the video. Yet, if I didn't, I'd worry about it and only make my anxiety worse.

"Is it bad?" I asked.

She nodded and wouldn't meet my gaze.

"Did... did you put it up there?"

"Oh, my gosh!" she shouted, stepping away while her brow furrowed in anger. "Of course not!"

So it must be terrible for her to have such a visceral reaction to my question. "Let me see it," I said, waving her back. "Please."

She groaned, but held up her phone. A few taps later, my face appeared again.

The picture was from a few years ago. I stood on stage at the Emmy's wearing a stunning purple sequined gown. As I held up the trophy, I beamed with pride, my smile wide, my eyes glistening with tears. Along the bottom, writing appeared. *This is...*

The second photo was from my fall at the Emmy's where I'd toppled backward and shown everyone my red thong. I cringed as I recalled the horror of that night and how thrilled I'd been when I learned my hideous moment hadn't been televised... but that didn't mean it hadn't been filmed. Now, it was out on TikTok for everyone to see.

How to...

The final picture flashed—Jordan and I dressed in Santa suits trying to prevent Mary from killing her lover, Terry—one that had been plastered on the front of the L.A. Times.

...Fail at life.

Laughter emojis ran across the screen.

I'd forgotten about social media. People didn't even need to show up at my door to mock and ridicule me. A larger reach could be found on the internet.

Annabelle shoved the phone back in her pocket. "I'm sorry you had to see that."

"Who put it up?" I asked, trying to steel my spine so the video didn't cut too close.

"Your former co-star, Bradley Bass."

Ah, yes. Good old Bradley—the highly functioning drunk I used to work with who always smelled of whisky. It didn't surprise me he'd stoop so low.

I sighed and twisted a curl around my finger, determined not to let it get to me. There was nothing I could do about a stupid video placed on social media by a stupid man who only wanted to demean me. I had my life directly in front of me that needed my attention.

"Thanks for showing that to me," I said.

"He's just a big idiot," Annabelle said. "You shouldn't think about it."

I nodded and wished I could do that, but unfortunately, that video would eat away at me until I became exhausted and could no longer give the energy to care anymore. That was the way I handled most embarrassing events.

"Anyway," Annabelle continued, "I was wondering if you wanted to go to On The River and get something to eat?"

"Is Sally open today? Even after the party last night?"

"Oh, yeah. She's got a huge buffet going."

"Sure. That sounds good. I'd like to get—"

"Did you just hear that?" Annabelle interrupted.

Both of us remained quiet, then a scream sounded from outside. Annabelle's eyes widened. We rushed out onto the deck just as Mrs. Mason came stumbling out her door. She cried out again.

"Mrs. Mason!" I yelled, hurrying over to her, Annabelle right behind me. "What's wrong?"

She pointed inside Knit Wit as she covered her hand with her mouth. Slowly, Annabelle and I walked inside. The back room was lined with shelves stocked with yarn. The front of the store had display tables showcasing some sweaters, mittens, and blankets.

"I don't see anything," Annabelle whispered.

My gaze darted all around. "Do you think she saw a mouse or something?"

"In the small alcove off the back room!" Mrs. Mason yelled.

We retraced our steps and rounded the corner to find a man lying, lifeless, in a pool of blood.

CHAPTER 2

"Ewww, gross." Annabelle turned her head away from the sight. "I'm pretty sure he's dead."

If he wasn't, I'd be surprised. "Who is this?" I asked.

"I think that's Mr. Mason. I haven't seen him in a while, but it looks a bit like him beyond the blood and gore. He wasn't very friendly."

I tried to recall having seen Mr. Mason in my time in Heywood. Maybe from a distance when he stopped by Knit Wit, but we'd never been properly introduced.

"Let's go back outside," I sighed, wishing I had a more visceral reaction to finding another dead body. I should be upset, sick to my stomach, horrified... but instead, I simply felt numb.

"Is that your husband?" I asked as we approached a sobbing Mrs. Mason.

She nodded as her body shook. "We should get you a chair," I said, worrying she was going to collapse at any moment. We didn't want two dead bodies.

"I'll grab one from our workroom," Annabelle said. I gently embraced Mrs. Mason while partially holding her upright. Her sobs soaked through my sweater and I suddenly realized I was freezing. I should've had Annabelle grab my jacket as well.

She returned moments later with the chair as well as our coats. "Thanks," I said after we got Mrs. Mason settled on the seat. I slipped on the coat and stuffed my hands in my pockets.

"We need to call the police," Annabelle said.

"Yes, we do," I replied, dreading it. Once again, I was caught up in a murder investigation, and the cops were the last people I wanted to see.

"I'll run inside and get a blanket from the display in the store for Mrs. Mason," Annabelle said. "You call."

Wonderful. I pulled out my phone and stared at it. In times like these, I usually phoned Jordan directly, but now I wasn't sure what to do. Honestly, he probably wouldn't pick up when he realized it was me. Instead, I dialed 9-1-1 and explained the situation. They promised someone would be out soon.

Annabelle returned from inside and wrapped the blanket around Mrs. Mason. We'd most likely contaminated the crime scene by stepping foot in the building, but how could we not? Mrs. Mason sat with wide eyes, her face paler than usual, trembling. I was afraid she was going into shock or about to have a heart attack, so the police could take their crime scene contamination and shove it. We were caring for the living.

Moments later, sirens sounded in the distance and quickly stopped in front of the building. I steeled myself, hoping it was someone besides Sheriff Mallory or Jordan. Footsteps sounded from within the store and a moment later, both Mallory and Jordan exited and stood before me. The day just kept getting better and better.

I met Jordan's steely gaze as he nodded my way. Keeping my features as passive as possible, I turned to Mallory. "I take it you saw the body?"

"We did," she said, narrowing her stare. "Why am I not surprised to find you here?"

I smiled and tilted my head. "I guess you're just lucky."

Mallory placed her hands on her gun belt and returned my grin. "Yes, we're all so lucky to have such a celebrity in our midst. Aren't we, Jordan?"

He grunted and pulled out a notebook from the inside pocket of his coat. "I'll take a brief statement, then you two can go back to your store," he muttered. "One of us will be by to interview you later."

Goodness, did I hate the sheriff. The less time I found myself in her presence, the happier I'd be. And frankly, I felt the same about Jordan. "Fine," I replied. "Here's my statement: Annabelle and I were over at Sage Advice talking about going to breakfast. We heard a scream. We rushed out onto the deck to find Mrs. Mason here, staring inside her store. She told us to go in, and we did. We found Mr. Mason on the floor."

Jordan jotted down a few notes while Mallory pulled out her phone and stepped out of earshot to make a call.

"Annabelle? Do you have anything to add?" he asked, not looking up from his paper.

She stuck her tongue out at him before answering. "Nope."

Jordan pointed toward Sage Advice and met my gaze. "Okay, you two head back to the store, but stay there, please. I'm going to have other questions after we go over the scene and have the body removed."

I glanced down at Mrs. Mason. Her tears had dried up and she stared at the deck. I wasn't sure if her eyes were open or closed. After placing my palm on her shoulder, I gave her a quick squeeze. "Call me when you can, okay?"

She nodded and patted my hand. Annabelle and I returned to Sage Advice and sat on the stools in the workroom. My cat, Catnip, was still curled up in front of the space heater.

"So much for breakfast," she muttered.

"Want some coffee?" The cups she'd brought in had grown cold and there was nothing I hated more than reheated coffee.

"I suppose so. But eggs and pancakes sound better."

"Sorry, can't help you there. I need to get to the grocery store."

I fixed us each a cup, then sat down with a sigh.

"You think he was murdered, right?" Annabelle asked.

"Well, considering he had a hole in his head, I would say yes."

"That's what I was thinking. A gunshot."

I nodded and took a long sip of brew. Oddly enough, the murder had provided a much-needed distraction from the horrible video my former co-worker had placed on social media, until Annabelle brought it up again.

"So, what are you going to do about the video?" she asked. "You need to exact revenge."

I snorted and shook my head. "I'm not going near Bradley Bass."

"We don't have to," she replied. "We can do something from afar."

"Annabelle, he lives in a fortress protected by high-tech security and a guard at the gate. No one is getting anywhere near him."

"We don't have to," she repeated. "Do you have his email address? We can sign him up for all sorts of annoying email lists, giveaways, and scams. Like I did with Sarah Billings."

I shook my head. "It was in my phone, which I left in Los Angeles. I'd just prefer to put it behind me, if that's okay. You don't have to exact revenge on him."

"Sure I do," she said, narrowing her gaze. "No one messes with my friends."

"Annabelle, I—"

A light tapping sounding at the back door interrupted us. I stood and walked over to open the door for Jordan. The fact he used to walk in and was now knocking wasn't lost on me, and I realized he was inserting customs into a relationship that used to be quite informal.

"May I come in?" he asked.

I rolled my eyes, not bothering to answer and returned to my chair. This distance he'd created between the two of us irritated me to no end. I didn't offer him a stool or a cup of coffee as I usually would. Two could play that game.

"It looks like Mr. Mason was murdered," he said.

"Duh, Sherlock," Annabelle muttered.

"Was it a gunshot?" I asked.

Jordan nodded. "Did you hear anything?"

I shook my head. "Nothing at all, except Mrs. Mason screaming."

"Hmm... I wonder if you would hear the shot with the windows and doors in both buildings closed."

I shrugged. "Is there anything else?"

"Where were you last night?" he asked.

"Why?"

"A man was shot at close range, so we're questioning everyone in the vicinity."

I narrowed my gaze on him. "Here. I was right here."

"Did you have any company?" I noted how his stare once again fixated on the pad of paper.

"Yes," I replied.

For a second, he froze. Then his gaze met mine, his eyes wide. "Who? Who was here?"

"Catnip," I said, silently pleased with the reaction I'd pulled out of him. "Catnip was here with me."

He sighed and returned to his notes. "And what about you, Annabelle? Where were you?"

"I was at On The River all night, then I came over here to see what Sam was up to."

Jordan arched an eyebrow and gazed at my friend. "All night?"

"Yes. Until about five, then I went home, showered, and came here."

Yikes. Annabelle was running on no sleep and tequila shots. I hadn't realized this. She should be home in bed, not driving around Heywood.

"Did either of you have any type of relationship with the deceased?" Jordan asked.

I shook my head. "I may have seen him a time or two at Knit Wit from a distance, but I'd never met him."

"That seems odd," Jordan mumbled. "You two are neighbors."

"He wasn't very friendly, and I'm busy," I replied.

"I knew Mr. Mason," Annabelle said. "But I've lived here my whole life so I know just about everyone."

"How well did you know him?" Jordan asked.

"Enough to, like, say hello. He didn't get out much these last few years, though. Well, I never saw him around, anyway."

"He didn't spend much time at Knit Wit?" Jordan asked.

Annabelle and I shook our heads. "Not that we noticed," I replied.

Jordan shoved the pen and pad of paper into his jacket pocket. "Thank you for your time, ladies. We'll be in touch if we have any more questions, okay?"

Annabelle and I both nodded, his formalities once again irritating me.

Jordan cleared his throat. "On a personal note, if you two were responsible for breaking into my home and placing plastic wrap around my toilet seat, I would appreciate it very much if you would please refrain from doing such things in the future."

I burst out laughing and no matter how hard I tried, I couldn't stop. Tears ran down my face and my stomach ached. Minutes passed, and no matter how much I tried to control myself, I couldn't. All of my anxiety seemed to be pouring out of my body.

"So it was you," Jordan said.

"N-no," I gasped. "I had nothing to do with it." I glanced over at Annabelle who smiled like a Cheshire cat.

"It wasn't me!" she yelled, holding her hands up to her shoulders as if she was surrendering to the police. "I promise, I had nothing to do with it!"

When I finally caught my breath, I met Jordan's gaze. Our stares locked for a moment, and I realized he'd be laughing if he wasn't the victim.

"That must have been a mess when you peed," Annabelle said innocently. "Who would do such a thing?"

"Yes, it was," Jordan muttered. "I'll leave you two to your day."

He strolled out the back door and up the side of the building to the main street, Comfort Road.

I turned to my friend when he was out of sight. "You can't break into people's homes!"

She shrugged and studied her cuticles. "He deserved it."

"How did you do it?" I asked. "How did you break into a cop's house?"

"It was easy," she said. "I found a hide-a-key and waltzed right in. He doesn't have any cameras or anything. Cops think they're immune from crime because of their badge."

Jordan didn't have cameras because they reminded him of losing his wife and daughter. Well, that was my assumption. I'd never come right out and asked.

"He's being a total jerk," Annabelle continued. "You'd think he'd be excited to have a celebrity as a girlfriend."

"I'm not his girlfriend," I blurted out.

"Right," she replied with a sigh. "Only coffee every morning, dinner most nights, lots of laughs, that kiss that brought the room temperature up a few degrees at the Christmas Festival… yeah, not his girlfriend. Deny it all you want, Sam."

Okay, so maybe she had a point.

"Jordan got what was coming to him," Annabelle continued. "I just hope he opens his eyes and sees he's made a grave mistake in treating you the way he has."

I sighed and glanced out the window. Maybe he would, maybe he wouldn't. Right now, I had more important things to worry about, like who killed Mr. Mason.

CHAPTER 3

THE NEXT DAY, Mrs. Mason entered the store while I was helping a couple of other customers. She walked around and studied the displays, but I couldn't help but think she wasn't interested in the products. She seemed to be picking up random things, turning the products in her hand but not really seeing them.

Once I finished up with the last customer, I hurried over to her, taking note of her haggard face and deep circles under her eyes. Bending down, I gave her a hug. "How are you?"

"Oh, I'm okay," she said, her voice muffled against my shoulder. "I was at the police station until late into the night."

I held her at arm's length. "Why?"

"That's why I wanted to talk with you."

"Let's go in back and have some tea," I said.

"That sounds lovely. Thank you, Sam."

I led her into the back workroom and pointed for her to sit on a stool. "I'll run up and make it in my apartment. All I have down here is coffee."

"Thank you. No coffee for me. My nerves are fried."

I hurried upstairs and returned moments later with two steaming cups of chamomile tea. "Here you go," I said, smiling. I pulled up a stool next to her.

"I can't believe all the bottles of stuff you two have back here," Mrs. Mason said as her gaze caressed the shelving filled with mason jars chock full of herbs.

"Yes, it's a lot," I said. "We do good work here. I'm sure you're feeling a bit stressed over everything. I have something that may help you."

She reached over and patted my hand. "You're very kind, Sam. You're right, though. I'm terribly upset, so anything you have that you think would help, I'd greatly appreciate it. But first, I'd like to talk about my trip to the sheriff's office."

"Of course. Please, continue."

"They were asking me all sorts of questions about my relationship with Russell," she said. "I found them very intrusive."

"Well, it's a murder investigation," I said gently. "They have to question everyone."

"I have a feeling that Sheriff Mallory thinks I did it."

A chill of dread crawled down my spine. "Why would she think that? What did you tell her?"

"Russell left early in the morning and never told me he was going to the store. Then I showed up and found him."

How had Mallory come to her conclusion based on that?

"Anything else?"

"She asked me if we'd been fighting or not getting along. We've been married for fifty years, so of course we fought. The man drove me to drink more than once."

"So, she thought you two argued and then you shot him in the store?"

"I guess so," Mrs. Mason said, shrugging. "It doesn't make any sense to me, though."

Still couldn't connect the dots on how Mallory had considered Mrs. Mason anything but a victim.

"What did you two fight about?" I asked.

"Lately, the store," Mrs. Mason said. "Russell begged me to sell it so we could do some traveling. I spend a lot of time at Knit Wit, and he didn't like that."

"Did he still work?" I asked.

"He worked a couple of shifts a week down at Hammer and Nail Hardware. The rest of the time, he spent in front of that darn television watching gardening shows."

"Why didn't you retire and go travel, Mrs. Mason?"

She sighed, then sipped her tea. After setting down her cup, she leaned forward as if she were about to reveal a big secret. "I loved Russell very much, Sam. But that doesn't mean I liked him all the time. I preferred to be at the store. I love teaching kids how to knit. I adore my knitting group and the women in it. I find the store and what it offers to be much more exciting and fulfilling than watching gardening shows all day. I feel alive while I'm there."

I took a deep breath. A better understanding of what Mallory was thinking came into view. "So, when was the last time you and Russell fought?"

"Yesterday morning. We had a big argument about me opening the store on New Year's Day. He said enough was enough, and he wanted me to spend time with him. I said I'd made a commitment to the knitting club, and I had to honor my promises. He stormed out of the house."

"And you didn't know he was going to the store?"

She shook her head. "I had no idea."

Mallory's theory must have been that Mrs. Mason had enough of Russell, so she followed him to the store and shot him, then pretended to be upset by her husband's death.

Except, wouldn't Annabelle and I have heard a shot? Recalling the events of the morning, I had been out on my deck drinking coffee. Mrs. Mason had walked up from the Riverwalk and we'd said hello, then I returned inside and Annabelle showed up. It couldn't have been ten minutes later that we heard her screaming.

But wouldn't Mrs. Mason see the body when she first walked into the store?

"What did you do when you went inside after we spoke yesterday morning?" I asked.

"I went to the front of the store to turn on the heat. Then I gathered some yarn from one of the displays and set out some chairs. When I went to the back room to make coffee, I didn't see him in the alcove. I guess I wasn't paying attention. It wasn't until I needed some extra knitting needles—which I keep in the alcove—that I found him."

For a moment, I didn't buy her story, but then I remembered Annabelle and I hadn't spotted the body when we'd walked in either. Mrs. Mason had yelled at us where to look, so maybe her account did hold up.

"I'm just not sure what to do," she said. "I feel like I should get a lawyer, but then I wonder if it makes me look guilty."

Mallory had made a debacle of many murder investigations. Mrs. Mason needed to be protected from her ineptitude. "Do you have a lawyer you can call?"

She shook her head.

"Let me phone my attorney. He's got a friend who does criminal cases."

"Thank you," she said. "Also, I was wondering if you could help me with something else."

"Of course, Mrs. Mason. What is it?"

"Well, Russell was the one who did the accounting for the store. Numbers are so confusing to me, so he took over once he saw how badly organized our books were. Can you please take a look at them?"

I certainly wasn't an accounting whiz by any stretch of the imagination, but I'd learned a great deal since owning Sage Advice. "I can do that, but I would suggest you also get a certified accountant to help you out."

"Do you know of one?"

"Yes, I do. He's my lawyer as well as my accountant."

"Oh, my!" she exclaimed. "Imagine the amount of schooling he must have had!"

Hopefully, Colin Breckshire III was taking on new clients. He was getting up there in age so I figured he'd have to quit at some point, and I'd have to find someone else as well.

"He's quite smart with a lot of experience," I replied.

"I was hoping you could come to the store tomorrow," Mrs. Mason said. "They should have the crime scene cleared by then."

Despite the tears welling in her eyes, I found it odd how calmly she stated those words. I would think after fifty years of marriage, losing your spouse would be similar to losing an arm. In Mrs. Mason's case, she may not have liked that arm, but it still had to hurt to have it gone.

"Sure," I replied. "I can do that."

She stood and smiled. "Thank you, Sam. I can't tell you how much I appreciate your help during this difficult time."

I rose and gave her a hug. "Call me if you need me."

Just as she exited the back door, the chimes rang, indicating someone had entered the front. I glanced around the corner to find Jordan strolling in. As our gazes met, his mouth remained in a tight, fine line.

"Can I help you?" I asked. If he wasn't even going to give me a smile, I'd play his game.

"Hi, Sam. I was wondering if you could look at some security footage and tell me if you recognize the person in it."

A flat "no" sat on the tip of my tongue, but I held it. Instead, I nodded, curiosity getting the best of me.

He pulled his phone from his pocket, tapped the screen a few times, then turned it toward me.

A person slowly staggered up a path—almost as if they were drunk —then disappeared from view.

"That's it?" I asked.

Jordan nodded. "That's the security footage from Knit Wit yesterday morning."

"I didn't even know they had a camera," I said. "Can I see it again?"

This time, I noted the person wore jeans, a bulky parka, and a base-ball cap. The jacket had a stripe down the back. Maybe paint? Or some type of decoration sewn in. "I think that's a man?" It was hard to tell with the jacket and the angle of the camera.

"Agreed," Jordan said. "Did you see or hear him yesterday morning?"

I shook my head. "Is there footage of him leaving?"

"No. The system went down shortly after this. We figure he either disabled it or left the back way."

"Could that be Russell Mason?" I asked.

"We don't think so," Jordan replied. "Russell was thin but this guy seems to have some bulk to him, unless he's got layers on under the coat."

I sighed and stared at the phone before he shoved it back in his pocket.

"So what do you think happened?" I asked. "That guy went in, killed Russell, then snuck out the back? Or realized there was cameras at the front door and cut the cord?"

"Well, sort of," Jordan said. "You'd told me that you were on the back deck having coffee that morning. I thought there may be a chance you'd seen him."

"I didn't see anyone but Mrs. Mason." I pointed at the phone. "But you think I would've if he'd left that way."

"Are you sure?"

"Yes. Do you know who he is?" I asked.

Jordan shook his head. "I was hoping you'd be able to tell me."

"I have no idea."

We stared at each other a long beat, then he cleared his throat and broke our stare. "Well, if you think of anything, give me a call."

As he turned to leave, I asked, "Give you a call directly, or call the sheriff's department?"

"You can call the sheriff's department."

I nodded as he hurried out the door. I rubbed my chest as a painful stab of longing ripped through it. I missed him so, and I had no idea if I'd ever get him back.

With a sigh, I checked the clock to see when Annabelle was going to come in. When I realized she'd be here shortly, I broke my no-caffeine-after-noon-rule and texted her to stop at Cup of Go to grab me a vanilla latte. After I received a thumbs up from her, my thoughts returned to that video.

What had he meant that he "sort of" thought that man was the killer? What other theories did the police have? If Jordan was right, I'd have noticed someone coming out the back door, wouldn't I? But then again, I'd been pondering my life, my worries and losses pretty hard. Was it possible that I stood on my deck while a murder happened right next door, then the killer walked right in my sightline and I hadn't even noticed?

CHAPTER 4

ANNABELLE ARRIVED with my latte just as we started to get busy. She wore a flowing red and black ankle skirt and a black Psychedelic Furs t-shirt over a black turtleneck. Her hair was piled on top of her head in a ponytail, the strands falling around like a waterfall. Large silver earrings dangled from her ears and her lipstick matched the red in her skirt. She waved, handed me my coffee, shucked her pink parka, and immediately got to work.

I took a quick sip and helped a couple of customers while she did a consultation with a woman in her thirties who had been sick on and off for months, never fully able to recover. I listened in when I could.

"It's always my stomach," she said, laying her hand over her abdomen. "I'm queasy, sometimes throwing up and have diarrhea as well. I've lost twenty pounds!"

"Have you seen a doctor?" Annabelle asked, her brow furrowed.

"Yes. And they've put me on a couple different medications, including three rounds of antibiotics. I'm done with them."

"Have they done any tests?"

"Like what?"

Annabelle shrugged. "Scoped your stomach? A fecal test?"

The woman shook her head.

As Annabelle asked a few more questions, I rang up a customer, then returned my attention to the consultation.

"I'd like to try some thyme in your case," Annabelle said. "We'll start with a gentle tea."

"What is that going to do?"

"Thyme is wonderful for digestive issues caused by viruses and bacteria. Based on what you've told me, it seems like you may have gotten a flu that won't resolve or something to that effect."

"I can't imagine a tea would help me," the woman grumbled, eyeing Annabelle with a good dose of skepticism.

"You came to me asking for help because your doctor hasn't been able to cure your issue," Annabelle said, placing her fists on her waist and furrowing her brow in irritation. "Now I'm suggesting we try some thyme tea and see what happens. It could help, or it may not. But we've got to start somewhere, right? Unless you want to pay them a few thousand dollars to shove a camera down your throat, be my guest."

The woman hesitated for a moment, then nodded. "I'll try the tea."

"Okay, let me go in back and gather what I need," Annabelle said. I sighed in relief as her features softened and she headed for the workroom.

As I smiled at the sick woman, I hoped Annabelle could help her. I'd have to have a chat about her short fuse, though. I understood people could be irritating when she was only trying to help them but she needed to have a little more patience.

Speaking of helping others, I needed to phone my lawyer and see about a criminal attorney for Mrs. Mason.

I pulled out my phone, stepped into the back room, and dialed. Colin picked up on the second ring.

Elderly and bald with a fondness for bowties, I had grown to adore the man. Not only because he kept a tight rein on my business books, but he was also kind and had helped me out of a couple of legal jams. Well, he'd provided me with the name of a lawyer who could help my friends. I really needed to keep the criminal attorney's number in my phone, but I'd never imagined I'd know so many people in need of one, myself included.

"Sam, dear. How are you on this fine second day of January?"

"I'm well, Colin." Okay, that may have been stretch. I wasn't well. From minute to minute, I felt as though I was one wrong look away from tears. I was barely hanging on by a thread. "How are you?"

"Good, good. What can I do for you?"

"I need the number for that criminal lawyer you like to recommend to me."

He chuckled, then said, "Who do you know that is in a bit of trouble with the law now? Is it you?"

"No, not me. Thank goodness. Mrs. Mason, the owner of Knit Wit, has found herself in a bit of a pickle."

"Oh, my. What has Polly gotten herself into?"

Polly. Huh. I'd never known her first name. She'd always been Mrs. Mason to me. "Well, Russell was killed and she seems to think that the sheriff is looking at her for the murder."

"Has the sheriff arrested her?"

"No. It's just a feeling she has after being interviewed for hours. I thought it would be best for her to get some representation before the sheriff came for her again."

"Good thinking. Is there any reason Mallory believes Polly murdered her husband?"

"I have no idea," I said, not bothering to mention that my line into the sheriff's office had been abruptly cut off because of my past. "Nothing that I know of. Mrs. Mason is going on instinct."

"Another case of shoddy policework, I see."

Nothing new there. Mallory Richards had to be the worst sheriff in the country. I wish someone would run against her so I could start a grassroots campaign in favor of her opponent. "That's what I was thinking. I told her I'd call you and get the name of the lawyer."

"I'll text it over."

"And I promise I'll keep it in my contacts."

Colin laughed again. "Sam, I just wanted you to know I saw the Los Angeles Times article on you. I get that paper and a few others every morning. I'm sorry your cover was blown, dear."

So was I.

"But although I never watched your show, I think you're a very special lady, regardless of your past fame," he continued.

Tears welled in my eyes. That was the nicest thing anyone had said to me in a long while. "Thank you."

"It's been lovely chatting with you, Sam. If I don't talk to you in the next couple of weeks, send over your year-end books when you have them completed. We'll get an early start on taxes."

"Wonderful," I muttered. I hated tax season.

"Good day, Sam."

I hung up and glanced over at the computer and the pile of receipts sitting next to it. If I was going to help Mrs. Mason with her books, I should get my own in order.

After swearing under my breath, I returned to the front of the store to find my employee flipping through a magazine while standing at the cash register. "Annabelle, I need to get these receipts under control back here. Can you handle the store for a bit?"

"Ten-four, amigo," she said.

I sat down, turned on the computer and began the task I hated. Twenty minutes later, I was lost in numbers, but the door chime signaling someone had arrived tore me from my concentration.

"Can I help you?" Annabelle said as I focused on my job. We had not spent one million dollars on mason jars—only one hundred. Ugh. In this instance, extra zeros were not my friend.

"I'd like to speak to the owner," a man said. That got my attention. I set down the hundred-dollar mason jar receipt and listened.

"Are you, like, selling something?" Annabelle asked.

"No. I'd like to speak with her, please."

Okay, so he knew I was a woman. He could've lifted that information from public records. Shutting my eyes, I tried to calm my irritation at the interruption. I stood and walked to the front of the store. When I saw the man, I narrowed my gaze. I'd met him before, but I wasn't sure where.

Thin with a smarmy smile shining through his thick black beard, tattoos peeking out from under his jacket collar and black-framed glasses, he resembled someone from Hollywood. But I couldn't place him in my former life.

"Can I help you?" I asked.

"Ah! Ms. Jones. I'm Aiden from Chester Development Corporation. We've met once before."

Of course. It all came back to me now. I'd caught him sneaking around the building after Bonnie had died. He'd told me he was going to buy it and they would erect a huge resort. Little had he known, I was the new owner. The meeting hadn't gone well for him. "I remember you. And, just like last time, Sage Advice still isn't for sale. Save your breath and have a nice day."

Annabelle giggled and snorted, while Aiden's smile faded just a bit. "I think you'll like what I have to say."

"I doubt it," I sighed. I really didn't want to be any ruder, but if I needed to go there, I would. "I'm busy, Aiden."

"Five minutes. That's all I ask."

I could sit here and argue with him for five minutes or I could listen and then dismiss him. Arguing required too much energy that I simply didn't have. "Okay, Aiden. Whatever you say won't change my mind but go ahead. Say your piece."

"A man was murdered next door," he began.

"Duh, Sherlock," Annabelle muttered.

"We're aware of that," I snapped.

"As a woman living alone, does that bother you?"

Of course it did, but I wasn't about to admit it to this slimy jerk.

"I feel perfectly safe here," I lied.

"Are you sure?"

"Yes."

"Well, I'll be in town for a few more days, Ms. Jones." He slid a business card across the counter. "If you decide you're not comfortable living and working next to the building where a brutal murder took place, then I suggest you give me a call. I'll make an offer that will blow your socks off."

I was about to explain that the powers-that-be who ran the town had rules put in place about selling businesses and tearing down buildings, but I skipped that lecture. I was almost tempted to have him buy Sage Advice just to watch him try to get approval from the town leaders.

"It's dangerous for you," he continued, "being a single woman living here."

166

"Wait a minute," Annabelle interrupted. "Was that a threat?"

He smiled, his gaze never leaving me.

Arching an eyebrow, I crossed my arms over my chest. "I feel perfectly safe, thank you. And I think you should answer the question. Was that a threat?"

With a chuckle, he shook his head. "Of course not. What a silly thing to say. Please, just make sure to keep your doors locked. There is a murderer on the loose."

After giving me a wink, he tapped his business card with his finger, turned and strolled out the front door.

"Sam, was he threatening you?" Annabelle asked. "Because it sure seemed like it."

"I'm not sure," I murmured. "But I agree with you. It could be taken that way."

"This is not good," she said. "Not good at all. What if he's the killer?"

"How did you make that jump?"

"First, he's been here before looking to buy Sage Advice for his stupid resort and was told to pound sand. Second, how odd is it that he shows up the day after Russell was murdered?"

"It may just be a coincidence," I said.

"Maybe. But I think we'd better talk to Mrs. Mason and see if he's approached her about selling Knit Wit. If he has, maybe he murdered Russell to force her into it. Now, he's trying to scare you."

Far-fetched, but not completely unlikely. "It's something to think about," I said.

"Watch your back with that one, Sam. He's nothing but trouble and I'd bet my signed Billy Idol album that he's the killer."

If she was willing to bet the record, then she felt pretty strongly about her accusation.

The door chimes rang once again and two young girls entered, one with blonde hair, the other a brunette. Somewhere around twelve, they approached us shyly, their gazes never leaving me.

"What's up, ladies?" Annabelle asked.

They giggled and then one whispered something to the other.

"How can we help you?" I asked.

The blonde nudged her friend, who finally said, "We saw your video on TikTok and were wondering if we could have your autograph."

With a gasp, I took a step back and placed my hand over my mouth. They might as well have asked me to cuddle a rabid racoon. Their request horrified me but I couldn't place why, even though I had received it hundreds, if not thousands, of times throughout my career. I wanted them to leave my store.

Finally, the truth hit me like a fist to the gut.

My anonymity had been fully compromised. No longer was I Sam Jones, the herbalist who owned Sage Advice... but Samantha Rathbone, the fallen soap opera star hiding from her past.

And *everyone* knew it.

CHAPTER 5

"Um... can you ladies come back later today?" Annabelle asked.

My breath sawed and sweat dotted my brow. Was my throat closing? And why was my heart beating so fast?

I turned and hurried into the back room, feeling trapped. Run. I needed to run from Heywood because I couldn't take the scrutiny. That's what I'd always done in uncomfortable situations. First, my childhood when I'd escaped my drunk mother and gone to Hollywood. Life had been pretty cushy for a long time, but then my husband had stolen millions from our friends and the Hollywood elite. I'd run then, too.

But where would I go?

How would I start over?

"Sit down," Annabelle ordered. "On the steps."

I did as instructed because I could barely breathe. "Are they gone? Oh, my gosh, Annabelle. I think I may die. My chest hurts."

"The girls have left and you're having a panic attack," she said as she kneeled in front of me and took my hands. "I need you to focus on me, Sam, and do as I say, okay?"

"But what about—"

"We'll figure it all out later. Right now, you need to look me in the eyes and breathe with me. Understand?"

My mind spun so fast and was clogged with so much panic, I felt as if I may topple over.

"I have to—"

"Sam, if you don't calm down, I'm going to have to call an ambulance."

That caught my attention. More spotlight was the last thing I needed.

"Now, breathe with me," Annabelle repeated. As she took a deep breath, my lungs seemed to collapse in on themselves. I could barely get in any air.

"That's okay," she whispered. "Let's try again. Focus on expanding those lungs."

My second attempt was more successful.

"Good, Sam. Now, look at me. Your eyes are darting all over the place. Concentrate on the tip of my nose and let's get some air in those lungs."

Again, I seemed to be able to breathe a little better. I wasn't sure how long we sat together inhaling and exhaling, but I eventually began to feel more grounded. The whirlwind of panic that had swept me up had become a light breeze as I gently floated down from the turmoil.

"Good, Sam," Annabelle said. "Now, I'm going to put you on an herbal stress regimen. I think we can agree that you've got a freight train of crazy times coming at you, and we need to protect your nervous system."

I nodded, suddenly exhausted. Placing my elbows on my knees, I rested my head in my palms.

She stood and placed her hands on her hips. "I thought you were going to, like, have a heart attack or something. This isn't healthy."

"I did feel like I was going to have a heart attack," I mumbled. "I don't want children coming in and asking for my autograph. I want my quiet life back, Annabelle."

"Well, that ship has sailed." She handed me a glass of water. "Now we have to figure out how to navigate these turbulent waters."

The door chimes rang, indicating someone was in the store.

I glanced up, unable to put one foot in front of the other. I couldn't face whoever was in my store.

"Sam?"

I recognized the voice. Sally, the owner of On The River.

"Can you talk to her?" Annabelle whispered. "Or do you want more time to pull yourself together?"

Sally and I had become friendly since I started selling her specialty mushroom hot chocolate.

"Sam?" she called again. "Are you here?"

I stood and forced myself to go to the front of the store. "Hey, Sally." I tried to smile, but tears welled in my eyes.

"You look sick," she said, her brow furrowed in worry. She wore her long brown hair pulled into a ponytail at the nape of her neck. Thin with hefty hips and beak-like nose, she reminded me a bit of an ostrich. "Are you okay?"

I swallowed past the lump in my throat and nodded. Had she seen the video? Did she know my secret? Was she here to chew me out for my deception?

"Listen, Sam. I saw the video on TikTok. Some of my customers were watching it and discussing you, so I listened in. I just came by to tell you..." She glanced around and shrugged. "I don't know why I came by. I just felt like you needed a friend."

Tears cascaded down my cheeks.

"Oh, honey," she said, coming around the counter. "Please don't cry."

As she took me into an embrace, relief swept through me. I was finding out who my true friends were, and I felt so much better having Sally in my corner.

The difference between Hollywood and Heywood wasn't lost on me. At the first sniff of a scandal, Hollywood had turned their backs on me. People I'd known for decades were more than happy to forget I ever existed. In Heywood, people I'd known for barely a year were rallying around me, giving me strength.

"I hope you won't be mad that I've never seen your show," Sally said, patting my back.

"You're much too busy for daytime television," I said, pulling away from her as I wiped my nose with my sleeve.

"That's true," she said. "So, what's your gameplan, Sam? Just ride it out until it all dies down?"

I shrugged. "I guess so." Still, I felt like I owed her an explanation. "I wanted to disappear, to live a life of anonymity, Sally. Just to be normal, I suppose."

"The reason why you didn't tell anyone your true identity isn't any of my business," Sally replied. "And, I don't fault you for wanting those things."

"Thanks."

"But at some point, I'd like to hear a few Hollywood stories," she said with a wink. "I've never known a celebrity."

"She's got some good ones," Annabelle said.

"How long have you known?" Sally asked.

"Since she first arrived," Annabelle replied. "I watched the show every day until they got rid of her. After that, it wasn't worth my time."

My phone buzzed in my pocket and I pulled it out. Mrs. Mason. I'd been so wrapped up in my own life, I'd forgotten there'd been a murder next door and I had to help Mrs. Mason with her accounting.

"Mrs. Mason," I answered, holding up my finger to Sally. "How are you?"

"I'm okay, dear. I was wondering if you'd have a chance to come over to the store and look over my books."

"Of course. When?"

"Is now a good time for you?"

As I stared past Sally out the front window, the two girls looking for an autograph came into view, this time with another girl in tow. I may have felt better about my situation, but I wasn't ready to sign autographs. "Yes," I replied. "Now's a great time. I'll be right over."

"Thank you. I'll see you in a minute."

I hung up and smiled at Sally. "Thanks for coming by. I do need to head next door, though."

"No worries. I'm on my way back to the restaurant. You both take care!"

As she walked out of the store, I put on my coat. "Thank you for helping me earlier, Annabelle," I said.

"That's what I'm here for!"

"I really appreciate it," I said. "You know, I don't think I've ever really known what it's like to have a true friend, but I do now."

She smiled while her cheeks turned crimson. "Thanks, Sam. That means a lot to me."

"And *you* mean a lot to me," I said, gathering her in an embrace. After a moment, I released her. "I need to go see Mrs. Mason for a bit."

"No worries," Annabelle chirped. "I'll hold down the fort."

I slipped out the back door and headed over to Knit Wit. Despite the sunshine, biting, cold air nipped at my cheeks as I stepped onto Mrs. Mason's deck.

She met me at the back door with a cup of tea and a smile. "Thanks so much for taking a look at the books."

"Of course. Happy to help. I also have the number for the attorney we discussed."

"Oh, my goodness. What a wonderful doll you are. What would I do without you, Sam?"

I grinned as she led me inside. It was nice not to be in the spotlight but instead, helping someone.

"Here you go," she said. The computer was in the back room tucked into the corner. I hadn't noticed it during any of my prior visits. I glanced toward the alcove where we'd found Mr. Mason and noted a blue curtain had been hung in the doorway.

"I don't want to look in there," Mrs. Mason said, following my gaze. "It's... it's so painful."

"It is," I said, recalling my own husband's death and the agony it had caused. "Have the police said anything more to you?"

She shrugged. "Nothing. I suppose they'll have a chat with me when they have something to tell me."

I stepped over to the chair in front of the computer, slid off my coat, and sat down. A large pile of receipts sat on the lefthand side and a smaller pile to the right. "Let me guess," I said, tapping the papers on the right. "This is the to-do pile?"

Mrs. Mason snickered. "Unfortunately, yes."

"Okay, let's see what program you have running here." I pushed the power button on and the computer came to life. After a few clicks, I found what I was looking for. "I think I have what I need here," I said. "I'll give you a call if I have any questions."

"Of course, Sam. I'll be out in the store."

The last thing I needed was her standing over my shoulder watching me, especially if she really had no idea about how the business ran. As I moved the arrow around the screen and clicked a couple of icons, I realized Mr. Mason had kept the books very much like the way we did at Sage Advice.

An hour and a half later, the din of people coming and going from the store had faded in the background. I'd finished entering everything, but according to my calculations when I compared the books to the bank statements, I was exactly twenty-five thousand dollars off. I'd gone through everything twice and couldn't locate my mistake. Maybe it was something similar to the error I'd made in my own books when I'd entered that we'd bought one million dollars in mason jars instead of a hundred.

What had I done wrong? I studied my transactions once again and still couldn't spot the error. According to the bank statements, Mrs. Mason was barely holding her head above water, yet, the accounting software showed her account held more than a thirty-thousand-dollar balance... and then it had disappeared.

Possibly, it wasn't my mistake so I had to dig deeper.

I did a quick search for twenty-five thousand dollars and found a transaction that had been posted two months ago—an influx of cash from a name I didn't recognize.

Juan Vasquez.

Was this an investor? If so, where had the money gone?

I sat back in my chair and waited until the store was quiet, then I called for Mrs. Mason.

"Yes, dear? What can I do for you? Do you need some more tea?"

I shook my head. "Mrs. Mason, who is Juan Vasquez?" I pointed to the entry on the screen.

She stepped back, gasped, and covered her mouth with her hand. "Oh, my word!"

CHAPTER 6

I HAD EXPECTED A SIMPLE EXPLANATION. Someone who had invested in the store was the first thing that came to mind. A typo was the second. I was caught completely off guard at Mrs. Mason's visceral reaction to the name. You'd think I'd just pointed a gun in her face.

"Who is he?" I asked.

"I think I need to sit down," she said, grabbing a shelf while her cheeks paled.

I stood and pushed my chair under her and helped her lower herself to the seat. "Do you want some water or something?" I asked, now very interested in who exactly Juan Vasquez was and what he had to do with Knit Wit and the Masons.

"Yes, please."

I found a glass next to the sink in the bathroom and used the faucet to fill it since I couldn't locate a refrigerator or water cooler. I guessed it was behind the curtain that led to the alcove where we'd found Mr. Mason.

When I returned, I leaned against the wall facing Mrs. Mason and waited for her to finish the water. She set the half-emptied glass down on the floor next to her, then, she began her story as she wrang her hands.

"Juan Vasquez was a friend of my son's when they were boys. We lived in the Phoenix area at the time, in the same neighborhood as the Vasquez family. The boys attended the same schools."

She shook her head and snickered.

"Those two were thick as thieves," she continued. "Always spending time at each other's houses. Russell and I actually bought an extra bed for our son's room so Juan would have a place to sleep besides in a sleeping bag on the floor. We kept a swimsuit at our place so he didn't have to run home to enjoy our pool. I stocked up on his favorite snacks. Every Halloween, I'd carve pumpkins with the boys. At Christmas, we'd build gingerbread houses."

She smiled and her features softened as she stared at the floor. With a faraway gaze, I guessed she remembered a time of her life she thoroughly enjoyed. "Juan was a good boy, and I did love him as my own. Our house felt empty when he wasn't around."

I hadn't known Mrs. Mason had children. She'd never mentioned them, and I assumed he didn't live in the area. "Will your son be coming to help you with the store and for the funeral? Or another one of your kids?"

Tears welled in her eyes as she shook her head. "He died years ago. Cody was his name. And he was my only child."

My heart skipped a beat as my breath caught in my throat. How very sad. "I'm sorry to hear that. I didn't know."

"I never talk about it," she replied, wiping the falling tears with her fingers. "Cody was one of the unlucky ones who couldn't untangle himself from the drugs. He died of an overdose. When he passed, we hadn't seen him in over a year. The last time we met with him, I barely recognized him. The drugs had eaten away at not only his soul, but his body. My vibrant, handsome young man was gone and replaced by a ghost of his former self. He looked as if he walked hand-in-hand with the Grim Reaper."

I sighed. The amount of heartbreak in this woman's life astounded me, and I couldn't help but think of Doug, the homeless drug addict who lived under the bridge down by the Riverwalk. When it had started to get cold, he had mentioned he was heading for warmer temperatures. I hadn't seen him since. Would he one become a statistic like Mrs.

Mason's son? Every time I passed the bridge when he lived there, I worried I'd find him dead. "I... I don't know what to say. I'm so sorry."

She waved her hand in front of her face as if to clear the air. "My boy died long before his body was found. He hadn't been our son—the one we knew and loved—for a very long time."

Although my heart ached for the woman, I didn't understand how the nice kid who spent a lot of time at her home fit into the accounting issue.

"But anyway, back to Juan," she continued as if I'd voiced the question. "As he entered his teens, he became a bit of a trouble-causer. At first, it was foul language, which I didn't appreciate at all in my home. More than once I'd asked him to leave. Then, I started noticing things going missing. Maybe a couple of dollars I kept in a drawer in the kitchen. A pair of earrings I swore I left on my bathroom counter. Russell said he thought he had a twenty-dollar bill disappear from his wallet. All this seemed to happen when Juan was around."

"It sounds like the sweet boy turned sour," I said.

"You can say that again. Little did we know, he wasn't just sour, but downright rancid."

"What happened?"

"As time went on, Juan got into drugs. Not taking them, but selling. By then, the boys were in their late twenties. Juan led Cody down the rabbit hole directly into addiction. My son was one of his regular customers. When Russell and I finally figured out what was happening, we confronted Juan. I'll never forget that day. Juan strolled into the restaurant where we'd asked him to meet us, looking healthy and well taken care of. Meanwhile, my son was rotting away physically and mentally. Juan said he never used his own product, but I could tell by the watch and fancy suit he was wearing, not to mention his shiny expensive car, he was reaping the benefits."

"What did you three discuss?" I asked.

"We begged him to quit selling to Cody, and if he had ever cared for his friend even a little, he should look at what our son had become and want him to gain his health back... to live a better life. Because if you don't have your health, you have nothing."

"I take it that didn't go over well," I murmured.

"Actually, it did."

My gaze widened in surprise.

"Yes, we were as shocked as you are," Mrs. Mason said, a small smile turning her lips.

"So, Juan agreed to stop selling to Cody?"

"Not only that, but he placed Cody in an expensive rehab facility and paid for it. Russell and I couldn't afford it, and we couldn't convince Cody to go. Somehow, Juan persuaded him and then footed the bill. He said the reviews on the place were excellent, and they'd get Cody cleaned up."

"That was generous of him," I replied, still surprised. A drug dealer with a soul who realized he was killing people? And he tried to fix the issue... How often did that happen? My guess was as close to zero as one could get.

"It was generous. Too bad the rehab didn't stick. Cody was back to his old ways twenty-four hours after he was released from his thirty-day program."

"You must have been so disappointed," I said.

"Oh, yes, but I somewhat expected it. Don't get me wrong, I hoped for the best but was ready for the worst."

"Why is that?"

"I appreciated Juan's gesture... I truly did. But when I visited the place, it seemed like more of a retreat for the rich. I didn't see anyone who resembled Cody there. They were healthy and sipping on their green smoothies while sunbathing. I didn't notice any real work being done on the addiction issues. His counselor explained that Cody was making great progress through his yoga and saunas—that his detox was going wonderfully. He needed to detox *and* get his brain rewired. I felt they were missing that part."

"What did Juan say?"

She shrugged. "He said he tried, and if there was anything he could do for us, to please call."

Finally, things were starting to make sense. "Did you call?"

"I most certainly did not," she said haughtily. "Years went by. Cody died. My hatred for Juan only grew. It became all-consuming, so Russell and I decided to get out of the Phoenix area. We moved up here, to Heywood."

It wasn't lost on me that another resident had chosen the town to give themselves a fresh start.

Pointing to the computer, I asked, "What's his name doing in your accounting software?"

She stared at the computer a long time before answering. "This store doesn't earn much money, Sam. Every now and then, I can give myself a paycheck, but Russell and I lived off Social Security. If I'm honest, the store's a money pit, but I love it. I love teaching people how to knit. I love the clubs I host, the people who come in. Knit Wit is an important part of my life, and Russell knew that. The only thing I can think of is that he was doing the books and realized what bad financial shape we were in, then he approached Juan for money."

"And do you think Juan would give it to him?"

She nodded, a tear slipping down her cheek. "I do. He may be a hardened criminal now, but underneath the flash, there's a boy who remembered his best friend and his parents who always welcomed him into their home. If all the kindness in his heart had been killed because of his occupation, my guess is he would've given Russell the money out of guilt."

"Guilt?"

"For getting Cody addicted and not being able to fix him."

We sat in silence for a long moment while I tried to reconcile with the idea of a conscientious drug dealer.

"He paid for Cody's funeral, but he didn't attend," Mrs. Mason finally said.

"I thought you didn't hear from him again after Cody went to rehab?"

"We didn't. I put Cody's obituary in the paper with details on where the service would be held. We received a phone call and were told it had been paid in full by Mr. Vasquez, but we never saw him again."

I wasn't sure what to make of the whole story. I'd never imagined a drug dealer to act that way.

But back to the books.

I cleared my throat. "Do you know where the money went? It's not in your bank account."

Mrs. Mason shrugged. "Maybe Russell paid bills with it? Like I said, I didn't have much to do with the financial side of the business."

I stared at the computer for a moment. I wasn't an accounting whiz by any stretch of the imagination, so perhaps I simply missed the payments. Maybe they'd happened in months prior, and the receipts hadn't been entered. That must have been it.

Suddenly, I wondered why the computer was even in the store. "Did the police look at it?"

Mrs. Mason nodded. "Sheriff Mallory sat down and poked around on it, but she told me she didn't see it as being part of the investigation."

Figures. "What did she look at?"

"Email and some search history. Of course, she didn't find much there except me looking up new, fun projects for my classes and groups, as well as the reminders and newsletters I send out to my customers."

I would've thought full forensics would have been done on the computer, but what did I know? I wasn't a cop or a computer expert. And besides, what could it have had to do with someone putting a bullet in Mr. Mason's head? Frankly, the guy on the camera sounded most promising as the murderer at this point.

"You know, Sam, I just had an idea."

"What's that?"

"If Russell borrowed the money from Juan, he'd want to be repaid."

I furrowed my brow. "Why? He never asked to be reimbursed for sending your son to rehab, or for the funeral, right?"

"You're correct, but this had to be business. This wasn't about him clearing his conscience."

Okay, that made sense. "What do you think happened?"

"What if Russell didn't have the money when it was time to repay the loan? What if... what if Juan killed him because of it?"

CHAPTER 7

USUALLY I'D CALL Jordan and discuss my conversation with Mrs. Mason. The money from Juan Vasquez was right there in the books, but not in the bank account. Where had it gone? I had no idea what other accounts the Masons had, or for all I knew, Mr. Mason could've pulled it from the bank and hid it in their mattress. First, someone should look into that debacle, but also take a listen to Mrs. Mason's theory. Was it possible the stranger walking up to the front door had been Juan? Perhaps Mr. Mason had agreed to meet him at the store for repayment of the loan and Juan had shot him when he realized he wasn't getting one dime back? After all, he was a drug dealer. I assumed violence was part of his day-to-day life.

Or was it as simple as Mr. Mason using the money to pay bills and the person caught on camera was some random sicko out to gun people down? A chill went down my spine. If that were the case, I really didn't feel safe. What's to say that wouldn't happen to me or someone else in town?

Instead of calling Jordan, I shoved my phone back in my pocket. I wasn't a police investigator and he wasn't speaking to me. The police would have to get everything figured out by themselves.

But still, didn't I have a duty to report what I knew?

Yes, I did, but what did I know as fact? Nothing. Mrs. Mason should be the one to share her theory with the sheriff about Juan Vasquez and the money. It was really none of my business. In fact, I'd stumbled into the whole mess.

I arrived through the back door at Sage Advice to find a line going out the front door. A few people in that line waved and smiled. Some I recognized as regular customers, others I'd seen around town, while the rest were strangers to me.

"What's going on?" I whispered to Annabelle as I smiled at the crowd.

"In the back room. *Now.*"

Pivoting, I hurried to follow her.

"All those people want your autograph," she hissed as she pointed to the front of the store. "I've told them that the only way they're getting an autograph is if they spend twenty bucks."

Horror washed through me as I gasped. "Annabelle! That's just wrong! It's bribery or—"

"It's extortion," she muttered. "I'm aware of that. But we can't have these looky-loos clogging up the store for our regular customers."

"I see some regular customers out there," I whispered.

"Yes, and they're happy to spend twenty. Some don't even want your autograph. They just want their product."

"Why can't we kick everyone out who just wants an autograph? Or send them to the back deck and I'll sign there?"

"Because you've given enough of yourself. It's time to make the best of this. It's a hard stance to take, but I'll take the blame for it, okay?"

I shook my head and peeked around the corner. If we didn't get some of these people out of the store, someone would bump into a display table and knock over our items.

I crossed my arms over my chest. "I don't feel good about this. It seems... greedy."

"Okay." Annabelle sighed. "Then they either buy twenty dollars from the store or make a donation to Heywood Hounds."

"I don't know. I don't feel right taking money for my signature."

Annabelle stomped her foot and rolled her eyes. "You realize that there are celebrities who charge hundreds of dollars for their signature, then more money on top of that for a picture?"

I'd heard of such events, but I'd never participated in one. "That's their prerogative. I'm not comfortable with it."

"Then what are you comfortable with?"

Having my life back where I wasn't a recognizable figure would be nice, but as Annabelle had said, that ship had sailed.

She didn't wait for me to answer. "Here's what we're going to do. I'm going to, like, give them the choice of either buying a product or making a twenty-dollar donation to Heywood Hounds, and either way they get your John Hancock. Then everyone wins."

She wasn't giving me much of a choice. I glanced around the back room, then out to the store once again. Where was all this going to take place?

"Grab a small table and sit by the back door," Annabelle ordered, as if I'd spoken out loud. "I think there's one in the closet. After I collect the money, I'll, like, send them back here. You can sign really quick, then move them out onto the deck and they can walk up to the street."

My head spun. I was still unsure if what she had in mind was the right thing to do. Instead of trying to think it through, though, I did as she instructed. I found a fold-up table and chair and sat down while Annabelle rushed to the front of the store and explained to the crowd what was happening. Some groaned and protested, but Annabelle shut them down right away.

"Not going to hear it, Betty! If you want Sam's autograph, this is the way it's going to be!"

The cash register dinged and a moment later, one of our regular customers stood in front of me. Tall, thin, and in her thirties, I wished I remembered her name, but my nervousness had clouded my brain. Or was it menopause? Either way, I didn't recall.

"It's really nice to meet you," she said shyly, handing me a piece of paper.

"Well, we've actually met many times before, right?" I smiled as I scribbled Samantha Rathbone across the page. "I'm still the same person."

"But I didn't know you were famous then," she said. "It's not every day we have a celebrity in our midst. Well, as far as I know, Heywood has never seen anyone famous." I handed her the signed paper. "Thank you. I'll see you soon."

"My pleasure. Have a good one!"

I took the next piece of paper and chatted a moment with another woman who had actually watched *As The Years Turn*.

"That one time you killed the rapist... man, I loved that. He really got what he deserved."

"Yes, he did," I said as I signed my name. "Here you go."

"Awesome. You're the best, Sam! I loved your show and I'm so glad you chose Heywood to live in! It's so exciting for us normal folks!"

I smiled, but that's what I longed to be: one of the "normal folks." Hopefully, after all this died down and the novelty of having a soap star in their midst faded, life would go back to normal.

So, maybe signing autographs wasn't the horrible thing I imagined. I'd done it plenty of times in Hollywood, but that was to be expected. I wasn't hiding my identity there. I didn't care who recognized me.

An hour went by while people filed through the store either buying something or making their donation to Heywood Hounds. I assumed Gina would be very happy with the influx of cash. Although, I wasn't quite sure what she'd done with the money Annabelle had stolen from Gina's dead ex-husband's house. She hadn't mentioned moving or any improvements to her current residence. Maybe she was just sitting on it, or perhaps she was saving to send her son, Jacob, to college. He would be graduating in a few short months.

By the time the store was almost empty, I was elated. People had been kind to me, appreciating my autograph and my time. The community discovering my true identity had gone much smoother than I had expected. If all these acquaintances, customers and strangers could accept me, why couldn't Jordan?

I muttered a few curses under my breath, then glanced up to see two men walking toward me—one bald and the other with thick brown hair —while Annabelle stood behind them staring at me with wide eyes.

For a second, I thought I was seeing things. But no, there they were, in the flesh. As they approached, the smell of cigarette smoke engulfed me, causing my stomach to turn. At least they weren't in their business suits, but instead wore jeans and parkas, as if trying to fit in with the locals.

"Ms. Rathbone," the bald one said, smiling. "Do you remember me?"

I simply stared at him.

"Well, to jog your memory, I'm Detective Gunter and this guy is Detective Smith from the L.A.P.D."

"I remember," I muttered. Leaning against the back of the chair, I crossed my arms while my light mood deflated. "I'm assuming you didn't purchase a product or make a donation to Heywood Hounds to get yourselves back here?"

"We didn't," Smith said. He pulled a badge from his pocket. "This got us past your gatekeeper."

"Sorry," Annabelle called.

I waved her off. Of course she should've let them through, but that didn't mean I had to like it. Glancing at the front of the store, I noted it was empty. Had they waited until everyone was gone before approaching me, or was I just lucky?

"You left us in California while we were in the middle of an investigation," he said. "With your house on fire."

"I'm aware of that. I sent you everything I had regarding my husband's business dealings, as well as the evidence to nail Richard Crewer for Gerald's murder."

"Yes. I received the information. It was quite helpful. We arrested him, of course."

"Then what are you doing here?" I asked. But I knew. They had more questions.

"We have to finish our conversation," he said.

"I thought we had."

"Why didn't you tell us where you were going?" Gunter asked. "Why hide like you did?"

"Maybe I just wanted to be left alone after my life was burnt to the ground," I said shrugging. "It was nothing nefarious, if that's what you're insinuating."

"Did you start the fire that consumed your house?"

"No. I don't know how it began. You know Los Angeles—there are fires every summer. The flames came over the hill behind my house very quickly. I left just as they spread to my backyard."

"And where did you go?" Smith asked, running a hand through his thick brown hair.

"I came to Arizona," I replied. No sense telling them about the bank account Gerald had left me. "I ended up in Heywood by accident, but it's worked out well for me."

Detective Gunter glanced around. "We understand that this is your store?"

I nodded.

"So you must've had some money with you when you left in order to afford to buy a business."

"No," I replied. "I was close to penniless. To refresh *your* memory, you froze all our assets, including *my* money I'd earned playing Cassie on *As The Years Turn*. Sage Advice was given to me when the owner died. I was the beneficiary of her will."

"Wow. How convenient for you."

I recalled Bonnie's death and how very inconvenient it had been for me. I'd been the subject of a murder investigation. "Not really." I stood and gave them both a cold smile, one that Cassie would have flashed at the unwanted police presence. "If there's nothing else, I have a business to run."

"Actually, we do have more questions," Detective Smith said.

"Then come back tomorrow afternoon after four," I snapped. "Right now I have things to do."

Neither moved. I sharpened my glare as well as the tone of my voice. "I'm asking you to remove yourself from my premises and come back tomorrow."

"Are you planning on bolting again, Ms. Rathbone?" Smith asked.

The thought had occurred to me, but I'd quickly squashed it. "No. I'll be around. I have too much to live for here in Heywood. I'm not going anywhere."

CHAPTER 8

THE NEXT MORNING, I met Gina and Annabelle at Cup of Go. I used to meet Jordan there every morning, but that wasn't happening anytime soon. Besides, it felt good to be with my girlfriends. I kept telling myself that men—especially cops named Jordan—were highly overrated.

"What happened to your face?" I asked Gina as I sat down across from her in the chair by the window, my vanilla latte firmly in hand. Annabelle grabbed the chair next to me.

"I was on a rescue," she replied, picking at her muffin. "I ran into a tree."

The gash above her eyebrow appeared angry and painful. "How in the world did that happen?" Annabelle asked while pushing her crimped hair over her shoulder, only to have the heavily sprayed strands return to their original place.

"One of the rescues in Sedona received word from a couple of hunters of a dog out in the forest in the snow. They couldn't catch her, so they called the rescue. They in turn called me to come out and help since the dog was located halfway between here and Sedona."

"And you ran into a tree?" I asked. "While chasing her?"

"Yes. She was cold, wet, and faster than any dog I'd ever seen. We were finally able to corner her and catch her, though. Thankfully, she's not dangerous."

I studied my friend who wouldn't meet my gaze. "Have you seen the doctor? Do you need stitches?"

She pushed her tortoiseshell glasses up her nose. "No. I'm fine."

"Where's the dog?" Annabelle asked.

Gina sighed and lifted her gaze to the ceiling. "At my place. I have *another* dog who needs a home."

"What kind is she?" I asked. "How old?"

"Why? Are you interested?" Gina countered, her voice hopeful.

"No. I can barely take care of myself and Catnip. We don't need a dog around. I was just wondering."

"She's a Jack Russell Terrier / hound mix. We think she may be about two. Sweet little thing. I should bring her by so you can meet her."

I took a sip of my latte and shook my head. "I'm fine meeting her, Gina, but I can't adopt her. I don't have the time for a dog."

"They aren't much trouble," Annabelle said. "Jack's very easy."

Jack, Annabelle's beagle, was easy, but he was also older and spent his days chasing rays of sunshine to nap in.

"She can be a handful, but... we're getting along quite well," Gina said, although her tone didn't indicate she meant it.

"What's wrong with her?" I asked.

"She's... she's bossy."

Annabelle and I exchanged glances, then she burst out laughing. "How in the world is, like, a dog bossy?" she asked through gasps. "They can't say anything!"

I'd seen Gina with her dogs many times, and I swore she could talk to them. The idea was silly, so I'd never brought it up. But Annabelle was right: how was a dog bossy?

"Trust me, she is," Gina muttered. She glanced around the store, her gaze suddenly focused on one spot. "Well, well, well. If it isn't lover boy himself."

Lover boy could only mean one person. It didn't take me long to find Jordan standing in line. I knew his order by heart. Turning my head, I focused on my latte. I didn't need to be caught staring at him.

"He's pulling out his phone," Annabelle said. "I don't think he's seen us. Do you, Gina?"

"Nope."

My phone began to buzz in my pocket. Was he calling me?

I pulled it out and glanced at it. He most certainly was. A little flame of hope sparked inside me, but I stuffed the device back into my parka. It wasn't the time or place to have a discussion with him.

"So what are your plans today?" I asked Gina.

"I have some writing to get done and a couple of appointments at the nail salon."

Gina was one of the busiest people I'd ever known. She worked as a ghostwriter and also owned File It Away, the local nail salon. On top of that, she had her dog rescue and was singlehandedly raising a teenager. How she found the time for all of that, I didn't understand. She obviously had more energy and hours in the day than me.

She wouldn't meet my gaze. Instead, she stared out the window at the river and the forest beyond. "Are you sure you're okay?" I asked.

"Fine," she replied. "But please don't push it."

I let the matter drop, but I realized she was anything but fine. In fact, she seemed quite rattled. If she wanted to talk, she knew where to find me.

"Excuse me." The three of us turned to find a woman standing at our table. In her sixties, I recognized her as one of the checkers at the grocery store. I hadn't even noticed her approach, but her gaze focused directly on me, so I knew what she wanted. "Can I get your autograph?"

Just as I was about to reply, Annabelle shot to her feet. "Now is not a good time," she said. "If you want to come by Sage Advice later and either buy a product or make a donation to Heywood Hounds, you can have your autograph then."

My cheeks heated with embarrassment. Annabelle had become worse than any vicious guard dog when it came to protecting me from the general public.

"Oh, okay," the woman, said, taking a step back while her gaze flickered from me to Annabelle. "I'll be by the store later, then."

As she took her leave, I groaned and sat back in my chair. I appreciated what she was trying to do, but her tactics didn't place me in a positive light.

"What do you mean, make a donation to Heywood Hounds?" Gina said, furrowing her brow.

Annabelle sat down, her Cheshire grin indicating she was quite pleased with herself. As she explained her grand master plan of using my autograph to make everyone money, I watched Gina carefully. After Annabelle finished, the woman nodded. "That sounds good. I could use the money."

I had expected more of a reaction from my friend, but she quickly changed the subject. "Have they found out who killed old man Mason yet?"

Shaking my head, I took a quick peek at Jordan, who was now in the front of the line waiting for his Americano with sugar and cream while on the phone. "Not that I'm aware of."

"I overheard two guys in Hammer and Nail Hardware talking about it," she continued.

"What did they say?" Annabelle asked.

"That they think Mason got what he deserved."

"He worked there," I said. "Mrs. Mason told me he was a part timer."

"Well, he wasn't very well liked," Gina replied, reaching for her coffee. "One of the guys even mentioned he was glad Mason was dead so he could pick up his shifts."

"That's not very nice," Annabelle said.

"No, it's not," I agreed. "Did you tell the cops about it?"

Gina shook her head.

"Did you see who it was?" I asked.

"Nope," she replied. "I was busy trying to figure out what dog food to buy and then get home to finish up a project and make sure my kid had a hot meal for dinner."

"I wonder who it could have been." I bit on my bottom lip. If they were discussing Mason's demise and were happy about it, maybe they had something to do with it. The only way we'd find out is if Gina could identify them.

"No idea." She shrugged and took a long drink from her cup as she pulled out her phone. "I need to go."

Grabbing her wrist, I asked, "Do you think you could identify the voices if you heard them again?"

Gina rolled her eyes and sighed. "Jeez, Sam. I don't know. I wasn't paying much attention. I was literally looking at dog food and overheard the conversation. It barely registered. The only reason it did was because Jacob used to work there. I remember thinking I was glad he quit if those jerks were his co-workers."

I stared at my friend with incredulity. She'd overheard two men discussing a murder and hadn't thought to identify them? My confusion and disbelief must have been written all over my face because then she added, "Sam, that murder isn't my circus, and it's not yours, either. You aren't in an episode of *Murder, She Wrote*."

"I would think you'd at least go to the police and tell them what you heard," I muttered, releasing her hand.

"Fine. Get lover boy over here and I'll share my fifteen seconds of information."

Looking for Jordan, I found him striding out of the store, coffee cup in hand.

"Too late," Gina said, standing. "If it'll make you feel better, I'll stop by the department later today and tell them."

"Yes, it would make me feel better," I said. "There's a murderer on the loose, so I do think the killing is a circus that belongs to everyone in town. Who knows if there's a psycho out there or if an idiot at Hammer and Nail killed him for more work hours? And considering it happened in the building next door to me, I'm feeling a little uneasy about it all."

She stared at me a long moment, then nodded. "You're right. I'll go back to the store and slink around to see if I can recognize any of the voices there."

"We can come with you," Annabelle piped in. "For, like, moral support."

"Sounds good," Gina replied. "I do have to run, though. I'll catch up with you two later."

We watched as she hurried out, then Anabelle turned to me. "She seems totally preoccupied and a little grumpier than usual."

"Agreed."

"I wonder if she needs to see a doctor with that knock to the head."

"Maybe," I said. "If we don't hear from her today, we should stop by after we close the store. If she's still a little off, we'll try to convince her to visit the clinic."

"Sounds like a plan, Stan."

As we stood, I wondered if Jordan hadn't seen us or if he'd simply ignored our presence. Cup of Go was pretty busy and he'd also been preoccupied.

Annabelle and I decided to head to the store via the Riverwalk. As we strode down the path leading to it, we discussed weekend plans. She was going to try skiing again.

"I haven't been in twenty years, but I figured I'd give it another shot. You should come with me."

My weekend plans included a blanket, my couch, some hot cocoa and my cat. While living in Hollywood, I'd gone to some amazing ski resorts and even tried to ski a couple of times. I finally came to the conclusion that I hated being cold and preferred to spend my time around a hot fire or in a hot tub. "Skiing really isn't my thing," I muttered.

The river slowly meandered by to my right. The bare tree branches looked dead and sad, and I hoped spring would come around sooner rather than later.

As we walked under the bridge where Doug usually lived, I was pleased to see it still empty. It was too cold for anyone to be out in the elements twenty-four hours a day. Although, I did have to admit, I missed our chats and hoped he'd return as soon as it warmed up.

Once we reached Sage Advice, we walked up the pathway between our store and Knit Wit. How had I not seen someone leave that place the morning Mr. Mason was shot? Had I been so caught up in my own thoughts? I shook my head, unsure if I believed I'd missed a killer leaving a crime scene. There had to be another explanation.

Annabelle unlocked the back door and we hurried inside. Thankfully I'd turned the heat up before leaving, and the store was toasty warm. After shucking my coat, scarf, and gloves, I went to open the front door.

There, I found Jordan, waiting.

CHAPTER 9

WITH A SIGH, I hurried over and unlocked the door, a cold blast of morning air hitting my face. "What's up?"

"Did you miss this?" he asked, holding up a piece of paper by the corner.

"Where was that?"

"Taped to your front door."

"I didn't see it. What is it?" I tried to take it from him, but he stepped back.

"Just read it. I can't have your fingerprints on it."

Uh oh. What now? I pushed my glasses up my nose.

ROSES ARE RED,
Violets are blue,
It would be a shame,
If you were found dead, too.

I GASPED and placed my hand over my mouth. Dread weighed heavily on my chest. "T-That was on my front door?"

"Yes. Can I come in?" he asked. "It's pretty cold out here."

"Sure," I mumbled, still horrified by the note. I glanced at it again. "Why are you here?"

"Mrs. Mason called the police a while ago. She found something similar on her door. After talking with her, I thought I'd come by and make sure you were…"

His voice trailed off as I met his gaze. "I was… what?"

He took a deep breath and shoved his hands into his pockets. "Just making sure you were okay."

So he hadn't seen us at Cup of Go. One of the phone calls he received must have been a request to head over to Knit Wit, and then he'd called me. My heart leapt and I couldn't hide my smile. "So… you were worried?"

"Yes," he sighed. "That note at Mrs. Mason's says basically the same thing, except with a different rhyme. I wanted to make sure no one had followed through with any threats here. I tried to call, but you didn't answer."

He still cared. If he didn't, he never would've bothered to come over to Sage Advice after visiting Mrs. Mason. A small spark of hope flamed within. "Is Mrs. Mason okay?" I asked.

"She's shaken up, but she seems okay. You may want to stop by in a bit and make sure, though."

"What's going on?" Annabelle said as she came from the back room.

"I'm receiving death threats." I huffed, crossing my arms over my chest. "Both Mrs. Mason and I did."

"Oh, my gosh!" she yelled. "Who wrote them?"

"We don't know," Jordan said. "I'm hoping it's a couple of kids messing around."

I looked at the note again, still held by his gloved fingers. The rhyme was pretty simple, so maybe he was right. "Let's hope so," I said.

Annabelle read it and shook her head. "That's not very original."

"I agree," Jordan replied. "Not very original at all. When do you think this could've been placed on the door?"

I pondered the question. "Well, I left this morning through the front door and didn't notice it then. I was gone about an hour, and when we returned we came in through the back door." I glanced up at the clock on the wall. "So maybe it was left sometime between seven and eight?"

He went over to the cash register and pulled out a plastic bag from his inside coat pocket. Carefully, he slid the threat inside. Then, he retrieved a notebook from the same pocket and wrote down what I'd said.

"Was there anything strange going on here last night?" he asked.

I shook my head. I'd crashed with Catnip. "Nothing caught my attention. What did Mrs. Mason say?"

"She left Knit Wit around seven last night and didn't return until this morning when she found the threat taped to her front door."

I sighed and ran a hand over my curls.

"Do you know who could be responsible?" Jordan asked. "Have you upset anyone lately?"

"No," I said. "Not intentionally." I glanced at Annabelle. Maybe her plan of charging people for my autograph had really rubbed someone the wrong way. That had to be it. It wasn't like I'd accused anyone of murder lately. Although that didn't explain why Mrs. Mason had also gotten one.

"Let's check your security," Jordan said. "Are the locks on the window and doors working properly?" He hurried over to a few of the windows and pushed and pulled, then walked over to the front door and examined the locks.

"Everything is fine," I said.

He glanced around the store, then his gaze focused on the motion detectors. "What about the alarm? Any issues there?"

I shook my head.

"Well, I have a feeling that this was a prank." Jordan returned to the cash register. "Not a very funny one, but there doesn't seem to be any reason to threaten you."

If my assumption was correct about Annabelle's autograph rules, then I certainly didn't have anything to worry about. Someone was probably letting off steam because they didn't want to spend twenty bucks.

The three of us stood in silence for a moment, then Jordan cleared his throat.

"I'll be in back," Annabelle said. "I hope whoever that is slips and falls and hits their funny bone on the cement."

I grimaced, having done exactly that a few weeks ago. It hadn't been pleasant. Waiting until she was out of earshot, I then lowered my voice and shared my theory with Jordan.

"It's a possibility," he said, not bothering to hide his smirk. "How much have you raised?"

"I have no idea," I replied. "She said she was going to add it up. I think I'll just give the portions she's collected for Sage Advice to charity. I don't feel comfortable keeping it. I mean, it's my *signature*. It all seems kind of stupid to me."

He stared at me a long time as his smiled faded. "I've never known anyone whose signature was worth anything. It's... it's a bit mindboggling to me."

It was then I realized it may have not been the lie I'd been living that upset him so much. Was it the celebrity factor that had scared him off?

"You know, I'm the same person I was before you knew the real story," I said. "Nothing has changed. Only now, you know the full truth about me."

"Why didn't you tell me?" he asked, shaking his head. "Why lie?"

"I lied by omission because I wanted to start my life over with a clean slate," I replied. "I've told you this already."

He frowned and ran a hand through his salt and pepper hair, looking absolutely nothing like George Clooney. "I, uh, did some digging into the case."

"Good," I replied, throwing up my hands. "Dig all you want. My husband stole millions from some very powerful people and was killed for it. I knew nothing about his business dealings."

"I don't know if I can believe that."

Grounding my jaw, I simply stared at him for a long moment. "Why not?"

"If you didn't have anything to do with it, I don't understand why you ran from Hollywood and hid your identity."

"I just told you why, Jordan. I wanted a clean slate."

"Some of the papers say otherwise," he shot back. "That you were an accomplice and you ran when the heat became too much for you."

"The papers say a lot of things that aren't true, especially about people in Hollywood."

"I don't know, Sam." He shook his head. "I wonder if—"

"Here's what the papers didn't tell you, because the police haven't released the information," I interrupted, now furious. The press? Really? Had they printed anything without bias in the past decade? "*I* found a secret office my husband used. *I* discovered my husband's records of everyone he'd stolen from. *I* was the one who brought the whole case to the police. And as you've shared with me many times, the police can't comment on an ongoing investigation!"

"And then you just up and ran away, ending up in Heywood, of all places. Things have worked out well for you since," he said, gesturing around the store. "You own a nice business, you were dating a cop, made some friends... things were pretty cushy for you. It all lined up so perfectly, I can't help but wonder if it was all planned."

"What does that mean?"

"It means I wonder if you did kill your boss, Bonnie, and if you're using everyone in your life," he spat.

His statement hit like a punch to the gut. It took everything I had to remain upright. Pursing my lips, I fought back tears as dread and pain tore at my insides. "I was cleared of murdering Bonnie," I said, my voice barely above a whisper. "The real killer gave a confession. Her death was so difficult for me. She was the one who had given me a second chance. Her murder hurt like nothing I'd ever experienced, including the death of my husband."

I saw a flicker of doubt, but I wasn't sure if it was because I'd put a crack in his story, or if he didn't believe a word I said.

"And what would I be using you for?" I asked. "Annabelle? Gina? Do you really think I'm that shallow, that conniving?"

"You were an Emmy winning actress, Sam. So yes, I do think you could pretend to care about people and we'd all fall for it, hook, line, and sinker."

The knives were out and the cuts had gone deep. I swallowed to keep the tears at bay.

He shook his head. "I don't know what to believe anymore."

"Then I don't know what to tell you," I replied, shrugging. "Because everything I've said is the truth."

Suddenly, a brilliant idea came to me. The L.A.P.D. was going to be at my store. "The cops investigating my husband's case are going to be here this afternoon at four. They have more questions to ask me. Come by, Jordan. Question them. Listen to them, and to me. If that doesn't convince you of my innocence, I don't know what will."

He arched a brow. "They're here? In town?"

"Yes. The publicity has flushed me out and they have other questions for me. Come by. It will be a great time." I couldn't keep the sarcasm out of my voice.

"Aren't you going to have a lawyer present?" he asked.

I shook my head. "I probably should, but I've got nothing to hide."

"At least have Colin here with you," Jordan said. "He may not be a criminal lawyer, but you'll have representation. It's the smart thing to do."

He was right. Even though I did want this part of my life firmly placed in the history books, I also had to protect myself. Perhaps the cops were looking to railroad me, to bring me down and make me pay for a crime I didn't commit. "I'll give him a call and see if he's available."

"Good." He turned to leave and I wondered if he'd be by when the big city cops showed up. "I'll see you later, Sam."

If me being interrogated by the L.A.P.D. didn't curb his doubts, I had no idea what would.

In the meantime, I had to check on Mrs. Mason. First her husband was murdered and now she was receiving death threats. If the warnings had rattled me, I worried about what they'd do to her.

Who in the world would intimidate a woman in her seventies who had just lost her husband?

CHAPTER 10

I GRABBED MY COAT, left the store to Annabelle, and covered the short distance to Knit Wit's back door. After I knocked, I cupped my hands around my eyes and glanced inside. Empty. Had Mrs. Mason gone home? Finding the note may have scared her away and I wouldn't blame her for closing up shop for the day. I tapped again and a moment later she came into view. I grinned and waved. A sad smile turned the corners of her mouth as she opened the door.

"Sam. How are you, dear?"

"I think the question is, how are you?" I replied, stepping in. "Jordan was just at my store and told me you received a threat."

She shut the door and turned to me. "Yes." Her eyes welled, then the tears cascaded down her pudgy face. "I'm... I'm not well, Sam. It's all so... so much. I keep asking myself, why me?"

With a sigh, I took her in my arms and held her. Her body shook as she cried. After a few moments, she pulled away and wiped her cheeks with the back of her hand. "Can you stay a bit? I was just making some coffee."

Annabelle was running the store and always did so with efficiency. There wasn't any reason why I couldn't have a cup of coffee with Mrs. Mason. She seemed like she'd appreciate the company. "Of course."

She smiled and led me into the room where the computer resided. As I took a seat in front of it, she pulled over another chair. "Let me get our mugs. The coffee should be done by now. Do you need cream or sugar?"

"A little cream, please."

"Be back in a jiffy."

While she fetched our drinks, I glanced around the small space. I noted the knitting needles that had once been kept in the alcove where the body had been found now resided on the shelving. I tried to imagine being in Mrs. Mason's shoes. How difficult it would be to remain in the building where my husband had been murdered. I wouldn't be one bit surprised if she was in talks with Aiden to sell.

My elbow accidently hit the computer's mouse and the screen came alive. Mrs. Mason's email inbox came up, but I didn't have a chance to study it because she returned. "Here you go," she said, handing me the steaming cup.

I blew on my coffee, then set it down on the far edge of the table and made a mental note to keep an eye on it. I didn't want to be responsible for spilling it on the computer keyboard when it was cool enough to drink.

"So, Jordan told you what happened?" she began. "With the threatening letter?"

"Yes. I got one, too."

She gasped and shook her head. "Unbelievable. What is this world coming to? What did yours say?"

I repeated the rhyme but realized I didn't have it quite right. "Or something like that," I finished.

"Mine was similar," she replied. "I wonder who did this?"

I had to tread lightly. Having been the subject of an unwanted spotlight, I didn't want to cast blame where none was due. "Have you had anyone from Chester Development Corporation come to see you?"

"Why, yes, I have!" she proclaimed. "Quite a smarmy guy, if you ask me. What was his name? Andy? Alexander?"

"Aiden," I replied. "And your assessment of him isn't wrong."

"So he's been to see you, too?"

"Yes."

"Do you remember when he first approached you?" I asked.

"Let me think... it must have been a day or two before Russell was... was..." Tears welled in her eyes again. "I'm sorry. I can't finish the sentence."

I reached over and squeezed her hand. "It's okay. Do you remember what Aiden said?"

She nodded. "He started off being quite friendly and amicable. When I told him I wasn't interested in selling, he became a bit more forceful and said the town needed an upgrade. His resort would provide many jobs and stimulate the Heywood economy."

I nodded, having heard it all before when he'd visited me after Bonnie died. "Did he say anything else?"

"Yes. That you were in talks to sell to him and that you'd be making a very nice profit. He wanted to offer me the same deal." She studied my face for a moment. "Is that true, Sam? Are you in discussions to get rid of Sage Advice?"

"Of course not," I assured her. "He'd love it if I was, though. He approached me once a while back, right after Bonnie was killed. I told him to go pound dirt then. The day after Russell died, he was back, saying that I shouldn't feel safe because..."

Wait a minute. I recalled Annabelle's theory: Aiden had waltzed into town the day before Russell's untimely demise. He'd wanted both Knit Wit and Sage Advice for his resort. He could've killed Russell to scare Mrs. Mason into selling to him, and also thought a murder would frighten me enough to want him to buy my store.

"Because what, dear?" Mrs. Mason asked.

"Annabelle had an idea about Aiden," I said. After explaining it to her, she stared at me with wide eyes.

"That makes a lot of sense," she whispered. "My goodness. What if that man on camera was Aiden? Maybe when he was here he somehow stole a key from me without me noticing? He let himself in and waited until Russell came by the store that morning, then shot him?"

"To scare us both into selling," I muttered, balling my fingers into a fist, now angry that we could've been played this way, that a man may have lost his life for this, and that I hadn't taken Annabelle seriously when she'd brought it up before. "But how did he leave?"

"The police assume by the back door," she replied. "But the security system also went down, so he could've left through the front."

"I was out on the deck," I said, shaking my head. "I didn't see anyone come out of your store."

"Well, going out the front door gave him much more of a chance of being caught by folks out and about around town. With the back door leading to the Riverwalk, it offered cover, especially now with it being cold so no one wants to be by the water."

She wasn't wrong there. The water made the air chillier and the Riverwalk had been dead except for the odd person walking. If I was going to kill an old man, that would be the way I'd want to escape. However, I still had my doubts.

"I don't know," I said. "I think I would've seen him."

"You've had a lot on your plate, Sam." Mrs. Mason patted my hand. "You were probably preoccupied and no one would blame you." She took a sip of coffee then clucked her tongue. "I heard it through the grapevine that the Los Angeles police are in town to question you. That must be quite difficult."

The grapevine. Wonderful. Any hopes I had of the cops quietly coming into town and leaving the same way were dashed. I wondered where the information had originated. "Who told you that?"

"Well, the police checked into one of the bed and breakfasts and a maid there knows a barista at Cup of Go. She overheard the two detectives discussing you. The barista is dating a checker at the grocery store. He was talking to one of the women in my knitting club about it, who then told me about them. There may have been a few other people involved in that timeline, but that's the version I remember."

Word had traveled swiftly, but I supposed I shouldn't be surprised. An actress running from her past living in the small town of Heywood hoping to forget her former life, only to have the big city cops come to speak to her about her dead husband's bad business dealings? Sounded like the perfect recipe for a soap opera or a Hallmark movie.

"Did she give any indication of exactly what they had to say?"

Mrs. Mason pursed her lips and shook her head. "Just that you were in trouble."

"I didn't do anything," I said in a morose tone.

"I'm sure you didn't, dear. I believe you. But let's return to Andy. Do you really think he could've killed Russell?"

I shrugged. "Not sure. Like you said, it all fits. He's got motive—buying our stores. Besides, he could've purchased a gun down at Locked and Loaded and that morning, he sure had the opportunity."

"We should call the police about him," Mrs. Mason said. "Tell them our thoughts."

I nodded, wondering if I should phone Jordan directly or go through the main number. If I went through the receptionist, there was a chance I'd be put in touch with Sheriff Mallory Richards, and I'd rather eat cat food than speak to her. However, Jordan may not appreciate me calling, even if we'd just discovered a suspect for the murder.

"I'll go ahead and call the sheriff," Mrs. Mason said. "I'll keep you posted on what she has to say."

Well, that took care of my dilemma and I sighed in relief. "I better get back to the store," I said. "Are you sure you're going to be okay here?"

"I'll be fine," she replied. "I've got a class coming in soon, so they keep me out of my own thoughts, and I appreciate the distraction."

Wouldn't that be nice? I wish I had a nice interference into my own life. "All right then. Call me if you need anything, okay?"

"You're so good to me, Sam. Thank you."

We stood and hugged, yet something felt off. All the evidence lined up for Andy to be the killer, but I'd take a step back and let the police figure that one out. I had my own problems to worry about and didn't need to be sticking my nose in a murder investigation.

Neither the local nor the visiting California police were very fond of me.

CHAPTER 11

I RETURNED to the store and phoned Colin, who agreed to come represent me during my friendly chat with the Los Angeles police. Would Jordan show? That remained to be seen. He'd said he sit in, but things could change. After all, there was a killer on the loose.

The day proceeded smoothly and we were less busy than the previous day when we had a long line for my autograph. Only a few people came in, but Annabelle stuck hard to her rule of a product purchase or a donation to Heywood Hounds in order for people to get it. No one complained, which made me happy. And it would've been a perfect afternoon if I didn't have the meeting with the L.A.P.D. and maybe Jordan hanging over me.

"I think I'll take them upstairs," I said to Annabelle when I explained about the meeting. "Do you think that's a good idea?"

She nodded and crossed her arms over her chest. "I do. You don't need anyone seeing you talking to all those pigs."

"Annabelle! It's Jordan you're calling that disgusting name!"

"He deserves it," she muttered. "The saran wrap on the toilet wasn't, like, enough revenge for the way he's treated you."

I sighed, finding myself wanting to defend him for his behavior. "He just wants to make sure I didn't have anything to do with my husband's business dealings."

"Well, in my opinion, he should just believe you. I did."

I appreciated her loyalty, but sometimes it worried me. In her eyes it seemed I couldn't do any wrong. I didn't look forward to the day she discovered I wasn't as perfect as she thought.

With nothing else to add to the conversation, I glanced at my phone. Everyone would be arriving in fifteen minutes, so I decided to head upstairs and take a few moments to pull myself together. "Can you send them up when they get here?"

"Yes, ma'am, and I'll hold down the fort while you're being grilled."

"Thank you."

I hurried to my apartment, then immediately wondered if I should change my plan. After studying the small space, I came to the conclusion that I was a bit of a slob. I quickly picked up the dirty dishes from the coffee table and set them in the sink, then put away my sweaters thrown haphazardly over a chair. Why I cared what Detectives Gunter and Smith thought of my living arrangements, I had no idea. But, I did. I wanted them to understand that I'd left a bad situation and landed firmly on my feet, with a clean apartment.

Just as I was considering whether I should serve any coffee or tea, a tapping sounded on the doorframe.

"Knock, knock, Sam!" I'd left the door open and turned to find Colin.

"Thank you so much for coming," I said, noting his pink bowtie and gray pinstriped suit under a black wool trench coat. He always dressed like a 1920s gangster, but today, it seemed he'd donned his finest.

As he removed his fedora, he grinned. "I wouldn't miss this for the world," he said. "To hear the story of what happened in your former life in your own words? How could I resist?"

He stepped in and slid out of his coat, then carefully hung it over the chair where I'd just gathered all my sweaters from. After setting down his fedora, he pointed to the chair. "Do you mind if I rest my old bones here?"

"Of course not," I said. "Wherever you're comfortable."

He lowered himself to the cushion and smiled.

"Do you think I should serve coffee or tea?" I asked, now suddenly nervous about the meeting.

"Not unless you want them to stay a while. I personally wouldn't allow them to get too comfortable."

Good point, and advice I'd follow. "Okay, then. I guess we just wait."

"I hope they aren't pulling the tactic of delaying the meeting so your nerves get jumbled. It's just so tiring."

When I'd first invited Colin, I wanted to be certain I had legal representation, even if he wasn't a criminal attorney. Now, I was finding his presence very comforting. He'd been through this rodeo before and seemed to know the plays.

Footsteps sounded up the stairs, but I only detected one set. When Jordan came into view, Colin stood. "Well, well, well. Not only does she have legal assistance, but a friend as well. How nice to see you, Deputy."

Jordan shook his hand, then our gazes locked. "Sam."

"Hi."

As he glanced around the room, I noted he was out of uniform and wore jeans and a button-down black shirt under his parka. Perhaps he didn't want the Los Angeles police to realize he was also a cop? When he didn't take a seat, I realized he didn't want to sit on the couch with me, which was fine. I didn't mind him keeping his distance. "You can grab a couple kitchen chairs," I said.

With a grunt, he headed into the kitchen and returned with two. To my surprise, he then took the cushion next to me and left the chairs for Gunter and Smith. Silence enveloped us as we waited for the detectives.

"Seems they are up to their games," Colin murmured. "I despise tardiness."

A moment later, my phone dinged. I pulled it out of my pocket and read the text from Annabelle just as footsteps sounded on the staircase.

THE PORKIE-PIES ARE *on their way up*

. . .

"HERE WE GO," I sighed.

Detective Gunter and Smith appeared in the doorway. Smith frowned as he glanced from Jordan to Colin. "I thought this was going to be a private conversation," he said.

Colin stood and stuck out his hand. "Colin Breckshire, the third. It's lovely to meet you, sir. I'll be Sam's legal representation today."

Smith shot me a glare before taking the man's hand. "Nice to meet you. Who's that?" He pointed at Jordan.

"He's my assistant," Colin said.

Arching an eyebrow, I glanced over to Jordan. His face remained passive as he waved.

"Okay." Smith's mouth pursed into a fine line. "Let's get this done. We need to get back to Los Angeles."

Thank goodness.

"Do you mind if we record the interview?" Gunter asked.

I glanced over to Colin for a final answer. I had nothing to hide, but maybe he wanted me to decline.

"If it's okay with Sam, then I'm fine with it," he said.

I nodded as Gunter pulled out his phone. He set it down on the coffee table and said, "For the record, Sam, you've given us permission to record."

The little blinking red dot suddenly made me even more nervous. My hands began to sweat and my heartbeat picked up. "Yes," I said softly. "It's fine."

Was the furnace on the fritz again? The temperature had read seventy-five, but it seemed awfully hot.

Smith smiled and began the interrogation. Or interview. To me, it felt as if I were in front of a firing squad. "As we stated in our first conversation yesterday, we greatly appreciate the thumb drive containing all the information of your husband's business dealings."

"You're welcome," I mumbled.

"However, you claimed time and time again that you knew nothing about them. So, I must ask: where did you get all the account information and data you sent us if you were in the dark?"

I took a moment to gather my thoughts. I was going to admit to a crime, yet one that not only caught my husband's murderer, but also provided the information I'd given to the police.

"You had told me to stay out of my husband's office because it was a crime scene," I said. "But I didn't."

Gunter swore under his breath.

"It doesn't matter now," I said. "The house is gone."

"Please continue," Smith murmured.

"I wasn't looking for the files on who my husband stole from. I was looking for information on who killed him, but I had a hunch they went hand-in-hand."

One of Hollywood's most important men—namely, my boss—had been the murderer. However, there simply wasn't any proof.

"But I think it's best if I start at the beginning," I said.

"Please do," Smith urged.

I took a deep breath, hoping my words emerged coherently instead of a jumbled mess. I equated the situation to a final act in this soap opera, the one where I would convince everyone of my innocence and make them all realize I'd done nothing wrong.

Well, nothing I should serve a life sentence for, anyway. Leaving the way I had probably wasn't the smartest move and may fall on the side of slightly illegal.

Slip into character and get this over with!

The character? Calm, collected, intelligent.

Action!

"When my husband and I bought the house, we'd gutted the inside. He'd been the one to draw up the plans, and I didn't know about his secret space located between the wine cooler and his office which, if you recall, is where he was murdered."

Gunter glanced at Smith and shook his head. "This sounds far-fetched."

"I'm sure there were a bunch of hoops he needed to jump through to get those plans approved," I said. "They have to be on file somewhere."

"Didn't you help your husband design the house you were going to live in?" Gunter asked.

"I worked twelve-hour days," I said. "When we bought the house, he told me he would take care of the layout, and I was happy to allow him to do so. I may have glanced at the plans once or twice if he had a question for me, but I never studied them in great detail."

Smith nodded. "How did you find this secret office?"

I sighed, surprised how much it pained me to revisit my old life. That final day in Los Angeles had been a turning point for me and changed the course of my very existence. "The wine cooler was set at a certain temperature and made a clicking noise when it went on and off. When I was in the office looking for proof of who murdered him, I heard it and felt cold coming from under part of the bookcase."

Gunter rolled his eyes. "Which you never noticed before?"

Pursing my lips together, I tried to find the words to describe my marriage, and frankly, my life before Heywood.

"No, the sound never registered with me," I said. "I didn't notice a lot of things, like how my marriage was so empty, how my friendships were a farce, and how my job held little meaning. I rarely visited my husband in his office and if I did, I stood in the doorway. Our talks were never more than a minute or two, without a lot of depth, Detective. We were each playing a role of the devoted spouse, until we decided we were done with that act and decided to divorce the night before he died." I shook my head, both disgusted and sad. How had I lasted so long in such a toxic place? "For all I know, he had a secret family as well. It took me being forced to leave my fame, and to have my fortune taken away from me, in order to realize it was all just a façade."

I clasped my hands in my lap and stared at my interlaced fingers, feeling everyone's gaze on me. What I said next, I wanted to say directly to Jordan but I couldn't meet his stare, even though it practically burned me. Could my heart beat any faster? Maybe. Sweat dotted my brow, and I was certain it wasn't a hot flash, but pure nerves.

"Only when I arrived in Heywood did I understand how full life could be," I began quietly. "People accepted me, even if they didn't know the truth. I found true friendships, people who wanted to know my thoughts and cared about me, and... well, I think..." I paused as my mouth went dry. To say this was putting myself out there would be an understatement, but I had to do it.

"I think I fell in love," I admitted at last, each word I uttered falling at my feet like a ton of bricks. Jordan gasped beside me, just loud enough for it to register. "The crash and burn of my life in Hollywood was the best thing that could've happened to me, but I also know that my husband hurt many people."

I squared my shoulders and raised my gaze to the detectives. "That's why I sent the thumb drive, so you could build your case and get the victims reparations. If I had anything to do with his business, why would I give you the evidence? You never would've had it if it weren't for me finding that room and doing the right thing."

"And you gave us the thumb drive to give yourself cover if you were involved," Gunter shot back.

I shrugged and nodded. "Yes, I could've done that. However, it would've been the stupidest move, don't you think? Why would I hand over anything that could incriminate me?"

Heavy silence fell over the room as everyone considered my words. I didn't dare glance at Jordan as I was afraid of what I'd see there. Disbelief? Disgust? Understanding?

"Did you find anything on there to incriminate me?" I asked. "Or was it simply the ledger of accounts and people my husband defrauded? Was my name mentioned anywhere on that thumb drive?"

I held my breath, waiting for them to answer. Yes, I'd glanced over the data, but I hadn't studied it. My question was a dice-toss, one I hoped paid off.

After a long moment, Colin stood and clasped his hands in front of him. "If you gentlemen don't have any further inquiries for my client, I think this chat has come to an end."

Gunter and Smith traded stares, then slowly rose to their feet. "We don't have anything else, Sam. Thank you for your time."

"And just to be clear," Colin continued, "I'll be filing paperwork for my client to petition for her money to be returned. The joint bank account doesn't mean you get to keep it all to pay back those who experienced fraud, especially since Ms. Jones had no knowledge of her husband's business dealings."

I pursed my lips to hold back the tears. I'd talked about petitioning for my money, but never pursued it because it seemed easier to just leave the past where it was. With Sage Advice, I did okay. I could pay my bills and live comfortably, but the money that I'd left behind... that would be life changing.

"We'll be in touch if we have any further questions," Smith said.

As they walked out the door and their footsteps sounded down the stairs, I had a feeling I wouldn't hear from them again. They'd gotten what they needed, and their goodbye felt final.

I sighed and finally glanced up at Jordan. He nodded and his lips curved slightly. "I'll call you later."

Relief swept through me while a weight seemed to lift from my shoulders. No matter what happened with him, the tether to my past had been snapped, and I was truly free.

Or so I thought.

CHAPTER 12

THE NEXT DAY, I met Gina and Annabelle for coffee again. Our plan was to caffeinate, then head over to Hammer and Nail Hardware and try to discover who Gina had overheard talking positively about Mr. Mason's demise. I didn't believe someone would kill another because they wanted more hours at their job, but unstable people could do terrible things.

As we sat at our table and chatted, I picked at my chocolate chip muffin, still feeling light and free. I seemed to laugh a bit more loudly, my pastry tasted a little better than usual, and the view of the river and forest beyond appeared even more beautiful than yesterday. My discussion with the L.A.P.D. had set me up with an amazing pair of rose-colored glasses.

Jordan hadn't phoned, which was fine with me. After the interview, the urge to curl up with Catnip, stare at the television, and fully decompress overrode any need to be in contact with him.

"This dog... she's just too funny," Gina said, smiling. "She's so darn cute." She spoke of her new rescue named Daisy. I'd yet to meet the dog, but Gina called her a Jack Russell Terrier / hound mix. The way she described the mutt made me think she would be keeping it instead of trying to adopt her out.

"Sounds like you've found quite the companion," I said. "Will she be a full-time employee of Heywood Hounds?"

"I think so," Gina replied, shaking her head. "I can't believe I've become so attached to her. I really try to keep an arm's length between me and the rescues, but this one... she's wriggling her way under my skin."

I always admired the relationship Gina had with animals, particularly dogs.

"Anyway," Gina continued, "she does this thing where—"

"Would you ladies mind if I joined you?"

I glanced up at the familiar voice, my stomach flipping as I met Jordan's gaze. Today, he definitely resembled George Clooney and I realized that meant I probably wasn't too mad at him any longer. He smiled warmly as Gina and Annabelle both turned to me.

"That's up to Sam," Annabelle said. "Well, and how big of a jerk you plan on being. On a scale of, like, one to ten, where are you at today?"

"Okay, I deserved that," Jordan said. "But I'll say I'm at a one or two, if that makes you feel better."

"Well, then, you can join us," I said, pointing to the empty chair next to Annabelle.

After taking a seat, he asked, "What's on everyone's agenda today?"

"We're going to Hammer and Nail Hardware to see if we can, like, smoke out the two guys Gina overheard the other day who were glad Mr. Mason was killed because they want more hours at work."

It took a moment for Annabelle's explanation to sink in for everyone, including me. Jordan stared at her as her words registered, then his eyes widened. "What?! Why hasn't anyone told the police about this?"

"You haven't been around much." Gina snickered as she tossed her blonde hair over her shoulder. "You left the faction of free-flowing information we've got going on. So, you not knowing? That's on you, buddy."

With a sigh, he hung his head. "You're right. And I might as well say this now. Sam, I was wrong. I'm so sorry for the way I've treated you. I've been an absolute—"

Annabelle listed off a quick string of colorful language, all which perfectly described Jordan's behavior.

"That about covers it," Jordan muttered. "Anyway, I'm truly sorry."

"We can talk about it later," I said. Or, he could grovel later. Heck, yes, I was willing to take baby steps to rebuild my relationship with him, but I did want him to squirm, just a bit.

"Do you think I can reclaim my place in the faction of free-flowing information?" Jordan asked. "I do have a murder to solve."

I traded glances with my girlfriends and shrugged. "I guess so, although we don't have much to tell you."

Gina repeated what she'd heard while buying dog food at the hardware store. "I really don't think it's much to go on, but these two convinced me we needed to poke around and see who exactly I heard saying those things."

Jordan's brow had furrowed as he slowly nodded. "We'll see about that if it's anything worth a follow-up. When are you heading over?"

I picked up my cardboard cup and found it empty. I'd also consumed my pastry. "Whenever everyone is ready. And if that's not anytime soon, I'll need a refill."

Jordan jumped up. "I'll get it."

As he hurried over to the short line, Gina and Annabelle grinned mischievously. "He's working hard to get back into your good graces," Annabelle said.

"I hope it takes more than a coffee run," Gina grumbled.

"It's a start," I said. "But he's got a long way to go."

WE DECIDED people would talk more freely if Jordan wasn't with us. I promised I'd call him after and fill him in on the details of our visit, especially if we discovered anything worth noting.

With me owning my building, I spent quite a lot of time in Hammer and Nail Hardware, but that hadn't always been the case. During my first visit, I'd been so out of my element, it was like I'd landed on a different planet. Everything seemed foreign to me. Now, I felt more comfortable and could identify most of the tools hanging from the

racks. Annabelle had taught me most of what I knew about self-suffi-
ciency, and I'd also gathered some knowledge through trial and error.
For someone who once dealt with household chores with a phone call or
a quick discussion with my housekeeper, I was pretty proud with how
far I'd come and the skills I'd gained. I could take care of myself and my
property. It felt darn good.

As we meandered around the store, the three of us pretended to
be shopping while listening to the conversations around us. One guy
asked for directions on setting up a drip system for his summer
garden. Another asked about retooling the plumbing in his house.
Exciting stuff to be heard in the aisles of Hammer and Nail
Hardware.

"I think we should split up," Annabelle whispered. "I'm going to
the other side of the store and we'll meet up in the middle."

As she scurried away, Gina and I studied the dog bones.

"I wonder if my mutts would like these," she said, picking up something called a Yak Chew. After turning it over and glancing at the back
packaging, she quickly set it back on it's hook. "Not for that price." She
shook her head. "Ridiculous."

We continued our wandering through the aisles. A few minutes
later, Gina said, "This is dumb. I saw Ericka was working today. Let's go
talk to her and find out what she knows."

I followed my friend to the front. Gina had always been blunter and
more direct than me, and I was curious about who exactly Ericka was
and what she would have to say. At the front of the store, we found a
female cashier wearing a nametag that read Ericka.

In her late twenties, she wore her long, shiny black hair in a curtain
down her back, dark makeup circled her eyes, and I had a hard time not
staring at the thick, drawn-on eyebrows. While trying not to stare at
them, I noted her turquoise nails and realized she must have been one of
Gina's clients.

"Hey, girl!" Ericka said, her smile wide. "What's up?" She glanced at
me and her eyes widened. "You're that famous person!" And then she
squealed and heat radiated up my neck into my cheeks. "Oh, my
gosh! Hi!"

"Hi," I said quietly. "It's nice to meet you, Ericka."

"She knows my name!" The young woman hissed at Gina. "How? How does she know me? Is it my TikTok channel?"

I didn't have the heart to tell her it was her nametag.

"That must be it," Gina whispered. "Do you want her autograph?"

Ericka gasped and laid her hand over her heart as she gaped at me.

"I'm happy to give it to you," I said, keeping my voice low and praying Annabelle didn't find out.

After reaching under the counter, she slapped down a piece of paper, took a pen from the cash register, and handed it to me.

To Ericka –
Wishing you happiness and much success with your TikTok account.
All the best,
Samantha Jones

"This is so awesome!" she whispered, holding the paper to her chest. "Wait until I show it on TikTok!"

I laughed as Gina leaned over the counter. "Ericka, I need some information."

The girl's face fell, and I felt a little bad her exciting moment had deflated like a pinpricked balloon. "What information?"

"There's two men here who were talking about how happy they were that Mr. Mason was murdered," Gina continued. "Who were they? And why would they be happy about it?"

Ericka sighed and rolled her eyes. "That would be Oly and Adam," she said. "They're so annoying."

I filed away the names to share with Jordan.

"Why are they happy Mr. Mason is gone?"

She glanced around before answering. "Mr. Mason was older and really cranky. He didn't like people sitting around doing nothing, especially when inventory came in. On the other hand, Oly and Adam will do just about anything to avoid putting away inventory, so the three of them clashed a lot."

"I thought I heard one of them say they were happy he was dead so they could pick up his shifts," Gina said.

Someone cleared their throat behind us and I glanced over to see a couple people waiting to be checked out. I grabbed Gina's arm and stepped away. "Let's leave Ericka to take care of these people."

We waited as she chatted amicably with the customers and rang up their purchases. She was friendly, knew most by name, and asked about families and pets. Yet, she performed her job fast and efficiently. I wasn't looking to hire anyone, but if I were, I'd steal Ericka away in a heartbeat. What a wonderful employee.

When she finished her duties, we hurried back over to her. Hopefully, we could finish our conversation before the next wave of customers needed to pay for their purchases.

The three of us huddled around the counter again.

"I thought I heard one of them say they were happy he was dead so they could pick up his shifts," Gina repeated. "If they don't like working, then why would they feel that way? Did I hear them right?"

"You may have," Ericka said. "Neither of them mind helping customers or talking shop. It's just the inventory that drove them nuts."

"Huh," Gina said, shaking her head. Then she turned to me. "I told you this would be a waste of time."

"Did Mr. Mason die from a gunshot wound?" Ericka asked. "That's what the gossip vine claims."

I nodded, curious to see where her questioning was headed. "I can confirm that," I said. "I found the body."

"Ewww." Ericka's face twisted in disgust. "That's so gross."

"Yes, it was," I replied. "But why are you interested in how he was killed?"

"Well, I'm not a tattler or anything, but a few weeks ago, the three of them were arguing about inventory," Gina said. "Oly made a gun with his fingers and pointed it at Mr. Mason. Then he said something like, 'I'm going to shoot your brains all over the floor if you don't shut up, old man.'"

Which was exactly what had happened.

CHAPTER 13

After a long day at work, I curled up on the couch with Catnip and began reading about herbal antibiotics. The fact that our society was losing the war on superbugs because of our overuse of antibiotics both fascinated and scared me to death.

My goal was to educate myself on herbal remedies that acted like antibiotics within the body and fought off the most common bugs, such as urinary tract and sinus infections. If there was a way we could formulate something, it would not only be a win for my bank account, but for society in general. The brews would have to be potent. A small part of me looked forward to seeing the town's doctor, Garrett Butte, melt down when he discovered what we'd achieved. He hadn't been around to harass me lately, so I hadn't given him much thought. According to him, our plants were useless and harmful. I intended to prove him wrong, just as Annabelle and I had done for many ailments.

I'd called Jordan earlier in the day to share what we'd discovered at Hammer and Nail Hardware. Unfortunately, there'd been an over-turned semi that spilled eggs all over the road just outside of town.

"You can't believe the mess," he'd muttered. Raw eggs all over the pavement? Thank goodness it wasn't warm out or the smell would become horrendous in a short period of time.

"Call me when you can," I'd replied. "I have information that may be helpful in finding Mr. Mason's killer."

Hours had gone by since I'd closed up shop. I whiled away the time reading and trying to understand the different types of bacteria while Catnip purred on my chest. I'd completely lost track of time when the phone rang, causing me to jump. With a yelp, I dropped my book and jolted to a seated position, which sent Catnip running. "Hey," I spoke into the phone. "Have you kept the highways free of dangerous egg whites?"

He chuckled. "Aren't you funny."

"Thank you. I do my best."

"I'm just heading back to town," he said with a grunt and I glanced at the clock. Almost midnight. "I was wondering if you'd join me for breakfast in the morning, so I can once again tell you what a jerk I've been."

"Are you buying?" I asked jokingly.

"Of course."

"What time?"

After we agreed to meet at On The River at eight, we continued our conversation, which had always flowed so easily between us. I shared what we'd discovered about Oly and Adam at Hammer and Nail Hardware, and he said he'd stop by and ask them about it.

"I've missed you, Sam," he said after we'd been on the phone for over twenty minutes. "I was foolish."

"Yes, you were," I countered with a sigh. "And I appreciate the apologies, but I'd really like to move forward, if that's something you want."

"I do," he said quickly. "I just hope you can forgive me."

As someone who hated conflict, I did want to forgive him, but maybe the hurt I felt by him not believing me in the first place would take time to pass. I didn't want to push it aside, which was exactly what I'd done with my husband—ignoring the red flags in our relationship. I never sat with my feelings and tried to unpack them. I wouldn't make the same mistake again.

"I'll be able to," I said quietly. "It may not be right away, but it'll happen."

"It's still weird for me to think of you as famous," Jordan said. "I've watched a lot of your stuff. You were really good. It seems like you don't belong in Heywood—that your true calling is Hollywood."

"No," I replied firmly. "I'm right where I belong. Even if someone could wave a magic wand and offer me my old life back, I wouldn't take it, Jordan. And as for you having a hard time wrapping your mind around me once being famous, if we're to move forward, you're going to have to accept my past and forgive me for not sharing it with you. I had my reasons."

A long silence ensued.

"I guess we're going to have to both work on offering each other amnesty," he said at last.

I smiled at his use of words. "Amnesty it is," I said.

When Catnip sauntered into the living room and sat down in front of the apartment door with his tail swishing, I groaned. His actions were compatible to when he'd heard mice beforehand.

"What's wrong?" Jordan asked.

"I think Catnip is tracking a mouse outside the apartment," I replied, standing. As I walked to the door, my knee and back popped, reminding me of a bowl of Rice Krispies cereal. "Go get it," I said to Catnip after I opened the door. "And please don't bring it back to me as a present."

Jordan laughed as Catnip ran out and I sat back down on the couch. "What's wrong with dead mice, Sam? He's showing you his love and affection. It's a present."

"At this point, I don't even mind the dead ones," I said. "It's when he brings them to me barely alive and still moving that I—"

What was that noise?

"Sam? You cut out. I didn't hear what you said."

A scraping sound came from downstairs. I tried to place what could have caused the racket but came up empty.

Then, glass broke.

With a gasp, I shot to my feet, unsure of what to do. "Jordan, some-one's in my store," I hissed while my hands shook and my heart thundered.

"What?!"

"Someone's here! Glass just broke downstairs!"

Footsteps sounded in the store. Whoever was down there made no attempt to hide their presence. More glass shattered. I stared at the open doorway, frozen in fear. Logically, I understood that if someone came up to the second floor, it would be best if the door was closed because it became a deterrent. Right now, they had a free pass directly to me.

The door. I had to shut the door.

"Where are you?" Jordan asked.

"I-in my apartment."

"Lock that door, Sam, and stay on the line with me. I'm on my way." Sirens wailed through the phone as I was finally able to hurry to the door and closed it quietly, flipping the lock.

"Why isn't the alarm on?" Jordan asked.

"I hadn't set it yet." I listened intently to the ruckus downstairs and tears pricked my eyes. "They're ruining my store, Jordan."

"Don't worry about that now," he replied. "We need to make sure you're safe." I nodded and swiped away at the tears now tracking down my cheeks. "Where's your stun gun?"

"On top of my fridge." I imagined me running downstairs and attacking whoever it was. As I jammed the gun into their body, I'd watch them shake and quiver while writhing around in a pool of tinctures and oils. The fantasy gave me a strange satisfaction.

"Don't you dare leave that apartment," Jordan said, as if he'd read my mind. "Get your stun gun and go into the bedroom. Lock every door between you and the intruder."

Despite my desire to watch my prowler get electrocuted, I did as instructed.

I hurried into the kitchen, grabbed the stun gun, and hustled back to my bedroom. The commotion downstairs continued and hopefully, Catnip was steering clear of it. If anything happened to my cat, I'd not only be devastated, but also looking to harm someone with something more than a stun gun.

After locking my bedroom door, I moved behind my bed and sat down. I was at the farthest point away from the store. Holding the weapon out in front of me, I held the phone between my shoulder and ear, terror ripping through me. My breath came in short spurts as an anvil seemed to land on my chest.

"I'm almost there," Jordan said. "I've called for backup. You still with me?"

"Y-yes," I whispered.

Suddenly, I heard footsteps on the stairs. "They're coming up here, Jordan!"

"Remain calm," he ordered. "They have to break down doors to get to you and that's no easy feat."

The intruder was banging on a door, but it wasn't mine so I assumed they were at Bonnie's apartment.

I pulled the phone away from my ear, setting it on the floor next to me when I heard sirens outside. The police were close.

Silence filled the air for a long moment, then my burglar clamored down the stairs. I felt the emptiness when I thought he'd left the building. Or was it wishful thinking?

The sirens came to a full stop. Fear paralyzed me once again when I heard someone walking around downstairs. I had to assume it was Jordan, but I was too afraid to move. Glass crunched under their feet and I shut my eyes against the sound. Had the store been demolished?

The quiet, except for his footsteps, weighed heavily like a wet blanket, suffocating me. Sweat dripped down my temples. What if Jordan ran into the intruder and was hurt? I could swear the burglar was gone, but what if I'd been wrong?

Moments later, heavy fists landed on my apartment door. With a screech, I shut my eyes.

"Sam!" Jordan called. "It's me! Open up!"

I still couldn't move.

"Sam! Are you okay? The place is clear!"

Slowly, I stood. Pins and needles poked at my legs that had fallen asleep. I awkwardly teetered out of the bedroom and into the living room where I flung open the door. Jordan met my gaze, his mouth in a fine line, his brow furrowed in anger. "Are you okay?"

I nodded and crossed my arms over my chest. Then I realized I'd set down my stun gun on my bed and left my phone on the floor of my bedroom. Stupid.

"The downstairs is clear and Bonnie's apartment is locked," Jordan continued. "Is that the way you left it?"

"Yes. It's been locked."

"Can I get the key just to make sure?"

"They were banging on that door before you got here," I said. "But let me grab it for you."

I hurried into the kitchen to fetch the key, which hung on a white plastic hook on the side of the refrigerator. Returning to Jordan, I handed it over.

"Stay here," he ordered. "I'll be right back."

He shut the door and I stood rooted in place, listening for any signs of a confrontation.

Jordan moved silently. I wasn't sure he was still in the building until he returned to my apartment and holstered his gun that I hadn't noticed him carrying before.

"How... how bad is it?" I whispered. The destruction seemed to have gone on for hours, even though it had been mere minutes. Each shattering of glass had resembled a direct cut to my heart and I was both curious and afraid to see what I would find at the bottom of the stairs.

"It's bad," he said. "But nothing you can't rebuild."

The use of the word 'rebuild' indicated destruction. Tears welled in my eyes again. Rebuild with what? I was able to support myself and Annabelle with the store, but I didn't have rivers of money flowing around me. Surely, insurance would help.

"I better go look."

Jordan nodded and ran his hand through his salt and pepper hair. "You'll need shoes."

I retrieved my sneakers with shaky hands, then Jordan followed me out onto the landing and down the stairs. I tried to steel my spine against what lay before me, but the devastation was too much.

The back room was mostly clear. For some reason, they hadn't touched the walls of mason jars filled with herbs. They had kicked over a couple of stools and flipped over the small table I'd used to sign autographs. Stepping into the front of the store, I found another story.

As the glass crunched under my feet, I took in the carnage. All the tables lay shattered on the ground along with the product they once held. Our cold and flu display was decimated, as were our anxiety tinctures. I waited for some sort of emotion to hit me, but instead, I stood and stared at the mess, completely numb.

"You can put it back together," Jordan said. "It's not like the building burnt down. It's all superficial."

Except it wasn't. The hours and painstaking preciseness Annabelle and I had used to create the products couldn't be regained. I turned to the wall holding our soap baskets and skincare to find everything once again on the floor. A message had been spraypainted in the products' place: *We don't want your kind around here.*

CHAPTER 14

I STARED AT THE MESSAGE, unsure of what it meant. My kind? Female? Menopausal? Previously famous?

"Do you know who would do this?" Jordan asked. "Have you had any run-ins with anyone?"

Doctor Butte would be considered my main nemesis, but I hadn't seen or heard from him in months. I shook my head. What in the world did 'your kind' mean?

"Sam, I need you to think. We'll do a full workup, including prints, but I need some direction."

I picked up a bath basket that had somehow made it through the carnage unscathed, still unable to believe the damage that had been done in such a short amount of time. They had come in through the window and quickly destroyed everything they found in their path, leaving the back room alone. Then, they'd headed upstairs and banged on Bonnie's door. Whoever it was either didn't know which apartment I resided in, or they were trying to scare me.

"Sam?"

"I don't know," I whispered.

Spinning around in a slow circle, I couldn't figure out where to start. How did one recover from the destruction? So many emotions swirled through me: confusion, utter sadness, and defeat. Would I be able to rise from the devastation that was now my store?

"What am I going to do?" I breathed out, the weight of my problem crushing me until I fell to my knees. Gut-wrenching sobs wracked my body while my insides seemed to split open with pain.

"Shhhh, come on, honey," Jordan said, pulling me upright. "Let's go upstairs, ok?"

"T-The window," I said, pointing to where the glass used to be and now cold air rushed in. "What about that? Anyone can come in."

"I'm staying tonight," Jordan replied. "No one is coming in here, Sam. Let's get some rest and tackle this in the morning."

"There's no way I can sleep," I said, shaking my head. "No way. They've ruined my store!"

"Come upstairs," he said, pulling my arm. "You need to rest, Sam. I'll be here, so no one else is going to come in without meeting the business end of a bullet. This can all wait until tomorrow when you can look at it through fresh eyes and a clear head."

It had to be past midnight, and he was right. The adrenaline had subsided and my shoulders slumped with exhaustion. But my store...

"It's okay," he continued. "We'll get it figured out tomorrow."

As he led me upstairs, I said, "Thanks for coming over so quickly."

"Of course."

We entered my apartment and he left the door open. A strange thing to do, but I figured he wanted to hear if my intruder returned. Catnip appeared from the bedroom and greeted us loudly, as if he were telling us what he'd witnessed.

"I know, buddy," I said, scooping him up, probably more for my comfort than his. "I saw it, too."

"I'll be on the couch," Jordan said. "Go and try to sleep, Sam."

Absently, I nodded and walked down the hall to my bedroom with Catnip purring in my arms. My thoughts were cloudy, as if I wandered in a fog. Maybe I'd gone into shock. I fell onto the bed and stared at the ceiling while Catnip made himself comfortable at my side. After a few moments of trying to figure out what my next move was going to be, I shut my eyes, doubting I'd ever be able to drift off.

~

How wrong I'd been.

I woke the next morning, surprised by how easily sleep had come. Sometime in the previous hours, Jordan had thrown a blanket over me. As the night's events came flooding back, the heaviness of dread settled through me and I shook my head. How in the world did I fix everything downstairs? Tears flowed freely again.

Then I heard pounding.

Sitting upright, I listened as the noise continued, my pity party forgotten. It definitely was coming from downstairs. For a second, my stomach tightened with fear. White hot anger quickly overrode it. I marched out of my apartment—noting Jordan had abandoned his station on my couch—and down the stairs with my fists at my sides.

What I found astonished me, and my anger quickly ebbed.

Annabelle sat in the back room at her workbench, the space full of tincture bottles, herbs, and alcohol. Wearing a purple and teal tracksuit, I noted her hair hung limply around her shoulders, and her face was makeup free. A rare sight. When she saw me, she stood and ran over.

"Oh, my gosh, Sam! I'm so glad you're okay!"

I glanced at the clock as we embraced. Eight in the morning. Based on the contained chaos of her workspace, she'd been here for hours. "What's going on?" I asked. "Why are you here?"

"To get the place back up and running as soon as we can," she said, holding me at arm's length. "What did you, like, think we were all doing?"

"We?"

More pounding came from the front of the store. She took my hand and led me around the corner.

Jordan was hammering a piece of plywood up over the broken window. Another deputy took pictures, while Sheriff Mallory filled out paperwork. Gina and Sally both stood at the ready at the front of the store with brooms and dustpans in hand. Both waved when they saw me. I simply stared, unable to move.

"Gina brought you a latte," Annabelle said, handing me a cardboard container from Cup of Go. "And, they've found some blood on the glass. Jordan said they may be able to get a DNA match and find out who did this!"

I absently took the coffee and studied the people who had come to my rescue. Jordan must've called everyone and explained what happened. Dear Lord. What had I done to deserve such good friends? Once again, my eyes welled, but this time with gratitude. Maybe everything would be okay, even though it didn't feel like it.

"Ah, Ms. Jones," Mallory called when she noticed me. "Glad you're finally awake. We need to talk."

I took a long sip of my latte, pretty certain there wasn't enough caffeine on the planet that would prepare me for a chat with Mallory about the raw, open wound of my trashed store.

As she tiptoed around the perimeter of the carnage, she pulled out a notebook from her jacket pocket. I detested the short, muscular woman, but still I was grateful she'd showed up at my store to help me file a police report.

"I'm going to get back to work," Annabelle said.

"I appreciate you," I whispered, giving her arm a squeeze, then I turned my attention back to the sheriff.

"Thank you for coming," I said, my voice raspy.

"You're welcome," she replied. "If Jordan hadn't been on the phone with you when this happened, I would've guessed you had done it yourself for the insurance money."

I glanced down at my coffee to keep from rolling my eyes. "Well, you would have been wrong," I said. "I'd never destroy something I'd worked so hard to build. I can't imagine someone would go to such lengths."

She snorted and shook her head. "Oh, you'd be surprised the lengths people will go to in order to get what they want."

I took a sip of my coffee. My plan was to say as little as possible to her and stick to the facts so I could join in the cleanup sooner rather than later.

"Jordan gave me the rundown of what happened last night, but can you tell me in your own words?"

Recalling the fear sent shivers over my skin, but I gave her a blow-by-blow of the night's events to the best of my recollection. Some parts seemed a bit fuzzy—like how long I'd sat on the floor of my bedroom before Jordan showed up—but I attributed that to the fright I'd experienced.

"And who do you think did this?" Mallory asked.

"I really have no idea." I stared at the spraypainted wall, still unsure of what exactly "your kind" meant.

"Well, have you made anyone angry lately?" Mallory asked. "You seem to have a knack for that."

Again, I ignored her dig and focused on the past few days. Could it have been someone who wasn't happy with Annabelle charging for my autograph? Destroying my store seemed a little extreme, but my former life as a famous person was one thing that set me apart from everyone in Heywood. There were plenty of menopausal, middle-aged women around.

"I really don't know who could've done this," I murmured, noting the deputy taking pictures was also dusting for prints. Of course, they'd find quite a few, including mine and Annabelle's. Customers came in and picked up multiple products, studied them and set them back at their display. Finding who was responsible through fingerprints would be akin to finding a needle in a haystack, in my opinion. But hopefully the blood would provide them with the identity of my destroyer.

We both turned when someone tapped on the back door.

"Are you expecting anyone at this time in the morning?" Mallory asked.

I shook my head.

She hurried over and opened it. Mrs. Mason stood out on the deck, her gaze wide. "Sam! What's going on?"

Mallory stepped aside and waved her in. "I was coming to see you next, Mrs. Mason. Glad you saved me the trip."

The older woman ignored her and rushed over to me, taking my hands in hers. "What happened?"

"Someone broke in and destroyed my store," I said, hitching my thumb over my shoulder. "You can't go in there, but you can take a look."

She moved to the archway that separated the back of the store from the front. With a gasp, she put her hand over her mouth. "Oh, my word," she whispered. "Who did this?"

"I have no idea," I said.

"This is awful, Sam," Mrs. Mason replied. "But I was afraid someone had been murdered in your store. Frankly, even though the destruction is terrible, at least you're all alive."

"I was going to speak to you about this break-in when I was finished here," Mallory said, stepping next to Mrs. Mason. "Were you at your store last night?"

"No, I wasn't," she replied, crossing her arms over her ample chest.

"What time did you leave?"

She blew out some air, causing her lips to make a motorboat sound. "I guess it was around nine, maybe a little beforehand. The knitting club ended at eight, but there were some stragglers. I didn't pay much attention to what time I locked up."

"And where did you go?" Mallory asked.

"Well, I went home, Sheriff." Mrs. Mason furrowed her brow and smiled. "That seems like a silly question. Where do expect a woman in her seventies to go? The local bar for tequila shots?"

Placing a hand over my mouth, I hoped to hide my snicker.

"So you didn't see anything or anyone out of the ordinary?" Mallory prodded.

"No, I didn't. Not last night. But yesterday afternoon, that horrid man came to see me again."

"What horrid man?" Mallory and I asked in unison.

"That guy... what's his name? From the Chester Development Corporation."

"Aiden?" I replied.

"Yes, that's him. I can never remember his name."

"What about him?" Mallory asked. "What did he say?"

"He was pressuring me to sell," Mrs. Mason continued. "He kept telling me I wasn't safe in my store."

Mallory arched a brow, then turned to me. "Has he been around to see you?"

"Yes. And he said the same thing to me after Mr. Mason was killed. I wasn't safe in my store, and if I wasn't comfortable working and living next to a building where a murder had taken place, he had an offer that would blow my socks off. That's almost a direct quote."

"So, he's trying to get both of you to sell," Mallory stated. "Interesting."

"Maybe he figured if he killed my husband, I'd be willing to hand over Knit Wit," Mrs. Mason said. "But when Sam didn't budge, he decided to ruin hers. Maybe put her in financial peril so she'd have to."

I nodded, now seeing where she was going with her thoughts. "And if the murder hadn't scared you away, then maybe the break-in would."

Mallory pursed her lips and jotted down some more notes. "I think I better speak with Aiden."

CHAPTER 15

AS THE CLEANUP PROGRESSED, I began to feel better about everything and actually had a shred of hope that Sage Advice would survive.

Annabelle worked tirelessly on her tinctures while Gina, Sally and I swept up the glass, scrubbed the floors, and tried our best to soak up the oils. I debated whether or not I should just refinish the hardwood floors but decided against it for monetary reasons. We'd simply have to reconfigure the store to hide the stains and maybe add a few throw rugs to the décor. With every problem we encountered, a solution was easily found.

For instance, since all our display tables had been smashed to bits, we were able to afford a few to get us up and running before the insurance company reimbursed me by using the autograph money. The gratitude and love I felt when the delivery truck rolled up almost brought me to my knees.

Sally had lunch and dinner delivered to us from her restaurant on the day she couldn't make it. Jordan called a friend from Sedona, who also happened to install windows. The replacement pane had been ordered and Jordan had convinced him to install it at a discount. I'd heard the bartering, which involved an all-paid fishing trip at Jordan's expense.

I wondered once again how I deserved such amazing friends.

Yet, a cloud of doubt hung over me, mainly because of the unanswered questions. Who had ruined the store? And why? Could the answer be as simple as Aiden wanting Knit Wit and Sage Advice so badly for a resort, he'd murder someone and destroy my inventory? How could I prove it? And what was to stop him from doing it again once we were up and running?

For the millionth time, I chastised myself for not setting the alarm that night. But honestly, the damage could've been done even if the alarm had been on. Whoever was responsible had been determined to destroy a lot of property in a short period of time, and the alarm wouldn't have mattered.

Our inventory was scarce, but we were able to open two days after the debacle. Word of what had happened to the store had spread quickly through town, and I was thrilled when customers came in to support us.

I checked in a few times with Jordan, and the police had been unable to track down Aiden. In my eyes, this only made him look guiltier. My store was broken into and trashed and the main suspect with the best motive disappears? However, I had a feeling he'd show up again sooner or later.

Mrs. Mason arrived two days after what I'd come to call "the event." Like a good neighbor, she'd been checking up on me and my cleaning crew many times, often bringing us coffee or snacks, which we all appreciated. If anything, between her husband's murder and the break-in at Sage Advice, it had only brought us closer together—we shared misery and fear, I supposed. Whatever it was, I was proud of myself for placing my trust in her without questioning her every move as I had done in the past with most people. Perhaps now that the secret of my prior life had been set free, so had my distrust.

We chatted for a bit, then her pudgy face turned scarlet. "I have a favor to ask, but I know I'm imposing, Sam." She glanced around the store and gestured toward the bare shelves. "You've got so much going on."

"Don't be silly," I replied. "You've been so helpful. Please tell me what I can do."

She sighed and shook her head. "My computer is on the fritz. I was wondering if you could come by and see if you have the magic touch. I don't know what I did wrong and Russell was the one who always fixed it when I made a mistake..." Tears welled in her eyes before she shut them. "I feel so incompetent."

I reached out and laid my hand on her shoulder. "Of course I'll come by. You don't need to explain anything." I glanced around the store and found one customer, which Annabelle could handle. "Let's go right now."

After conveying my mission to Annabelle, she gave me a salute and turned back to her worktable. I grabbed my coat, and Mrs. Mason and I left through the rear door.

"Have you seen that man again?" she asked as we ambled from my deck to hers. "Aiden?"

"No. Have you? I know Jordan wants to speak to him."

"I haven't," she sighed. "I hope they catch up to him quick, because I'd sure feel better if he was behind bars for murdering Russell. It would give me a bit of closure."

"You sound certain that it was him," I said as we arrived at her back door. She shoved the key into the lock and opened it. A nice blast of heat licked at my cheeks and I hurried inside.

"Well, I figure it's him because he wanted our stores for his resort."

I took a seat at the computer and hit the space bar. Nothing. "What about that drug dealer?" I asked. "You seemed pretty convinced he could be a suspect."

"Yes, and I still think that," she said.

Things had been so crazy the past few days. Jordan and I had barely had time to talk, let alone sit and toss around ideas on murder suspects. We were supposed to go to dinner, so hopefully he'd fill me in a bit about the Mason investigation.

"I don't have any secret insight into the investigation," I said. "With Jordan being so confused and angry about my past and my lies, we haven't talked much."

"Well, at least he's finally pulled his head out of his bottom." She pulled over a chair.

"Let's see what happens when I pressed Control-ALT-Delete," I said.

"I should make notes on what you're doing so I can handle my mistakes by myself," she replied.

When that didn't work and the black screen remained dark, I tried a couple other ideas that also failed. I was out of tricks. "I think it's best if we just unplug it," I said. "What were you working on?"

"Nothing important. If it's gone, that's okay."

I stood and pulled the plug, counted to ten, then shoved the prongs back into the wall. A second later, the computer powered back up and Mrs. Mason and I exchanged smiles.

"Thank goodness," she said. "I was beginning to worry I'd have to get a new computer. Russell was always barking at me about backing it up into some cloud somewhere, but I never fully understood that."

"I can show you if you like," I replied as the screen lit up and the mail app opened.

Glancing over at the inbox, one name caught my eye. Juan Vasquez.

"That's Russell's old email," Mrs. Mason said, reaching for the mouse. She clicked the corner of the app and the mailbox disappeared. "I was going over his email looking for some tax documents."

"Did you find them?" I asked. "I can help you look for them."

"Yes, yes, I did. Thanks."

I noted a couple of receipts by the keyboard. "Did you want me to help you enter these?" I asked, tapping them.

"You're so sweet, but no, thank you. I actually called Colin Breckshire, like you suggested. He's going to be taking over my books. I figured I'd leave those for him."

"Good. That's smart. He's very capable." I couldn't help but wonder if having a professional help with the accounting was the right move since so little money moved in and out of the store. Speaking of money... "Did you ever find where that large sum I found went?"

She pursed her lips and shook her head.

I recalled her theory that Russell had contacted Juan about a loan, and when it came time to collect, the Masons didn't have the ability to pay it back. According to Mrs. Mason, it could have been motive for Juan to kill her husband. "Have you heard anything from him?"

"No, and each day that goes by, I thank my lucky stars. If he shows up here, I'll probably end up dead, just like Russell. That man is a nasty piece of work."

"Why do you think he'd kill you?" I asked.

"Because if I'm right, Russell owed him money, which in his eyes most likely means that I owe it, too." She clucked her tongue and shook her head. "I hope that's not the case."

The stories she'd told about Juan paying for her son's rehab and later, his funeral still resonated with me. A drug dealer with a conscience stood out to me as a unicorn walking down Comfort Road would. Yet, he would have to have ice running through his veins to shoot a man who practically raised him, then come after that man's wife. "Have you talked to the police about him?" I asked.

She nodded. "Mallory came by again and we discussed him." Lowering her voice, she said, "She's not very bright. I'm not sure how she became sheriff."

That made two of us.

"But I have another favor to ask you," Mrs. Mason said, laying her hand on my knee. "I'm having a small service for Russell out on the deck, and then I want to throw his ashes into the river. Will you be able to join us? It'll be a small group."

Considering I'd barely spoken to the man, I didn't really feel I belonged at such an intimate gathering. However, after-death services weren't for the dead, but for the living. If Mrs. Mason wanted me there, I'd oblige. "Of course. Just let me know the day and time."

"I will," she said. "I'll text you. I'm supposed to get his urn tomorrow or the next day."

Glancing over at the computer, I longed to poke through the emails I'd seen. I hadn't caught the date on that email from Juan, but if Mrs. Mason had been looking at past dates, it could've come in then. Unless Juan was emailing Mrs. Mason still trying to collect the debt. But then she'd said she was looking at her husband's email, not her own.

Something didn't feel right, but I quickly brushed it aside and stood. "Well, if you don't have anything else for me, I better get back to the store."

"That's it, Sam." Mrs. Mason rose from her chair and took me into an affectionate embrace. "Your friendship means more to me than you'll ever know, especially during this difficult time."

I patted her back and smiled, so glad I could help. Warmth spread throughout my chest and I sighed. This had to be what life was about, right? Helping others in need. Building a community. Loving thy neighbor.

As I walked back to Sage Advice, that niggling of doubt resurfaced. Was it my own trust issues coming to the forefront, or was something truly wrong?

CHAPTER 16

THAT NIGHT, I met Jordan at On The River. I'd put on a bit of makeup and wore my best blouse. I even dabbed a little perfume behind my ears. I was excited to see him, to get our relationship back to normal ground where we laughed and enjoyed each other. I'd missed him terribly.

"Don't you look nice," he said, giving my cheek a quick kiss. "I could've come and picked you up."

"I know. I need the exercise, so the walk did me good. You can drive me home though. It's way too cold."

"Deal," he said, opening the door for me.

Sally greeted us at the hostess stand. "Two of my favorite people enjoying each other's company once again!" she proclaimed with a grin. "All is right in the world!"

Jordan and I smiled as she led us over to the table where we usually sat—toward the back and very private. After we each slid into our usual places, I picked up the menu. For a brief minute, I debated whether to get something besides my usual, but decided I'd go with the oatmeal and mushroom hot chocolate.

"I think I'll have a beer," Jordan murmured, then glanced over his menu at me. "You know, change things up a bit."

"Then I'll get crazy as well and have some wine."

Forget the hot chocolate.

Sally returned a few moments later and took our order, then hurried away with the menus. Jordan reached across the table and took my hands in his. "I'm glad we finally got the chance to spend some time together. Alone."

"Me, too," I replied. "I've missed you."

"The feeling is mutual, Sam. And again, I'm sorry for the way—"

Sally set down our drinks. "Sorry to interrupt. I'll be back in a bit with your food."

I took a sip of wine as Sally scurried away. "Let's look to the future, okay?"

Jordan nodded and raised his glass. "To the future."

"What's going on with the Mason murder?" I asked. "What about Oly and Adam at Hammer and Nail?"

"You know I can't comment on an ongoing investigation," he replied, grinning.

I rolled my eyes. "Okay, Detective, but I have a feeling this conversation will be going there in the very near future. I was trying to cut to the chase."

"You're right," he sighed, tapping his finger on the side of his beer glass. "I did get a chance to talk to Oly and Adam. They're just two dumb local guys who couldn't find their own rears with two hands. Basically, we're looking at a couple of different things, but overall, we're at a loss on who killed Mr. Mason."

"Well, run it through for me."

"Mr. Mason arrived at the store early in the morning through the front door. The video footage from Knit Wit shows this. A moment later, a man stumbled up to the store, and we don't see him again."

"Mrs. Mason said the video feed was cut."

"Yes. The working theory was that the man walked into the store and shot Mr. Mason, then left either through the front or back door. With you being out on your deck during that time, we have to assume he exited through the front."

"I've been thinking about that," I said. "I really don't see how I could miss someone leaving that store, especially if they followed the path down to the Riverwalk. I *may* not have noticed them if they snuck out then headed up to Comfort Road on the walkway between Knit Wit and Sage Advice, but there's a small possibility. I was really distracted that morning."

"With what?" he asked.

"My life," I sighed. "I hadn't spoken to you in days. I knew you were angry and my secret was out. I was feeling pretty low."

And just like that, we were back in the past, not talking about our future together. Although I would prefer to move on, maybe it needed to be revisited every now and then, and one day, we'd be able to laugh about it.

"I'm sorry, Sam," Jordan said. "Frankly, the revelation of your past life caught me off guard. I was surprised but also hurt that you felt the need to lie."

Reaching across the table, I interlaced my fingers with his. "I've told you why, but be honest, Jordan. Were you a little intimidated by my fame?"

"Heck, yes!" He chuckled and shook his head. "Like I told you, I'd never known anyone who could charge for an autograph."

"Yeah, that was Annabelle's idea," I grimaced. "I won't be doing that again. Hopefully, the excitement of having a washed-up celebrity living in Heywood has died down."

Jordan chuckled as Sally set down our food. "Anything else, folks?" she asked.

We both shook our heads, and my mouth began to water as I eyed my oatmeal.

"Good. You two look like you're solving the world's problems over here, so I'll leave you to it."

"Washed-up is not a word I'd use to describe you," Jordan muttered. "You've just moved on to a better phase of your life, Sam. You aren't irrelevant and ruined. You matter to a lot of people—you just aren't standing on a world stage anymore."

As I sipped my wine, I bathed in my gratitude for not being under the spotlight any longer.

"But getting back to the case," Jordan said, "that's where we are. We think that guy went in, murdered Mason, and then left. My guess is out the front door, then Mrs. Mason walked in later and found him. You saw her when she arrived, right?"

"Yes. We spoke for a few moments, then we both went to our stores."

We ate in silence for a few moments, my mind churning.

"I wonder who turned off the video feed?" I mused. "And why? It had to be someone familiar with the store."

"It may not have been disconnected," Jordan said. "But, yes, you're correct. If it was, someone had to know how to do it."

"What do you mean it might not have been disconnected?" I asked.

"Mrs. Mason did mention that the whole system had been on the fritz for a while," Jordan replied, dipping his spoon into his bowl.

Huh. She hadn't revealed that to me. "I thought someone had disabled it."

Jordan shrugged. "Could be. We just don't know."

"Isn't there an off/on switch?"

"Yes, and the way it's configured, if there's a power surge or something, the system goes off, switch and all. In these old buildings, power surges aren't unheard of. Mrs. Mason said it happens frequently, so she wasn't that surprised when we mentioned the video feed being off."

"So that guy who stumbled into the doorway is your main suspect?" I asked.

"Well, after what happened to your store and what we've learned about Aiden and Chester Development Corporation, we have some digging to do there."

"Oh, really?"

"Yes. When he was mentioned as a suspect, I didn't think much of it. I mean, he buys property and builds stuff. Is Knit Wit worth killing over?"

"I wouldn't think so, but he's been very persistent in his goal of buying the two stores. What have you found out about his company?"

"There were a couple of incidents reported, mainly in Montana, from people who say they use scare tactics to get owners to sell land and buildings they want."

"Like what?"

"One farmer testified they killed off twenty-five cattle and almost bankrupted the ranch."

I pushed my bowl of oatmeal aside, my intrigue overriding my hunger. "Did he have proof? Did it go to court?"

"He couldn't prove it, but the situation sounded similar to what's happened here. Someone from Chester Development Corporation approaches the landowner, they tell the representative to go spit in the wind, and then something terrible happens."

"Any murders?"

Jordan shook his head. "Not that we could connect. But there was another case of harassment where Chester Development was named. Once again though, there wasn't any proof."

As I sipped my wine, I turned over the new information in my mind. It did have a ring of familiarity, especially with my store being trashed. But how did harassment lead to murder? "Maybe they escalated with Mason," I said. "Or maybe they'd simply wanted to scare him and the gun going off was a mistake."

"But if you want to scare someone, why do it with a loaded gun?" Jordan asked.

Good point.

"The fact we haven't been able to catch up with Aiden and ask him about the cases in Montana and what's happened here worries me," Jordan continued. "Did he leave town or is he laying low, waiting to strike again?"

"I can't help you there. I've been too busy cleaning up the mess it sounds like he made."

After picking up my spoon, I concentrated on the rest of my oatmeal. When finished, I again pushed the bowl aside. "What about Mrs. Mason?" I asked. "Mallory seemed to see her as a suspect."

"At first, she interrogated her pretty hard, but she's kind of fell off the radar. She didn't have much to offer up."

"She's having a service for Russell on her back deck at some point in the next couple of days," I said. "I was invited. Do you want to be my date?"

Jordan took a long sip of his beer as he stared at me over his glass. When he set it down, he smiled.

"What?"

"I've never been asked on a date to a funeral," he replied. "It's really not very sexy."

"Well, think of it as a more practical date," I said. "We get to spend a little time together and maybe you'll find the magic clue to solve the murder."

As we laughed, Sally came over and cleared our plates. "Another round of drinks for you two?"

I shrugged and glanced at Jordan. "Do you want to live dangerously and have a second beer?"

"Sure thing," he replied.

While Sally went off to fetch our beverages, I asked, "What about Juan Vasquez?"

"Who's that?" Jordan's brow furrowed.

"It's that guy Mrs. Mason knows... the drug dealer from Phoenix."

Jordan stared at me a long while before saying, "I don't know who that is."

An uncomfortable feeling settled in my chest. "Mrs. Mason said she's been talking to Mallory about him as a potential suspect. Don't you two discuss the case at all? Compare notes?"

If not, the sheriff's department was in worse shape than I ever imagined. It wasn't a huge place employing thousands where paperwork could get overlooked and miscommunication would be easy. However, Mallory was running the place, so I supposed anything was possible.

"Well, of course we do," he replied. "We share information. Maybe she's deemed him not worthy of our time, or she wanted to do a little digging before she mentioned him."

"Oh, okay," I said. Hopefully, that was it and she was doing her due diligence, not completely neglecting a great lead.

Sally brought our drinks over and we spent the rest of the evening laughing and talking about everything but the murder and my past. I was sad when the lovely night came to an end, but both of us had to get to work early in the morning.

Jordan drove me back to Sage Advice and just as I was about to exit the car, in the dim nightlights coming from my store, I noticed a man lying at the entrance wearing a dark coat, his back to us... with a neon green stripe down the back. It was then I realized it wasn't part of the jacket as I'd thought it had been in the short video Jordan had shown me. It was reflective tape.

I laid my hand on Jordan's forearm and pointed to the store. "Who do you think that is, and why is he camped out in my doorway?"

CHAPTER 17

"Isn't that the same coat that was in the video you showed me?" I asked. "I remember the stripe down the back."

"I think you're right," Jordan said. "Stay here."

After he exited the car, I debated whether I should follow his orders and decided against it. What if that person was the one who trashed my store? If so, I had some choice words for them. Also, what if Jordan needed help? I pulled out my phone and readied it to dial 9-1-1. Then, I opened the car door and followed him up the walkway.

"Hey, buddy," Jordan called, approaching slowly. I noticed he hadn't brought his gun. Oftentimes he did, but apparently, not tonight.

The man groaned and moved slightly. At least he wasn't dead, but he would be if he didn't get out of the cold.

Once Jordan stood over him, he gave him a light push with his boot. Another moan escaped the intruder, and then he said, "Where's Sam?"

Jordan glanced over his shoulder at me. Furrowing my brow, I stepped closer. Who was this?

When the man rolled over to his back, I gasped. The long beard, the thin face... yes, I knew him. I dropped to my knees. "Doug! What are you doing here?!"

Taking his gloved hand in mine, I stared at my homeless friend that I hadn't seen in months. The last time we'd met at his place under the bridge on the Riverwalk, he'd told me he was leaving for a warmer climate until the spring.

"Sam." He slowly sat up. "I didn't know where else to go."

"Jordan, help me get him to his feet," I said.

Without a word, Jordan reached down and lifted Doug. Upon studying him closer, I noted his quivering lips and red nose.

"Come inside," I said. "Let's get you warmed up with some tea and something to eat."

"I don't know if this is a good idea," Jordan muttered as I unlocked the door.

"My friend is freezing and hungry," I replied. "It's the best idea I've had in weeks."

As I hurried inside, flipped on the lights, and turned off the beeping alarm, Jordan led Doug in. I moved through the store quickly and ran upstairs to turn on the heat in my apartment and get some water brewing. Catnip stared at me as I shucked my coat, then turned his attention to the footsteps sounding up the stairs.

"Be nice," I said, knowing full well he would act any which way he wanted, depending on his mood.

Jordan and Doug entered the apartment and the smell of body odor quickly permeated my small space. Catnip ran for the bedroom, and I didn't blame him. Despite the chill, I opened a window for some fresh air and tried to keep the grimace off my face. After making a sandwich and a steaming cup of tea, I set them down in front of Doug and took a seat.

"Thank you," he murmured, barely loud enough for me to hear. "You're so kind, Sam. Like I said, I had nowhere else to go."

I waited until his plate was clear before questioning him. "I thought you left for a warmer climate," I said once he finished.

He shook his head. "I was going to, but then my cousin asked me to move in for the winter."

His cousin, being the mayor of Heywood. I'd never understood their relationship, but I also knew very little about it. I did recall the mayor's son being a bit of a troublemaker and was currently in prison.

"Did he kick you out?" Jordan asked.

Doug nodded and sat back against the cushions. "He did. I had to stay clean, and I was for a few months. Then I slipped, and he booted me."

So many emotions swirled through me at once. Anger that the mayor had chucked Doug out the door, elation he'd remained off drugs for so long, and utter heartbreak that he'd fallen once again. "I'm so sorry to hear that," I said.

"Yeah, me too. I went to the shelter for a couple of nights, but there's tons of drugs there. I've been clean for two days now and I want it to stick this time." He glanced around the apartment. "You're one of the nicest people I know, Sam. I'm here to ask for your help."

"We can get you a spot at one of the bed and breakfast places," Jordan said. "A shower, a bed, and a hot meal."

"No," I said, shaking my head. "He's staying here with me."

Jordan cursed under his breath and frowned.

"With a couple caveats," I continued. "You need to remain sober, you stick to the herbal regiment we put you on, and you're in charge of keeping our store clean."

Doug's eyes widened while Jordan swore again.

"Seriously, Sam?" Doug asked.

"Yes. If you don't meet my requirements each and every day, then you're out. No second chances."

I had no doubt that Doug would be able to abide by my rules—as long as he could keep his demons in check.

"What do you think, Doug?" I asked.

"I'm very flattered that you have so much faith in me, and yes, I'd love to take you up on your offer."

Jordan stared at the floor, his mouth in a tight, fine line. Of course, he was concerned for my safety.

"Great! Just give us a moment," I said, standing and grabbing Jordan's hand. I pulled him to the staircase landing in the hallway.

"What are you doing?" he asked, his voice quiet.

"I'm helping a friend."

Shaking his head, he pointed at my apartment. "Sam, for all we know he murdered Mason!"

"He didn't," I replied. "I know it in my heart."

"Where's he going to sleep? Your couch?"

"Bonnie's place," I said. "It's still furnished. For some reason, I've never been able to clean it out—it's been too difficult—and now I know why. Bonnie gave me a second chance by allowing me to live here, and it's my turn to do the same."

Jordan closed his eyes, placed his hands on his hips, and tilted his head up to the ceiling, not even attempting to hide his exasperation. "You barely know this guy."

"No, you're wrong," I said. "I've spent a lot of time with Doug. We talk all the time when the weather is warm and he's living under his bridge. He's so smart, Jordan. Smarter than you and I will ever be. He just needs a helping hand."

"I ask again, what if he's the killer?" Jordan hissed. "If we're right, he's the guy who was in the security footage. And you're just inviting him in to live with you. Are you out of your dang mind, Sam?"

Okay, Jordan did have a point, but I knew in my heart Doug didn't have anything to do with Mr. Mason's murder. Well, at least I hoped not. Maybe I was wrong. My gut churned with the doubt creeping in.

"He may have killed Mason for drug money," Jordan continued. "We just don't know, and I'm not about to leave him here with you."

"Let's go talk to him," I said. "We can hear his side of the story on what happened that morning."

"And you're going to believe whatever he has to tell you?"

I ran a hand over my curls, trying to keep the trembling in check. "Doug is a lot of things, but a violent liar is not one of them." Gosh, what if I was wrong?

"Fine," Jordan said. "But if I feel anything is off, he's not staying here."

Not a fan of people trying to run my life. Heat rose in my cheeks and I forced a smile as I ground my jaw. "I really don't think that's your call, Jordan."

He stared at me a long moment then nodded. "You're right, and I'm sorry." After he took my hands in his, he gently squeezed my fingers. "I'm just worried about your safety."

"I understand that and appreciate it, but I have faith that Doug had absolutely nothing to do with the killing, and you seem certain that he did. Again, let's go talk to him and I'll make my decision then, okay?"

We covered the few steps to my apartment hand in hand. I smiled at Doug as we entered, relieved that Jordan and I had come to an understanding without much of an argument.

"I don't need to stay here," he said, standing. "I appreciate the sandwich and tea, but I'll leave now."

"No," Jordan replied, pointing at the couch. "Have a seat, Doug. I have some questions for you."

I exchanged glances with my homeless friend and nodded.

"Listen, I don't want to cause any trouble," Doug continued. "I can—"

"Doug, it's fine," I assured him. "Just sit down for a minute, okay?"

As he lowered himself to the couch, he glanced between me and Jordan. "I don't want to cause any trouble," he repeated.

"You haven't," I said. "There's just a couple things we need to discuss."

"I noticed the stripe down the back of your coat," Jordan began. "It looks like reflection tape?"

Doug nodded. "It's so if I'm out and about after dark, drivers can see me. We don't have a lot of streetlights around this area."

"Fair enough," Jordan said. "Now, your coat looks similar to the one that was found in some security footage the morning Mr. Mason was killed."

Doug's gaze widened. "I didn't even know he'd died. What a tragedy. Can you tell me more?"

"You didn't know there was a murder in town?" Jordan asked incredulously.

"I'm sorry, deputy," Doug replied. "I've been alone the past few days. No television, radio... nothing. If you tell me more about the video, maybe I can help."

"There's footage of a man, which I am assuming is you, stumbling into the Knit Wit doorway in the early morning hours. The sheriff's department assumed that whoever that was could possibly be the killer."

"How did you come to that assumption?" Doug asked, furrowing his brow. I studied the deep circles under his hollowed-out eyes. Exhausted was the only word I could think of to describe him.

"Well, Mr. Mason was then murdered, the cameras ceased working, and after that the killer left."

"And you think that was me?" Doug asked.

"We have to ask. Were you there that morning?"

Doug didn't hesitate to answer. "Oh, yes. That was the night my cousin kicked me out. I was higher than the gates of Heaven, Deputy. I passed out in the Knit Wit doorway."

His explanation made perfect sense to me. When I'd first seen the video, I had assumed the person had been drunk. In fact, if I'd known Doug was still in town, I would've probably guessed it was him, or at least mentioned him then. I'd seen him stumble around high more than once.

"Tell me what happened then," Jordan said, leaning forward and placing his elbows on his knees. Who came by? What did you see? When did you wake up?"

"I can't tell you any of that," Doug said. "I was passed out. A herd of elephants could've walked by and I wouldn't have known. If the killer stepped over me to get to Mason…" he shrugged. "I'm sorry, deputy, but I have nothing to tell you."

"Are you sure?" Jordan pressed. "What time did you leave the doorway?"

"I don't know."

"Did you hear a scream?" Jordan asked. "Does that ring any bells?"

Doug shook his head.

I appreciated Jordan trying to figure out Doug's timeline, and to prove his innocence if only for his own peace of mind. He sighed in frustration while anger heated his neck and cheeks.

We sat in silence for a long moment. Doug stared at the coffee table while Catnip decided to make an appearance. He sat at Jordan's feet and glared at him until the man sat back and made his lap available. Catnip quickly jumped up, curled into a ball, and closed his eyes.

"I do remember one thing," Doug said.

"What's that?" I asked.

"A light. At first I wondered if I'd finally died, but then I realized it was a light coming from Sage Advice."

Jordan glanced at me and I shrugged. "Maybe when I first got up? It was dark."

"Anything else, Doug?" Jordan asked.

He shook his head.

"Well, at least that helps us narrow down the timeline," Jordan muttered. The sun rises about seven thirty, so the light went on before then."

"Which means that Mr. Mason arrived when it was still dark," I said.

"I'm sorry I can't be more help," Doug said. "I just don't remember."

"Where did you go after you left Knit Wit?" I asked.

"To the shelter. I was cold and hungry."

"Maybe they would know what time he arrived," I noted.

Jordan nodded, then asked, "Do you remember if the sun was up when you got to the shelter?"

"Maybe?" Doug replied, furrowing his brow. "It's all a blur."

"Okay," Jordan said. "At least we have a timeline narrowed down a bit."

"You're one step closer to figuring everything out," I said. "And that's a great thing."

But I was still confused on whether the harassment Mrs. Mason and I had experienced was connected to the murder. Or could it possibly be two separate incidents?

CHAPTER 18

DOUG DID END up spending the night in Bonnie's apartment, and Jordan stayed in mine. When I woke, Jordan had already left and I didn't hear anyone in Bonnie's place, so I assumed Doug was still resting. Either that, or he moved like a cat.

After a cup of coffee and a little yoga to resolve a few kinks in my hips and back, I hurried downstairs. Annabelle would be arriving soon since she was putting in extra time to produce more products. I reminded myself to tell her about Doug so she didn't scare when she saw him.

I put on the pot of coffee downstairs and began my morning duties, which included a list of things that Doug would need. Pants, sweaters, underwear, socks, some food for the apartment, shower stuff and soap, toothbrush and toothpaste, shave cream and maybe a razor. I planned to go gather everything after I spoke to Annabelle.

A short time later, she entered looking extra flashy with her silver eyeliner, matching ribbons in her hair, and more silver bracelets bouncing around her arm than I could count. As she shucked her neon pink parka, I noted her Madonna t-shirt over her neon green turtleneck which coordinated with her legwarmers.

After exchanging pleasantries, I handed her a cup of coffee. "We need to talk about something."

"Sure," she said, her brow furrowing. "As long as you aren't going to, like, tell me that you're shutting down Sage Advice or I'm fired."

"None of the above."

"Okay, then. Talk away. I'm listening."

I shared our run-in with Doug the previous night, the conversation we'd had, and explained that he now lived upstairs. Late into the night I realized I should've run my plan by Annabelle since she spent a lot of time at the store. I wanted her to feel safe. If she had a problem with Doug living at Sage Advice, I'd have to find other arrangements for him. Some of the bed and breakfasts were reasonably priced, but I'd also look into weekly rentals in the area. Whatever the case, I was one hundred percent dedicated to giving him a second chance and helping him stay clean.

After I finished, she nodded. "Oh, that's good." She pulled some mason jars filled with herbs from the shelf. "I'm going to make up some capsules for him right now, and then get a tincture started. I'm so glad he wants to get clean. I mean, if Elton John can do it, so can Doug."

I sighed with relief. Annabelle was on board and ready to help.

"Thanks a lot, Annabelle. I appreciate your understanding."

"Everyone needs a second chance," she said. "Bonnie gave us both one, and now it's our turn to do the same. It feels good to help people."

"Agreed," I said, turning to the computer and firing up our online store and shipping program. I printed out the labels for a couple of orders that had come in overnight. Looking them over, I realized I hadn't updated the online inventory after my visitor had destroyed our product. I muttered a curse and began forming an email to explain that the wanted product was out of stock but would be available again soon.

"Did you ever meet him?" Annabelle asked.

It took me a moment to realize she meant Elton John. "No," I shook my head. "I did see him once in concert, though. And that's where I met Prince."

She gasped as I turned around. "You met Prince?!"

"Yes," I replied, bathing in her reaction. She loved hearing stories from my past, and I loved sharing them simply because they excited her so much. "But it was only for a second. There wasn't any deep conversation. Just a handshake and smile."

"Oh, my gosh," she sighed. "His movie, *Purple Rain*... holy cow. It was *so* good!"

As she continued her review of the movie, I returned to my online tasks and decided I'd need to watch it again. According to Annabelle, it was a classic, right up there with *Breakfast Club* and *Pretty in Pink*. I also listened for footsteps upstairs and wondered if I should prepare a quick meal for my guest. Last night he'd appeared worse for wear, and he definitely needed to put on some weight.

When the front door chimes rang, I stood, then peeked around the corner. Without thinking, I threw my pen to the floor and rushed out into the store, my blood boiling with fury.

"What are you doing here?" I yelled. "Get out of my store, right now!"

Aiden from Chester Development stared at me with a smirk on his face. If I wasn't so low on product, I'd throw some essential oils onto his floor-length camelhair coat and stain it.

"Is that any way to greet the person who's offering you a bunch of money for this old place?" He gestured around my beloved store. "Are you ready to accept my offer for this dump?"

"I'm ready to put my fist through your pretty teeth." I pulled out my phone and dialed Jordan. "I have Aiden here," I muttered, then hung up. Not only did I want Jordan to speak to him and discover if he was the one who had trashed my store and killed Mr. Mason, but I was also afraid of what I may do to the man. I believed he tried to ruin my livelihood in order to enhance his own, and a police presence may just be the deterrent I needed for him to keep his veneers intact.

"Who were you just talking to?" he asked. "What's going on?"

Annabelle came around the corner, her gun in hand at her thigh. She stared at him, her mouth in a fine line as she dragged a stool around the corner and pointed to it. "Sit your smarmy butt down."

His smirk slowly faded as he caught sight of Annabelle's weapon. "Is that necessary?"

"Yes. Now sit down."

Well, things had escalated quickly and I could tell Annabelle meant business. Aiden did as he was told just as Jordan rushed in. He must have been close.

Shaking his head, he eyed the gun. "Put it away," he ordered.

"I feel as though our lives are in danger," she replied. "This man has left threatening notes and probably destroyed our store. He probably killed Mr. Mason too, and I'm afraid for my safety, Deputy. Who's to say he's not here to do bodily harm to us?"

"What note?" Aiden sputtered, his brow furrowed. "I'm not a killer. What are you talking about?" He seemed quite perplexed. Was he lying, or did he truly know nothing about the note and Mr. Mason's death? And what about the destruction of the store?

"Let's head to the sheriff's department," Jordan said. "We've been intending to have a talk with you."

Aiden shot up from the stool. "About what? Am I under arrest for something?"

"We have to speak to you about a couple of incidents that have happened in town," Jordan said, his voice calm and professional. "You aren't under arrest. We've been looking for you, though."

"I went back to California!" Aiden shouted. "I haven't even been in town!"

Jordan placed his hands on his hips and sighed, apparently losing his patience. "Will you come with me down to the station?"

"No," Aiden stated flatly, then turned to leave.

The next few moments shouldn't have surprised me. In fact, I should've seen it all coming.

Annabelle placed the gun on the empty stool, then lunged at Aiden. Wrapping her arms around his neck with her legs encircling his waist, she held on for dear life as he spun around and clawed at her, stumbling around the store. Thankfully, there weren't very many display tables out and he managed to avoid those that were.

While Jordan screamed at Annabelle to let go of him, I grabbed her shirt and tried to pull her off. God help me if I ripped her Madonna t-shirt. I'd never hear the end of that travesty. She clawed at his jacket while he continued to attempt to separate himself from her. Seconds later, she stumbled back against me with his coat in hand, sending us both into the wall.

"What in the world has gotten into you?" I hissed. "He's going to sue us!"

"No, he won't," she muttered. "Look at his hands, Sam."

When he turned to us, fury raged in his eyes, his slimy demeanor disguised as couth now gone. I studied his hands and the portion of his forearms that were visible. Various cuts and scratches had scabbed over... as though he'd been wrestling a large rose bush... or maybe a bunch of glass.

"What the heck's gotten into you?!" Aiden shouted, approaching us.

"Stay right there," I said, keeping Annabelle behind me. "Why don't you tell us what happened to your arms?"

His face quickly shifted from anger to surprise. Heat colored his cheeks as he turned away from us and shoved his hands in his pockets.

Jordan glanced at Aiden's hidden hands. "Let's see the rest of your arms."

"There's nothing to see."

"Looks like there's plenty to see, buddy. Annabelle, could you hand him back his coat so he can accompany me down to the sheriff's department?"

She stepped out from behind me and threw it at Aiden's feet. As he reached down to grab it, the sleeve of his turtleneck rode up and I noted more cuts and scrapes. If the timeline worked out, I was certain we'd just found the person who destroyed Sage Advice. But had he killed Mr. Mason?

"I'm calling my lawyer," Aiden said as he slipped on his coat.

"Probably a good idea," Jordan muttered. "Let's go."

After they left, I turned to Annabelle. "Do you think he wrecked the store?"

She nodded. "I do. You don't get all those cuts on your hands and arms from everyday life, unless you're wrestling something with claws, and he doesn't look like an animal lover to me."

"I'm so glad you noticed." I shook my head. "Thank you. Hopefully, Jordan can nail him to the wall."

"With travel records, I don't think it'll be a problem. He'll be able to figure out when Aiden was in town, and maybe even match his DNA to some of the bloodied glass we found."

"He was probably thinking that small town cops don't have a clue on how to do all that," I replied. "Good thing Jordan has the big-city experience. If Aiden did it, I'm sure he'll get all the evidence he needs."

"And we won't have to deal with him any longer," Annabelle said, crossing her arms over her chest as she smiled. "Case closed."

"But do you think he murdered Mason?"

Her grin faded. "I don't know. Hopefully. Otherwise, there's still a killer on the loose."

We both turned when someone cleared their throat. Doug stood in the doorway of the store and back room, still in the same clothes from yesterday. I'd forgotten he was even in the building.

"Are you two okay?" he asked.

Annabelle and I exchanged glances and nodded.

"Is it always this crazy around here? Because if it is, I think I'd rather go back to living under my bridge."

Frankly, after the drama the week had brought, I didn't blame him one bit.

CHAPTER 19

AFTER SHOPPING FOR DOUG, I brought back my purchases to the store and handed everything over. "I didn't know if you wanted to keep the beard," I said. "If not, there's a couple razors in there."

"You're so kind. Thank you. I think I'll go up and enjoy that lovely shower."

"Great," I said. "Have at it."

I would also appreciate not having to breathe the smell of body odor.

My phone rang as he headed upstairs. Mrs. Mason.

With a sigh, I answered. I really needed to get the online store's inventory straightened out. "Hey, Mrs. Mason. What can I do for you?"

"I know this is last minute, but I wanted to have Russell's goodbye ceremony this afternoon. I just received the urn. Will you be able to make it?"

With a grimace, I rubbed my forehead. There was so much for me to do, but how long could the service take? Maybe an hour, tops? "Sure," I said. "I'll be there. What time?"

"Five."

"I'll see you then."

I hung up and sent a quick text to Jordan:

You're invited to the sexiest date of your life today at 5

A MOMENT LATER, my phone buzzed:

Looking forward to it

I spun around in a slow circle as I tried to figure out what to do first. The online store seemed to be the most important thing at the moment. I sat down at the computer and began archiving products and lowering the inventory numbers for the ones I did have in stock while my ire rose once again. I hoped Jordan got a confession out of Aiden. If so, I planned to sue Chester Development and Aiden for anything and everything I could. Destroying property and harassment were two crimes that came to mind. Maybe illegal breaking and entering as well? I'd leave that up to the lawyers. I should call Breckshire and get him on the lawsuit once I had a definitive answer from Jordan.

An hour later, footsteps sounded down the stairs and Annabelle and I turned to find Doug. In his new clothes and fully shaven, I wouldn't have recognized him if I'd seen him on the street. Although his face was overly thin, I'd still call him handsome.

Both Annabelle and I said nothing—we only stared.

"I... uh... I was going to vacuum the apartment, if that's okay," he said.

"Sure, sure," I replied, standing. "Let me show you where we keep the cleaning supplies."

After showing him the closet with the vacuum upstairs, I said, "I'd like to have the store cleaned after hours so we don't interrupt any guests coming in."

"Of course, Sam. Just let me know when to start." He glanced down at the floor, then at me again. "I appreciate this opportunity, and I won't let you down."

"I hope not," I said, laying my hand on his shoulder. "Annabelle's working on some herb mixtures for you, so that should help with the detox and cravings."

"This won't be easy."

"I know. And that's why you're here. You have my full support, and I'll do whatever I can to help you."

He nodded and I thought I may have seen a tear in his eye. When he turned and dragged the vacuum back to his apartment, I hurried downstairs.

"Hubba, hubba," Annabelle whispered once I sat down. "He's, like, hot as heck! I'm going to get me some!"

Oh, for the love of... "Please remember he's at a very vulnerable place in his life and the last thing he needs is to be hunted down by a cougar, Annabelle."

She snorted. "Maybe that would be the best thing for him!"

"Just stop," I said with a chuckle. "Leave the poor man alone."

"He's, like, the only guy in town I haven't dated. Well, except for the super short ones and the fat ones."

"Annabelle—"

"Oh, fine," she muttered. "I don't need to be involved with a drug addict anyway, no matter how cute he is."

With that settled, I turned back to my computer. Every now and then, the chimes would ring, and either Annabelle or I would hurry to the front of the store to help our customers. Throughout the morning, only two came in wanting autographs, which I gave without collecting any money. It seemed the novelty of having a celebrity in town had almost fully faded. Maybe in another week or so, there wouldn't be any further autograph seekers.

When the chimes rang again, I glanced up to find the woman with the stomach issues strolling in with a huge smile on her face.

"I take it the tea is agreeing with you," I said as she approached the counter.

"Yes, it is," she said, shaking her head. "I never would've imagined that a tea could help me so much."

Annabelle emerged from the back room and they discussed the benefits of thyme.

"It's also wonderful for inflammation," Annabelle said.

The woman nodded and held out her hands. "My mom has arthritis, and I've noticed in the past year or so that my joints are starting to ache, especially in the morning. Since I've been using the tea, it hasn't been as bad."

After glancing at the clock, I realized I needed to head over to Mrs.

Mason's soon. The day had flown by so quickly! A moment later, Jordan walked in. I smiled and waved him into the back room while Annabelle and the customer continued their lovefest of thyme.

"How's your day been?" I asked after he gave me a quick kiss on the cheek.

"Good. Old Aiden confessed to trashing your store."

I gasped, surprised he'd caved so easily. "He barely put up a fight!"

Jordan nodded. "At first, he was indignant and rude. Then I explained to him we were going to match the DNA on the blood he left behind as well as track the time he was in town with his credit card records and flight itineraries. After that, he pretty much folded."

"He sure made your job easy."

"Don't get me wrong... he confessed after hours of me questioning him. He's been my main focus all day. My persistence paid off, though."

"My hero."

"It warms my cold heart to hear you say that," Jordan said, grinning.

"I want to sue that company for everything they've got," I spat.

Jordan shrugged and raked a hand through his hair. "You could certainly do that, but they're a huge conglomerate, Sam. They have deep pockets. It would be a David versus Goliath situation, and they could keep the case in the legal system for years."

I sighed and nodded. Of course, he was right. "What about murdering Mr. Mason?" I asked.

"That, he wouldn't admit," he said. "But then again, killing someone can get you executed, ruining property can't. We're putting together the timeline on his travels in and out of town and we took his prints so we can hopefully match them with what we have at the scene. He also owns a gun, which was registered in the state of California. I contacted the Sacramento police department today to get a liaison going there so we can all work together."

"Did they sound like they wanted to be helpful?"

"Oh, yeah," Jordan said. "I think it's going to be a great partnership, and we'll nail Aiden, trust me."

"That's fantastic news," I said.

"There's only one thing that's bothering me," he continued. "The note that was left on your front door."

"Why does that bother you?" I asked.

"Aiden wasn't in town the morning it was left. He had a flight the night before."

"Maybe he placed it on my and Mrs. Mason's door the night before."

Jordan shook his head. "I did a little test. The tape used, which was just regular old tape that you can pick up at any store, doesn't stick for very long in the cold. Something about the makeup of the glue—it doesn't function in below-freezing temperatures, which is what we had. That note wasn't placed the prior night, but that morning."

"So right before you found it."

"Exactly."

"I guess it was some stupid prank."

"Probably," he replied. "It's the only thing that makes sense. It was a coincidence that Aiden was pressuring you and Mrs. Mason at the same time."

"Speaking of which, we better get going."

"Sure. But I have to say, I do hate funerals, so you owe me for going with you."

I smiled and wrapped my arms around his waist, then kissed the tip of his chin. "It's not really a funeral. More of a remembrance ceremony."

"Same thing in my book."

After I disentangled myself from him, I pushed open the back door. "What about Juan Velasquez?" I asked. "Did you get the chance to talk to Mallory about him?"

"No." Jordan shook his head and took my hand in his. "She was out most of the day. I'll get with her tomorrow about him. He's in Phoenix, right?"

"That's what Mrs. Mason told me."

"Maybe I can talk Mallory into footing the bill for a road trip. Do you want to join me?"

"To go interview a potential murderer?" I asked. "Thanks, but I think I'll pass."

About fifteen people had gathered on Mrs. Mason's deck and all the chairs had been claimed. Jordan and I stood against the building and waited. A few moments later, Mrs. Mason exited Knit Wit carrying a golden urn etched with black writing. I couldn't see what it said, but I had to assume it denoted Russell's remains. She smiled at a few people, then moved to the front of the deck which overlooked the river and forest beyond. She set the urn on the railing.

"Now that everyone's here, I think we should begin," she said. She stared at the papers in her hand, as if gathering her thoughts. "Thank you all for coming."

She glanced around, her gaze moving over the crowd. "Russell and I had been married for a long time. With that came ups and downs, good times and bad. And we had all that." Pursing her lips, she stared at her paper again for a long moment, then continued. "Especially with the death of our beautiful boy, his life destroyed so needlessly. His passing almost shattered my husband and I, but in each other's arms we found strength, we found hope, and we kept our love alive."

As she continued to list their trials and tribulations, tears welled in my eyes as I looked around the crowd. Others were dabbing their cheeks as well. The service was far more difficult than I had imagined. Mrs. Mason's grief had become an almost tangible source, weighing heavily on the crowd. As Jordan placed his arm around my shoulder, I leaned into him and wished I had brought a tissue, never imagining that I'd cry for a man I barely knew.

But then I realized I wasn't teary because of his death. I was upset for the huge losses Mrs. Mason had endured and the pain she suffered. At the same time, I admired her because I didn't think I would still be standing if I were her. What she'd been through made all of my problems seem silly and trivial.

"Because of the troubles we faced together, our good times were happy. We learned to embrace them, to appreciate them, to..."

As her voice faded out, her gaze didn't falter. She stared at the back door, then brought her hand up to her heart and stepped backward, grabbing the railing with her hand. "No!" she yelled. "Don't! Don't kill me!"

CHAPTER 20

I moved away from the building to see beyond Jordan while Mrs. Mason continued to beg for her life. In the doorway stood a medium-height man, about my age with tanned skin and black hair. He wore a black leather jacket, matching jeans, and boots. His eyes widened as Mrs. Mason continued to scream.

He swore under his breath when he realized everyone was staring at him. Slowly, he backed up into the store.

"Please don't hurt me!" Mrs. Mason wailed. "Someone, help! Help!" She pointed at him. "He's here to kill me!"

"That must be Juan Vasquez," I said, nudging Jordan. "That's who Mrs. Mason thinks murdered Russell. We have to catch him!"

Jordan hurried after him while I followed close behind. "Hey!" Jordan said as the guy made his way to the front of the store. "Buddy! Can you stop a second?"

He turned around.

"Are you Juan?" Jordan asked. Why wasn't he throwing cuffs on the killer?

"Yes," he responded with a slow nod, his gaze traveling up and down Jordan, who wore his uniform. "I don't want to talk to any police."

"What's she yelling about?" Jordan asked. "Why does she think you're here to kill her?"

"I have no idea. She invited me here."

"Are you armed?" Jordan asked.

Juan lifted his hands to his sides. "Nope. Pat me down, man. After that, let me off this crazy train. I'm headed back to Phoenix."

"We'll see about that," Jordan responded.

Personally, I didn't think he'd be going anywhere, except to jail. I smiled smugly, thrilled the murderer had been caught.

Mrs. Mason burst through the door as Jordan conducted his search for a weapon. "Thank goodness you were here, Deputy. This man killed my husband."

"I did not," Juan shouted. "Quit trying to pin it on me!"

As they argued, my gaze bounced from one to the other.

"Pin it on you?" Mrs. Mason yelled. "You killed my Russell because he couldn't pay you back!"

Juan's gaze widened as he slowly brought his hands to his sides when Jordan had finished his weapons search. "Are you out of your mind?"

Mrs. Mason lifted her chin defiantly. "Of course not," she spat. "I'm a law-abiding citizen, while you most certainly aren't. You're the scum of the earth... a killer and a drug dealer!"

I studied Juan carefully. His surprised expression softened until it settled into resignation. "Well played, Mrs. Mason. Well played." He shook his head.

And suddenly, the situation didn't seem as cut and dried as I'd thought.

"I haven't played anything," she said, her gaze narrowing with hatred. "Hopefully, this kind deputy will do his job and send you to prison for the rest of your life."

My stare found the floor as Jordan asked more questions. Mrs. Mason's screaming faded out, as did Jordan and Juan's calm replies.

The woman had said her husband had probably borrowed money from Juan and couldn't pay it back, so he'd driven up to Heywood from Phoenix and shot him. She'd also claimed that Aiden had probably killed Russell as a warning to sell the building to his company.

But none of the evidence led down those two roads. However, it did lead back to Mrs. Mason.

I glanced at the raging woman who was now calling Juan a bunch of names while he stood stone-faced, taking each one as if he deserved it. Had her story about him and her son been true? Had they grown up together and had her son, Cody, died from a drug overdose? Had Juan put him through rehab?

Jordan pulled out his radio and called for backup while Mrs. Mason demanded Juan be arrested not only for killing her husband, but attempting to kill her, as well.

It was all just... too much. And none of it made any sense to me anymore.

I stepped in between them. "Juan, did you grow up with Cody Mason?"

He nodded as his brow furrowed. "I did."

"Why are you talking to him?" Mrs. Mason yelled. "He's a killer, Sam! Don't get too close to him or he may stab you or something!"

Except he'd been cleared of all weapons. I was slowly coming to realize Mrs. Mason was completely unhinged.

Another deputy entered the store and Jordan asked him to take Mrs. Mason outside while we talked to Juan.

She screamed the whole way. Once the back door was shut, I turned to Juan.

"Did you lend Mr. Mason a large sum of money recently?" I asked.

"No," he replied, shaking his head. "But I did *give* it to her. It wasn't a loan."

"Why?" I asked.

"Guilt money. Hoping she'd finally leave me alone. Because she's never let me forget that I killed her son."

"How did you do that?" Jordan asked.

Juan glanced at me, then pursed his lips together and stared at the floor.

"He's a drug dealer," I said. "Quite successful, from what I under-stand. Cody overdosed on his product, and Mrs. Mason blames him."

Jordan arched an eyebrow. "Is that true?"

Juan didn't answer.

"I'm not interested in your business dealings," Jordan clarified. "I'm interested in finding Mr. Mason's killer."

After a long moment, Juan relented. "Yeah, it's true."

"And did you send Cody to rehab before he died?" I asked.

"Yes."

I glanced at Jordan. At least everything Mrs. Mason had told Mallory and me was true. But what about her husband's death?

"I didn't kill Mr. Mason," Juan said. "I'm a lot of things, but I wouldn't kill the man who practically raised me."

If what Juan was saying was true, he gave her the money, then... then what happened? Why had Mrs. Mason gunned down her own husband?

"Can I talk to you for a second in the back room?" I said to Jordan, hitching a thumb over my shoulder.

"Mr. Vasquez, would you mind waiting here?"

He glanced at the door and then back at Jordan.

"I promise you I'm not going to arrest you for murder... or anything else unless you're guilty of it," Jordan said. "Right now, I don't know what to think, so I'd appreciate you sticking around. We just need a few more details and a statement from you would be helpful."

"Yeah," he said in a low tone. "I can wait."

Turning his back to us, he stood with his hands laced in front of him and studied the knitting projects Mrs. Mason had hung on the walls. The dichotomy of the drug dealer appreciating the baby booties, blankets, and mittens wasn't lost on me.

I wondered if he hated Mrs. Mason, or if he ever believed he could've somehow fixed everything that had happened with her son and changed the course of everyone's life. Would the situation be much different if he'd never given Cody his first taste of drugs? Or would Cody have found his forbidden fruit elsewhere and gone down the same path?

I stepped into the back room, but Jordan stayed in the doorway so he could keep an eye on Juan.

"She's trying to set him up," I said to Jordan. "And he knows it."

"I'm getting that feeling."

"I don't understand why she killed Russell, though."

He paced back and forth for a moment, then stopped. "I guess we have to ask. Tell her the game is up and hope she tells us the full story."

A sinking feeling hit the pit of my stomach. She'd manipulated everyone, including me. All of the clues came rushing back. How she'd made a point to speak to me the morning she'd found her husband dead, so I'd assume she wasn't at the store. The money in her books, and how quickly she'd fingered not only Russell, but Juan. How she deflected guilt in every direction, particularly placing blame on Juan and Aiden. She threw theories and ideas at a wall and then stood back to see what stuck.

As long as she didn't get any guilt on her, she didn't care who went to jail.

But I had a feeling her true target had been Juan—she'd wanted to see him go down for her son's death.

Why had I trusted her? Was it because she was a kind old lady and I couldn't see through her charade? Maybe I didn't want to? Or was my judgment of people really that terrible?

"Let's find out why she killed her husband," Jordan said. As he grabbed my hand and led me to the back deck, I wanted to run, my hurt so great at her betrayal.

Mrs. Mason sat in a chair outside with the deputy and stared out over the river with the urn in her lap. Everyone else had left. Jordan sent the other cop to go inside and keep an eye on Juan.

At least she'd quieted down. I'd been worried she'd give herself a heart attack. Now, I wasn't so sure I cared. Probably a little harsh, but she'd broken my trust, something I didn't dole out without a lot of thought, and it pained me she'd so blatantly taken advantage of it.

Jordan dragged a chair over and sat in front of her. "Do you want to tell me what happened?" he asked.

"I already did," she said calmly. "Russell borrowed money from Juan and then he killed him because he couldn't pay it back. He's here to kill me."

The fear was gone from her voice, defeat taking its place.

"But Juan says that's not the way it went down," Jordan replied. "Russell never approached Juan for the money. You did."

"And you're going to believe a drug dealer over a tax-paying citizen?"

"I don't know what to believe," Jordan said. "That's why I'm asking questions. Is what Juan said true? Did you ask him for the money?"

For a second, guilt flickered in her gaze and I knew I was right. The details and motive were fuzzy, but she'd killed her husband. "The game's up, Mrs. Mason," I said. "Now that the police know the real murderer, it won't be hard to trace the evidence to get you jail for the rest of your life."

She smirked and shook her head. "You silly woman. I've been jailed my whole existence."

"What does that mean?" Jordan asked.

For a long moment, she stared out over the river and I thought she'd decided to remain silent. Jordan would haul her down to the department and maybe they'd elicit a confession after presenting her with all the evidence. Or perhaps she'd stick with her story until the bitter end, involving a trial.

But I was wrong.

"When my son died, I was a prisoner of grief," she began. "It ripped me up from the inside out. Such intense pain, it wouldn't have hurt as bad if someone stabbed me a thousand times."

"But what does that have to do with you killing Mr. Mason?" I asked.

"When we moved up here, I finally found a small spark of joy. Well, I don't know if I'd even call it that. I can't remember what that feels like. I found something that gave me a little relief from my pain... Knit Wit."

As she stroked the urn, she sighed. "Russell wanted me to sell the store because it's a money pit. We'd put most of our savings into it, and Russell was forced to come out of retirement and take a job at Hammer and Nail Hardware. He resented me for it, but I still wouldn't give up the store."

"Tell me what happened the morning Russell died," Jordan said softly.

"We were both up early," Mrs. Mason replied, her stare still far away. "We argued. He'd done the accounting and realized I had taken money from Juan, and he was furious. I couldn't take any more of his yelling, so I left and came down to Knit Wit while it was still dark."

I realized that her story was going to be filled with half-truths. She'd told me that morning that Russell had come down to the store first.

"And from where did you enter the store?" Jordan asked. "The front door or the back?"

"The rear," she replied. "Russell showed up shortly after me and came through the front door. I wasn't expecting him. When I heard the noise, I pulled out the gun we keep on the shelves and shot him, thinking he was a burglar." Tears welled in her eyes. "I didn't mean to shoot him."

I had my doubts. Mr. Mason had been shot in the alcove. Unless all the lights were out, she would've had to have recognized him before pulling the trigger. Or maybe she hadn't. I doubted we'd ever know the truth.

"What did you do then?" I asked. "Why not call the police and tell them what happened?"

She glanced up at me and shook her head. "I was going to, but then I realized I had an opportunity to right so many wrongs."

"Let's get to that in a minute," Jordan said. "Tell me what you did after you shot him."

"I sat with him for a bit and worked out my plan. Sam was out on her deck, so I couldn't leave that way. But I also had the camera recording the front door. I disabled it and hurried down Comfort Road, then to the Riverwalk. When I got back to the store, I chatted with Sam, giving myself something of an alibi."

I recalled how rosy her face had been that morning, indicating she'd been out in the cold for a while, much longer than it would've taken her to walk from home. At the time, I hadn't paid much attention, but it should've been my first clue.

"And then?" Jordan urged.

"She went inside, waited a few minutes, then screamed. Annabelle and I ran over. Juan was right. She's played everyone, Jordan. Especially me."

I stared at her a long moment as she stroked the urn but didn't meet my gaze.

"When you found the money, Sam, I realized I could have everything I wanted. My store, no husband to hound me about the one thing that brought me a little peace, and I could get my revenge on Juan."

"But you needed a backup plan," I spat. "So you threw Aiden under the bus for good measure."

"You're right. I figured if I could play up the angle of him harassing us so we'd sell our stores, that would also deflect blame from me."

"The notes left on the doors?" Jordan asked. "Was that you, or is there some prankster out there I need to hunt down?"

"It was me."

"You're a despicable woman," I said. "I can't believe you'd kill your husband."

She smiled and shook her head. "Neither can I, Sam. Grief has made me into someone I no longer understand, a woman I barely know."

EPILOGUE

Six Months Later

The sun shone high in the sky as a warm breeze caressed my cheeks. I strolled hand-in-hand with Jordan, perusing the offerings and art at the Farmers Market.

We stopped at a booth where a woman I recognized as one of our regular customers was showcasing her paintings and exchanged pleasantries. At the next table, the bakery, Skippity Scones, had some cookies and pies for sale.

"Oh, we can't walk past those," I said, eyeing the chocolate chip cookies.

"Probably a bad idea to not buy them," Jordan agreed.

After we collected our dozen cookies, we strolled over to Too Hot To Handle, the local hot sauce company. Their products always made me giggle with names like, Devil's Juice, Hot Mama, and Tear Jerker.

"Are you going to sample any?" I asked Jordan as we perused the offerings.

He shook his head. "Heck, no. I like my tastebuds intact."

"Aw, come on, Deputy," the owner, Chris Raves chided. He stood about my height but was a few years younger than me. It was my understanding he grew all the peppers he used in his products. "Give it a go."

"No, thanks," Jordan said.

"I'll give the Devil's Juice a try."

Turning, I found Doctor Garrett Butte snickering. Our gazes met and he quickly looked away.

"Sure," Chris said. "Here you go. Try a little Devil's Juice with the crackers."

Butte grabbed the cracker and poured a little hot sauce on it, then shoved it in his mouth.

Describing the satisfaction I felt as his cheeks turned red and his eyes bulged would be impossible. I smiled as he coughed and sputtered, then bent over to place his hands on his knees.

I laughed out loud as he gasped for breath, thrilled to see him so miserable.

When he went down to the ground and slowly rolled over to his back, my smile slowly faded.

Jordan bent over him and gave his shoulder a shake. "Okay, Doctor. Time to get up. I appreciate the antics."

Except, he didn't move. His eyes stared up at the perfect summer sky while his hand twitched slightly.

With a curse, Jordan fell to his knees and began chest compressions. "Call an ambulance!" he yelled.

I did as instructed, unable to take my gaze off Butte. I'd seen that faraway stare before. I knew he was dead.

But I did wonder, could hot sauce really kill a man?

CHAMOMILE AND CHAOS

A SMALL TOWN CONTEMPORARY COZY MYSTERY

ABOUT THE BOOK

When the town doctor dies at the Farmers Market, it is quickly discovered he was poisoned.

The gossip vine turns its sights on Sam because she was one of the last people to see the man alive, and if anyone wanted him dead, it was her.

As Sam fights to maintain her reputation as well as find the real killer, she discovers that once again, her future is going to be deeply affected by her past.

Will Sam find the murderer before her life is left in tatters?

CHAPTER 1

"SHUT IT DOWN! Shut it down! Shut it down!"

The chanting voices filtered into my store, Sage Advice, from the street. At first I thought I was hearing things. But when I glanced around the corner from the back room to the front door, a sinking feeling settled into the pit of my stomach. Six people stood outside, and I realized they were chanting to shut *me* down. Or at least, my store. The line between me and my beloved business sometimes blurred.

Crossing my arms over my chest, I leaned against the archway and stared at them while trying to decide what to do. Call the police? They weren't on my property. Spray them with the hose? A nice idea, but it seemed like a lot of work to haul it from the back deck to the front and hope the stream of water would hit them. After a moment, the ring-leader became apparent—Doctor Gerald Butte waved his fist in the air as he screamed. Five people joined him in the protest. Three even held signs.

Butte had been fighting the existence of my store since before I came to Heywood. As someone who deeply believed in over-prescribed pharmaceuticals, he hated that my herbal apothecary assisted people in getting well with the power of plants.

I turned as my friend and employee, Annabelle, entered through the back door carrying two bottles of wine. Since Mrs. Mason murdered her husband, the store next door, Knit Wit, had closed. A younger couple had opened a wine shop, aptly named Never Quit Wining. I couldn't ask for better neighbors. Adrienne and Wayne were wonderful, kind people, and I'd developed a serious love affair with their organic chardonnay.

"What's all that noise?" Annabelle asked, setting down the bottles on her workbench. We'd decided an afternoon cocktail was in order, and she'd run next door to purchase our favorite wine.

"Apparently, Butte is protesting our store," I muttered.

Her brow furrowed as she ran a hand over her crimped blond hair. Pastel ribbons had been interwoven into a couple of small braids that matched her tie-died ruffled skirt and yellow t-shirt tied at the waist. "Who's out there with him?"

"I have no idea."

We watched them for a few more minutes.

Annabelle shook her head. "I think we should turn the hose on them."

"Great minds think alike," I sighed.

"I wondered what happened to make him, like, do this?" Annabelle mused. "I mean, he's always been a pain in the butt, but why protest our store like this? Why now?"

Suddenly, they became quiet, and my hopes soared that they'd leave. But they'd only taken a moment to change the chant.

"Pills over Plants! Pills over Plants!"

"That's dumb," Annabelle said.

Footsteps sounded down the stairs, and we turned to find Doug. I'd taken him in after the New Year and helped him stay sober. In return, he did odd jobs around the store and the apartments upstairs. The old building had many issues, so he was usually quite busy.

"Hey, Sam," he said, flashing a smile. "That sink upstairs is fixed." He then met Annabelle's gaze. "Hi," he said softly.

"Hi," she replied, meeting his tenor.

For the past six months, I'd watched the two of them dance around each other like moths to a flame. He needed to concentrate on remaining sober—which he'd done—not getting tangled up in a relationship, so I'd forbidden the romance. No, I really didn't have the authority, but Annabelle had abided by my wishes and kept her claws to herself.

Doug lifted his handsome chin to the front of the store. "What's going on out there?"

Sobriety had been kind to him. He'd put on weight, had a nice tan from painting the outside of the building, and his hazel eyes sparkled with curiosity and life.

"They're picketing the store," Annabelle said. "We were just discussing whether we should take the hose to them or not."

"Are they really saying pills not plants?" Doug asked.

We nodded.

"That's ignorant." He shook his head.

"Exactly what I said," Annabelle said with a huff.

"Let's get back to work and hopefully the temperatures outside will make them scatter," I said, eyeing the wine. Maybe cocktail hour should happen sooner rather than later.

I'd complained about the snow in the winter until no one wanted to listen to me. Now, the temperature soared and I almost missed being cold. None of my picketers would be out there very long—I hoped.

Glancing over at Doug, I quickly grabbed the bottles and ran upstairs. Even though he insisted that alcohol didn't entice him, I didn't want to tempt him. He'd worked so hard and come so far, my love affair with organic wine wasn't going to ruin it for him, regardless of what he said.

After shoving the wine into the fridge, I gave my cat, Catnip, a quick scratch behind the ears as he stretched out on the couch. I then returned downstairs and tried to figure out the problem at hand. Having never been on the receiving end of a protest, I was at a loss.

"I think you better call Jordan," Annabelle suggested.

"Do you really think he can do anything?" I asked. "They're on the sidewalk, which isn't my property."

"Call him anyway," Doug said. "A couple of people just looked like they were coming into the store and then walked away when they saw the picketers."

I didn't want to bother my boyfriend. Yes, I said it. Jordan is my boyfriend. As a sheriff's deputy, his day had started early with a car crash on the freeway and gone south when he had to respond to a domestic abuse case which had sent the woman to the hospital. I could handle Butte on my own.

"I'll go talk to him," I muttered. "But film it all, Annabelle. If this jerk lays a hand on me, I'll file a police report."

"Aye-aye, Captain!" she yelled, giving me a salute.

Closing my eyes for a second, I took a deep breath and brought forth my character on *As The Years Turn*, Cassie. It didn't take long for me to slip into the role of the take-charge murderer who always got what she wanted.

I pushed open the front door and marched over to Butte. "What are you doing?"

The protesters silenced and circled me. Fear settled in my chest. Surely, they wouldn't attack me in broad daylight on the main road in town?

"We're here to have you shut down," he said loudly. "You've poisoned this community for long enough!"

I shook my head, angry I had to deal with the elderly man. "I haven't poisoned anyone," I hissed. "I've done nothing but help everyone who comes through my door."

"Tell that to Kathy Richmond!" Butte shouted.

"What does that mean?" I asked. "Who's Kathy Richmond?"

"You can't even remember the name of the woman you killed," he hissed.

Butte might as well have punched me in the stomach. Now he was accusing me of murdering a woman?

"We don't—"

"Of course you did!" Butte yelled. "Her name was Kathy Richmond! You killed her!"

Before I knew it, everyone was chanting, *You killed Kathy.*

I tried to place the woman and her ailments, with no luck. But we'd most certainly have a record.

However, I wouldn't stand outside arguing with Butte. "If you don't quit your stupid protest, I'm going to stand out in front of your medical clinic with a sign that says you're a drug dealer," I said, shaking my finger under his nose.

He narrowed his stare. "You wouldn't dare."

"Don't test me, you condescending jerk. What's good for me is also good for you. I'll just make it ten times worse."

As we continued the stare down, more people gathered around to watch. I realized me wagging my finger in the elderly doctor's face wasn't a good look, but I was so, so sick of this man trying to close my business.

"That's enough!" Annabelle yelled as she hurried out of the store with her phone held up in front of her face. "Back off, Butte, or I'm going to put this on social media so everyone can see what a bully you are! How dare you pick on a woman!"

Ah, yes. Social media. The great equalizer. It had bitten me in the rear end not too long ago. People could say anything about anyone, and only the powerful elite were able to keep the truth in check... or promote the lies.

Butte's face softened just a bit and he stepped back.

"Now, take your crew of ill-informed people and, like, skedaddle, fish face!" Annabelle yelled, still filming.

I turned my head, unable to meet Butte's gaze as I fought a smile. Many months ago, Annabelle had hidden a dead fish in his car as retribution for being a jerk. She loved getting revenge on those who had slighted her or her friends. Did he realize the fish found inside his car and the insult Annabelle had slung at him were related?

Glancing at the store, I caught Doug watching Annabelle, grinning. Was that pride I saw in his stare?

"I'll see you closed down for the death of Kathy Richmond!" Butte yelled before pivoting and stomping down the sidewalk, his crew following behind.

"Who's Kathy Richmond?" I asked when they were out of earshot.

Annabelle lowered her phone and shoved it into her pocket. "She was a customer. Why does Butte think you killed her?"

"I don't know." I shrugged. "Do you remember what she was treated for?"

"Let's go look. It's been a couple of months since I saw her, and I always get her confused with Holly Bale for some reason."

Doug held open the door as Annabelle and I marched inside. Worry curled my stomach. We'd treated Kathy, and now she was dead. What if we were responsible? It could mean lawsuits, not to mention the horrible weight of guilt I'd carry. Just because a product was natural didn't mean it couldn't be dangerous if not used correctly.

Annabelle rifled through her customer journal while mumbling to herself. I tried to wait patiently, but now I was horribly anxious. A hot flash ripped through me from head to toe and I took a deep breath to attempt to calm it.

"Here she is!" Annabelle shouted. Her brow furrowed as she read her notes. After a moment, she said, "This doesn't make any sense."

"What doesn't?" I asked. I craned my neck to try to read her handwriting.

"She was here for stress. We put her on a chamomile tincture."

I sighed in relief. "There's no way the chamomile could kill her, is there?"

"I don't see how," Annabelle said. "Unless the tincture was somehow tampered with or went bad."

"Do we still have some of what we gave her?" I asked, glancing around the store. What if we had it out on our shelves?

Annabelle nodded. "Let me check the batch numbers."

As she hurried into the back room, Doug gathered a few bottles from our anxiety display. "I think we should pull these until you have everything figured out."

"Yes. Thanks, Doug." I grabbed a plastic bag from under the register and he gently settled them inside.

"I'm sure everything is okay, Sam," he said gently.

With a smile, I tried to put on a brave face. "I hope you're right."

Because if my products had killed Kathy Richmond, I didn't know how I was going to live with myself.

CHAPTER 2

THE NEXT DAY, Annabelle and I set up our booth at the Farmers Market. With all the tourists pouring into Heywood to enjoy the river rafting and our idyllic, small mountain town, we'd expected to sell a boatload of products, and we'd been correct. By the afternoon, almost everything had been cleared off our table.

I'd made the decision to keep the chamomile tincture off the shelf, even though Annabelle seemed quite certain there was nothing wrong with it. I thought it would be best to start a new batch, just in case. I'd looked up Kathy Richmond's obituary, but it didn't offer any insight as to how she'd died, only that she'd left behind two grown kids and a husband. If my product had truly been involved in her demise, I guessed Sheriff Mallory Richards would have been knocking at my door. She'd love nothing more than to see me behind bars.

As Jordan approached our table, I smiled while heat rose in my cheeks. The swagger, the grin... yes, he was giving off all sorts of George Clooney vibes.

"Hey, you," he said, leaning over and giving me a quick kiss. "Looks like sales have gone well."

"It's been a great day," I replied.

"Care to walk around with me and check out the other vendors?" Jordan asked.

I glanced at Annabelle. "Go," she said, shooing me away. "I'll be fine."

As I took Jordan's hand, I looked across the park and noted Doug approaching, his gaze firmly set on Annabelle. Were they carrying on behind my back? I shouldn't try to police any adult, but in my defense, I was only trying to help Doug.

"See you in a bit," I said, waving to Annabelle.

The afternoon sun shone high in the sky as a warm breeze caressed my cheeks. I strolled hand-in-hand with Jordan, perusing the offerings and art my beautiful town had to offer.

We admired the handmade jewelry from the local shop, Jemisphere, and the leather goods from Sedona's shop, Boots n' Bags.

My friend, Gina, also had a table for Heywood Hounds and we stopped to say hello. Today, she had Daisy, a dog she'd rescued and eventually adopted, and another mutt, who resembled a chow. As we walked up to her table, her gaze was firmly on Daisy and she was speaking to the little brown and white dog.

"I'm not going to give you any more of those treats before bed," Gina said. "They give you horrible gas. Don't argue with me about it anymore, either."

I swore she was having a conversation, but people couldn't talk to animals.

A second later, she turned to us, her gaze wide in surprise as if she hadn't seen us coming. Daisy wagged her tail and ran over to me. As I leaned over and petted the cute little thing, I smiled and said hello.

"Hey, Gina," Jordan said. "That's a nice-looking chow you have there."

She nodded. "His name's Sing and he needs a home. You interested, Deputy?"

"I wish I had time, but my twelve-hour days wouldn't be fair to him," Jordan said, stroking the dog's head. "Sorry."

"He's super lazy," Gina continued. "He'd love nothing more than to lie around all day."

"I can't, Gina."

She sighed and rolled her eyes. "Fine. If you know someone who wants a lazy dog, let me know. Sing just wants a place to call home. He's no trouble."

As I stared at the cute, fluffy face, my heart ached. I also didn't have the time for a dog. How Gina remained upbeat as a dog rescuer, I never understood. It had to be one of the hardest jobs in the world.

We chatted a few more minutes and Gina and I agreed to grab a coffee in the morning then walk her dogs. She stood and stretched her arms above her head. "I've got to head home. The rest of the mutts need to be let out and fed. I'll see you tomorrow, Sam."

Jordan and I continued our perusing of the offerings. My mood slowly deflated when I noticed Doctor Butte a few tables away.

"What's wrong?" Jordan asked.

He'd become so in tune with my emotions, I didn't even have to utter a word for him to sense when my demeanor changed. "Butte." I frowned. "He was at my store yesterday."

Jordan glanced over his shoulder. "What happened?"

I had hoped to put the fiasco behind me and allow it to die down, so I hadn't shared it with Jordan. After explaining the antics that had taken place, he shook his head. "Do you want me to say something?"

"No. I just want him to leave me alone and quit spreading rumors that my products are killing people."

"That's a fair request," he said. "If he stops by the store again, please tell me, okay? I'll ticket him for harassment."

Dating a protective cop had its perks.

"Maybe you could just toss him in jail?" I asked, batting my eyelashes.

Jordan laughed and kissed the tip of my nose. "Anything for my girl."

"Be careful. I may hold you to that."

As we turned to the next vendor, someone tapped me on the shoulder.

I glanced back and found Butte.

"Your boyfriend should put your murdering heart in jail," he said. "I know what you did."

"What are you even talking about?" I asked. "I had nothing to do

287

with Kathy Richmond's death!"

"Oh, yes you did, Samantha. And I'm going to prove it."

A small crowd had gathered and some people pulled out their phones to record the argument. It wasn't a secret in town that the good doctor and I butted heads.

"Soon, everyone will know you're a killer!" he shouted, spreading his arms out to his sides. "Everyone!"

Fury rose within me and I fisted my hands. "Watch it, Butte, or you may be next!"

"Okay, okay," Jordan said, stepping in between us. "Doctor Butte, if you have a shred of evidence to support your claims, you can come down to the station. Until then, you can quit slandering her. For now, stay away from Ms. Jones."

"She just admitted murder!" he yelled, pointing at me over Jordan's shoulder. "You should arrest her!"

"No, I didn't!" I screamed, losing all sense of control. When I lunged at the man, Jordan grabbed my arm and pulled me behind him again.

"Go!" Jordan ordered the doctor. "Stay away from her!"

As Butte narrowed his gaze, I sneered right back. All I wanted was to be left alone and live a quiet life. Butte apparently had other ideas and accusing me of murder was one of them.

When he turned and walked away from us, Jordan grabbed my hand and led me in the opposite direction. "You really lost your cool back there," he muttered, just barely loud enough for me to hear.

"Can you blame me?" I asked, yanking my hand away. "He's accusing me of killing a woman!"

"Did you?"

My mouth hung open in shock. "Did I... kill her? Is that what you're asking me?"

"Yes."

"Of course not!" Well, I hoped not, anyway. No one had told me I had.

"Then can we please have a nice afternoon?" Jordan begged. "We're both so busy, it's hard for us to get time alone. I want to enjoy it—not argue, not worry about Butte. Just spend time with you."

My anger softened slightly. He was right. I hadn't done anything wrong and Butte was a jerk. I shouldn't have allowed him to get under my skin.

"Okay," I sighed. "Yes. Let's enjoy the afternoon and maybe I can talk you into letting me take you out to dinner."

"Twist my arm," he said.

I smiled and grabbed his elbow, determined not to let Butte ruin the rest of my day. However, I would most likely toss around some sneaky ideas for revenge with Annabelle. The man had become an even bigger thorn in my side than usual, and if I couldn't do anything legally, I'd get back at him somehow. Maybe another dead fish would be in order.

We stopped at a booth where a woman I recognized as one of our regular customers was showcasing her paintings and exchanged pleasantries. At the next table, the bakery, Skippity Scones, had some cookies and pies for sale.

"Oh, we can't walk past those," I said, eyeing the chocolate chip cookies, suddenly starving.

"Probably a bad idea to not buy them," Jordan agreed.

"Yes. It's important to support our local businesses," I said. "To not do so would be a crime."

After we collected our dozen cookies, I also grabbed a few chocolate chip scones to keep on hand in case anyone wanted them with tea at Sage Advice.

We then strolled over to a juice vendor, aptly named Berry Good. Butte seemed to be trailing us. Was he trying to aggravate me?

"Hey, there," the tall, thin, bald man working the Berry Good booth said. I pegged him about my age and I'd probably seen him around town, but I didn't know his name.

"Good afternoon," I greeted him.

"Would you care to sample?"

I thought he'd never ask. With a smile, I reached for a little paper cup on the plate labeled cherry mango.

"Oh, here," he said, removing the platter quickly. "These are fresher."

"Thank you," I replied, taking a cup from the offered tray. "I appreciate that."

I sipped the liquid while Jordan tried the peach juice.

"This is delicious," I complimented. "Do you have a business card? I'd love to get more."

"Sure," he said, pulling one out of his wallet. "I sell out of my home. No storefront, so please give me a call so I can get your order ready."

"Perfect." I shoved the card into my skirt pocket as Butte stepped up next to me. I shot him a glare, then turned to the vendor. "Have a lovely afternoon."

Almost every business in Heywood had a booth. Subs and Smiles was giving out samples of their sandwiches. Sally from On the River was featuring her new breakfast burritos. Never Quit Wining gave out small paper cups of their organic wine. I indulged in two. As we ate and drank our way around the park, I wondered if dinner would be such a good idea. I was becoming stuffed from all my nibbling. All the way, I kept my eye on Butte. He visited every vendor we did and seemed to be mirroring our movements, and I came to the conclusion he was definitely trying to irritate me.

We moved toward Too Hot To Handle, the local hot sauce company. Their product names always made me giggle: Devil's Juice, Hot Mama, and Tearjerker were a few of my favorites. The owner, Chris Raves, was in his thirties and it was my understanding his wife had just given birth.

"Are you going to sample any?" I asked Jordan as we perused the offerings.

He shook his head. "Heck, no. I like my tastebuds intact."

"Aw, come on, Deputy," Chris chided. He stood about my height and was one of the few African Americans who'd made Heywood home. "Give it a go."

"No, thanks," Jordan said.

"Don't be a wimp," I said, elbowing his ribs.

Chris chuckled as Jordan shook his head. "A few years ago, Chris here bet me he could make me cry. I tried the Tearjerker and lost the bet."

The three of us laughed, then Chris said, "Yeah, that was a funny one." He turned to me. "My wife loves your old show, Sam. Before you left it, she'd record it every day. She said your character was inspirational."

"You realize she played a murderer, right?" Jordan asked. "Better watch your back if your wife finds that inspirational."

More laughter ensued and I signed an autograph for his wife, Melanie.

The hair on the back of my neck stood on end when a voice behind me said, "I'll give the Devil's Juice a try."

Turning, I found Doctor Garrett Butte snickering. Somewhere during the day, he'd acquired a large red stain down the front of his white shirt. Wine would be my guess. Our gazes met and he quickly looked away.

"Sure," Chris said. "Here you go. Try a little Devil's Juice with the crackers."

Jordan tried to pull me away, but if Butte had the same reaction as Jordan had had when he'd tasted the Tearjerker, I wanted to stick around to witness it. I hoped his eyes popped right out of his head.

Butte grabbed the cracker and poured a little hot sauce on it, then shoved it in his mouth.

Describing the satisfaction I felt as his cheeks turned red and his eyes bulged would be impossible. I smiled as he coughed and sputtered, then bent over to place his hands on his knees.

I laughed out loud, thrilled to see him so miserable, as he gasped for breath.

When he went down to the ground and slowly rolled over to his back, my smile faded.

Jordan bent over him and gave his shoulder a shake. "Okay, Doctor. Time to get up. I appreciate the antics."

Except, he didn't move. His eyes stared up at the perfect summer sky while his hand twitched slightly.

With a curse, Jordan fell to his knees and began chest compressions. "Call an ambulance!" he yelled.

I did as instructed, my hands shaking almost uncontrollably. Unable to take my gaze off Butte, I realized I'd seen that faraway stare before. He was dead.

But I did wonder, could hot sauce really kill a man?

CHAPTER 3

I'D BEEN FORCED to wait at the park until after dark along with all the other vendors. Jordan had eventually sent me home with the promise he'd be around at some point the next day. I wasn't allowed to gather the remaining product at our table to bring back to the store, but neither were the other vendors. Anything edible was held, and a lot of moaning and groaning ensued, particularly from the folks at Skippity Scones, Berry Good, and Too Hot To Handle.

Although my leftover soap baskets smelled heavenly, they weren't edible. I figured Mallory was keeping them simply out of spite.

As I tossed and turned all night, I kept debating if hot sauce could actually kill someone. The internet wasn't very helpful. Maybe it could cause a heart attack? But then again, I'd thought I'd seen white, frothy spittle around Butte's mouth. Or had I imagined it? And if I had seen it, that would have indicated Butte had been poisoned. However, I'd been pretty shaken up after watching him die. I'd found a quiet corner of the park and sat down for a bit and tried to process what I'd witnessed. Yes, I'd found dead bodies, but I'd never watched anyone die in real time. Was I upset? Yes. Did I carry even the slightest amount of sympathy for the man? No. I felt nothing but numb. There were no tears to be found. What did that indicate about my overall character?

Was I a horrible, hateful person? Or was I in shock? I still didn't have an answer.

The paramedics had arrived very quickly and surrounded Butte. Maybe my mind had been playing tricks on me, or the afternoon light had hit his face at a strange angle and it only appeared like white foam on his lips.

After my third cup of coffee the next morning, I realized there wouldn't be enough caffeine to wake up my sleep-deprived brain, but I poured another one and hoped for the best.

"Good morning, Sam," Doug said as he trotted down the stairs and helped himself to a mug of java. I did enjoy having him around, but I hoped there wouldn't be any deep conversations this morning. Oftentimes, he liked to start the day with ruminations on God, the universe and the concept of a spiritual-self versus our corporeal-self—things I had trouble understanding even after being fully caffeinated. I would never claim to be anywhere as smart as my friend.

"Hey, Doug. How did you sleep?"

He shook his head. "I have to admit, sleep is an issue with me. Annabelle said she was going to work on a new tincture to help with it."

Maybe I should get in on that, too. "Great," I replied. "I'm sure she'll find something that soothes your system."

"I agree. She's an herbal artist."

Pride gleamed from his gaze as he smiled, as though he spoke of someone he loved.

But I'd told Annabelle to give the poor guy some space. Not that I had any right to police two adults, but Doug needed to focus on his sobriety. I wanted him well, and I also didn't wish to be the bad guy and kick him to the street if he slipped up, as I promised him I would. I was already feeling quite ugly since I couldn't conjure any remorse for Butte's death.

"She's quite amazing," I agreed. It wasn't the time or place to question him about his private life. Frankly, it was none of my dang business. "Can you take a look at the front display table? I think one of the legs needs to be adjusted. It's a bit wobbly."

"Of course. After that, I'll get the tables and chairs set up for afternoon tea on the deck."

293

"Thanks, Doug."

We'd been leaving the seating out overnight until someone had come by and tossed it all over the side down to the Riverwalk. My guess had been Butte. Jordan had said it was most likely some kids. Now we brought in the furniture to the back room after dark.

Butte wouldn't be bothering me anymore and for some reason, that made me terribly uncomfortable. Dread settled in my stomach as I picked up my phone to see if I'd missed a text or call from Jordan.

Nothing.

"Good morning, good morning!" Annabelle sang as she swept into the store in a pair of neon green leggings and a pink and green oversized shirt with a matching bandanna in her hair. As she approached Doug and me, a headache began to form behind my eyes. Probably from the neon.

"Good morning!" Doug chirped. "Can I get you a cup of coffee?"

"That would be very chivalrous," Annabelle said as she shoved her purse under the counter. "Thank you, sir."

After Doug set down the cup, he walked to the front of the store and methodically removed the product from the table, setting it aside where he wouldn't accidentally knock it over. I appreciated that he handled my inventory with such care.

I lowered my voice. "Can I ask you a weird question?"

"Oh, you know me, Sam. The weirder the better. Ask away."

"Did you see Butte up close after he went down?"

"No," she said, furrowing her brow. "We saw the crowd form by Too Hot To Handle but when we got there, we couldn't really see anything. There were too many people around. When Mallory arrived, she told us to return to the booth. I never saw him. Well, maybe his foot or something. Why?"

I sighed, unsure if I should share my concerns. "Well, I thought I may have seen a white foam form around his mouth, but I'm not sure."

She gasped and brought her hand up to her lips. "Oh, my word, Sam! I thought he dropped dead of a heart attack or something!"

"Me, too. But I'm not sure if I saw the white stuff on his lips, or if I imagined it."

"If you did, that means someone most likely poisoned him!"

"I know. I'm not sure what I saw, though. I was pretty upset. Maybe I was just imagining things and he died of natural causes."

"Well, if you can die from being mean, then yes, he dropped dead from being a jerk. It's really bad for the heart."

If that had been the case though, why had the police taken the products of each vendor at the scene? Perhaps they were simply covering their butts just in case it came back that he'd been poisoned?

"Have you heard anything from Jordan?" she asked. "Has he called and given you the inside scoop?"

I shook my head. "I thought he'd phone me by now, but he's been radio silent."

"Let me know when you hear something. If Butte was killed, that's a little scary."

I couldn't agree more, but I think we were afraid for different reasons. She was most likely worried about a killer being on the loose. Of course, that concerned me as well, but my anxiety hit a little closer to home. She hadn't been the one to threaten Butte mere moments before he died.

The day stretched on without many customers coming in. Annabelle, Doug, and I spent more time chatting about innocuous things than actually working. We argued about what eighties band had had the best hair: Whitesnake or Bon Jovi? As we hunched over her phone and compared pictures of the two bands, Annabelle insisted it had been Bon Jovi, but Doug and I voted for Whitesnake. When we'd been debating for almost an hour, I became bored. How in the world did I get entrapped into a discussion about big hair?

I picked up my phone to see if I'd missed any calls or texts from Jordan. Nothing.

"What in the world is going on here?" I asked, gesturing toward the empty store. "Why are there so few customers today? We don't even have anyone here for afternoon tea!"

"Maybe people are out enjoying the hiking trails," Doug suggested.

"Possibly, but it's tourist season," I replied. "We should have a bunch of loony-loos flowing through the door."

A few moments later, two women entered. I figured them to be in their mid-thirties—one with black hair, the other blonde. Annabelle and I sprang into action while Doug retreated to the back room. Why he always disappeared when customers walked in, I'd never understand. With his good looks and beaming smile, he was an asset to the store.

They perused our offerings while Annabelle and I stood ready to answer any questions. Based on their conversation about their husbands being on the golf course for the day and the bed and breakfast they were staying at, I knew they were tourists. After they'd chosen some pain salve for the blonde's neck—the pillows at the B&B were terrible—they meandered to the cash register where they noticed the sign about our afternoon tea service.

"It's perfect!" the blonde said. "I'm not very hungry, but I sure wouldn't mind enjoying the beautiful weather."

"Have a look at our tea menu," I said, pulling it from under the counter. "I'm sure we have some blends you've never tried. All are very good."

"Chamomile and mint sound so refreshing," the black-haired woman said. "That's cold, right?"

"Yes, and we grow both the chamomile and mint ourselves, so it's very fresh."

After a couple more minutes of discussion, I led them through the back room to the deck. They gasped in delight at the view and took a table as close to the railing as possible.

"Do you have an umbrella?" the blonde asked as she rubbed her hands over her pale arms. "I'm going to fry alive."

"Sure. Let me have Doug bring one out for you."

When I'd implemented my deck idea, I hadn't given any thoughts to umbrellas until customers started asking for them. I debated purchasing the portable ones, but the space was far too small. Instead, I decided on the umbrellas that slid into the hole in the middle of the table. They were easy to move, lightweight, and Doug had become a pro at assembling them into the tables.

"Doug, they need an umbrella," I said, hurrying past him and up the stairs. There simply wasn't room downstairs for a refrigerator, so we kept all the cold tea in my apartment refrigerator and made it fresh every other day. When we were busy, I couldn't keep track of how many times I ran up and down the stairs.

After fetching the chamomile and mint as well as the raspberry, I hurried back downstairs and pulled out the glasses. Annabelle dressed the cups with sprigs of chamomile flowers and raspberry leaves.

"They also want chocolate chip scones," Annabelle said.

"Good thing I got some from Skippity Skones yesterday," I replied. "Can you grab some plates?"

Annabelle hurried over to the cupboard and pulled out the white plates decorated with small flowers along the edges. After placing everything on a tray, I hurried out to my guests to serve them.

Sometimes, the way my life had changed hit me square in the jaw and I'd have to stop for a moment to appreciate it, as well as marvel at the twist and turns. I'd gone from someone who worked at a car wash to a daytime soap opera star, to serving tea and scones to two women who sat on my deck.

Having the money my former life had provided me would be nice, but I wouldn't change my place in the world for anything. I smiled as I set down the tea and scones. Yes, life was very good.

When I hurried back into the store, I found a few more customers up front where Annabelle was tending to them. Maybe things were looking up for the day.

My phone buzzed in my pocket, and I pulled it out to find a text from Jordan.

On our way over.

Our. That indicated he had someone with him.

I waited a few moments, then his truck pulled up out front. He burst into the store and weaved through the display tables at top speed in civilian clothes. I thought he had been working, but apparently not. I smiled until I noticed his furrowed brow.

"What's going on?" I asked.

297

"Mallory's following me," he growled. "You better keep your cool, and don't say a word."

I glanced over his shoulder to find the sheriff parking her car behind Jordan's. She strode in with a smile on her face, and I had a feeling my day was about to take a big downturn.

CHAPTER 4

AS MALLORY RAN a hand through her short black hair, I realized the store had quieted and Annabelle had disappeared into the back room. The customers stared at me while the sheriff approached. Unfortunately, they were regulars. They were used to seeing Jordan around, but a visit from the sheriff herself piqued their interest. Word would spread through the gossip vine like wildfire.

"Ms. Jones!" Mallory boomed. "It's so good to see you!"

I wished I could say the same. "Hello, Sheriff. What can I do for you?"

The customers meandered through the tables, making their way closer to the cash register. I'd been in this town long enough to realize they weren't shopping but attempting to get within earshot to gather the details of the conversation. What constituted good gossip? Details. Details always mattered.

"I wanted to discuss Doctor Butte's death," Mallory said.

Wonderful. "Okay. Should we step in back?"

Mallory shrugged. "I'm fine right here."

I smiled, despite my ire. She wanted my customers to overhear this conversation. She knew I was a private person and would like to keep my business as my own, but she had other plans. "What about it?" I asked. "I'm assuming he died of natural causes?"

She shook her head. "No. The coroner thinks he was poisoned."

I *had* seen the foam around his mouth. Someone had killed Butte. My discomfort grew, and I shifted my weight from one foot to the other.

Mallory smiled, clearly enjoying watching me squirm. "It's come to my attention that you didn't threaten his life once, but twice."

One of the customers gasped as a heaviness plummeted in my gut.

"That's not true," I said loudly to make sure the clients heard me. "Who told you that?"

"Well, I have video of it," she said, pulling out her phone. "Some of the good citizens of Heywood were very kind to provide me with the documentation yesterday at the Farmers Market. They were quite eager to share it."

Crud. Why did everyone have to film everything? Why couldn't we just go about our lives and mind our own business?

I sighed and fought back tears. "Look, Sheriff. Doctor Butte and I had a long history. He didn't like me and I didn't like him. If I said anything of the sort, it was because I lost my temper. Butte was really pushing my buttons. I'd never actually hurt anyone."

She grinned again and narrowed her gaze while crossing her arms over her chest. "It's also interesting that you were standing right next to him when he died."

I pursed my lips and tried to put my thoughts in order over the sound of the blood pounding in my ears. "What does that mean?" I asked, although I had an idea of where she was headed with her questions.

"Well, let's see," she said, her voice dripping with sarcasm. "You threatened the man twice. Then you were standing right next to him when he died, so maybe, just maybe, you went through with it."

"So you think I poisoned him?" I asked. The customers weren't bothering to pretend to be interested in the products before them. Instead, their gazes bobbed from me to Mallory, as if they were watching a tennis match.

"It's definitely a theory that I like," she replied. "Of course, I'm looking into everyone who was in attendance when he died."

Okay, she had to find another idea to interest her because I didn't want to be a suspect in a murder investigation once again.

"And let's say that I did indeed kill Doctor Butte," I said. "How exactly did I deliver the poison?"

"Is that a confession?" she asked, her eyebrow raised.

"Of course not," I snapped, now losing my temper. "It's a valid question. If you think I killed the man, I'd like to know how."

Jordan cleared his throat as a reminder to keep myself in check.

"We're working on that," Mallory said. "My guess is that you stuck him with a needle or something."

I ran a hand over my curls hoping my features didn't show my exasperation. I was trying hard to be civil, but I was slipping. "And the fact that he was eating hot sauce and a cracker at that time? Do you think perhaps the food could've been poisoned?"

I didn't want to get Chris Raves, the owner of Too Hot To Handle, involved. I really didn't. Guilt washed through me at the possible implication of my words. However, Mallory was once again focused on me for another murder. I needed to push the spotlight elsewhere.

"Yes, I've thought about that," she replied. "But what Chris Raves doesn't have is a motive, Ms. Jones. And, he's never threatened Doctor Butte for all the world to see. Not even once, let alone twice."

"And what's my motive?" I asked.

"You said it yourself. You and Doctor Butte had never gotten along. I've heard him refer to your store as a witch's hut, and that your plants kill people. For the sake of your business, you can't have someone saying those things about you. Get rid of Doctor Butte and the problem goes away."

She had me dead in her sights. Although she claimed to be interested in other parties, I was too familiar with her. Mallory was coming for me.

I understood why Jordan wanted me to keep my cool. I was in a huge amount of trouble and anything I said could very well make it a lot worse.

Time to end the conversation, but Mallory had other ideas.

"I'd like to take a look around your place," she said, gesturing to the back room. "Your business and your apartments."

As I glanced over at Jordan, he shook his head ever so slightly. I shouldn't allow it.

"Do you have a warrant?" I asked.

"Do you have something to hide?" Mallory shot back.

"No," I said sweetly. "But before I allow the police to snoop around my personal space and my store, especially during business hours, I'd like a warrant."

As expected, Mallory's smile faded. I'd quickly learned she was lazy and preferred to take shortcuts whenever she could.

"Very well," she said. "I'll be back after I speak to the judge."

"See you then," I muttered under my breath as she turned and marched out of the store.

One customer followed her out, while the other two stared at me, their mouths slightly ajar.

"I didn't do anything," I said. "The sheriff is barking up the wrong tree, so to speak."

The desperation in my voice irritated me and anger warmed my cheeks. The women slowly nodded and quickly exited.

Hanging my head, I sighed.

Jordan walked around the counter and took me in his arms. "It's going to be okay." I laid my head against his chest, reveling in the warmth and assurance he provided.

"I thought you were working today?" I stepped away from him. "Where's your uniform?"

With a sigh, he placed his hands on his hips. "Since I was with you, I'm under investigation as well. So, I've been put on paid leave."

"You've got to be kidding me!" I exclaimed.

"Nope. She's asked me a thousand questions indicating she either thinks I was involved in the murder, or at a minimum, I knew it was going to take place. Then she put me on leave."

"Oh, Jordan," I said. "I'm so sorry she's involved you in this. I apologize."

"No need." Placing his hands on my shoulders, he gave them a squeeze and smiled. "We know what she's capable of. We'll get through this, okay?"

Annabelle and Doug rounded the corner from the back room as he kissed the tip of my nose.

"We heard everything!" she said. "That woman is the biggest jerk ever!"

"Really, she is," Doug said. "There's not a person in town who would believe that Sam could kill someone."

Except the women who had listened to Mallory question me, and then left.

"Okay, okay, let's put our heads together," Jordan said. "We need to be rational about this. We know Sam didn't kill Doctor Butte."

"Right," Doug and Annabelle said in unison.

"Then who did?" Jordan asked.

His question was met with silence.

I stared at the floor and tried to recall the moment Butte had collapsed. He'd eaten the cracker with hot sauce and almost immediately began coughing and sputtering. Who had been around us? Of course, Chris Raves. But there had been people there. I just hadn't paid any attention to who they were.

"Did you notice who was close by when Butte hit the ground?" I asked Jordan.

He shook his head. "I remember a couple other people there, but no, I didn't place any names with faces."

"It seems silly to me that Mallory believes someone stuck him with a needle," Doug said. "Why would anyone do that when they could simply poison the offerings at the Farmers Market?"

He had a point.

"Mallory must think that's a valid theory or she never would've kept all the vendor offerings, right?" I asked. "She's going to have everything tested and then she'll find out who really killed him!"

I smiled, now satisfied that the truth would prevail. Relief washed through me. Her coming to my store and questioning me had to be part of a game she was playing to make me uncomfortable.

"I don't know, Sam," Annabelle said. She crossed her arms over her chest. "Mallory seemed pretty intent on taking you down for this."

"Annabelle's right," Jordan said. "I think you're giving her too much credit."

"You don't know that for sure because you're out of the loop," I replied as I clung to my last shred of hope.

"Not totally." Jordan smiled and pulled out his phone. "Trevor has agreed to pass me information. He knows I'm being railroaded."

Trevor. Of course. The deputy who had arrested the dance instructor who had tried to kill me a few months ago. He'd also reported to Jordan about that case behind Mallory's back.

"Are we back to using burner phones?" I asked.

Jordan shook his head. "I don't think so. Trevor will let us know, though. The only way I see that happening is if he feels like Mallory is suspicious and he's worried about her seeing his phone."

I glanced over my empty store.

"You can't count on Mallory to do the right thing, Sam." Jordan gently laid his hand on my shoulder. "I think we better do some digging ourselves."

I slowly nodded, realizing he was right. Word that I was the center of a murder investigation would spread like wildfire throughout town. People wouldn't come into the store. As much as I wanted her to do her job, Mallory had a solid record of looking for the easy way to solve murders. For the death of Doctor Butte, she'd found it in me. I had motive and opportunity. She even had video of me threatening him.

I was done for if I didn't fight back.

CHAPTER 5

TWO LONG DAYS passed as we waited for word from the sheriff's office. I'd been right—the store was dead because people thought I'd killed Butte. Everyone was talking about it according to Gina, who owned File It Away, the local nail salon.

"And I mean *everyone*," Gina said, tucking a lock of blonde hair behind her ear. She'd come into the store with her dog, Daisy, which had caused Catnip to make a run for the apartment upstairs. The cute brown and white mutt sniffed around while Gina leaned against the counter. "I had the salon open for business yesterday, and I swear every other person was talking about you."

"What exactly were they saying?" I asked.

"That if anyone knew how to kill in a non-lethal way, it was you," Gina said.

I appreciated her lack of sugar-coating, but I still winced. "What does that even mean?" I asked.

"The plants," she said, gesturing around the store. "Plants can be poison!"

"Only some of them," I muttered. "When used correctly, most have wonderful medicinal value."

"I bet you can name five plants right off the tip of your tongue that are poisonous."

Water Hemlock, Deadly Nightshade, White Snakeroot, Castor Bean, Rosary Pea.

Dang it. She was right.

"Ha!" she yelled while pushing her glasses up her nose. "I knew it! I can tell by the look on your face!"

I sighed and rolled my eyes. "But I didn't kill him."

"Well, as one woman pointed out, you played a murderer on your soap opera, so you were quite familiar with the art of taking a life."

"That was a television show!" I exclaimed. "I couldn't get away with any of the stuff I did on TV!"

"Well, you killed a lot of people on that show in a lot of different ways."

I stared at my friend and shook my head. "Why are you making a case against me?"

She snorted and glanced at the dog. "Hang on, Daisy. Just a minute."

Turning my attention to Daisy, I tried to figure out how Gina knew what she wanted. The canine had taken a seat on the floor and watched us carefully.

"What does she need?" I asked.

"Bathroom."

I arched an eyebrow at my friend. The last thing I needed was to have the dog urinating in my store.

"Don't worry. She's got a rock-solid bladder and I'll leave in a minute," Gina said. "Let's get back to the gossip going around."

"Let's not," I groaned.

"What are you going to do about it?" she asked. "You have to clear your name, right?"

"I was hoping Mallory would do the right thing and look elsewhere for the killer."

"Not going to happen. You know that, Sam. You aren't that naive. So, what's the plan?"

I leaned over the counter and lowered my voice as if my store was teeming with customers I didn't want to overhear me. Unfortunately, that wasn't the case. "We're waiting to see what Trevor has to say," I said. "Since Jordan is on leave, Trevor's the one feeding us information."

"Has he said anything so far?"

I shook my head. "They're waiting for autopsy results. He said he'd let Jordan know as soon as they come in."

"Trevor's a good guy," Gina said. "He grew up here. I've known him practically my whole life."

"He seems like it," I said. "He knows Jordan and I aren't killers and that Mallory is wrong."

"Well, just about everyone knows that," Gina said.

"You just got done telling me that the ladies at the nail salon thought otherwise."

"That's true. I should've said that anyone with half a brain knows you two are innocent. I swear, some of my clients are operating at a quarter of a brain at best."

Daisy whined and Gina looked over to her again. "I better get this one outside. I'll see you later."

I waved as they exited and disappeared up the street. With a sigh, I tried to ignore the silence of the store. We'd been so dead, Annabelle had taken the afternoon off, and Jordan and Doug had gone fishing. I was left by my lonesome to manage a place that didn't need managing.

"Better to keep busy than wallow in worry," I muttered, then headed to the back room to check the online store. Thankfully, we had customers all over the world who didn't keep up on the local Heywood news. I had a few orders to fill. As I walked around and picked up the items ordered, I did so with gratitude in my heart. The sales hadn't been large, but with the way business was going, I appreciated every dime.

After packing up the orders and getting them labeled, I sat down on the back stairs and played a game of solitaire on my phone. Perhaps I should close the store and take a walk? If I did that, I would be missing out on any possible business. "But if I don't do something, I'm going to go crazy with boredom," I muttered.

When the front door chimes rang, I sprung up and hurried to the front room where I found Trevor.

"Hey," I said. "What are you doing here?"

Blond with a piercing green gaze, he eyed me warily. "I can only stay a second, and you never saw me. Understand?"

With a nod, I furrowed my brow as a feeling of dread spread through my chest. "What's up?"

"I wanted to give you and Jordan the run down on what's going on with the investigation."

"He's not here," I said. "He went fishing."

Trevor rolled his eyes. "Figures. Okay, Sam, listen up. There weren't any needle marks on Butte's body. He was poisoned by ingesting something."

"Well, that takes me off the hook," I sighed. "I didn't give him anything to eat."

"Sorry, no. Mallory thinks that maybe you poisoned the cracker and hot sauce before he ate it."

I stared at him, slack jawed. "How the heck did I do that?"

"That's what she's working on. I don't know how she's going to prove it." He glanced over his shoulder. "Listen, I need to run. Tell Jordan to text me when he's back."

When he turned and walked out, I closed my eyes for a moment. I hated Mallory with such a passion, I wanted to smack her in the face.

Instead, I decided to take a walk. A stroll down the Riverwalk would calm me down and, on my way back up Comfort Road, I could mail my online orders and stop in to see Chris at Too Hot To Handle. He was the obvious murderer. After handing Butte the cracker, he'd died. But what was Chris's motive?

Besides Chris, I really needed to think about who else was there that day and why they'd want Butte dead.

Just as I was packing up, Annabelle burst through the door. "What are you doing here?" I asked. "I thought you were taking the afternoon off?"

"I had to show you this," she said breathlessly. "You aren't going to believe it."

She pulled out her phone as sweat trickled down the side of her face.

"Were you running?" I asked.

"Yes." She swiped at her face. "I knew you had to see this, like, right away."

"What is it?"

"Shh! Just let me find it. Oh, my gosh. It's so perfect!"

I waited patiently while she tapped at her phone with shaky fingers. TikTok came up and I groaned. My old co-star, Bradley Bass, had put up an video of me around the beginning of the year, which hadn't been very flattering and quite embarrassing. That had been one of the core drivers in my true identity being revealed. "I don't want to see anything, Annabelle," I muttered. It had taken me months to get over the humiliation I'd felt the last time I'd been on TikTok.

"You'll want to see this," she said.

I began to argue, but then Bradley's face popped up on the screen. "Here it is!" Annabelle squealed. "It's amazing!"

After she pushed play, he said, "Hey, there! My name's Bradley Bass. You may know me from *As The Years Turn*, the soap opera that is really terrible now. And just so you know, I'm the biggest loser Hollywood has ever seen."

Narrowing my gaze at the screen, I wasn't sure I was hearing him correctly.

"Not only can I not act, I'm also a functioning drunk. And I have a small—"

"Oh, my gosh!" I yelled. "Annabelle, what is that!"

She dissolved into a fit of giggles. "Look! It's got ten thousand views and it's only been up for three hours!"

I pulled off my glasses and squinted at the image again. It looked like Bradley Bass, but there was no way he'd ever say any of those things.

Then a sickening feeling settled in my stomach. Annabelle spun around in a circle, giggling maniacally. She'd obviously been responsible for the video.

"You didn't," I whispered.

"I did!" She jumped up and down. "I told you I was going to get revenge on this jerk for what he did to you, and I finally did it!"

"How? What did you do?"

"Well, my usual methods of revenge weren't going to fly with him because he's out in Hollywood living under his own lock and key. So, I had to, like, get creative. I saw an article about deepfakes, and I started asking around in some chatrooms online. It didn't take long to find a guy in Romania who had some talent."

I stared at the paused screen again. Yes, it did resemble him, but there was something off. Most likely people who were familiar with him would be able to detect it, but the average person certainly wouldn't.

A quick thrill ran through me. Karma, in the form of Annabelle, had hit Bradley Bass square in the face.

"He'll look for whoever did this," I said, slipping my glasses back on.

"I know. And he'll never find him. He routed through twelve different countries, and if Bradley does go down that rabbit hole, he'll find that one of the I.P.s is his own house."

"How long are you going to leave it up?" I asked. "It can be deleted, right?"

"Probably a day or so," she said. "Then I'll take it down. Just long enough for him to get the same treatment you did."

Pursing my lips, I tried to imagine Bradley when he got a look at the video. Enraged wasn't a strong enough word. I couldn't imagine the hell he'd rain down on those around him. I'd been around him enough times during my long career at *As The Years Turn* to see it more than once, especially when he'd been drinking.

I hated being petty and admitting that I was secretly thrilled with the video, but then my heart went out to the crew who would suffer from his wrath. Those people had been good to me, and a lot of them I considered friends. "Take it down, Annabelle."

"No!" she wailed, her gaze wide. "After what he did to you, he deserves it!"

"I agree," I replied. "But he's a jerk and he's going to make people's lives miserable, if he hasn't already. Some of those people were very kind to me and I don't want to see them suffer."

She sighed and stared at me a long while, then nodded. After a few taps on her phone, she smiled, then set it down. "You're such a good person, Sam. I didn't give thought to any of that."

"You don't know him," I said. "He's a drunk and a jerk."

"I just wanted to get back at him for what he did to you."

"I know," I said, taking her into an embrace. I wasn't sure this focus

310

on revenge was good for her, but I sure found it amusing. "I appreciate you looking out for me."

After a moment, she stepped away and exclaimed, "Oh! I found out how Kathy Richmond died."

The woman Butte had accused me of murdering and we'd treated for stress. "How?"

"She was mountain biking and went over the handlebars, then smashed her head on a rock."

Wincing, I said, "That's awful."

"Yeah, but at least we didn't kill her like Butte said." She pointed at my bag. "Where are you going?"

"For a walk," I said. "Then, hopefully, to catch a killer."

CHAPTER 6

I HEADED out the back door and took the path to the Riverwalk. For a few brief moments, I forgot my troubles as the river rafters floated by. Screams of joy and laughter echoed around us, and I smiled while trying to figure out why I'd never gone rafting. I wanted to, but I'd never gotten around to it. Maybe this summer I'd dip my toes in the water, so to speak.

The Riverwalk was crowded with both locals and tourists while the restaurant decks above were packed with people enjoying their day in the sunshine with Heywood's finest food offerings. I passed a few locals I was acquainted with who wouldn't meet my gaze. Gina had been right. People were talking and spreading rumors about me being a murderer and now I'd become the town pariah.

As I approached the end of the Riverwalk, I eyed the grassy area where the geese hung out with a wary eye. Thankfully, they all seemed to be napping. I'd witnessed them chase people before, but I never understood what set them off. Trying to make myself as inconspicuous as possible, I hustled up the hill to Comfort Road, relieved the birds didn't give me a second look. The last thing I needed was to be pursued by geese.

I mailed my packages, then walked up the road a bit to Too Hot To Handle.

It quickly became apparent no one besides me suspected Chris Raves of murder. His store was packed.

I meandered around and studied his offerings as I listened to him charm his customers with stories of how he grew his peppers in his backyard, give recommendations on what hot sauces complimented which foods, and tell a few really bad jokes.

How do you tell how hot a red hot chili pepper is?

Give it a weigh, give it a weigh, give it a weigh now.

WHAT DO you get when you cross a chili pepper, steam shovel, and a Chihuahua?

A hot-diggety dog.

As his customers laughed, I rolled my eyes and turned away. Terrible jokes. Absolutely terrible.

After a while, the store finally cleared out.

"Sam!" he greeted me. "How good to see you! What can I do for you?"

I smiled as he embraced me, then I stepped away to put some space between us. How odd for him to hug me as if we were long lost friends. My internal alarm bells sounded danger. Had a killer just wrapped his arms around me? But I couldn't leave, no matter how badly I wanted to. I had to clear my name.

"I wanted to stop in and see how you were doing after... well, you know," I said.

"Butte's death?"

"Yes."

His bright grin faded. "That was horrible. I'd never seen a man die right in front of me." He glanced around the store as if to make sure no one was there. "I'm guessing he had a heart attack or something? Have you heard?"

Interesting. Apparently the gossip hadn't reached Chris, or he was playing ignorant. "I don't believe so."

"What then?" he asked, his brow furrowed in confusion. "A stroke? Or did he have some other medical issue?"

How much did I tell him? Eventually, he'd know the truth, so I decided to be an open book. "Word around town is the authorities think he was poisoned."

His gaze widened while his jaw slackened. "Poisoned?!"

I nodded and studied him, searching for any indication that he was aware. Nothing. Just surprise.

"How? How was he poisoned?" he asked.

Pursing my lips together, I shrugged. "Well, a little birdie told me it may have been something he ingested."

"At the Farmers Market? Or somewhere else?"

"The market," I replied. "It was a pretty quick death, so they're guessing he ate or drank something there."

"Dang it," he replied shaking his head. "What a tragedy. What do they think killed him?"

"I'm not sure," I said. "I would guess the coroner would look at the stomach contents and figure it out from there. But I really don't have any idea how all that works."

Slowly, his mouth drew into a tight line. "Wait a minute. I gave him a sample, and then he dropped to the ground. Do they think I did it?"

I chose my answer carefully. It had been said Mallory was looking to pin the killing on me because I had the motive and opportunity. But what I didn't possess was the means. However, Chris had. I didn't want to offend him, but I also had other questions—ones that were tough to ask. "If they haven't been here to speak with you, then I doubt it."

His shoulders sagged. "Good. I didn't have a problem with Butte. I have no reason to kill him."

Of course not. In my experience, every killer said something similar about their victim.

I picked up a bottle labeled 5 Alarm Fire, which was rated five peppers, and debated whether to buy it. Maybe a drop or two would add a little life to my taco recipe.

"That's really good on eggs," Chris said.

"Good to know," I muttered, and set it down. "Did you have a relationship with Butte? Were you friends?"

"No. I'd been to see him a few times in the past decade as a patient, but I wouldn't say we were friends."

"Is that when you moved here?" I asked. "Ten years ago?"

"Yes. I moved up from Phoenix."

"Why?"

"Mainly the summers," he replied. "I hated the summers. I prefer four seasons. Some days, I don't even mind the snow."

I wished I could say the same. "And you met your wife here?"

"Yes. We dated four years before we tied the knot. Just had our second baby. Cute little girl. Doesn't sleep worth a darn, but we've decided to keep her."

I laughed, despite the fact I thought I may be staring at the murderer. I just needed to figure out his motive.

"Did you think Butte was a good doctor?" I asked. When he furrowed his brow, I quickly added, "I've heard different rumors. I was wondering what your experience with him had been."

"He was fine. I'm not a big fan of going to the doctor, so I only go when necessary. Like the one time I had strep throat that wouldn't clear up on its own. Or when I sliced open my foot and he put some stiches in."

I nodded, grasping for anything that would give me a motive. "What about your wife? Did she see him as well?"

A shadow passed over his face so quickly, I wondered if I'd imagined it.

"Yeah, she did," he sighed. "But no trouble there, either."

As he glanced all around the store, I realized he was lying. So something had happened between Butte and his wife.

"What's Jordan up to?" Chris asked, changing the subject. "Usually he stops in while on patrol."

"He's been off work for a few days." No sense telling him the full story. He may not want to speak with me any longer if he knew Jordan and I were both suspects.

"You and Butte sure went at it," he said. "I heard about him picketing your store the day before he died, and I saw you yelling at him at the Farmers Market."

I nodded since there was no sense denying anything. "Yes. We butted heads quite a bit."

"Over what?"

"He believed my herbs were doing harm. He preferred pharmaceuticals over plants. We just had different views of what is good for people's health and what isn't. He wasn't nice about it, either."

"That's too bad, Sam. Has Mallory talked to you about the murder?"

I shook my head and waited for my nose to begin growing. "No, she hasn't."

"I'm surprised to hear that," Chris said. "It sounds like you've got a motive to kill him, especially with him picketing your store."

Well, well, well. He was turning the tables on me.

"I mean, that can't be good for business," Chris continued, a small smile playing his lips. "No one wants to visit a place that's being picketed."

"It didn't help, no," I replied with a snicker. "I can't believe you're accusing me of murdering Butte."

"Oh, I didn't accuse you," Chris said, smiling. "I was just making an observation. It would seem to me that if anyone in town wanted Butte dead, it would be you. But that doesn't mean I think you did it."

Based on the satisfied smile, I had a feeling that was exactly what he meant. "I didn't expect this conversation to go quite like this," I said, crossing my arms over my chest.

"Why not? Isn't that what you came in here to do to me? Accuse me of murdering the good doctor?"

"No," I shot back.

"Really? Asking me all those questions about my relationship with Butte? If I ever had a problem with him?" He shook his head and crossed his arms over his chest, mirroring my stance. "All that sounds like you're looking for a motive."

Okay, so I hadn't been as sneaky as I thought. "I'm not trying to pin Butte's death on you."

I was caught by surprise as he threw his head back and laughed. Almost maniacally... Or was it my imagination? "Why don't you leave, Sam?" he asked. "I really feel like you're trying to gather information so you can take it to the sheriff since I was the one who gave him the cracker and hot sauce."

"I'm really not trying to do that," I replied. "I just—"

"Get out!" he yelled, then took a couple steps toward me.

With a yelp, I headed for the door, my heart racing at his threatening actions.

As I hurried down the street back toward Sage Advice, my fear turned to rage. Okay, sure, he'd been right and I was trying to fish for information. But for him to come at me like that?

I may have been probing around for a motive, but his reaction made me wonder if I'd hit a nerve and I had just been in the company of Butte's murderer.

CHAPTER 7

I ARRIVED BACK at the store to find Annabelle hunched over her tinctures while Bon Jovi's *Wanted, Dead or Alive* blasted from the boom box so loudly, she didn't hear me walk in.

After I turned off the sound, she shrieked and lurched away from me. "You just scared me to death!"

"Sorry," I muttered while setting down my bag.

"What's wrong?" she asked. "You seem angry."

How astute. "I was just at Too Hot To Handle, and Chris accused me of murdering Butte."

She narrowed her gaze. "Well, we need to prove him wrong."

I sighed and sat down on a stool next to her. "How?"

"You need to find the killer yourself, Sam." She elbowed me in the ribs. "Come on. You've done this before."

"Where do I start?" I asked, laying my head down on my hands on top of the table. "I'm too tired."

"You better shake yourself out of that nonsense," Annabelle muttered. "Or you're going to jail for killing Butte. And I can tell you right now—orange isn't your color."

My phone rang in my bag, but I ignored it.

"Come on, get up," she ordered. "We're leaving."

"Where are we going?"

"To Gina's. We're putting together a rock-solid plan to find the killer."

Right. A plan. It may have been a good idea to come up with one before I decided to question Chris.

Annabelle's phone dinged and I sat up.

"Let's go," she said, studying the screen. "Gina's at home. We'll put our brains together and figure out who killed Butte."

With a groan, I rallied a little energy and grabbed my bag once again. I followed her out the front door to her car, then slid into the passenger side. Van Halen—David Lee Roth, not Sammy Haggar—blasted from the speakers as she pulled out onto Comfort Road.

As we drove, she turned down the music. "Did you ever meet David Lee Roth?" she asked. "He was so darn cute back in the best decade ever."

I smiled and nodded. "Yes, I met the whole band."

"Oh, my gosh!" she screeched, almost driving into an oncoming car. I grabbed the steering wheel and yanked it to bring us back into our lane. Horns from every direction sounded and I clutched my chest, certain I was about to have a heart attack.

"Tell me everything!" she shouted, completely oblivious, or simply not caring about the chaos she'd caused. "Eddie Van Halen... oh, my word! That smile could melt paint off a wall!"

"I'll tell you when we get to Gina's," I muttered. I didn't want to risk another accident.

Annabelle grumbled something indecipherable then we rode the rest of the way in silence.

I sighed with relief when we pulled into the driveway of the white house with blue trim and a little sign out front that read, *Heywood Hounds*. Driving with Annabelle sometimes scared me to death, and I was happy to be at our destination unscathed.

As we walked up the path to the front door, the dogs began barking from inside. I'd never been to Gina's house when it was quiet, and with her dedication to rescuing dogs, I imagined I never would.

"Hey!" she said as Daisy and Sing ran out to sniff Annabelle and me.

I waited for the dogs to become acquainted with me and give me a pass, then I brushed by Gina and went inside.

"Let's go into to the kitchen," she said.

A little white terrier stood at the food bowl, glaring at us.

"Who's that?" I asked.

"Banshee," Gina replied. "Don't ask how she got her name. It's a long story."

The dog began to bark, her high pitch yapping stinging my ears. Daisy hurried over to her and stared down at her as if willing her to be quiet. When the barking continued, Daisy laid her paw on Banshee's head and growled. That settled her down.

"Daisy seems to have taken her place as queen of the castle," I said.

"More like the overlord, but yes. She's in charge."

We sat at the table and the dogs curled up under it.

"So what's this meeting of great minds about?" Gina asked.

"Sam needs a plan," Annabelle said. "She, like, needs to find the killer."

"Here we go again," Gina muttered, shaking her head. "I take it you found out Butte was murdered?"

I nodded. "Trevor confirmed it today. There weren't any needle marks on the body, so they're assuming he ingested something."

"It seems the person who would be responsible for Butte's death would be Chris Raves," Gina mused. "He gave him the cracker and hot sauce, then Butte dropped dead. Case closed."

"I agree," I replied, "and I'm not taking his name off the table. I was at Too Hot To Handle earlier today and he became very caustic toward me when we were discussing the murder."

Gina pushed her glasses up her nose. "I'm assuming he didn't confess."

"Not in the least," I said. "In fact, he accused *me*, saying that I had a motive."

"Well, he's not wrong," Gina pointed out.

"True, but I didn't do it."

"We know that," Annabelle said, patting my hand as if she were talking to a child.

"Okay, so who did?" Gina asked. "Since the old coot was poisoned by something he ate or drank, we have to look at all the vendors there, right?"

"Exactly," Annabelle said. "And figure out why someone would want him dead."

I thought back to the bright, sunny afternoon at the Farmers Market. "You know, Jordan and I visited almost every booth there for samples, and I remember thinking Butte was following us."

"Now we're getting somewhere," Gina said, shooting to her feet. She turned and hurried to the counter. After pulling open a drawer, she rummaged through it, muttering something about needing to clean up the mess. It made me think of my own kitchen junk drawer. Didn't every house have one drawer that became the catch-all for miscellaneous things?

Gina returned to the table with a pad of paper and a pen. "Okay, let's take some notes and make a map. How many vendors do you think were there?"

I closed my eyes and tried to mentally count the tables.

"Maybe twenty?" Annabelle said.

"I think there may have been more," I said.

"Well, Sage Advice and Heywood Hounds were present," Gina said, chuckling as she wrote down the names. "That I remember."

"Never Quit Wining, Berry Good, and Skippity Scones," I replied. "I remember those."

"Oh! Don't forget about On The River!" Annabelle exclaimed. "Sally was there! Weren't her burritos to die for?"

"And Too Hot To Handle." I tapped the table between Gina and me. "Write him down."

After making our map and labeling the drawn squares with the corresponding vendor, conversation slowly drifted from Sally's amazing burritos to the artists who had been present.

"You know, just because they didn't outright serve any type of food or drink doesn't mean they didn't poison him," Annabelle said. "A lot of them had little candies and stuff."

"That's a really good point," I muttered. "It literally could've been anyone there."

We sat in silence for a long moment and my mood deflated even further. How in the world was I going to prove I didn't kill Butte?

Daisy came out from under the table and laid her head on Gina's thigh.

"In a minute," Gina said.

Narrowing my gaze on my friend and her canine, I wondered how Gina knew what Daisy wanted. Was she that in tune with the dog? Or had some secret language passed between them?

"Okay, so here's what you should do," Gina said. "You mentioned that it felt like Butte was following you. Therefore, you need to go see the vendors you visited, the ones where you're sure the doctor was right after you."

"And ask them about Butte," Annabelle finished. "But be sly about it, Sam. Don't, like, accuse anyone of anything."

Gina tapped her pen on the table and remained quiet for a long moment, as if in deep thought. "There's one other avenue I think we better explore."

"What's that?" I asked.

"Butte's wife."

For some reason, her words stunned me. I never imagined in a million years that Butte would be married. I guess I considered him such a huge jerk, I couldn't picture someone putting up with him.

"What about her?" Annabelle asked.

Gina cleared her throat and glanced from Annabelle to me then back again. "I don't like to gossip."

At File It Away, Gina heard all the chin-wagging in town. In fact, I'd say her store, along with the coffee shop, were the two places I'd go if I wanted to listen to the rumor mill and gossip vine in full swing.

"Oh, for goodness sake, Gina," I said, rolling my eyes. "You *do* like to gossip almost as much as you like to breathe, so spill it!"

"Yeah!" Annabelle shouted. "Spill it!"

"I do not!" Gina yelled. With a harrumph, she crossed her arms over her chest and glared at me, but a small smile played on her lips. "I don't tell anyone even half of what I hear. I distribute information as I see fit."

"Well, distribute the information on his wife," I said. "Please."

Gina sighed and placed her forearms on the table. "Okay, but you didn't hear this from me. My job requires confidentiality."

"Go on," Annabelle encouraged.

"I heard at the nail salon that Pam Butte was leaving her husband."

"How long have they been married?" I asked while Annabelle gasped.

"Forty years, give or take a year or two," Gina replied.

Annabelle let out a slow whistle. "You'd think by that point, you'd, like, just put up with each other because untangling forty years of marriage would be too much work and require too much energy."

Gina snapped her fingers and pointed at Annabelle. "Exactly. Right on the money, Annabelle. Makes you wonder, doesn't it?"

I stared at my friend for a moment, thoroughly confused. Glancing at Annabelle and her furrowed brow, I realized she wasn't tracking Gina's line of thought either.

"What does that mean?" Annabelle asked. "I don't get it."

"Think about it," Gina replied. "You've been married forty years. *Forty years.* That is such a long time. Half a lifetime for some people. Everything is in both your names. You've spent decades buying things together. Time has passed and you've had disagreements. He's driven you crazy, and you've done the same to him."

She stood and began pacing the small kitchen and continued. "Then, one morning, he's eating his cereal and you can't stand anything about him. Just the sound of him chewing makes you want to stick a knife in his eye, and you realize that you're past the point of no return. There's nothing but disgust and irritation in your heart toward your husband, but gosh darn it, when you think about what it takes to unravel forty years of marriage, who would get what, how much is in the bank accounts... there has to be an easier way."

Having been in a similar situation, I now understood what Gina meant. When my dead husband, Gerald, and I had discussed divorce, splitting our money had seemed like an impossible task, especially since we had so many bank accounts—his, mine, and ours. One thing we had decided upon was to figure it out on our own so that lawyers wouldn't eat up a good portion of our funds.

What if Mrs. Butte had suggested a divorce, and the good doctor had vowed to fight her? Or after forty years of marriage, she just assumed he would? What if she was tired, angry and just sick of him?

"I know what would be easier," I muttered.

"What's that?" Annabelle asked.

"Murder."

CHAPTER 8

I CHEWED my lip as I stared at my friends. Goosebumps crawled over my skin. Holy moly. We were on to something.

Except...

"Was she even at the Farmers Market?" I asked.

Annabelle shrugged. "I didn't see her, but I doubt she'd come near the Sage Advice table, especially after what her husband put us through. For all we know, she felt the same way as him."

"She was there," Gina said. "She stopped by to see Sing and Daisy. We chatted for a hot minute while she petted the dogs, then she continued to walk around."

"Was she there with Butte?" I asked.

"That I don't know," Gina replied. "I didn't see them together, and I didn't pay attention to her after she left."

"If she was there with Butte, she could've easily poisoned him," I said. "She could've gotten him something to eat or drink, slipped in the poison and given it to him."

"That's, like, super cold," Annabelle said. "Especially if she stood back and watched him die."

I recalled when Butte went to the ground. There hadn't been any hysterical elderly women around worried about him. Yes, it would've been cold to poison your husband and watch him die, but wanting someone dead didn't equal to a whole lot of warm and fuzzies in someone's heart. "Maybe she poisoned him and then left," I mused. "Maybe she wanted him dead but didn't want to actually witness the whole process."

"That's possible," Gina said. She stood, opened the back door, and Daisy led the pack outside. As they chased each other, I smiled. To be one of Gina's dogs and not have to worry about going to prison for murder—what a wonderful feeling it must be.

After a moment, she shut the door and sat down with us again. She picked up the pen and wrote across the page: *Mrs. Butte.*

Then she underlined it twice.

~

ANNABELLE and I headed back to Sage Advice to find Jordan and Doug had returned from the fishing trip and once again, zero customers in my store. Stress knotted my stomach. I needed customers to keep the lights on and food in Catnip's stomach, not to mention Annabelle's.

As I gave Jordan a kiss, I watched Annabelle and Doug carefully. There were no signs of affection, no sly looks, no quick hand squeezes. My imagination must have gotten the best of me. Nothing seemed to be going on between the two.

I quickly explained my plan of action to find the killer: interview all the people who had manned booths I knew Butte had visited and figure out if they had a motive to kill him.

"You have a lot of people to talk with," Doug said. "He wasn't well-liked."

"I know," I sighed. "Jordan and I stopped at almost every booth, and I feel like I saw Butte everywhere I was. I'm heading over to Never Quit Wining since they're right next door." I turned to Jordan. "Do you want to go with me? You've got some skin in this game since Mallory thinks you may be involved."

"Sure," he said. "And I'd feel better if you took me to see all the people you want to speak with. If you do run into the killer, things could be dangerous for you."

I snorted and shook my head. "You should've been there when I stopped by Too Hot To Handle this morning. He was very defensive and rude."

"Chris was?" Jordan asked, his eyes wide in surprise. "I've never seen him be rude. Usually he's as friendly as can be and tells really bad jokes."

"Well, that was my experience."

Jordan ran his hand over his whiskered chin. "Huh. That's really odd."

"It makes him look guilty," Annabelle said.

I couldn't agree more. In fact, he was still fighting for first place on my suspect list. "Let's go next door and see Adrienne and Wayne," I said, grabbing Jordan's hand.

We hurried through the store, out the back door and over to Never Quit Wining. I tapped on the back door, glad that I'd become such fast friends with the younger couple.

"I don't think they had anything to do with Butte's death," I muttered.

"Why?"

With a sigh, I shook my head. "I just don't feel it in my gut."

"You don't solve a murder on gut feelings alone," Jordan said. "Those are important, but evidence is necessary."

"Right," I sighed. "They have the means, but they're really nice people. If Butte—"

The door swung open and Wayne smiled at us. Tall, lanky with shoulder length, straight brown hair, he reminded me a bit of John Lennon's late-Beatle days when he protested war from his bed. "Hey! Are you out of wine already, Sam? If so, I think we need to have a talk."

"Ha, ha," I said. "Not quite. I was hoping to steal a few minutes of your time, though."

"Sure. Adrienne's up front with some customers. Come on in and she'll be with us in a minute."

I loved what they'd done to the back room. The small alcove was gone, which really opened the space. They'd also taken down the shelving and replaced it with oak wine racks. I inhaled the earthy scent as I took a seat at the small table. It happened to be set up where Mr.

Mason's body had been found when the building was Knit Wit and Mrs. Mason had killed him. I tried not to think about it.

"It sounds like business is good," I said as laughter filtered from the front of the store. All the stores in town but mine seemed to have customers.

"It's been great," Wayne replied. "The locals have really supported us."

Must be nice.

"What can I do for you?" Wayne asked.

"You're familiar with Doctor Butte, right?" Jordan began.

"Sure. If you've lived in this town long enough, you've visited Butte."

"Did you see him at the Farmers Market?" I asked, knowing full well they had. I'd been at their booth and Butte had stopped by shortly after. I recalled trying to guess if he was a red or white wine drinker.

"I don't remember," Wayne said. His brow furrowed while he stared at the table. "There were a lot of people there."

I also remember the large red stain down the front of Butte's shirt. At the time, I thought it had been wine.

"What's going on?" Adrienne asked as she came into the room and fell into a chair with a sigh. Tall and also lanky with curly red hair and the palest skin I'd ever seen, I often wondered if she'd ever done any modeling, but I'd never felt comfortable asking. "Did I hear you talking about Butte?"

"Yes," Jordan said. "We're trying to piece together what happened that day he died. Do you remember seeing him?"

"Sure I do," she said. "I spilled wine all over his shirt. It was an accident, but he wasn't very forgiving."

"Oh! That's right!" Wayne exclaimed, snapping his fingers. "We were out of the Merlot he likes, and you were attempting to get him to try a new one."

"He didn't have anything nice to say about that either," Adrienne sniffed. "He was as nasty as a customer as he was a doctor."

"So he's treated you in the past?" I asked.

Wayne and Adrienne exchanged glances, almost as if they were deciding how to answer.

"Yes," she finally said. "It's been years since I've seen him, though. I've been seeing a naturopath in Sedona for years."

"Why did you leave Butte's practice?" I asked.

"I just didn't appreciate his approach to medicine," she replied, shrugging. "I don't think every little ailment needs a pharmaceutical."

Smiling, I nodded in agreement. But her feelings on medicine didn't necessarily mean that they'd killed Butte. There had to be more to the story.

"Weren't you two involved in an accident a year or so back with him?" Jordan asked. "I seem to recall something about that, but I didn't respond to it."

Wayne nodded. "Yes, we were. Just outside of town. Traffic had come to a full stop to allow a deer and her fawn to cross the road. The fawn was terrified, so it took a while for mom to coax him to follow. Butte rounded the corner going full speed and slammed into the back of our car."

"I remember now," Jordan said. "Trevor from our department responded. He was angry at the way Butte had acted."

"Yes, like it was our fault," Wayne said.

I glanced over at Adrienne and noted her eyes welled with tears. "It wasn't our fault," she said, angrily swiping her fingers across her cheeks. "But because of him..."

Her voice trailed off and the front door chimes sounded. She shot to her feet and raced out of the room to help the customers, seemingly glad she didn't have to continue the conversation.

"Because of him... what happened because of Butte?" I asked.

Wayne sighed and crossed his arms over his chest, then studied the ceiling for so long, I actually glanced up expecting to see a spider or something. "We don't like to talk about it," he said quietly before meeting my gaze. "But we were coming back from visiting the naturopath in Sedona when Butte hit us. We'd just found out Adrienne was pregnant. She lost the baby the next day."

A sharp pain stabbed at my heart and I brought my hand to my chest. "Oh, my," I whispered. "I'm so sorry."

"We were too," he said. "We'd been trying for two years."

Jordan cleared his throat. "So the accident caused the loss of the baby?"

Wayne nodded. "The doctor had told us the fetus looked great. We got into the accident and Adrienne was rushed to the hospital. She then had the miscarriage. Butte was responsible, but we couldn't prove it."

"He must've hit you guys hard," Jordan probed.

"Butte was going way over the speed limit," Wayne said. "He even tried to turn it around and say it was our fault for being stopped in the road, despite the fact there were about ten cars ahead of us."

"What happened then?" Jordan asked.

"Butte's insurance paid for our car. That was the end of it." The chimes rang again and Wayne glanced over his shoulder. "If there's nothing else, I should help Adrienne."

I nodded as the three of us stood. Wayne turned toward the front of the store but stopped at the doorway. "You know, Adrienne isn't able to have kids because of him. I try to keep my thoughts upbeat and positive, but I'm glad he dropped dead. This store is our baby now." He tapped the doorframe and disappeared to the front.

Jordan and I let ourselves out the back. As he shut the door, we exchanged glances.

"Do you think they could've killed him?" I asked.

"Sure I do," Jordan replied. "There's nothing quite like the pain of losing a child."

Unfortunately, Jordan was acutely aware of that agony since he'd lost his ex-wife and little girl to a gas leak in Chicago.

"They tried to get pregnant for so long," I said as we made our way to Sage Advice. "I feel so bad for them."

"I do, too."

"But they seem so nice," I said. "I can't imagine them killing him."

Jordan held up three fingers. "Revenge is their motive and giving him the wine was the means. Everyone was present at the Farmers Market. They could've easily slipped something into the wine, or maybe the poison was in the drink Adrienne spilled on him."

"What? And it just permeated the skin?"

"It's a possibility," he said, shrugging.

330

"From the sound of it, they think he died of natural causes, or they're pretty sure no one is going to figure out they killed him."

Jordan smiled and reached out to run a finger over my cheek. "They are a bit too confident for me," he said. "They definitely have to be investigated further. I'll call Trevor at the station and see what he has to say about the accident."

"Okay, good," I said. "I feel like we're making progress."

"Me, too. We're going to figure out who murdered Butte, and we're going to bring his killer to justice, whether he deserves it or not."

CHAPTER 9

THE NEXT DAY, I met Gina at On The River, my goal being three-fold. First, I got to spend some time with my friend. Second, I would shovel Sally's homemade breakfast burritos into my mouth until I couldn't stand another bite. Third, I had some gentle questions to toss Sally's way about Butte's death. I'd seen him stop at her booth and I wondered if she had a reason to kill him.

Did I think she murdered Butte? Probably not, but I also hadn't thought my dead husband would steal millions of dollars from our friends and business associates, either. I still didn't fully trust my judgment of other people's character. And a burrito would be a perfect way to hide poison—a few drops mixed in with home-cooked goodness. Heck, he probably wouldn't even had tasted it.

As I waited for Gina, I noted a few locals giving me snide looks. They still thought I'd murdered the town doctor. In return, I simply smiled and hoped my fury at my situation didn't show on my face. I really wanted to stand up and scream that I didn't have anything to do with the man's death, but I'd keep my cool for now.

Gina walked in, late as usual. It used to bother me but I'd grown to accept it. She was one of the busiest people I'd ever met, so I tended to excuse her.

"Hey," she said, sliding into the booth across from me. "I won't apologize for being late because it seems no matter how hard I try, I can't get out the door in time."

"No worries," I said, then sipped my coffee. "Maybe try setting your clocks ahead ten minutes."

"But then I'd know they were ahead ten minutes and it wouldn't matter. I'd still be late."

Perhaps I should have Annabelle break into her home and reset the clocks for her. Something to consider.

"What are you having?" she asked, picking up the menu.

"Definitely the breakfast burritos. I sampled some at the Farmers Market and they were delicious."

"I thought you liked her oatmeal?" Gina asked as she tucked a lock of blonde hair behind her ear.

"Oh, I do, but for some reason I prefer that at dinner."

"That's weird, but okay. I'll take your word for it and then I don't have to make a decision."

Sally stopped by to top off my coffee and set a mug down in front of Gina. "What are you two lovelies having today?"

"Breakfast burritos," we said in unison.

"Good choice. Just made them an hour ago, and they are one of my better batches, if I do say so myself."

"Do you think you'll have a minute to talk?" I asked, handing the menus to her.

She glanced around the restaurant and nodded. "Let me get your food and take care of a couple other tables, then I'll be able to sit for a bit."

As she scurried away, Gina pushed her glasses up her nose and leaned over. "Why do you want to talk to Sally?"

"Because we're friends," I said.

She shook her head and smiled. "No, I think there's more to it. What's going on?"

I glimpsed around the restaurant before answering. "She was at the Farmers Market handing out samples of breakfast burritos."

"And?"

I shrugged, not wanting to admit that I was thinking my friend could possibly be the killer.

"Oh!" Gina exclaimed. "You think she killed Butte!"

"Shh!" I hushed her. "I don't want anyone to hear you!"

"Especially Sally," Gina laughed. "She'd spit in your burrito if she knew you suspected her. Either that or poison you."

"I'm sure you're right." I laughed. "I'm trying to cover all my bases and see who had a motive to want him dead."

"You're probably better off trying to figure out who *didn't* want him dead, Sam. The man was a menace."

She smiled and turned to Sally who was hurrying toward us with two large plates. As she set them down on the table, my mouth began to water. The freshly made tortilla, the scrambled eggs, the fresh herbs, the bits of bacon, onion and pepper—it was heaven on a plate.

"Oh, heck, yes," Gina whispered while she picked up her fork. "I'm so glad I have on my stretchy shorts today."

"I'll be back in a bit," Sally said.

We didn't speak for the next few moments because both of us got to shoveling food into our mouths as if we hadn't eaten in days. Frankly, I wished I had on my stretchy shorts as well. My button and zipper seemed to be barely holding together. I'd have to take the rest of my breakfast home for lunch or dinner.

"So, what's going on?" Sally said. She edged in next to me and I scooted over.

Gina pointed at her plate. "This is amazing."

"Thanks! Everything is purchased directly from the farms surrounding Heywood, so it's very fresh."

"It tastes like it was made with magic," Gina groaned.

"Nope. Just fresh herbs," Sally replied, grinning. "Glad you're enjoying it." She turned to me. "What's up, Sam?"

I'd decided to go with a different tactic instead of questioning her directly about the murder... one birthed by Gina's comment. "We were just talking about Butte, and how everyone in town seems to dislike him. What about you? What was your experience with him?"

Sally sighed and pursed her lips together. After a long moment, she said, "I don't like to gossip, Sam."

"It's not gossip," Gina replied. "It's sharing experiences. Like the time I went to see him because I had a horrible sinus infection and he put me on two different antibiotics. Was that a smart thing to do? And what is the area going to do now that he's gone? Does a new doctor move in?"

I nodded. "And what do we look for in a new doctor?"

"See, it's not gossip," Gina said. "It's understanding his flaws as our community doctor and planning for the future."

I took a long sip of coffee, impressed with the way we'd turned the discussion from a gossip session to something productive. I just hoped Sally fell for the new angle.

"Well, I never really had any problems with him," she began. "He may have complained that the bacon in the BLT wasn't done well enough, or his iced tea needed more ice, but overall, he wasn't too bad."

"What about his wife?" I asked.

"She's actually pretty nice," Sally replied. "Quiet, but nice."

"You always have to watch out for the quiet ones," Gina muttered.

I shot her a glare and hoped Sally kept talking. "So, no indication that they were having marital problems that you ever saw?" I asked.

"No, but like I said, she was quiet. Almost docile. If they were having marital problems, they kept it out of my restaurant. I don't think I ever saw them fighting in any way that I would've noticed."

"How often did they come in?" Gina asked.

"A couple times a month," Sally said, shrugging.

"So they were regulars," I offered.

"Not really," Sally replied. "I have some people who come in three times a week, like clockwork. Heck, I sometimes see you and Jordan more than that."

We sat in silence for a long moment. I stared at my half-eaten burrito and contemplated getting another one to take home.

"You know, now that I'm thinking about it, I did see them at the Farmers Market," Sally said, snapping her fingers.

"Who?" Gina asked. "Butte and his wife?"

"Yes," Sally replied. "Her name's Pam."

"When you saw them, were they there together?" I asked.

"I'm just not sure." She sighed and laced her fingers together on the tabletop. "She was at my booth and we were chatting about the new breakfast burritos. When he walked up, she did a double take... like she was surprised to see him. They didn't say much to each other, but I handed her two samples, figuring she'd give one to him. Someone else caught my attention after that."

"You didn't see her give him the plate of food?" I asked.

She shook her head. "I just don't know about him having a heart attack, though," Sally mused. "He seemed so healthy."

My eyes widened when I realized she hadn't heard he was murdered.

"There wasn't a heart attack," Gina said, lowering her voice. "He was poisoned."

With a gasp, Sally placed her hand over her mouth. "I didn't know," she whispered. "Where did you hear that?"

"Sheriff Mallory confirmed it," I said. "But you didn't get that from me. I don't want anyone to get into trouble."

"Right. Of course. Who do they think killed him?" Sally asked.

Gina pointed at me.

Sally turned and arched her eyebrow. I smiled and shrugged.

"Well, I guess I can understand that," Sally said. "You two have had more run-ins than a pair of Bighorn sheep during rutting season."

"I know," I said, not exactly sure what 'rutting season' consisted of, but if Sally believed it to be a time of severe headbutting, I'd go with it. "But I didn't kill him."

Sally grinned and shook her head. "I get it now. You didn't kill him, but the sheriff thinks you did. Now you're fishing around for who would want him dead."

Arguing would be futile, so I went with the truth. "You're correct. Mallory is coming after me. She's even put Jordan on leave because she thinks he had something to do with it."

"We should really look at replacing her, along with Doctor Butte," Sally muttered. Crossing her arms over her chest, she glanced around the restaurant.

"What is it?" I asked. "You look like you have something on your mind."

"I was just thinking about the possible food handoff between

Butte's wife and him. What if she poisoned him then, with my darn burritos?"

Gina and I exchanged glances.

"It's a possibility," Gina said. "Especially if she's divorcing him and doesn't want to go through the hassle of divorce."

"They were divorcing?" Sally asked.

"Yes," Gina replied. "I heard that at the nail salon."

"Wow," Sally said, sighing. "I hadn't heard that. I'm so out of the loop and I didn't even know it. What a shame."

"Maybe she just got tired of him," Gina said.

"There were plenty of people who had issues with Butte," Sally said. "I just didn't realize his own wife was one of them."

"Who?" I asked. "Who had trouble with him?"

"Off the top of my head, I remember Wayne and Adrienne from the wine shop coming in here and talking about a car accident they had with him. She was terribly upset. That was a while ago, though."

A tingle traveled down my spine. This was the second time I'd wondered if Wayne and Adrienne could've been upset enough to kill him.

"I was also talking to Chris Raves, and he mentioned he was angry with Butte about something."

Yes, he was, but we still didn't have the details. Whatever Butte had done to upset Chris, he wasn't letting on what it could be.

"But honestly," Sally continued, "I don't think I've ever seen anyone as upset with him as his daughter."

"His daughter!" Gina and I said in unison. I glanced across the table at her and imagined my eyes were as wide as hers.

"Would you two lower your voices?!" Sally hissed. "I can't let my customers know I'm gossiping!"

"Sorry," I whispered. "I didn't even know he had a daughter."

"Me neither," Gina muttered.

"She went to boarding school, then to college somewhere back east... she hasn't been around."

"That's really sad," Gina commented. "What's the point of having kids if you're not going to spend time with them?"

"I agree," Sally said.

"So what did his daughter say? What were they arguing about? When was this?"

"A few weeks ago," Sally said. "Pam, the doctor, and their daughter came in. We were very busy so they had to sit at one of the middle tables —not a usual booth—and Butte wasn't happy about that."

"What's the daughter's name?" I asked. "How old do you think she is?"

"Molly is her name, and I think she's maybe in her thirties. Pam is a bit younger than Butte by maybe a decade or so. You can tell they're mother and daughter. From a distance, it's hard to tell them apart."

"What did you hear Molly saying to him?"

"It was terrible," Sally said. "From the snippets of conversation I caught, I got the impression they were discussing wills and such. She didn't seem happy to be there... well, none of them did. But the one thing I did hear for sure was when she told him what an awful father he'd been and she hoped to see him dead sooner rather than later. Then she marched out of the restaurant."

CHAPTER 10

EVEN THOUGH MY store remained almost empty, I felt I had to be there—a captain going down with the sinking ship. Over the next few days, a dozen or so tourists came in and a few even purchased some goods. However, my regulars had evaporated. A few new clients called to cancel their consultations with Annabelle. Even the online orders had slowed.

If things didn't change soon, Butte would be getting his wish—there'd no longer be a Sage Advice. He'd win from the grave.

When my husband stole from our friends and associates, our bank accounts had been frozen to pay for reparations to his victims. Since I wasn't aware of his bad business dealings, I'd had my lawyer, Colin Breckshire III, petition for innocent spouse relief in the hopes of getting my earning from *As The Years Turn* back in my pocket. Unfortunately, such proceedings could take years. I wasn't holding my breath that a large check would appear in my mailbox at any day. I needed customers to pay my bills. And therefore, I had to find Butte's murderer to clear my name.

While on my own personal version of the Titanic, it gave me a lot of free time to think things through. Although Butte's wife was leaving him and his daughter hated him, I had a difficult time believing that one of them had killed him. No one could say for sure if they even saw the daughter at the Farmers Market. Annabelle was pretty certain she was there, while Gina said she wasn't. Jordan hadn't noticed her. My mind had spun many tales, including one where the mother and daughter conspired against Butte and killed him so they'd get all the money. Most likely they'd end up someplace warm with a beach view and a cute personal butler serving them drinks.

It all sounded great, but I couldn't help but consider that the killer had to be someone Butte had hurt in his medical practice. How many times had people come into Sage Advice with stories of Butte not being able to help them, or they'd been given medicine that didn't work, or worse yet, a prescription that did more harm than good? This line of thinking led to me going down the rabbit hole of the Arizona Medical Board's actions against doctors.

Of course doctors are only human, and they call it a "practice" for a reason. No doctor is infallible. Yet, reading the current actions against doctors in the area gave me a violent headache. Physicians giving known addicts opioids. Another doctor seeing patients while drunk. A surgeon arrested for disorderly conduct. Aiding and abetting in the intentional possession of a controlled substance. As I scrolled through all the interesting stories and downed another couple of Motrin, it felt like I was looking at a terrible car crash. I wanted to divert my gaze, but couldn't. The cases both horrified and fascinated me, and I truly hoped the doctors had their licenses suspended before they'd killed someone or done life-altering harm. If they'd been caught for their crimes, there had to be other victims.

"What are you doing?" Annabelle asked from behind me.

"Looking at the doctors who are in trouble with the state."

"Why?" she asked.

I'd hoped to find something on Butte, my thinking being that a past patient had been so upset, they'd filed a complaint with the board. Perhaps then, if the board hadn't given Butte a big enough punishment, the patient had killed him. Even though I'd spent hours scrolling through the online paperwork, I realized that even if I had found a case against Butte, I wouldn't know the name of the patient. They weren't listed.

My efforts had been a waste of time. "I don't know," I sighed as I rubbed my temples.

"I still think it's the wife," Annabelle said, her bracelets jangling up and down her arm as she flipped her hair over her shoulder. "She's got the most to gain, and I'd be tired of him after forty seconds of marriage, let alone forty years."

"Yes, it makes sense, but I just can't imagine the quiet woman Sally described as a killer."

I glanced up the stairs. "Where's Doug?"

"The hardware store."

"Ugh. What's broken now?" The way things were going, I may need to put off further repairs until I actually had an income.

"Nothing. I'm not supposed to say anything, but he'd like to replace the carpet in his apartment with hardwood flooring, so he went to get some samples."

Well, I certainly couldn't afford any cosmetic upgrades at this time and made a mental note to talk to him when he returned.

The front door chimes rang. I shot to my feet, startled. It had been hours since we'd heard the noise.

I glanced around the corner to find a woman walking in. Annabelle gasped. Small in stature, thin with an erect spine, I placed her in her late sixties. But a very fit late sixties. There were little signs of age in her demeanor or stride. Time had taken its mark on her wrinkled face. She slowly moved around the store while Annabelle whispered in my ear.

"Oh, my gosh! It's her!" she hissed. "That's Pam Butte!"

We stared at her for a moment.

"This is fate," Annabelle said. "We were just talking about her and now she's here. The universe is trying to tell us something!"

I wasn't so sure. "What's she doing here?" I whispered more to myself than to Annabelle. I narrowed my gaze as she studied the skincare products.

"I just told you! Fate has struck like lightning! That woman has never stepped foot in the store before! She's going to drop a clue of who the murderer is!"

My jaw worked as I stared at Pam Butte. Did she feel the same way about my herbal apothecary as her husband had?

"I suppose I should go speak with her," I muttered, even though I wished she'd go away.

"Maybe she'll buy something," Annabelle offered. "After she confesses!"

"We can hope." After taking a deep breath, I plastered a smile on my face and walked around the corner. "May I help you?"

She turned to me and grinned, even though her blue eyes held a cast of sadness. "I'm just looking for now, thank you, though."

"Let me know if you have any questions," I said.

I sat on the stool behind the counter and pulled out the clipboard that held our inventory and pen and pretended to study the numbers. Since we hadn't had much traffic, the inventory was exactly the same as it had been that morning.

How depressing. Maybe I should put everything on sale, set out a large sign on the front walkway, and pray some more.

"You aren't as scary as my husband described you," she said. I glanced up to find her just a couple of feet away. She moved quietly, like Catnip. Or a serial killer, which I supposed described my cat as well.

"Scary?"

"He said you were out of your mind, that you threatened him."

Uh oh. I didn't think we'd bond over hatred of her husband, but I didn't expect her to be so forward. I decided to play stupid.

"I'm sorry," I said, setting down my clipboard. "Who's your husband?"

"Garrett Butte."

"Ah. I see. Yes, we didn't see eye-to-eye on many things."

She glanced around the store again. "He made it sound like this place was filled with snapping plants that would eat me alive if I stepped foot in here. I see that's not the case."

"No, there's nothing violent here." I didn't bother to explain that there were carnivorous plants, but a human had never been consumed, according to my research. Apparently, Butte had watched too much sci-fi television.

"And you don't seem like the harlot he described, either."

"Harlot?" I stood and crossed my arms over my chest. "He called me a harlot?"

She nodded. "Among some other things."

I shook my head. The woman was trying to get under my skin, and I wouldn't allow it. The conversation was close to over, as far as I was concerned. Unless, of course, she decided to confess to the killing. Then she could call me all the names she wanted. "Is there something I can do for you, Mrs. Butte, or did you simply come in here to throw insults at me?"

She smiled again. "I'm sorry. I expected something else when I walked in here. See, Garrett forbade me to enter this store. He said you were a horrible human, that everything in the store was dangerous and I should stay away at all costs. Now that he's gone, I had to come and see for myself."

"We're pretty harmless here," I replied. "We always have been."

"But are you?" she asked. "I've spoken to the sheriff, and she seems to think the conflict between you and Garrett caused his death."

Well, that escalated quickly. "How did our differences cause his death?"

"Not so much the difference, but *you*. You caused his death."

"I didn't kill your husband."

"She seems to think otherwise since you were standing right next to him when he died."

"I didn't kill your husband," I repeated.

Pam Butte stared at me a long while, then turned and walked around the store once again, stopping at each table to examine the products. "You sure aren't very busy."

I bit my tongue and shut my eyes for a moment. The woman was almost as horrible as her husband, except not as brash and loud.

After about ten minutes, she turned to me again and smiled. "Thank you for your time. Even though you seem like a nice person, I hope you rot in prison for what you've done."

"I didn't do anything," I said calmly. "And even if I did, why would you care? You were divorcing him, right?"

A slow blush crawled up her neck as she narrowed her gaze. "Where did you hear that?"

"I may not have customers right now but at times, the store gets very busy. People talk, and your marriage has been a hot topic of conversation."

Although Gina had been the one to share the news with me, I would keep her and File It Away out of the discussion.

"My marriage is no one's business."

I shrugged, happy to see I had flipped the tables and gotten under her skin just a bit. "Well, that may be true, but the timing between the divorce being initiated and your husband's murder... it's a little coincidental."

"What does that mean?" she shot back. Maybe I was irritating her more than just a little.

"It means that people are saying you killed him so you'd get everything. Money, house, savings accounts, investments... *everything*. No splitting assets down the middle for you."

Her face turned a shade of red I'd only seen on tomatoes. "How dare you!" she hissed.

"Don't shoot the messenger," I said, holding my hands to my shoulders in surrender. "You shared with me what the sheriff thought, I'm sharing with you what everyone in town is talking about."

Okay, maybe not everyone, but it sure sounded good, and her cheeks reddened a shade darker.

"I didn't kill him!"

"You disliked him enough to divorce him."

She squared her shoulders and lifted her chin. "You'll be seeing the inside of a jail cell."

As she turned to leave, Annabelle came from the back room and set her hand on my shoulder. "Don't let her, like, get to you."

I placed my palm on top of hers. "I'm trying, Annabelle. I'm really trying."

"She did it, Sam. I feel it in my bones."

Turning to my friend, I asked, "What makes you say that?"

"Because if she wasn't guilty, she'd be concerned that someone innocent may be going to jail."

"Then why come here?"

"My guess is to see who she thinks is going to go down for her husband's murder. As long as it's not her, who cares, right?"

"That would be... I don't know... Cruel."

Annabelle rolled her eyes and snickered. "Sam, she killed her husband. She's cruel to her core and just wants to meet who's going to take the fall. She'll finally have all her money and freedom."

And it was a perfect reason to murder her husband.

"Let's follow her," Annabelle said. "Look! She's getting in that car parked across the street."

"Why?"

"Why not? It's not like we're doing anything here, and besides, maybe we'll be able to uncover some clues."

Annabelle turned and ran into the back room. A moment later, she returned with both our bags and flung mine at my chest.

I caught it just as she shouted, "Let's tail that murderer!"

CHAPTER 11

I HURRIED OUT AFTER ANNABELLE. In the middle of the day, I should be at the store. But I'd been there for hours without any customers and that was because the townspeople thought I'd killed Doctor Butte. I didn't know what Mrs. Butte was up to, nor was I sure following her would be anything but a waste of time. However, Annabelle was right. Maybe she'd drop some clues as to the killer's identity and motive.

After locking the door, I hurried over to Annabelle's car and slipped in. As she turned the ignition, Guns n' Roses blasted from the speakers. I reached for the volume and turned it down. How in the world was she not deaf?

"Let's just turn it off," she said. "It helps me see better."

I did as instructed and didn't bother to question her on why the silent radio helped her see better, but simply accepted it as fact. We all had our quirks, and Annabelle possessed an overabundance of them. I took each in stride.

Pam had already pulled away from the curb and was down the road. Annabelle waited for a long moment, then swerved onto Comfort Road. "Keep an eye on her!" she shouted, then cursed at the car she'd just cut off when the driver began honking at us.

Driving with Annabelle was never boring—sometimes life-threatening—and I always felt as if I'd aged a few years when our trip was completed. Other times, I felt a renewed faith in a higher power because I survived.

Pam's white Mercedes was now three cars in front of us. I kept my gaze firmly focused on her right rear bumper that came into view and disappeared again, depending on the cars in front of us. For some reason, I'd expected her to head home, but instead, she pulled over and parked in front of Too Hot To Handle.

"What's she doing?" I asked. Annabelle drove by and illegally double-parked.

"You can't park here!" I said, pointing at the sign. "You're going to get a ticket."

"I know someone who's dating a cop," she said. "And we'll only be here for a minute."

Speaking of which, I should call Jordan and tell him about Pam Butte's visit. "How do you know she won't be in there long?"

"Locals know what they want when they go into Chris' store. It's not like she's going to look at every single bottle like the tourists do."

I glanced around, hoping she was right. We shouldn't have parked there.

Both of us stared at the building. Too Hot To Handle was busy once again. Hopefully, some of those people would get heartburn from the hot sauce and they'd need to come to me for a chamomile and ginger tincture to settle their stomachs.

As we stared at the door, I considered why Mrs. Butte had come to the store of the man who had served her husband a cracker moments before he died. Was it a coincidence? Was she a hot sauce fan? Or perhaps she and Chris had been working together to end the doctor's life?

A moment later, Pam emerged from the store emptyhanded, which only fueled my theory that they were working together. She hurried across the street to her car. Annabelle turned and looked over her shoulder, watching the woman with hawkish concentration. When Mrs. Butte merged into traffic, Annabelle floored it, backing up. I yelped and grabbed the dashboard as we barely missed an oncoming car. Thank goodness they had a great braking system.

We now had one car between us and Pam. "This is the way they do it in the detective shows," Annabelle said. "One or two cars."

I settled back into my seat and sighed with relief that we hadn't caused an accident.

Pam's blinker came on and she turned right off Comfort Road, up into the residential areas. "Now what do we do?" I asked. "She's going to see us."

"We'll stay back far enough so she won't notice us."

Annabelle slowed as she made the turn to follow Pam. When we got to the top of the hill, Mrs. Butte was already on the downslope about a quarter mile ahead.

"Where are you going now, husband killer?" Annabelle whispered.

She turned left and Annabelle followed. A few streets later, she veered right. "Okay, so we're going deep into old Heywood," Annabelle muttered.

"What's old Heywood?" Even though I'd been living in the town for over a year, I'd never heard the reference.

"Jeez, Sam," she replied, rolling her eyes. "Where all the super old houses are."

Well, maybe that should've been self-explanatory.

As we drove deeper into old Heywood, I couldn't help but feel uneasy. Did Mrs. Butte know we were behind her? If so, was she leading us somewhere to ambush us? If not, where was she going?

Annabelle, however, seemed to be completely immersed in the chase. She held the steering wheel at ten and two, her gaze firmly set on the car in front of us.

We turned down another street and Pam pulled up in front of a small, brown home with white trim. The yard was still somewhat tidy, but on the verge of being an unmanageable mess. Overgrown red rose bushes lined the front of the home, but still held their beauty, and the grass was a couple inches too long with a few dandelions sprouting. "Who lives here?" I asked.

Annabelle slowed until Pam exited her car and walked up to the house. Then she drove by at normal speeds, flipped around at the next intersection, and parked a few houses down, across the street. We wouldn't be noticed.

"What was she carrying?" Annabelle asked. "It looked like an envelope."

Some spy I was. I hadn't paid attention. However, Annabelle's parking had given us an excellent view of the house and I pushed my glasses up my nose and squinted in hopes of collecting any detail I could.

Mrs. Butte stood at the door, knocking. Annabelle had been right. It looked like she was carrying a white envelope.

No one answered.

She pounded her fist against the panel again.

The door flung open. "Who is that?" I asked.

"I can't see them," Annabelle said, leaning forward as if she were going to press her face against the windshield. "The door is in the way."

She was right. I could make out half a figure. Based on the jeans and t-shirt, I was guessing a male.

Mrs. Butte held the envelope in front of her, almost wagging it under the other person's nose.

As the homeowner waved his hand around, Mrs. Butte shook her head. He held out his hand and she slapped the envelope into it, then turned and walked back to her car. When the man slammed the door, she glanced over her shoulder then in our direction.

In unison, Annabelle and I slid down into our seats.

"Did she see us?" I whispered.

Annabelle poked her head over the steering wheel. "I don't think so. She's getting into her car." She sat upright and started hers.

"Whose house is that?" I asked again as she pulled away from the curb.

"I don't know. Write down the address and we'll figure it out later."

She slowly drove by the brown house and I typed in the street number into my phone. Then I turned my attention back to the white Mercedes.

"Mrs. Butte is really making the rounds today," I said.

"I'm, like, so glad we followed her," Annabelle replied. "I'm not sure what any of it means, but we're going to nail the hag to the wall."

To me, it looked like Pam was running errands, but maybe it would all make sense in the end.

Mrs. Butte meandered to the other side of town via Comfort Road. Traffic was particularly heavy thanks to the tourists.

When she made a turn, I recognized the neighborhood because Annabelle and I had been there when she'd placed the dead fish in the doctor's car. Pam was heading for her home.

As she pulled into the driveway, Annabelle once again drove by up to the next intersection, then turned around and parked down the road.

We watched the house for a few moments, then I turned to my friend. "I need to use the bathroom."

"Hold it," she said. "Something big is about to happen. I can, like, feel it."

All I felt that was going to happen was my bladder exploding. With a sigh, I crossed my legs.

A moment later, a moving truck pulled in, followed by a red Mercedes.

"Who's that?" I asked, squinting once again.

"I'm not sure. It looks like a younger version of Pam, though."

"Her daughter? Sally said her name's Molly."

"That's my guess."

As the moving truck pulled into the driveway, Molly parked on the street and exited her car just as the front door swung open.

The two women met in the middle of the lawn, each with their hands fisted at their sides, and began yelling at each other.

"Oh, I'd like to be a fly in the grass to hear that argument," Annabelle said as Pam stomped her foot.

"You can probably roll down the windows and not worry about being squished to death in the grass."

The driver of the moving van stepped out the moment Annabelle opened the vehicle's windows.

"It's half mine, so I'm here to take it!" Molly yelled. "That's what the will said!"

"You'll take what I give you, you ungrateful brat!" Pam screamed, shaking her fist in her daughter's face.

"He's not even buried and they're arguing about the stuff in the house?" I asked incredulously.

"Neither of them cared for him much," Annabelle sniffed. "Which is, like, completely understandable, but also sad."

As the two women shrieked at each other, I had to agree. After a few moments, the driver tried to step in between them. For his efforts, he received a fist to the face from Molly. He rubbed his jaw while returning to the truck, then pulled out his phone just as Pam grabbed her daughter's hair and tried to push her to the ground.

"Oh, my word," I whispered, shutting my eyes. "This is just awful to see."

I glanced over at Annabelle, who stared wide-eyed at the spectacle.

"Should we call the police?" I asked, immediately regretting the question. If we phone and Mallory found out we were sitting outside the house of the man I supposedly murdered, it wouldn't look great for me. But then again, the two women were having their own MMA match on the front lawn.

"We probably should," Annabelle sighed. "But I think that guy already did."

Despite not wanting to, I turned to watch the melee once again—another train wreck in action.

Both women were now on the ground hitting and kicking each other, screaming. The moving truck driver hurried over and pulled Molly away from Pam. In the distance, I heard sirens.

"We should probably go," I suggested. "If Mallory rolls up and sees us, I'm going to be in a lot of trouble."

Annabelle nodded and started the car. She slowly pulled away from the curb and we drove past the house. The women continued to yell at each other while the driver kept them apart.

"I have a new theory," Annabelle said.

"What's that?"

"I think the daughter killed him," she replied. "She obviously hated her father and based on what we just witnessed, she's not too fond of her mom. She knew they had a will and she'd get something out of it once he died. She killed him for the money."

I swallowed past the bile rising in my throat while I considered what she'd said. My mother had been a drunk and a terrible parent, but I never would have physically assaulted her.

But perhaps Annabelle was right and Butte's death came down to a daughter filled with rage who was in need of money.

CHAPTER 12

THAT EVENING, Jordan and I sat on my couch, enjoying a glass of the organic chardonnay from Never Quit Wining. Catnip had curled up between us and purred loudly as Jordan stroked his head.

"I couldn't believe what we saw today," I murmured. "It still makes me sick to my stomach. She attacked her mom, who fought right back. It was like something out of a movie."

"The wife and daughter need to be looked at more closely," Jordan said. "I spoke to Trevor earlier today, and he said they both have great motive."

"What's Pam's motive, besides her husband being a jerk?"

"Butte was having an affair with one of his nurses, and Pam found out," Jordan replied. "That was the start of the divorce proceedings."

"Gross," I muttered. I couldn't imagine talking to Butte for more than a minute, let alone having an affair with him. "So she finds out he's making time with the nurse, then... kills him? Why? Out of rage?"

"Or money," Jordan said, shrugged. "Like you guys suggested. She realized she'd have to split everything down the middle and decided if he was going to have a little side fun, she'd make sure she was compensated well."

"What happened to the nurse?" I asked.

"Not sure about that one," Jordan replied. "Trevor is trying to track down a name. He's going to talk to the staff at Butte's office tomorrow."

"I bet I could find out who she was before then," I said, picking up my phone and setting down my wine glass.

"How are you going to do that?"

I dialed Gina.

"What's up, Sam?" she greeted me.

"Hi, Gina. Listen, I was wondering if you knew the nurse at Butte's clinic who no longer works there."

"Let me think a minute... I did hear something about this not too long ago."

"Take your time."

I waited as she muttered to herself, then finally she shouted, "Jillian Goodwin! That was her name."

"Do you know her?" I asked.

"Yeah, but we aren't close. We went to school together, but she hung out with a different crowd."

"Do you know why she isn't working for Butte anymore?"

"No, I don't. Why?"

If Gina didn't know about it, the affair had to be a pretty tightly kept secret that I shouldn't be gifting to anyone. However, Gina was my friend and had just saved the police time in discovering the nurse's identity.

"She was having an affair with Butte," I blurted.

"Sam!" Jordan hissed.

"That's gross," Gina replied. "I wonder what was in it for her?"

"We need to find out."

"I'll go with you to talk to her," Gina suggested. "I wonder if she's working now?"

I didn't have an answer, but if she had kept up her work in nursing, there were only two places for her to go: Butte's office or the local emergency clinic. "Maybe at the emergency clinic?" I asked.

"Hmm. Maybe. Let me make some calls and I'll touch base with you in the morning."

"Sounds good." I hung up and laid my head back against the pillows.

"I wish you hadn't said anything to her about the affair," Jordan grumbled. "No one's supposed to be aware of it."

"It's Gina," I replied. "I had to give her the information so she'd help me."

"Hopefully she keeps her mouth shut."

Doubtful, but I decided to remain quiet. "We're going to see Jillian tomorrow."

"Maybe you should allow Trevor to handle it."

I sat up and turned to him. "Jordan, if I don't find this killer and clear my name, Sage Advice isn't going to exist for much longer. I'm currently the town pariah. My sales have crashed."

Tears welled in my eyes and he took my hands in his. "I get it," he said. "There's only so much Trevor can do with Mallory looking over his shoulder, too. I just worry about you possibly saying the wrong thing to the killer and getting hurt. Why don't I come with you?"

"Because everyone knows you're a cop."

"I'm not working, though. I'm on leave, remember?"

"People don't know that, Jordan," I sighed. "No one wants to talk to the police."

He squeezed my fingers. "Be careful, okay? Don't poke the hornets' nest too hard."

"I need to poke at it a bit or my store isn't going to survive."

Jordan nodded and sighed. "Just try not to get stung, Sam."

GINA CAME through and discovered Jillian was indeed working at the emergency clinic. The next morning, she picked me up and we drove over there. I'd never visited, although I probably should have. During the winter, I'd taken a couple of brutal falls that most likely should've been examined. My elbow still didn't work right.

When we strolled in, I noted a couple of people in the waiting room —a man with a bloody towel wrapped around his hand, and a very pregnant woman who held her belly while breathing deeply. There wasn't any feeling of urgency in the air.

"Can I help you?"

I glanced away from the patients to the receptionist. Young, blonde, and small in stature, she smiled brightly and didn't look a day over fifteen. I remembered reading somewhere that you knew you were old when everyone younger than you started to resemble children. She apparently loved plants, as well. Her desk was surrounded by ten pots, most of which I recognized as simple household plants. There were a few I couldn't name, but one in particular resembled white snakeroot. Why in the world would a hospital have a poisonous plant in their reception area?

"We're looking for Jillian," Gina said.

"Oh, she's in back. Let me call and see if she's busy."

My gaze once again wandered toward the two in the waiting room. If Jillian wasn't busy, then maybe she should be treating them. Both seemed like they could use some medical attention.

"She'll be up in a minute," the receptionist chirped as she set the phone back in its cradle. "You can take a seat."

The blood was now dripping past the towel onto the man's lap. "I think he needs to be seen," I said just as the woman groaned loudly.

"We'll make sure everyone is taken care of."

Was that a white snakeroot? Was it possible I had been mistaken? I snapped a picture and shoved my phone back in my pocket.

I debated whether to engage in a conversation about the poisonous plant. What place did it have in a hospital? Sure, the flowers were pretty. Maybe the receptionist didn't know it was deadly? But then again, I had to surmise no one was going around the clinic consuming plants, either. Except maybe kids. It was my understanding that kids would eat almost anything.

Gina and I sat down as I kept my eye on the pregnant woman and the bloodied man. If these two didn't have priority, I hated to see the people who were in back being treated.

A few moments later, a woman burst through the door leading to the back. In her forties or fifties, she wore her long brown hair in a ponytail. Her green scrubs strained over her thick hips and stomach. She glanced around for a moment, then her gaze landed on us. "Gina? What are you doing here?"

We stood and walked over to her. "I know you're busy," my friend began, "but we need to speak with you about Butte."

Jillian blinked a few times in rapid succession. "What about him?"

After clearing her throat, Gina leaned toward her and whispered, "We know you were having an affair with him and we just have a couple of questions."

She gasped and stepped away. "No one knows about that!" she hissed.

"Well, that's not true," Gina replied. "I know about it, and although I'm not that popular around here, I wouldn't exactly call myself a nobody. That's a little insulting."

Pursing my lips together, I hoped to hide my smile.

"I didn't mean it like that."

"I'll believe you," Gina sighed. "Can you tell us a bit about your relationship with him?"

Her lip began to quiver as her eyes welled with tears. "I can only talk for a minute. We're a little busy."

"That's okay," Gina replied. "We won't take much of your time. Now tell us about the affair."

Jillian glanced around, then led us over to the front door where we'd be out of hearing range for the receptionist and the patients. As the tears began to fall, she swiped her cheeks with her fingers. "He... his wife was horrible to him. He didn't deserve the abuse she gave him."

Well, that was interesting information. Maybe Gina was right and the quiet ones needed to be watched a little more closely.

"How long did the affair last?" Gina asked.

"A year. Then she found out and I was let go."

"What happened when she discovered her husband's infidelity?" I asked. "Was there a scene?"

She shook her head and sighed. "No. Garrett walked into the clinic one day, pulled me into his office, then told me he had to let me go, that Pam knew about us."

"Pam never confronted you?" I asked.

"Never. I haven't seen her since before he fired me."

"Did you talk to him after that?" I asked.

"No."

"Was Butte ever in trouble with the state over the treatment of his patients?" I asked. "Did he make a mistake with someone who would then want him dead?"

She stared at the floor for a long moment, then nodded. "There were two cases that he worried over. One was Melanie Raves."

"What happened with her?" Gina asked.

"She almost died," Jillian replied. "She came to Butte with severe stomach pain and he told her it was gas. She just needed some stomach medicine."

"And it wasn't?" I asked.

"Nope. It was her appendix. She went home and took some meds, then ended up in here hours later and almost died. He should've done some imaging, but he didn't take her concerns seriously."

That was why Chris Raves became so agitated when I'd brought up Butte and his wife's past interactions with the man. His dismissal had almost killed his wife.

"What was the other case?" Gina asked.

"Harold Shumaker," Jillian sighed. "Look, I've got to get back to work."

The woman waiting to be seen groaned loudly and a splashing sound filled the room. We looked over as she screamed.

"Her water just broke," Jillian muttered. "I need to get her in back."

"Do you want me to help?" Gina asked. The two rushed over to the woman, each taking an elbow and assisting her to her feet.

"How would you help me, Gina?" Jillian asked. Another nurse rushed out from the back and took Gina's place.

"Well, I've delivered a few puppies in my time. It can't be much different, right?"

The nurses rolled their eyes and disappeared through the back door with the woman about to give birth.

"Puppies, Gina?" I asked. "Really?"

She shrugged. "I was trying to get more time with her."

We turned and walked toward the door leading outside. As we stood on the sidewalk, my stomach howled and my brain begged for some coffee.

"Are you hungry?" I asked.

"A little. Do you want to come—"

The door to the clinic burst open and Jillian appeared, out of breath. "Listen, I'm needed in back but I have to tell you one thing."

"What's that?" I asked.

"I wasn't going to say anything, but the heck with the secrets. The man is dead."

Gina and I stared at her expectantly as she placed her hands on her knees and took a few deep breaths.

"When Garrett fired me, I asked if we could still see each other," she finally said.

"And?"

"He said that would be impossible. His wife, Pam, told him that if he didn't break it off with me, she'd kill him."

"And did you see him after he broke it off?" I asked. Holy cow, this could be the smoking gun the police needed.

Jillian nodded. "Twice. I've got to get back inside. We have a baby to deliver and a guy to stitch up who shouldn't operate an electric knife while drunk."

As she hurried off, I stood, stunned.

"Well, I think that's a really good piece of evidence to pass on to the police," Gina said. "Wow."

"Right? If Pam knew her husband was still seeing Jillian, she said she'd kill him."

"And maybe she did just that."

CHAPTER 13

THE NEXT DAY went by with a few people venturing into the store. Frankly, they didn't spend enough to justify me keeping the lights on.

I did a Google search on the plant in the clinic and compared my image to what I found on the screen. Yes. A white snakewood. Just to be certain, I also used a plant identifying app, which also confirmed my suspicions. To my surprise, I could buy the plant just about everywhere.

My mood had grown so foul, I was tempted to shut the store, board up the door and crawl in bed with my cat and my last bottle of organic chardonnay. As I sat at the computer and paid a few bills, I realized I was sinking into deep financial trouble—the kind I wasn't sure I would recover from. I didn't have time for a pity party.

Two things still bothered me about our talk with Jillian. First, why was a poisonous plant in the clinic? It could be something as simple as the receptionist finding the flowers pretty and not realizing that people had died by ingesting it. In my research, I recalled a story of a woman who had died because she'd drank the milk of a cow who had consumed the plant.

Or was there something more sinister? Did Butte spend time at the emergency clinic? Was the poisonous plant there to hopefully kill him by someone adding it to a meal or a drink? And maybe, when it didn't do its job, someone poisoned him at the Farmers Market instead?

Second, who was Harold Shumaker? Jillian had to run before I'd gotten the chance to question her.

So, it seemed I had to make another trip to the emergency clinic and poke around a bit more.

Based on what Jillian said, Chris Raves had come back to the top of my list. Butte had died at his booth after eating a cracker and hot sauce. What if Melanie's ignored appendicitis almost killed her. But then again, there was my wonderful next-door neighbors, Wayne and Adrienne. They had seemed certain that Adrienne's miscarriage and subsequent infertility was caused by the accident with Butte. And, Adrienne had said she'd spilled wine on him. For all I knew, there was some underground "I hate Butte and he needs to die" club in Heywood, and all those hurt by him had come together and killed him. A little poison in the wine to seep through his skin, a little more in the hot sauce to finish him off.

"Wouldn't that be something," I muttered to the empty building. Well, I didn't exactly know if Doug was upstairs or not. He moved quieter than Catnip. I picked up my phone and texted Annabelle.

THERE's no one here again. I'm going to run some errands.
Don't bother coming in.

TO MY SURPRISE, I received a thumbs up emoji. Usually, Annabelle came into the store whether I wanted or needed her, or not. Did she read the tides and know the ship was about to sink? Was she looking for a new job?

With a long sigh, I decided not to worry about things that could be. I had enough hard facts in my life to concern me.

After I shut down my computer, I grabbed my bag, ready to head out the door, my first stop being Too Hot To Handle. Chris Raves and I were going to have a chat and this time, I wouldn't allow him to intimidate me. I'd waltz into that store with my spine straight and I wouldn't flinch at any threats. He could scream at me all he wanted, but I wouldn't leave until I got the answers I wanted.

I scrawled out a note to leave on the door asking customers to write down their name, phone number, and the product they were interested in, or visit the online store. I hoped to return to a full sheet of information, but I had my doubts.

The chimes sounded, indicating someone had come in through the front. Setting down my purse, I took a moment to place a smile on my face and pray that it was someone who needed thousands of dollars of product, then rounded the corner.

Jordan.

"Hey, good looking," he said. The time off had agreed with him. His well-rested and stress-free demeanor only soured my mood further.

"Hi. What are you doing here?"

"Coming to see what you were up to," he replied, giving me a quick kiss.

"I'm off to talk to some people."

"Who would that be?"

"Number one," I held up my index finger, "is Chris Raves. Number two—"

"Wait a minute," Jordan interrupted. "Let's go back to number one. I thought he was a little less than friendly with you last time you were there?"

"He was. But I'm not fishing for information any longer. His wife almost died because of Butte's negligence."

Jordan arched a brow. "Where did you hear that?"

"From Butte's mistress."

"You've been busy and haven't shared what you've been up to."

"I know."

After recapping my conversation with Jillian, Jordan shook his head. "That really gives Chris a motive."

"Exactly. And he handed Butte the cracker, then the doctor dropped dead."

"You're off to talk to him right now?"

I nodded. "Do you want to go?"

Of course I wanted to spend some time with my boyfriend, but I also knew Chris wouldn't be so rude to me if Jordan was there.

"Do you want me to be your bodyguard?"

I threw my head back and laughed. He knew me too well. "Now that you mention it, yes."

"Let me use your bathroom, then we'll take off."

As he hurried upstairs, I grabbed my bag again. A shiver raced down my spine when chants sounded from outside. No catchy phrases like *pills over plants*. Instead, they simply yelled *killer,* over and over again.

I glanced outside and counted four people out in front of Sage Advice... the same who had been protesting my store with Butte before he died.

Jordan returned a moment later, his smile fading as the protestors' presence registered. "You've got to be kidding me," he muttered.

I shook my head, glad that I'd decided to close the rest of the day. No one would cross that line and visit the wicked witch of Heywood and her murderous plants.

"Let's go," Jordan growled, taking my hand. We walked out the front door and while I locked up, he told the protestors to get lost. After a little back and forth, he threatened to call in a favor to the sheriff's department and have all of them arrested. They hesitated only for a second. "And then I'll have them do a cavity search," he said. "Don't test me on this, people. I've never told a lie in my life."

I sighed in relief as they departed. Jordan took my hand again and we walked down Comfort Road. Some locals gave me a glare, while a couple smiled sadly in my direction, as if they pitied me. This nonsense had to end.

Once we arrived at Too Hot To Handle, Jordan opened the door for me and followed me in. It took a second for my eyes to adjust, but I did catch Chris' smile fading when he noticed us.

We waited patiently as he helped a couple customers. When the store emptied, he sighed loudly, then walked over. "What can I do you for?"

"Just stopping in to say hello," Jordan said, extending his palm. The two shook hands and grinned, yet I could feel the tension rising almost as fast as the testosterone.

And I didn't have time for niceties.

"Tell me about Melanie almost dying," I said. I may as well have produced a lit stick of dynamite. The pressure mounted, an almost tangible force sitting on my shoulders.

"How did you find out about that?" Chris asked.

"It doesn't matter," I replied, my voice strong, my chin lifted ever so slightly—a stance my character, Cassie, on As The Years Turn, had taken many times. Chris Raves wouldn't be intimidating me today. In fact, I could've probably handled him without Jordan in tow. "I just want details. Was Butte involved?"

He narrowed his gaze on me for a long moment, then his shoulders slumped as he sighed. "Yeah, he was. But that doesn't mean I killed him."

"Tell us what happened," Jordan said softly.

"Melanie woke up one morning with a bad stomachache. We thought maybe it was the shrimp she ate the prior night, but as the day went on, it became worse."

"How long did you wait until you went to see Butte?" I asked.

"We got the last appointment for the day," he replied. "When we arrived at his clinic, we were the only people in the waiting room."

"Why didn't you go to the emergency clinic?" Jordan asked.

"Because, back then, we trusted him. He'd never steered us wrong before."

"What tests did he run?" I asked.

Chris shrugged. "None. Joked around with us a bit and said it was probably the shrimp. Told her to take some anti-gas medicine and she'd feel better in the morning."

"Except she didn't," Jordan said. "What happened next?"

"That night, she couldn't take the pain any longer," he sighed. "We went to the emergency clinic. They did some imaging, and then put her in an ambulance to the hospital in Sedona. One of the nurses told me if we'd waited any longer, she would've died."

"I'm glad that didn't happen," I said. "But after that, you didn't see Butte in a professional capacity again, did you?"

"Heck, no," Chris said. "Don't get me wrong—I was steaming mad. Thought about heading over to his house and taking my baseball bat to his cars and windows. I wanted to scream from the rooftops that he was negligent."

"Did you ever confront him?" Jordan asked.

"Yeah, I did. Once Melanie was home and up and around, I waited outside his office. I told him what happened to her and that I blamed him for almost losing my wife."

"What did he say?" Jordan prodded.

"That Melanie was fine when she was in his office and the fact her appendix went bad so fast wasn't his fault. I told him he should've done some testing, and he said he didn't feel it was necessary. I knew right then and there that if I didn't walk away, I was going to hit him."

"I'm glad you didn't," Jordan muttered. "I would've had to arrest you."

"Yeah, well, it doesn't mean that I can't daydream about it."

As I stared at Chris, I wondered about my theory of other people in town being hurt by Butte, and all of them coming together to kill him so the murder couldn't be laid at the feet of one person. "Do you know anyone in town who's had a similar experience with him?"

"What? Who almost died because he was a neglectful hack?"

"Yes." I appreciated how succinctly he described the doctor.

"No," Chris replied. "I never brought it up to anyone. I never felt like talking about the day my wife almost died because of Butte. I finally realized it was time to let go of my anger and concentrate on the great things in my life, like our kid and the fact Melanie was healthy."

"That's good," I said. "Negative emotions can eat you alive." And yes, I was speaking from experience. After the death of my husband, my insides had been rocked with turmoil because of my raging anger.

The front door opened and a few people wandered in. After Chris smiled and greeted them, he turned back to us. "Is there anything else you guys need?" he asked.

"No, not today," Jordan said. "I appreciate you taking the time to talk with us."

"Sure, Jordan." The two shook hands again. "When are you getting back to the job?"

"As soon as we can prove that we didn't kill Butte," Jordan replied, glancing over at me. I didn't meet Chris' gaze. I'd told him Jordan was taking some time off, but I'd neglected to share he was also being accused of murder.

"I see," Chris said while I studied his shoes—a very nice pair of black and red Nikes. New, if I wasn't mistaken. Either that or he cared for them well. His gaze bore into me as my cheeks heated. "Well, as long as you don't go trying to pin it on me, you can ask all the questions you want."

Jordan cleared his throat. "Great. I'll see you around."

I glanced up at Chris and smiled, then followed Jordan out the door.

"What was that all about?" he asked.

"I never told him Mallory had accused you of murder as well," I said. "I just told him you were taking some time off, so now he thinks I'm a big liar."

We strolled in silence for a few moments, then Jordan turned to me. "What do you think? I feel like he's hiding something."

"I don't know what that would be," I replied. "He seemed pretty forthcoming about Melanie and her issue with Butte."

Jordan shook his head and placed his hands on his hips. "Something isn't right, though."

"Chris had motive, especially if he's lying about releasing all that anger he had built up," I mused. "And he did give Butte the cracker, then the man dropped dead."

"Exactly," Jordan muttered. "It sure seems like he killed the doctor. He had motive, means, and opportunity."

"I need to stop by the store and see if anyone left me a note," I said.

"Sure. I'll go with you," Jordan replied. "Should we take the Riverwalk?"

"That sounds nice."

We strolled down to the Riverwalk, hand-in-hand. Upon reaching Sage Advice, we huffed it up the path to the back door. When I opened it, I found Annabelle and Doug lip-locked in a passionate embrace.

CHAPTER 14

I SIMPLY STARED, unsure of what I was witnessing. George Michael's "Careless Whisper" blasted from the boom box, which was why they carried on as if we weren't there. They didn't hear us come in.

"Oh, my word," I whispered. I closed my eyes for a brief moment, sure I had been seeing things. When I opened them, I found them in the same position. "Annabelle!" I shouted.

She yelped and pulled away from Doug. Jordan hurried over and shut down the music. A heavy silence settled around us.

The two stood before me like scolded children, staring down at the floor. I'd asked her to stay away from Doug so he could concentrate on remaining sober. Sure, I'd had an idea that they'd been carrying on behind my back, but to actually witness it completely stunned me. My emotions spun from curiosity, to horror, to anger. "What... what is going on?"

"I think that's pretty self-explanatory," Jordan murmured.

Ignoring him, I said, "Annabelle, I asked you—"

"I know you did," she replied, finally lifting her chin defiantly and meeting my gaze. "But I've fallen in love with Doug and I'm done trying to hide it from you."

"I wanted Doug to concentrate on his sobriety," I said. "It's important that he doesn't slip."

"I won't," Doug said, wrapping his arm around Annabelle's shoulder. "She's the best thing that's ever happened to me. I want to stay the course for her. She's amazing. I've found my reason for sobriety."

Again, I felt like I was policing two adults and I had no business doing so. The thing that bothered me was that Annabelle had gone against my specific wishes. With Doug living under my roof, I felt responsible for him and his frame of mind.

"Now that you know about us," Doug continued, "I wanted to let you know that I'll be moving out."

Astonished, my thoughts began to spiral. If he moved out, he'd lose his sobriety. "Where will you go?"

"He's moving in with me," Annabelle said.

"I can still help around here if you want," Doug offered.

"And of course I'll still work here," Annabelle said. "We just want to be together, like, all the time."

"Of course." I forced a smile. "I understand."

"I'm going to grab some of my things," Doug said. "Can you give me a hand, Annabelle?"

"Sure!" she chirped.

"You're moving out now?" I asked, the heavy stone in my belly dropping further.

"Yes. I'll get the rest of my stuff by the end of next week."

I nodded and pursed my lips. It would seem that both of them under my roof for multiple hours a day hadn't been enough, which I understood. They'd been playing cat and mouse with me, trying not to get caught showing affection for each other. However, Doug moving out felt like a gut punch. I'd grown used to him being around and just the idea of him leaving made the building feel quite empty.

My world seemed to be crashing around me. First the murder and the consequences of Mallory announcing I was responsible, then Annabelle and Doug making their secret relationship official. Why wasn't I happy for them? Was I being selfish? Probably. Or maybe I was jealous they had found joy, while my life seemed to be falling apart, piece by piece, minute by minute.

Jordan's phone rang. Annabelle and Doug scurried upstairs, hand-in-hand. I did have to admit they were cute together and I adored the story of an underdog finding love. I wondered if he had Annabelle's appreciation for the 80s and I immediately concluded a firm *no*. He wasn't stuck there as Annabelle seemed to be, even though she aged right along with the rest of us.

"I better take this," Jordan muttered.

Standing in the back room, I tried to figure out what to do next. I hurried to the front door, unlocked it, and pulled the taped paper. Completely blank.

No one had left me an order.

After crumpling up the empty sheet, I tossed it in the trash and sat on a stool behind the cash register, feeling completely defeated. Jordan was still in the back room talking on the phone. I needed to get to the hospital and ask some questions about that poisonous plant.

A moment later, Jordan emerged from the back room. "I have to get to the station," he said. "Mallory said I could go of my own free will, or she'd bring me in with cuffs on."

"For what? Did she say?"

"Just more questions," he sighed.

"Did she say how long it would take?"

He shook his head. "It could be minutes or hours, Sam. Go and do what you need to do, and I'll catch up with you later."

Leaning over, he gave me a quick kiss and then hurried out the back door.

I sat in the store, staring out the front window while listening to Annabelle and Doug laughing upstairs.

Alone. I felt so alone, although I knew I wasn't. My close friends were rooting for me.

My phone rang and I reluctantly pulled it out of my pocket. My lawyer and accountant, Colin Breckshire, III was on the other line, and my dread grew deeper.

I answered anyway. It couldn't get much worse, right?

"Sam!" he greeted me. "It's wonderful to hear your voice."

"You, too, Colin," I said. "What's up?"

"Well, I was going over the books, and it seems there's a problem with your bank account."

"What's that?" I asked, shutting my eyes and mentally going over the past few days. There hadn't been many transactions—debits or credits—so I couldn't imagine what the issue could've been.

"It seems that the balance is reading zero."

"What?!" I shot to my feet. "There's no way it can be at zero! I had a few thousand dollars in there!"

"That's what I wanted to discuss with you," he said, his voice much calmer than I felt. I imagined him sitting behind his big desk, leaning back in his chair and straightening his bowtie as he cradled the phone between his neck and shoulder. "I called the bank, using the power of attorney you've granted me. They said that the account has been frozen by the authorities."

Sinking to my seat, the power punch caused me to fold forward onto the counter. "What? How... what in the world, Colin? Does this have to do with Gerald?"

"I believe so," he replied. "I have to make a few more phone calls, but from what I've gathered so far, yes. Apparently, you were summoned via letter to a hearing on the matter and you never showed."

"What?!"

"Yes. The judge, in his infinite wisdom, had the summons sent to your Los Angeles address."

"I never received a letter," I muttered as I shut my eyes.

"I figured as much. Anyway, I wanted to touch bases with you and inform you of the issue before I continued my investigation."

"They're supposed to be giving me my money back!" I yelled. "Not taking more of it away from me!"

"The money is still there. They've just zeroed out the account until they get permission to release it."

"This.. I don't even know what to say. This is the stupidest, most ignorant—"

"I understand," Colin interrupted, his voice calm. Unfortunately, it did nothing to soothe my nerves. "I wanted to tell you what has transpired, Sam. Believe me, I'm working on it. In the meantime, I would suggest that you don't take any credit cards since the money is deposited into that account. They're allowing deposits, just not withdrawals. Please take cash only for the next few days until I get everything worked out."

Was it possible I could hate Gerald even more than I did? His actions had cost me so much. If I'd been involved, I would've understood the authority's witch hunt, but they'd already questioned me multiple times. I was innocent and continued to be punished.

"It doesn't matter," I whispered as tears welled in my eyes. "Everyone in town thinks I'm the big, bad killer, thanks to the stupid sheriff. They're avoiding me, and therefore, my store."

"Butte? Does this have to do with his untimely demise?"

"Yes."

"Oh, my," he sighed.

"Just keep me posted on everything, Colin."

"Will do, my dear. Take care of yourself."

After tossing my phone on the counter, I took a deep breath and glanced around Sage Advice. The urge to take a baseball bat to the wall of mason jars filled with herbs curled my fingers. I longed to hear the smashing sound of the glass, the pleasure of destroying something.

But that wouldn't solve my problems. It would only leave me with more. If I didn't have any customers, and if one happened to wander in and I couldn't accept a credit card, what was the point of being in business? With my frozen funds, I couldn't even pay Annabelle, let alone the electric bill.

Wiping my cheeks, I pulled a piece of paper from under the cash register and scrawled *Closed* across it, then taped it to the front door.

Moments later, Annabelle and Doug trotted down the stairs. He carried a box, while she had a duffel bag slung over her shoulder. She smiled, her gaze sparkling with happiness. And for a brief moment, I hated her for it, as well as myself because envy ripped through me. Her life was so together, so simple. Why couldn't I find that? Why did my past keep coming back to haunt me when all I wanted was to forget about it and look forward to my future?

"I'll be in tomorrow," she said. "We should really look at restocking the—"

"Don't bother," I said. And I was about to blow her simple life up with the force of a bomb. "We're closed."

Her face paled as Doug furrowed his brow. "What does that, like, mean?" she asked.

"It means that we're closed. Sage Advice is no longer in business."

"Why, Sam?" Doug asked. "Does this have anything to do with Annabelle and me?"

"No," I said, firmly. "It's... it's a bunch of things, but I guess in the end, Butte got what he wanted. Sage Advice is done."

CHAPTER 15

It seemed the longer I stayed in the store, the more depressed I became. I had to try to find the positives in my life and focus on those. First, if I could prove my innocence, then maybe the locals would come back around. Second, Colin was working to get my bank account unfrozen. Hopefully, that would happen soon.

If all that fell into place, then maybe, just maybe, my life would return to normal. Sage Advice would be up and running again, I could employ Annabelle and Doug, and perhaps Jordan and I could slip away for a vacation. I needed one. However, his idea of a good time was camping and fishing, which I'd discovered were really not my thing. The couple times I'd ventured out with him, I didn't appreciate being covered in dirt and I'd lain awake all night worrying about bears attacking us in our sleep.

Maybe I could convince him that a beach in Mexico was also a pleasant experience and just as much fun. Of course we wouldn't travel the way I once did: private jet, a butler and chef on hand, or shacking up in a five-star hotel. Instead, we'd travel like normal middle-class people—fly coach, grab a taxi, and figure out meals on our own.

I locked up and hurried down Comfort Road toward the emergency clinic, hoping the receptionist who had been there previously would be working once again, and maybe I'd get a chance to talk to Jillian again about her affair with Butte. I didn't know what she could possibly add, but I'd push and probe and see what came up. Not to mention, I still had no idea who Harold Shumaker was, except that he may have something to do with Butte's demise.

As I walked into the clinic, I glanced at the waiting area, which was empty. Good. Not only was I happy no one needed immediate care, but hopefully it also meant people would have time to speak with me.

"Can I help you?"

At the reception desk was the same woman from before. I smiled as I approached while noticing the white snakeroot still in place.

"Yes," I said. "I was wondering if you could tell me where that plant came from?"

She looked to where I was pointing. "Oh! Okay, that's a weird question."

"It's very pretty," I hedged, hoping she'd give me more information. "I love the little white flowers. Did you buy it?"

"No, I didn't," she replied. "It was dropped off here for one of our nurses, Jillian."

"By who?" I asked.

"Well, I wasn't working when it happened," she said. "Why does it matter?"

"Did whoever was on duty when it was left mentioned who'd brought it?"

She stared at me for a long moment, probably debating whether she should just start answering me or continue to reply to each of my questions with one of her own.

I smiled again.

"Becky, the receptionist who works the other shift, said Doctor Butte's wife dropped it off with a really nice note for Jillian," she said. "Something about what a wonderful help she is to her husband. That's what I was told, anyway."

"Oh," I said, taking a step backward, caught completely off guard. That wasn't the answer I'd been expecting. "What did Jillian say when she saw it?"

"I don't know. I wasn't here, remember?"

Right. She had mentioned that.

"Is Jillian working today?" I asked.

"Yes, she's with a patient."

"Could you tell her Gina's friend is here? I was with Gina the other day speaking with Jillian."

"Oh, that's right," she said. "I thought I recognized you from somewhere."

"Right here!" I said, lifting my hands to my sides and hoping I was hiding my irritation well. "You recognize me from right here. If you could tell Jillian I'd like to speak to her again, that would be great."

She nodded and picked up the phone. Meanwhile, I turned to sit down in the reception area and leaned my head back against the wall, thoroughly exhausted, but determined to get my life back on track.

I became lost in the remodeling show playing on the television mounted to the opposite wall and imagined how I could update my own small kitchen. No black and white, that was for sure. The color scheme had been prevalent in my Hollywood home that had burnt to the ground. I preferred a warmer ambience... maybe some rich oak cabinets? Taupe granite? Definitely stainless-steel appliances.

But then I remembered a remodel required money, which I had very little of now since I hadn't taken my paycheck this month, and the bank had frozen my business account. A new kitchen sat on the far side of the horizon, completely out of sight. Daydreaming had been fun, though.

Jillian came out about an hour later. "What can I do for you?" she asked, plopping down in the chair next to me.

"I just had a few follow-up questions from when Gina and I were here."

"Sure. What's up?"

"Well, first... that plant up there." I pointed at the receptionist desk. "The one with the little white flowers. Did you know that was for you?"

Her gaze widened as she glanced at it. "No. I had no idea." We both stood and walked over. "Katie, was there a note left with the plant?"

Katie nodded. "Becky told me Pam Butte brought it. She said she appreciated you helping her husband."

"When?" I asked.

"A couple of days ago."

"Where's the note?" Jillian asked.

"Here," Katie said, pulling it out of the drawer. "I guess we forgot to give it to you. Sorry about that."

"It's okay," Jillian mumbled, then we returned to the chairs.

"Why is she giving me a plant?" Jillian whispered. "This is freaking me out."

"It should," I said. "Mainly because it's poisonous."

"Are you kidding me?" she hissed, glancing up at the receptionist again, then back at the note in her hand.

"Open it," I urged.

"I feel sick."

"It's okay. Open the note and see what it says."

She tore at the small white envelope, then opened the card.

JILLIAN,

Although we had our differences, I always noticed how
helpful you were to my husband. In his death, I am trying to
forgive those who have wronged me, to find the good in everyone.
I've said some horrible things to you, and about you.
I'm hoping you can find it in your heart to forgive me, to put
the past behind us. Please accept this lovely little plant as a
gesture of amnesty.
The little white flowers taste like vanilla and are very good.
Give them a try!

"OH, MY GOSH!" Jillian whispered. She dropped the card and envelope to the floor and brought her hand to her mouth. After a moment she turned to me, her face pale. "Are you sure that's poisonous?"

I nodded, both horrified and stunned by what I'd just read. "I-it's called a white snakeroot," I stammered.

Thankfully, that note had been shoved into a drawer and the plant forgotten, or Jillian may have actually tried to eat the flowers and been murdered. No one would've known how she died.

Pam Butte was either the most brazen women I'd ever met, or crazier than a four-dollar bill.

"She wants me dead," Jillian muttered. "The old hag tried to kill me."

"Perhaps you should call the police," I suggested. "I'm sure they'd be interested in both the note and the plant."

"But then I'd have to answer for the affair," Jillian said, shaking her head. "No one knows about that."

"I know," I said. "Gina does as well. She heard about it while working at her nail salon. It's out there, Jillian."

"They'll ask me what she means by 'putting the past behind us,' and 'forgiving those who have wronged her.' I just can't explain it all. I'm ashamed and embarrassed."

Understandable, but Pam Butte may have tried to murder her. Those emotions needed to be set aside. "Look, I'm not trying to tell you what to do, Jillian. But this looks like a death threat, and you never know... she may try again."

"Maybe she thought she was buying a different plant and all of this is true," she replied, tapping the note with her sneaker. "I mean, the little flowers are pretty. And who would know that a white snakeroot was poisonous unless they did their research?"

"Exactly," I whispered. I had very little doubt in my mind that Pam Butte hadn't dropped off the plant not as a show of goodwill. She was trying to kill her husband's lover.

"I'm going to suggest that you call the police," I reiterated. "If she sees you around town and this was meant to kill you, then you can be certain she's going to try again."

Jillian shook her head and leaned her head against the wall. Although I was pretty certain Pam had killed her husband, I still needed to figure out one piece of the puzzle. "You told us Butte worried about Harold Shumaker," I said. "But you didn't get a chance to tell us about him."

"Right. Gina thinks delivering puppies is the same as delivering a baby." She rolled her eyes as we both chuckled. "Harold's wife was a patient here. Butte was on duty. He volunteered a couple of times a week. Anyway, Harold's wife, Wanda, came in with an infected leg. It was bad. She said she'd cut it while gardening and thought maybe it came from a rusty nail in a planter. She hadn't done much with it—just poured some hydrogen peroxide on the wound and bandaged it up."

"She didn't come in right away to get a tetanus shot?"

"Nope." Jillian sighed. "I can't remember how long she'd gone before being seen, but that thing was nasty. We had to clean it, cut the skin around it... never mind. It was terrible."

"What happened with Butte?"

She pursed her lips together and crossed her arms over her chest. "She was allergic to penicillin. This was noted on the chart. She had the wristband in place indicating such."

"And he gave her penicillin for the infection?" I asked.

"Yes."

I sat back, unable to believe the blatant disregard for the protocols put in place.

"She went into anaphylactic shock and we were unable to revive her."

"When did this happen?" I asked.

"Maybe six months ago. In my opinion, Butte should've quit practicing about five years ago. That's when the mistakes started happening. I loved him, but he should've faded away into retirement and taken me with him. That's what I wanted."

"Did Harold Shumaker know what was done to his wife?"

She nodded. "Oh, yes. Butte tried to hide it, claiming she had a heart attack, but another one of the nurses here wasn't going to lie to Harold. She told him flat out."

And why hadn't this horrible neglect been reported to the Arizona Medical Board? Why hadn't Butte been formally charged by the police? Something wasn't adding up.

"Thanks for your time, Jillian," I said. Once again, I glanced at the white snakeroot. "Please call the police. I don't know Pam personally, but I've met her. I do think she's trying to kill you."

Jillian shook her head. "I just can't imagine it."

"Let the police handle it," I urged, squeezing her shoulder. Although, I didn't have much faith in them, at least it would be on record. If Jordan was working, I would phone him and have him come down and take a statement. Maybe I should mention it to Trevor, the deputy who was supposed to be feeding us information on the case—which he hadn't done.

Time to call a meeting and squeeze the information out of him.

"And Jillian?" I stood and slung my bag over my shoulder. "Make sure to lock your doors. Get some mace. And be careful. If I'm right and she realizes you're alive, you're in deep trouble."

CHAPTER 16

LATER THAT DAY, I was craving a glass of wine but decided I needed something a bit healthier. Then I recalled the juice I'd had at the Farmers Market and how delicious it had been. I needed to call that guy. Where had I put the card?

When my phone rang, I glanced at the screen. Jordan.

"Hey," I said. "What's up?"

"Trevor wants to meet tonight. Are you okay with that?"

"Sure. It's time. I feel like he's been radio silent."

"He kind of has," Jordan said. "Is meeting at your house okay?"

"Of course. What time?"

We agreed that after dark would be better.

"I'll see you then," I said. After hanging up the phone, I quickly glanced around the apartment and wondered where in the world I'd put that card. With a sigh, I headed next door to Never Quit Wining to pick up some chardonnay.

"Hey!" Adrienne greeted me. "How are you, Sam?"

"Pretty good," I lied, when a great thought struck. I should put together a liver cleanse tincture that Adrienne could sell along with the bottles of wine. A win-win for everyone.

I waited until the store had cleared, wondering if I'd truly had a good idea or if I was simply desperate.

As I watched the young woman smile and help her customers, I debated whether she and Wayne were killers. I'd never had children, but I'd always had the option. What if that had been taken away from me? I'd be furious. I'd always been too focused on my career and that time window had closed quickly without me even realizing it.

Yet, I'd had the choice. According to Wayne, that choice had been stolen from them by the accident. By Butte, the thief in the night. Both had been emotional when discussing it. But had that emotion transferred into murder?

Adrienne said she had spilled wine on Butte. Since they made their own, she could've easily poisoned a glass just for him. They'd mentioned how much he loved their merlot, so they could've hedged a bet that he'd be around to their booth at the Farmers Market.

Everywhere I turned, someone seemed to have a reason to want the man dead.

"What's up?" she said as the last customer walked out with a case of chardonnay.

"I wanted to get some wine," I said.

"Of course. The usual?"

"Yes. Thank you."

She hurried into the back room and returned a moment later, setting the bottle down on the counter. "One bottle?"

"Yes."

A strange tension grew between us that had never been present before as she rang up my purchase.

She flipped her red ponytail over her shoulder. "You know, I'm sorry I got so emotional when you were in here the other day."

Recalling our conversation, she'd stormed out of the back room with tears in her eyes. "There's no need to apologize, Adrienne. It was an upsetting subject."

"I hated that man," she said, shaking her head.

"A lot of us did."

"I always wanted to be a mother," she continued. "He killed my baby and robbed me from ever having another one."

381

Her pale skin reddened as she pursed her lips. There weren't any tears of sorrow, but instead, her gaze flashed with white-hot rage.

"I'm glad he's dead," she spat. "I hope he rots with Satan."

I nodded and fished out some cash. After setting it down on the counter, I said, "I don't blame you for feeling the way you do. However, I will tell you this: hate him all you want, but you'll need to release it eventually. It'll eat you up inside."

Her features softened. "That sounds like it comes from a place of knowledge."

"It does. You know my story, Adrienne. My dead husband burned my life to the ground. I was bitter for a long time, and even though I'm still dealing with the fallout, I've had to let the hatred go." Well, I'd tried, anyway. With my bank account frozen and my store closed, the fury raged pretty hot within me.

The door chimes sounded behind me, indicating someone had entered. I smiled and grabbed my bottle as she shoved my cash into the register. "I'll see you later," I said, then headed back to my store.

Jordan and Trevor would be arriving soon, and I wanted to make some notes on the suspects. Unfortunately, that also included Adrienne and Wayne. They had the motive, means, and opportunity.

WHILE I WAITED for the two men to arrive, I did some laundry and tried to ignore the emptiness of the building. I really missed having Doug around, even though he was as silent as a ghost. I *felt* his presence while he'd been living here, and I'd always found it comforting.

Jordan showed up first and let himself in through the back door. After I offered him a glass of wine, we both settled into the sofa with a long sigh. Trevor had insisted on arriving under the cover of darkness via the Riverwalk and into the back in case Mallory was watching him for any reason. I'd left it open and hoped he would show up soon because I was getting tired, even though I knew sleep wouldn't come easily. I was too wound up with stress.

When we heard the door open, Jordan and I jumped up from the couch. Trevor walked upstairs and smiled as he entered the apartment, then closed the door quietly behind him. "I feel like I'm doing something illegal by being here," he whispered.

"Well, you kind of are," Jordan replied, shaking his hand. "You're conspiring with the accused."

"I'm excited to hear what you guys have to say," Trevor said. "How's it going, Sam?"

Great. My business is tanking faster than the Titanic. I can't sleep. My stomach hurts. "I'm fine," I said. "Everything's fine."

Jordan rolled his eyes, then said, "Have a seat, Trevor."

Catnip had stretched out across the couch and refused to move when Trevor tried to sit down.

"Please don't be a jerk," I muttered as I scooped up the protesting feline. After I set him on the floor, he stalked to the bedroom, obviously quite offended I'd disturbed him.

"That cat has some attitude." Trevor said, chuckling.

"Tell me about it." I took a seat.

"What's Mallory saying about the case?" Jordan asked.

"Not going to waste any time, are you?" Trevor winked at me.

"Nope. We need the details," Jordan said. "So spill them."

"I'll get you a glass of wine if you want one," I offered.

"That would be great. Thanks."

Silence settled around us as I poured the wine in the kitchen, then joined the men once again and handed Trevor the glass.

"So, what have you got?" Jordan asked.

Trevor shook his head. "Why don't you tell me what you two have been up to? I'm tired, I've been talking all day and I'd just really like to listen for a bit, see if what you have lines up with what I know."

He ran a hand through his blond hair, took a sip of wine, leaned back against the cushions and shut his eyes. I traded glances with Jordan, then cleared my throat.

"There are a couple of people who really need to be looked at closer," I began. Trevor nodded, letting me know he was listening. "First is Pam Butte. She's a horrible woman, as is her daughter. Both of them hated the doctor, and there was an affair, as well as a large amount of money. Both stand to inherit from his death."

Trevor cracked an eye. "The daughter? How do you know that?"

"I saw them arguing in front of Butte's home," I replied. "The daughter showed up with a moving van, ready to clean out her inheritance from the house, whatever that was. She and her mother came to blows on the front lawn. The moving van driver called the police."

"She hit her mother?" Trevor said, sitting up. I now had his full attention, which led me to believe I was definitely feeding him new information. "I'll have to see who responded to the call and read the report."

"And her mother hit right back," I said. "She may be small and thin, but she's anything but frail. It was disturbing and fascinating to watch, all at once."

"Okay," he said. "Mallory had pretty much written off Pam because of her age."

"That's one mistake," I muttered. "How many more will we uncover before the night is through?"

"Who else is on your radar?" Trevor asked.

"Chris Raves for sure," Jordan replied.

I arched my eyebrow, surprised he was throwing a friend under the bus.

"What?" Jordan spread his arms wide. "Butte almost killed his wife. I'd think about going after the guy if the same thing happened to you, Sam."

I knew Jordan loved me, but to hear him be so protective gave me butterflies. You'd think in my mid-fifties I'd be over such nonsense.

"What happened to his wife?" Trevor asked.

"Exactly where have you been looking for other suspects?" Jordan asked. "Under a rock?"

"Just tell me about Raves' wife," Trevor grumbled.

"She had a stomachache and went to see Butte," I said. "He told her it was gas and didn't do any testing. Turns out it was her appendix, and she almost died."

"Again, that's a great motive, and he was the one who handed Butte the cracker," Jordan chimed in. "Motive, means and opportunity."

"Dang." Trevor bit on his bottom lip, his brows furrowed in thought. "Who else?"

"The two young people next door," Jordan said. I had to agree with him, even though guilt washed through me. He had been right in saying a case couldn't be solved by gut reactions.

"The folks who own the wine store?" Trevor asked incredulously.

I nodded. "They were in a car accident involving Butte. They lost the baby and she'll never be able to have kids."

Trevor winced. "Aw, man. I remember that accident. Butte acted like such a jerk. I knew she lost the baby, but I didn't know it made her infertile."

"The whole thing is absolutely tragic," I said. "But you may also want to look at Butte's girlfriend. Her name's Jillian, and she works at the emergency clinic."

"His girlfriend?!" Trevor exclaimed. "How come that old coot had a girlfriend and I can't even get anyone to have coffee with me?"

It was a good question, especially with his looks. Who didn't love a tall, blond guy with green eyes? I could easily see him on the big screen if he'd chosen to be an actor.

Jillian hadn't wanted the police to know about her affair and she'd never come across as a killer. But I was throwing possibilities at the wall to see what was going to stick. She was directly involved with the man, so she had to be considered.

"I also think Butte's wife is trying to kill her," I said, then explained about the plant. "It could be that she was sincere in her apology, but I wouldn't think so after what I saw between her and her daughter. I just don't believe it was an accident that she gave Jillian a poisonous plant and told her to eat it. Plus, she actually wrote in the note that the flowers taste good, which she couldn't ever have tasted or she'd be dead."

"Agreed," Jordan said. "If that was the case, it would be a huge coincidence, I don't believe in coincidences very often."

I told her to call the police about it," I said. "But I'm not sure if she ever did."

"Again, I'll check the reports," Trevor muttered. "If she did, the case wasn't assigned to me."

I didn't mention Harold Shumaker. I had nothing on the man and I didn't want to drag anyone into the investigation who didn't belong. Maybe once I had more evidence I'd tell Trevor about him.

"Well, once again I think Mallory's got this all wrong," Trevor said. "What do you think, Jordan?"

"I agree, one hundred percent. If I were you, I'd really press the wife. First, Butte cheated on her and she wanted a divorce. The assets would have to be split down the middle, but with him dead, she gets everything."

"Besides all that, she's just a horrible woman," I said. "I think that's your killer right there."

CHAPTER 17

THE NEXT MORNING, I folded my laundry and found the elusive business card I'd been searching for. Finally! The number for Berry Good. It had gone through the wash, but I could still make out the printed digits. I dialed and got a voicemail.

"You've reached Berry Good. Please leave a message with your order and your email address. Pick-up will be the following day if your order is placed before noon. Please listen for the menu and pricing after this message. Once the order is placed, I'll send an email with the address for pick-up. Thank you and have a good day."

Weird way to run a business. He should find a teenager to build him a website and make his life a whole lot easier. I listened to the menu, committed what I wanted to memory, then left the requested information. I set down my phone and went back to folding my laundry. Catnip meowed at me, so I opened the apartment door. When he didn't leave but continued to scream, I dropped the shirt I'd been folding and placed my hands on my hips. "You just ate," I said. "I watched you clean that bowl, Catnip. You aren't fooling me and I'm not feeding you again this morning."

He narrowed his gaze, then stalked out of the apartment.

I cursed under my breath and returned to my laundry. A moment later, the phone rang.

Annabelle.

"Hey!" I said, genuinely glad to hear from her. "How are you?"

"Sam!" she said. "We have, like, a big problem."

"What happened?" I asked. I wasn't sure I would be able to do anything to help, especially since I didn't have any money.

"The waterline to my house broke," she said. "The living room is like a swimming pool and we don't have anywhere to stay."

It took me a moment to realize what she was hedging at, but it finally registered. "Come live here!" I exclaimed. "Doug's apartment is open!" Giddiness caused goosebumps over my skin. I so wanted them to live with me!

"Oh, my gosh, Sam," Annabelle said in a relieved tone. "I was hoping you'd say that. This place is a mess. They've turned off the water. All my stuff is ruined. I feel like I need a life jacket or a boat to move from one end of the house to the other. The landlord said it's going to be weeks—maybe even months—before the house is livable again."

It sounded awful. From what Annabelle had described, she'd lost everything. Or at least it was all very waterlogged.

"You have a place to stay here," I said. "Do you want to come and get me so I can help you gather your stuff?"

"Aw. You're so sweet, but no. Like I said, almost everything is ruined. Thankfully, my signed Billy Idol album sits in a frame on my wall, and the water didn't get that high."

Yes, thankfully. I knew for a fact it was Annabelle's most prized possession.

"I can't say the same for my Billy Idol Christmas sweater though," she muttered. "It was in a box in the hall closet where I was storing it for the summer."

"Hopefully we can get it dried out and there's not too much damage," I said. The sweater was atrocious, unless one was a huge Billy Idol fan, as Annabelle was. The singer wore his famous sneer while donning a Santa hat. The thing had been hand-knitted by my former neighbor, Mrs. Mason, who had killed her husband. "Let me know if there's anything I can do and come on by when you're ready. I haven't been in Doug's apartment at all, so everything is just how you two left it."

There was a brief silence, then Annabelle said, "Sam? What's going on with the store?"

I sighed and closed my eyes. "Nothing. The same as before. I don't have any money to pay you, and I don't know if and when I will. My bank account is frozen and the sheriff has turned everyone against me by claiming I murdered Butte. No customers, no money." I shrugged, trying to not let it all upset me too much.

"What's going on with the murder investigation?" she asked. "I mean, once everyone knows you're innocent, they'll, like, beg for forgiveness and come back to the store, right?"

"I hope so, Annabelle," I sighed. "Come by when you're ready."

After hanging up, I set my phone down. It began ringing again almost immediately. Gina.

"What's up?" I greeted her.

"You should come bring me lunch. Make my day, and all that."

"I'm right in the middle of something," I said. "Annabelle is—"

"No, you should come bring me lunch. *Right. Now.*"

"Gina—"

"Perfect! A coffee and a sandwich sounds fantastic. If you can make it turkey and be here in twenty minutes, you'll be my best friend ever."

"And what happens if I'm more than twenty minutes?"

"You'll regret it," she whispered. "Trust me on this one."

"On my way," I replied. What was her deal?

I may not have any cash, but I went armed with a credit card and stopped at Cup of Go on my way to File It Away. The barista gave me a dirty look and whispered something to her co-worker, but I did my best to ignore them. Once I had Gina's sandwich and two coffees in hand, I went to the salon. For the record, I made it in fifteen minutes.

When I walked in, it took a moment for my eyes to adjust. Gina's dog, Daisy, ran over and jumped on my leg, whining with her tail going a thousand miles per hour. "It's nice to see you, too," I said, setting down my purchases by the cash register to free my hands so I could give her the attention she obviously craved.

Once she'd calmed down, I glanced up to find Gina. All three of her chairs were occupied and each person was in one stage or another of a pedicure.

"Hey," I said, walking over to her. "I brought you lunch."

"Great. Thank you. Have you ever met Molly Butte?" she asked, not meeting my gaze as she concentrated on the foot in front of her. The woman in the chair glanced up at me and gave me a quick wave. "Molly lives and works in Los Angeles," Gina continued. "I thought you two may have some friends in common."

Gina pushed her rollaway chair with her toe and moved on to the next client.

I realized she had called me under the guise of bringing her lunch so I'd have the chance to speak with Molly. Sneaky.

"I'm Sam Jones," I said, smiling. The resemblance to her mother was uncanny. "What do you do in Los Angeles?"

"I work for one of the big studios there in a production crew," she said. "You used to go by Samantha Rathbone, right?"

"Yes. Correct." My stomach coiled at the mention of the name. It was a life I no longer wanted, but I didn't seem to be able to untangle its talons from my back as I tried to run away from it.

"Yeah, I'm working with Bradley Bass right now," she said, rolling her eyes. "What a piece of garbage that guy is. Come sit with me while my toes dry."

"Let me grab a chair." As I walked across the room to where the dogs lay to fetch a seat, I smiled at Gina's cunning.

I brought the small stool over and took a seat next to Molly. Petite and blonde like her mom, she had an air of sadness around her.

"You don't look like a killer," she said, eyeing me. "And you seem nice."

"Thanks," I said. "I didn't kill your dad."

"I know," she sighed, looking at her pink toes and wiggling them.

Interesting. I'd been accused of murdering her father, and she didn't seem the least bit curious about the allegation. "You seem pretty sure of that," I hedged.

"I am," she said. "My mom did it."

Gina glanced over and met my gaze, but then reverted to her customer.

"And why do you think that?" I asked.

"Because both my parents are/were horrible people," she said, her voice calm with little inflection. "My dad was cheating on her, and she'd never put up with that. Heck she about busted a gasket when I got caught cheating at boarding school. She wouldn't accept it in her own home."

I was going to point out that cheating in school and cheating in a marriage were two very different things, but decided to allow her to keep talking instead.

"They sent me away to boarding school when I was six," she said. "That made it pretty clear they didn't want me. I don't care if he's dead, and I don't care if she goes to prison for it. In fact, I hope she does."

I cleared my throat, unsure of how to proceed with the conversation. I decided to be straightforward. If she thought her mother had been responsible for her father's death, I'd go along with it. "Have you shared your thoughts with the sheriff?"

"Oh, yes," she said. "That woman... what's her name? Mallory?"

I nodded. "Yes. Mallory Richards."

"She's dumber than a brainless frog, but I told her exactly what I thought."

Something wasn't adding up for me. This woman was ready to throw her mother to the wolves, so to speak. But what did she get out of it?

The satisfaction of her mother being in prison, but also a large inheritance.

What if Molly had killed her dad and was now setting up her mom to take the fall? But she also lived in Los Angeles, so if she was the killer, there'd be evidence of her leaving California before the murder—a plane ticket, or credit card receipts. Unless she paid cash to stay off the radar.

"When did you get in town?" I asked.

"The day after my dad was killed," she said. "Mommy dearest called me and told me about it. I was on the first plane."

"If you hate your parents so much, may I ask why you came so fast?"

She shrugged. "Obligation? I don't know. It's not the warm and fuzzies in my heart, though. I can tell you that. I spent a lot of years in therapy realizing that my parents would never be able to be the people I needed them to be while I was growing up."

We sat in silence for a moment as she continued to stare at her toes. "Maybe I should've gotten red," she mumbled. "Pink just seems so happy, and I'm not happy."

"That's too bad," I said gently, laying my hand on her arm.

"I never have been," she said softly. "But maybe now that he's dead and she's hopefully going to prison, I can get this monkey off my back."

Not sure what to say to this stranger who was opening up to me, I said, "I hope you find peace, Molly."

Her lips curved up slightly as she turned to me. "Enough about me. Do you want to hear the latest on Bradley Bass?"

Not really. "Sure."

"Well, his drinking has gotten way out of control," she said. "He was doing a scene for a Christmas movie... one of the ones for television, and he fell asleep while sitting on a couch during taping. Just conked right out."

"Were you working on the set when that happened?" I asked.

"Yeah. It was something else. He's such a loser."

I smiled in agreement but kept my mouth shut, not willing to add fuel to the fire.

"When do you think they'll arrest my mom?" Molly asked. "I need to get back to L.A. and I'd like to see her in cuffs."

The woman next to me had a heart so hard, I wondered if it could ever be softened. Her parents seemed to have done irreversible damage to her, and I found the whole situation very sad.

Unless she was setting up her mother to take the fall for the murder. Then she took the role of a cold, vindictive daughter with her sights on her inheritance.

And that was frightening.

CHAPTER 18

THE NEXT MORNING, I woke to a voicemail with the address of where I could pick up my juice. I did have to admit, with the store being closed and my regular duties coming to a halt, it was nice to sleep in—even if it did feel like a guilty pleasure.

Jordan's truck was on the fritz and he'd taken it to Tinkering on Trucks, so I called Gina and asked if she could drive me over.

"Did you find out anything about the murder from Molly yesterday?" she asked.

I frowned as I recalled the gloomy woman. "She's a very sad person, but I'm not sure if that's translated into being a killer or not."

"Yeah, she's got this black fog that seems to sit on her, doesn't she?"

"That's a really good way to describe it," I said, sipping my coffee.

"I feel sorry for her," Gina continued. "I can't imagine sending my son away to school for his whole life. I'd have missed out on so much. She must not have felt wanted while growing up. That would be a hard pill to swallow."

Having had that exact experience, I understood it was a painful thing to go through. My mother had been a drunk and we'd been living in poverty while Molly's mom had sent her away to some fancy school. It didn't really matter the status of a family. Irreparable damage could be done to a child whether there was money in the bank or not. It left a lot of baggage to carry.

For me, I had thrown myself into my work and never looked back. It seemed Molly had been weighed down by her past.

I heard a doorbell ring, then a cacophony of dogs barking. "Why don't the delivery services read my sign?" Gina muttered. "It says, *Don't ring the doorbell*, right there *next* to doorbell. It's so frustrating because these monsters won't shut up now."

They continued their chorus, and after a moment Gina yelled, "Shut up! He's gone! No one's coming into the house!"

A couple dogs tried to get in the last word and Gina swore under her breath.

When it was finally quiet, I asked, "Do you want to drive me to get some juice?"

"What? You need me to take you to the grocery store?"

"No. I have an address for Berry Good. I'm trying to cut my wine consumption, and his stuff I tasted at the Farmers Market was really good. I placed an order, and now I have to go pick it up."

"Sure. How about an hour from now?"

"That sounds good. Thanks a lot. I appreciate it."

After a quick shower, a snuggle with Catnip and two more cups of coffee, I hurried down the stairs when Gina texted me she was waiting.

I slipped into her car and was greeted with a kiss from Daisy, who met me from the backseat.

"Well, hello to you, too," I said, scratching her chin. "That's certainly a nice way to greet someone."

"She wouldn't get out of the car when I tried to leave her at home," Gina muttered. "Said she needed some fresh air."

I glanced at Gina out of the corner of my eye. Was my friend losing her mind, or was she just speaking about the dog in a very familiar way?

When she pulled away from the curb, Daisy stuck her head out the window and I watched her in the rearview mirror. With her tongue lolling out the side of her mouth and the wind pushing her ears back, she seemed like the happiest creature on the planet. A pang of jealousy railed through me. How wonderful to be so free, to not have a care in the world.

"What's the address?" Gina asked as we drove down Comfort Road. I gave it to her and she punched it into her phone while at a stop sign. "That's in old Heywood."

"Really?" I was surprised that I'd never heard of old Heywood in my time living there, but now I was venturing into the area twice in one week.

"Yep. I didn't know the Berry Good guy lived out there," she said.

"Me neither."

We drove in silence while old school rap sounded softly from the speakers. Naughty by Nature, if I wasn't mistaken.

As we meandered through the neighborhood, I realized things began to look quite familiar. We pulled up in front of a small brown house with white trim. The last time I'd been here, the grass and red rose bushes had been overgrown. Today, everything had been tidied up.

"Are you sure this is the right address?" I asked.

Gina studied her phone, then the house. "Yep. This is the place you wanted to go."

Annabelle and I had followed Pam Butte to this house and she'd given the owner an envelope. It seemed like they'd had a heated exchange.

"I wonder who lives here," I muttered, stepping out of the car. My heart thudded against my ribcage as I strode up the walkway, and then my hands began to shake. Why was I so nervous?

Danger.

If I knocked on that door, something horrible would happen.

Shaking my head, I took a deep breath and pressed the doorbell.

When it swung open, I immediately recognized the tall, thin man I'd met at the Farmers Market. "Hey, there," I greeted him in my friendliest voice, hoping my fear didn't bleed through. "My name's Sam Jones. I ordered some juice."

I stuck out my hand, hoping for an introduction. Instead, he waved me inside without a word.

As I stepped into the foyer, I glanced over my shoulder to make sure Gina was watching me. She was busy on her phone, but Daisy had her head sticking out the window and studied me intently.

"Wait here," he said gruffly.

He'd been friendlier at our first meeting.

I stood at the entry and glanced at the table. A stack of unopened mail sat there, so I studied the addressee. Harold Shumaker. Holy cow. I was standing in Harold Shumaker's house?

My heart continued to pound as sweat formed on my brow. I heard Harold in the kitchen, opening the refrigerator door. The sound of glass bumping glass tinkled through the air. After taking a few steps forward, I glanced into the tidy living room. There, on the mantle, sat an over-sized picture of Harold and who I could only assume was his dead wife. The photo stuck out, as if it didn't quite belong. It was definitely the focal point of the room.

My stomach coiled as I wiped my hands on my shorts. My internal radar screamed that I'd stumbled onto something big and important.

Okay, so how did all this play out?

Doctor Butte had killed Harold's wife by giving her penicillin for her leg infection and causing anaphylactic shock. I knew that as fact. Then... why had Pam Butte been at his house, handing him an envelope? And why hadn't he reported Butte to the Arizona Medical Board?

My mind spun, trying to come up with answers, but the pressure of time weighed so heavily, my mind blanked as he rounded the corner.

"Here you go," he said, handing me two bottles.

My breath caught in my throat and I became dizzy as I stared at them. At the Farmers Market he'd offered me a sample. I'd reached for the cherry mango and he'd pulled the tray away, saying that the other tray was fresher.

Butte had been right behind me.

"T-thank you," I stuttered.

What if Harold Shumaker murdered Butte as revenge for killing his wife?

But why had Pam Butte been here? And what had been in the envelope she'd handed him?

"Are you okay?" he asked. "You look a little pale."

"I'm fine," I said, smiling. "I'm excited to have some cherry mango."

"It's fresh. Just squeezed it yesterday after you left the message. Hope you enjoy it."

He stared at me a long moment and the urge to run almost overwhelmed me. Did he know I suspected him of murder? Did he feel the tension radiating off me? Was my face giving my fear and surprise away, or had I managed to settle my features into a calm mask? It certainly felt like the former. Why was he looking at me so intently?

"What?" I finally asked.

"Payment," he replied. "I'd like to be paid."

I made a sound that was supposed to be a laugh, but sounded more like I vomited in my mouth. After setting down the bottles on the table, I rummaged through my bag to find my wallet. I pulled out the bills and handed them to him.

"Thanks," he said before motioning me toward the door.

I picked up my purchase and hurried outside. I needed time to think things through. Perhaps I was so desperate to solve the case, I was seeing murder suspects where there weren't any. Harold Shumaker seemed like a grumpy man who made juice on the outside, but losing a beloved family member to incompetence... I assumed that could drastically change a person.

Bile rose in my throat while I raced to the car. Daisy barked as I slid in. "Go," I said. "Drive away. Now."

Gina side-eyed me but put the car in gear and pulled away. I glanced out the side mirror, half expecting the man to be standing in the street, pointing a shotgun at us.

When we rounded the corner, I released a ragged breath.

"What's going on?" Gina asked as Daisy whined and licked my cheek.

"I... I don't know," I said. "I just had this crazy theory about Butte's death."

"Well, don't keep us in suspense," Gina said. "Spill it."

I took a deep breath and fisted my hand in my lap. Was I out of my mind? "Harold Shumaker's wife was killed by Butte's incompetence," I said. "Butte was at his booth at the Farmers Market right after me. When I reached for a sample of the juice, Harold pulled the tray away from me, claiming that the other tray was fresher. What if that first tray had been poisoned?"

"And you think he served it to Butte?"

"Yes," I replied, my voice growing louder with excitement. "Then

Butte went to Too Hot To Handle, ate a cracker with hot sauce and the poison kicked in."

"And it looked like Chris did it," Gina said. "Or you, because you were there and you hated the doctor."

"I did hate him. He made my life miserable, but I'd never kill him."

Gina drove for a long moment in silence, her brow furrowed as she stared at the road. I did sound like I was losing my mind. The more I thought about it, the more ridiculous my theory was. Or was it? Had I almost consumed the poison that had killed Butte?

"I think you have something there," Gina said. "Most definitely." She yanked the steering wheel and pulled over to the side of the road, then turned to me. "We have to go back there."

"To Harold's house?"

"Yes. You have to confront him."

"I don't want to go back there by myself!"

"Call Jordan. Tell him to grab Trevor and meet us there. This has to be looked into because I think you're absolutely right."

I reached down between my legs and pulled up my bag, then fished out my phone. After dialing Jordan, I put it on speakerphone.

As I voiced my theory yet again, the certainty of being right settled into my bones. "Harold had a motive, the means, and the opportunity, Jordan," I said. "Why wouldn't he let me drink from that one tray of juice? The only reason is because it was poisoned."

"Or it wasn't as fresh as the other, just as he said," he countered. "Maybe it had been out in the heat longer." My nostrils flared as I ground my jaw in irritation. "But I think you're right," Jordan continued. "We don't have the proof, but it's a solid theory. Give me the address. I'll call Trevor and we'll meet you there."

I recited the number and street, then Jordan said, "And whatever you do, don't confront him by yourselves, Sam. If you're correct, he's a very dangerous man."

CHAPTER 19

GINA TURNED the car around and we drove back to Harold's house.

"Don't park directly in front of it," I said. "Park down there where we can still see the house, but it's not obvious we're watching it."

She did as instructed without a snarky comment, but when she burst into laughter, I glanced over at her. "What's so funny?"

"Daisy said it sounds like you've been watching too many cop shows."

I smiled and glanced back at the dog, who seemed to be grinning at me.

Gina maneuvered the car so we settled in up the tree-lined street a few houses away, but facing Harold's home. The woman shifted in her seat and crossed her arms over her chest.

"She *said* that, huh?" I questioned, now a little concerned about my friend. Sure, she'd always had a way with dogs and I'd mused that she could somehow communicate with them, but had I ever been really serious about the idea? No. Now she was claiming she heard this animal speaking, and not for the first time.

"Yes." Gina pushed some blonde strands behind her ear. "She *said* that. She's a talker and I'm tired of trying to hide it and pretend I don't hear it. I can talk to this dog."

Pursing my lips, I stared out the window at Harold's house. Did she need medical or psychiatric attention? It sure seemed like perhaps she needed both. "Can you speak with other dogs?" I ventured.

"Nope."

Okay, so there was only one canine she was conversing with. "And when did this happen, Gina? When did you decide you could have conversations with her?"

"When I rescued her. I hit my head against a tree, was knocked unconscious, and when I woke up, I could hear her speaking to me."

Daisy gave me another swipe of the tongue on my cheek, as if she were reinforcing what Gina had just shared.

My goodness. I'd have to convince Gina to get some medical help, but I wasn't sure how to broach the subject, especially when we were waiting for two police officers to show up so we could go question a potential murder suspect.

"I think we should talk about this later," I said. "You may want to—"

"Listen, Sam. If you're going to tell me I need to visit a shrink and need to see a doctor, I've already had that conversation with myself a hundred times. I can hear Daisy. We have conversations. After I hit my head, some screws came loose or some wires crossed. This is my life. Besides listening to her, I feel fine and everything is normal. I'm not seeing Bigfoot or spending my evenings on an alien ship. It's just this weird thing that's happened."

"People can't hear dogs speaking, Gina," I said. "You've always had a way with them, but maybe when you hit your head—"

"Is that Jordan and Trevor?" she asked, pointing at another vehicle pulling up in front of the house. It had parked the wrong way so the windshield faced us. We couldn't see the driver from the sun glaring off the glass.

I knew it wasn't Jordan's car, so I tried to recall what Trevor drove, but I didn't think I'd ever seen him outside a police cruiser. If I had, I didn't study the make and model of the car, and I was pretty sure he wouldn't drive a white Mercedes.

However, I knew who did.

"Is... is that Pam Butte?" I asked.

"No idea," Gina said, pushing her glasses up her nose. "I don't know what kind of car she drives."

"I think that's her," I replied. "She drives a Mercedes. What's she doing here? Delivering another envelope?"

"Again, I don't know, Sam. Can you please stop asking me these questions I don't have an answer to?"

"Sorry. Just wondering out loud."

I was going to question why Pam remained sitting in the car for so long, but just as I was about to voice my concerns, she exited the vehicle and marched up to the front door, her purple purse in hand, which matched her purple shirt. The way our car was situated placed her just out of our sight.

Once again I considered that perhaps Pam Butte and Harold Shumaker had worked together to kill her husband. The idea made perfect sense. Pam discovered her husband was cheating and went to one of the people she knew hated him. There had been many. Perhaps she even approached everyone she knew her husband had slighted or harmed and finally found a willing accomplice in Harold. They agreed to kill him and Pam would pay him to do it. Maybe she was delivering another installment?

As we waited for the woman to come back into view, I once again considered Gina's declaration of being able to hear Daisy.

"So you and the dog have outright conversations? You can talk to her about the weather? What she wants for breakfast?"

"Yes. She complains when it's cold but loves lying in the sun. I don't ask her what she wants for breakfast or I'd get a laundry list of stuff she shouldn't eat," Gina replied. A second later, she turned to Daisy. "No, I'm not making you chocolate chip pancakes." Shaking her head, she faced forward again. "Chocolate will kill you."

I glanced over my shoulder. "Chocolate chip pancakes, huh?"

Daisy wagged her tail and kissed me again.

As I was about to question Gina further, a loud popping sound rang through the air.

"Get down!" Gina yelled as Daisy began to bark.

I bent over, almost slamming my head into the dashboard. "What was that?" I whispered.

"Gunshots," she said. "Daisy get down on the floor!" Gina had laid herself over the center console. Her head rested near my back so I cranked my neck to meet her gaze.

Panic gripped my chest, causing me to struggle to breathe. "What?! Are you sure?"

"Oh, jeez, Sam! You've met my brother and father! Of course I know gunshots when I hear them! Now shut up unless you want to have holes put into you next!"

She had a point. I was indeed acquainted with her father and brother and at one time, I'd described them as the Corleones of Heywood. Not that they actually terrorized anyone or had bodies buried in their backyard that I knew of, but their vibe was very mafia-like. Vic, her brother, worked on a horse farm and had hit on me more than once. Gina had described him as a womanizer with a gift of making bad decisions. Her father was a sweet old man, but I always got the feeling his demeanor could flip if the wrong thing was said.

I shut my eyes for a moment, sending up a quick prayer that we wouldn't get shot. Breathing deeply, I hoped to avoid the anxiety attack I felt building.

"Do you think that's coming from Harold's house?" I asked.

"Shh! And yes!"

Oh, my word. Was Pam shooting Harold?

"Do you think we should drive away?" I whispered.

"No! Right now Pam doesn't know we're here. If she sees us driving away, she may start shooting at us, and I don't need any bullets in me."

I raised my head and peeked over the dashboard. Pam's car was still there.

"Get your dang head down!" Gina hissed, and I did as instructed.

We waited in silence for a long moment, then Gina slowly sat upright. "Stay right there," she muttered. "Don't move."

My heart thundered while my shoulders began to ache. My body was not meant to be bent forward for long periods of time. The blood rushed to my brain and I became a bit dizzy.

"Huh. That's weird. If I was going to shoot someone, I'd do it then leave. Why is she sticking around?" A few seconds passed, then Gina once again dove down. "I spoke too soon! She's coming out of the house!"

"Did she see you?" I asked.

"I hope not."

We waited for what seemed like an eternity. I kept glancing up at my passenger window, hoping I wouldn't find Pam with a gun pointed at us, ready to dispose of the witnesses.

Long moments passed. Neither of us dared to move. I twisted to look up at the window again. A figured appeared, and I screamed.

"What! What!" Gina yelled as Daisy began to bark.

My door opened, and I realized it was Jordan. "What are you two doing?" he asked.

Gina and I sat up and I pointed toward the house. "I think Harold may be dead!"

Jordan crouched down next to me. "Sam? Are you okay? What do you mean Harold's dead?"

"Pam was here," I said breathlessly. "We heard gunshots. Gina thinks it came from Harold's house."

Jordan grabbed my elbow, stood, and helped me from the car. My neck and back protested violently as my spine loudly snapped back into place.

Gina exited on her side. "Mercedes sure are quiet. I didn't even hear her drive off."

Trevor strolled up to the car, his brow furrowed in confusion. "What's going on here? Why were you two hiding?"

"They say shots were fired at the Shumaker house," Jordan replied. "The suspect is Pam Butte, who has now left the scene."

Trevor swore under his breath. "Let's go check it out, then I'll call it in. Heck, for all we know, one of these neighbors may have done so already. Gina, Sam, you two stay put."

The men walked across the tree-lined street as Gina and I exchanged glances. We then followed.

"Maybe they won't notice us," she whispered.

My heart thundered as we strode up the walk. The red roses I once admired now seemed to be an omen of what we would find. My hands began to tremble.

Jordan swore when the open front door came into view. I glanced around him to see Harold lying in a pool of blood.

CHAPTER 20

THE LAST THING I wanted to do was hang around to give Sheriff Mallory a statement. My stomach still twisted and turned from seeing Harold dead and I wanted to go home. Yet, having witnessed a murder, I had no choice but to stay. While we waited for her to show, Trevor secured the scene and began asking us questions. We recapped everything we'd seen during the day, and I shared my theory on Harold and Pam working together to kill Doctor Butte.

Once Trevor heard that, he hurried inside. How I'd have loved to go through Harold's things. I imagined finding a contract or some letter that would incriminate both him and Pam. The case would be solved, Jordan and I would be in the clear, and maybe the townspeople would get over their fear and dislike of me and shop at my store again. Although I did feel the killers did Heywood a service by disposing of Butte and should be considered for hero status, I'd keep that thought to myself.

My phone rang, but I didn't answer. I didn't even look to see who was calling. I was too happy to be in one piece and not full of bullets. Whoever was on the other end of my phone would have to wait.

Instead, I tilted my head up to the summer sun as Gina, Daisy, and I sat on the curb in front of Harold's house while Jordan chatted with the medics who'd arrived. Daisy sniffed around at the end of her leash, seemingly oblivious to being in the middle of a murder investigation. I longed to ask Gina about Daisy's thoughts on this morning's happenings but decided not to indulge in her fantasies of speaking to dogs.

I had a feeling this whole case was finally over. I'd been wrong about Chris Raves, and I felt horrible I'd even considered my friend Sally as the killer. Jillian, Butte's mistress, had nothing to do with Butte dying, but Harold and Pam did. All the pieces just needed to fit together and the evidence had to line up, but I felt confident we'd solved the case.

I didn't know how long passed before Trevor came out again. He knelt before Gina and me. "I found some of Harold's bank statements," he said, holding up a fistful of papers. "Six months ago, he began receiving large monthly payments. I checked with the bank, and they were from the Buttes."

"Pam was giving Harold money six months in advance to kill her husband?" I asked, my self-assuredness slowly fading. Okay, maybe the case wasn't solved, dang it.

"That doesn't make any sense," Gina said. "Why would a killer do a payment plan?"

Trevor shrugged. "In my experience with bad people doing bad things, there aren't any payment plans involved. It's money upfront, or the job doesn't get done. At minimum, it's half at the beginning and half after the contract has been completed. But you're right. I've never seen an agreement like this. It feels too... too clean. It's not a murder contract."

He was right. With an irritated sigh, I realized I hadn't figured everything out. "Why would Pam pay Harold for six months and then kill him?" I asked. I didn't really expect an answer... well, a right one, anyway.

Trevor shrugged. "Maybe she got tired of dishing out the money."

I shook my head. "I don't know. Something isn't adding up the way it's supposed to."

"Agreed," Trevor said, standing. "But if you figure it out, let me know."

As he walked back into the house, Gina turned to me. "What if we're looking at this wrong?"

"Well, we obviously are," I huffed.

Gina pursed her lips while stroking Daisy's head. "What if the payments weren't for something that was going to happen in the future, but something that had *already* happened? What if there was an event six months ago that caused the Buttes to start giving Harold money?"

I stared at the street for a long moment, thinking about everything I knew to be true.

Then it hit me like a fist to the face. "Harold's wife died six months ago," I whispered. "Butte gave her penicillin when he shouldn't have."

"Was the money a payoff?" Gina asked. "But for what?"

"For not turning Butte in to the Arizona Medical Board," I said, shooting to my feet. I began to pace back and forth in front of her and the dog, who were both staring up at me expectantly. "That has to be it. Butte bought off Harold and paid him monthly."

"Okay, but then who killed Butte?" she asked.

I tried to put myself in Harold's position. "Maybe he thought the money would lessen the pain of losing his wife and he was getting Butte where it hurt—in the checkbook."

"Then Harold didn't kill Butte," Gina said. "Why stop the gravy train?"

I recalled the oversized picture of him and his wife in his living room, sitting on the mantle. "Guilt," I replied. "The money didn't make him feel better, so he hoped murder would."

That had to be it. Harold hadn't filed a report with the Arizona Medical Board. Instead, he'd taken the hush money. But it hadn't dissolved his pain, so he'd killed the doctor.

"Butte never would've visited his booth that day if there wasn't some type of agreement in place between the two men," I mused. "He felt safe seeing the husband of the woman he killed."

"If that's true, then Butte was an arrogant, narcissistic, low-down pr—"

"Exactly. And you're right."

I recalled the Farmers Market. As I was leaving the Berry Good booth, Butte had come up beside me. I'd wondered if he was trailing me on purpose to annoy me or if he'd been following the foot traffic.

"Harold had planned to see him that day," I said. "*Everyone* was at the market. All he had to do was keep the poisoned juice away from the rest and serve it to Butte when he came by."

"What do you think he poisoned it with?" Gina asked.

I shrugged. "I have no idea. I'm assuming the toxicology report will tell us. We should ask Trevor if they've received it back yet or not. Since he hasn't mentioned it, my guess is no."

Glancing around the front yard, a thought occurred to me. The roses, the well-kept lawn... what did the backyard look like? My guess was we would find it very tidy and blooming with flora, or if he hadn't gotten around to cleaning up, something resembling a jungle. "Let's take a quick walk," I suggested. "Before Mallory gets here and chains me to a tree or something."

Gina snorted and stood. "Where are we going?"

"The backyard." I took a quick glimpse at the emergency personnel. Everyone seemed to be preoccupied. "Let's go."

We hurried around the side of the house and slipped through the gate.

I'd been right.

Roses, lilac bushes, and the last remaining tulips of the year sat in brick planters lining the fence. A perfect swath of deep green lawn covered the rest of the yard.

One planter was filled with herbs, and I recognized the small white chamomile flowers. Before we ventured in further, I glanced at the back of the house. I guessed the sliding glass door would lead into the kitchen and dining room area, but the shades had been pulled. The chances of Trevor or any other deputy inside seeing us was slim.

"Come on," I whispered, urging Gina forward. "If we get caught back here, we'll just tell them we're looking at the pretty plants."

"That's not a total lie," Gina muttered. "This yard is gorgeous. If I didn't have dogs, I'd attempt to do something like this."

As we slowly walked the perimeter, I admired the beautiful vegetation. Harold put in a lot of time and effort to keep his plants happy and healthy.

"My brother, Vic, grows weed," Gina continued. "His plants are really healthy, but he could probably learn a thing or two from Harold."

"If Harold wasn't dead," I reminded her.

"Right. Of course. Yes, Daisy. I know that was a stupid thing to say."

I looked more closely at the vegetation and ignored Gina's conversation with the dog. "Good thing marijuana is legal in this state," I said.

"Oh, you know Vic," she said. "He doesn't think troublesome things like laws apply to him."

In the corner of the yard, one particular plant caught my eye. It was on the small side with little purple flowers and purple berries. I bent down in front of it and pulled out my phone, noting that all the phone calls I'd ignored were from my attorney, Colin. I'd have to get back to him later.

I snapped a picture of the bush and used my plant identifying app, although I was certain of what I was looking at: deadly nightshade.

My phone confirmed my suspicions. I stood and looked at Gina. "I bet this is what killed Butte. He ground up the berries and put them in the juice. It took a few moments for it to settle in his system, but then it killed him."

"Just as he ate the cracker Chris Raves gave him," Gina sighed, shaking her head. "I really thought he did it."

"Yes, he was on my radar as well."

We stared at the deadly plant for a long moment, then I said, "We need to tell Trevor about this. All they have to do is match the toxicology reports and it's a closed case. We've got motive, means, and opportunity."

"That's all well and good," Gina said. "But why did Pam kill Harold?"

Right. Butte's killer was lying in his entryway in a pool of blood. "Let's go find out."

"You want to go to the Butte house and ring the doorbell?" Gina asked incredulously. "Did you forget she just blew out Harold's brains?"

"We aren't blackmailing her, though," I said. "We're just showing up at her house for a chat. We look pretty harmless."

"That's the dumbest thing you've ever suggested, Sam. And you've said some pretty stupid things in the time I've known you." She sighed and glanced around again as if searching for a valid reason as to why we should stay put at Harold's house. "Don't you think we should wait for Mallory like we said we would?" Gina asked.

I looked at her and arched an eyebrow.

"You're right," she muttered. "Let's go now. Everyone seems so busy, we can probably just walk away and no one would notice."

Hmm... if my calculations were correct, the Butte house would be quite the walk. Doable, but it would take a while.

"How far do you think it is to Pam's house?" I asked. "I don't think we should get in your car and drive away."

"No, that would call attention to ourselves," she said, handing me Daisy's leash and pulling out her phone. "But I have an idea."

CHAPTER 21

AFTER GINA FINISHED her phone call, she led me over to the back wall. She reached up and grabbed the edge, then pulled herself up to peek over.

"It's clear," she announced, falling back down to the ground.

"I'm impressed," I said. "I didn't realize you were so strong."

She rolled her eyes and pointed at the wall. "This is your dumb idea, so get up there and over. The other yard doesn't have a dog and it doesn't look like anyone's home. We'll cut through there to the street where Annabelle will pick us up."

I glanced at the wall and shook my head. "I can't get up there, Gina. Not by myself."

She cursed under her breath, then leaned over and made a stirrup with her hand. "Let's go."

With a long sigh, I placed my foot in her hand and reached for the ledge. She shoved me up so hard, I almost toppled over to the other side. I sat with one leg dangling in each yard.

"Take the dog," she ordered, lifting Daisy into my arms.

As I held the canine, I wondered how in the world I'd get down to the other side. I didn't think my knees could take the jump.

The next thing I knew, Gina was crawling up the wall, then straddled it, facing me.

"I'm going to jump down, then hand me Daisy," she said.

As she sprung off the wall, I admired her agility. She turned and reached up, and I gently placed the dog into her hands. All that was left to do was figure out how to get my uncoordinated butt back to the ground.

"Come on, Sam," she urged. "Annabelle will be here soon."

I lay down and brought my leg around so all I had to do was slide down the wall.

"You're going to regret that," Gina said.

And she was right.

The concrete scratched my stomach and arms. When I hit the ground, I fell backward, landing on my butt and hands.

"That was super graceful." Gina chuckled. "Now get up and let's get out of here before I come to my senses and decide to stay and wait for Mallory."

I stood and as I followed her, I studied my arms. Little tracks of blood began to rise on my forearms.

"Does it hurt?" she asked, glancing over her shoulder.

"Not yet."

She set down Daisy. "Let's go. Annabelle should be here shortly."

The yard wasn't nearly as nice as Harold's but I was thankful no dogs or humans came running from the house wondering why we were on their property.

We slipped out the back gate, then walked to the front of the house. A moment later, Annabelle whipped around the corner and came to a screeching halt in front of us.

"What are we doing?" she asked. Gina and Daisy took the back seat, while I slid into the front. "And what happened to your arms, Sam?"

As she pulled away from the curb, I said, "We're going to the Butte house and I'm not built for climbing cement block walls."

Annabelle giggled. "I could've told you that."

I ignored her, as well as the burning sensations that had started from the scrapes. "Do you have a tissue so I can clean up some of this blood?"

"In the middle console," Annabelle replied.

As we drove, Gina gave her the full rundown, including the gunshots we'd heard and how we'd witnessed Pam driving away from Harold's house.

"You guys have had, like, a super dangerous afternoon!" she said, shaking her head. "That's just nuts!"

"Tell me about it," I muttered as I dabbed at my arms. I assumed my stomach looked similar.

"Are we sure that we should be going to the Butte house if Pam killed Harold?" Annabelle asked.

"We shouldn't," Gina said. "We're doing dumb stuff today, Annabelle."

Annabelle nodded and stepped on the gas. "Got it. So what's the play at the Butte house? Shouldn't the police be questioning her?"

"Yes, but here we are," Gina said. "We're just digging around a little, trying to find the truth."

We were going to a murderer's home, which was dangerous and bordered right on stupid. Now that I'd given it some thought, it would've been better to let the police handle it. But as we pulled in front of the Butte home, curiosity got the best of me. Was I right in assuming that Butte had paid off Harold? I sent Jordan a quick text to let him know what we were up to.

I slid from the car and walked up the path. Gina followed at my flank. Glancing behind me, I noted Annabelle with Daisy sitting on her lap with the window down, both of them staring at us.

After knocking on the door, I waited. The sound of footsteps on the tile became louder, and the door opened.

"Can I help you?" Pam Butte asked.

I narrowed my gaze. "Do you remember me?"

She stared at me a long moment, then her eyes widened. "Why, yes! Of course. The one who owns the silly plant shop and killed my husband."

The urge to punch her in the face for the "silly plant shop" comment almost overwhelmed me, but instead, I lifted my chin and sucked in my stomach. For some reason that always made me feel taller and stronger. "I think we both know I didn't kill your husband."

Confusion flickered across her face. "Why would I think that?"

I took a deep breath. *Here goes nothing.* "Because I know that Harold killed Garrett. You and your husband were paying him off because the good doctor killed his wife. Hush money, if you will."

There it was—guilt and surprise passed through her gaze before she set her features neutrally. "I have no idea what you're talking about."

"Sure you do," I said. "I've seen you deliver a payment to Harold and today, we watched you gun him down in cold blood. Tired of buying his silence, Pam?"

"You're out of your mind," she said, chuckling. "I didn't kill anyone."

I noticed how she didn't deny the payments.

"So you *were* paying Harold so he wouldn't turn Butte in to the Medical Board?" Gina asked.

"And then what?" I continued. "You shot him because you realized he was the killer?"

"Why would Harold kill my husband?" Pam asked. "That's absurd."

"Because he felt guilty for accepting your bribes," I replied. "The money didn't help reconcile his wife's death, so maybe murder would."

"And you found out what he'd done to your husband and killed him today," Gina said.

"Today? No, I've been home all day, my dear. I have no reason to kill Harold." With a smirk, she crossed her arms over her chest. "I suggest you remove yourself from my property now."

"We know you and your husband were paying Harold," Gina continued. "The cops know it, too. The game's up, lady."

I glanced behind me at the white Mercedes parked in the driveway. Had the car I'd seen earlier been a Mercedes? Absolutely. Even Gina had mentioned how quiet it had been when the killer drove away.

But Mrs. Butte seemed to be telling the truth. So if it wasn't Pam that we'd seen at Harold's house, who was it? Who had killed him?

I turned to face Pam again and took in her yellow shirt. Of course, she could've come home and changed after killing Harold.

But then her daughter came into view behind her... wearing a purple shirt. The two looked so much alike, was it possible that Molly had driven her mother's car to kill Harold? And why?

"You did it," I whispered, my gaze locking with Molly's. "You killed Harold."

Sirens sounded in the distance as Pam gasped and looked over her shoulder at her daughter. Molly ran toward the back of the house and disappeared from sight. Gina pushed past Pam and began sprinting after her.

"What is going on?!" Pam yelled. "What do you mean she killed Harold?!"

I hurried past Pam and heard barking behind me. Daisy flew by in hot pursuit of Gina while Annabelle brought up the rear, screaming for Daisy.

I followed the dog and Gina's voice as she yelled at Molly. From the foyer we ran into a living room, then through a dining room where I found a purple purse hanging on the side of a dining room chair, and out the back door. When I glanced around the backyard, I found Gina launching herself through the air and tackling Molly to the grass. Impressive. The two rolled around for a moment, Gina throwing a few punches. Then Daisy grabbed a mouthful of Molly's hair and growled as she pulled.

Molly finally gave up the struggle and Gina straddled her back while digging her knees into the woman's forearms.

I ran over and threw myself over Molly's legs. Gina seemed to have everything under control, but I wanted to be somewhat helpful as I wasn't as educated in the art of fighting as Gina seemed to be.

"Nice tackle," I huffed.

"Thanks. Those are the skills you learn when you have an older brother."

Jordan and Trevor showed up seconds later with Pam not far behind. Molly struggled when Trevor pulled her to her feet and cuffed her while Jordan helped me stand.

"What the heck is going on here?" he asked.

"She killed Harold," I said, my breath heaving. "We didn't see Pam today at his house. We saw Molly."

"How can you be sure?" Trevor asked.

"The shirt," I replied. "The woman we saw walk up to Harold's had a purple shirt on with a matching purse."

Everyone turned to stare at Molly.

"What have you done?" Pam yelled. "Did you kill Harold?"

Molly smirked then nodded. "Yep. I found out you and Dad had been paying him off since Daddy dearest killed his wife."

"Why would you do that?" Pam whispered, her face falling in horror. "You monster!"

"Oh, relax, you old hag," Molly spat. "If these two hadn't interfered, you would have been next. Then, the whole inheritance would've been mine."

"T-the gun is probably in her purse," I stammered. Molly had come across as a hurt woman, and she most likely was. But the pain had turned into anger. Madness, even. "When your dad was killed and you realized you'd be getting part of the inheritance, you started digging around trying to find out what was yours. Then you came across something that showed the payments to Harold."

She sneered at me.

"And you decided to get rid of Harold so that in the end, there'd be more for you," Gina said. "Knock off Harold and your mom, play the part of the poor, victimized child, and you walk away with a boatload of cash." Gina glanced over her shoulder at the huge house. "Maybe even tell the cops you killed your mom in self-defense because she murdered Harold. After all, she was a terrible mother."

"I never would've killed anyone!" Pam shouted.

"It's actually not that far of a stretch to imagine it," Gina said, then pursed her lips together as if she realized she'd just voiced her thoughts out loud. Not that I disagreed. Pam Butte was as horrible as her husband, and it was easy to see how they'd produced Molly.

"How dare you!" Pam yelled. "How dare you say such awful things about me!"

As the woman fell to her knees and began to sob, I almost felt sorry for her.

Almost.

She'd been willing to have me go to prison for her husband's murder. It was hard to find empathy.

My phone rang, and this time I pulled it out.

Colin again.

I walked away from the scene of the crying mother and the daughter screaming obscenities at her while Gina, Jordan, and Trevor all looked on.

Now, it was truly over. Jordan and I were in the clear and wouldn't be going to prison for murder.

Phew.

"Hey, Colin," I said. "I'm sorry I've missed your calls. What's up?"

As I listened to him talk, my knees weakened. I ended up wobbling over to a bench in the yard where I sat down.

I couldn't speak.

When he finally finished what he had to say, I nodded, then ended the call and sat the phone down next to me.

"Sam, you okay?" Jordan shouted.

I nodded, then burst into tears.

EPILOGUE

~Gina~

As I STOOD in Sage Advice getting ready to say goodbye to Sam and Jordan, I had to admit, I held back a few tears.

That phone call Sam had received the day we'd solved Doctor Butte's murder? It was her accountant telling her that not only had the bank unfrozen her checking account, but he'd also retrieved a truckload of money that she'd earned on *As The Years Turn*. And when I say a truckload, I'm telling you that Sam will never have to work another day in her life.

She could've closed up Sage Advice for good and moved to some mansion with a full staff and fancy cars. Instead, she decided to turn over Sage Advice to Annabelle and Doug. With Jordan retiring from the police force, they'd decided to take a nice, long vacation. Something about lounging on a beach in Greece and hiking the Himalayan mountains. I was thrilled for her but dang it, I was terrible at goodbyes. I hated showing my emotions, but between Sam leaving and me just dropping off my son at college a few days ago, it was difficult to keep them in check.

I felt pretty lonely.

"When will you be back?" Annabelle asked. She had no trouble with emotions. The tears tracked down her cheeks, her mascara in long black lines down her face. Not the best look for her.

"Probably a month or so," Sam said, taking her friend into an embrace. "I promise to call often though, okay?"

Annabelle nodded and stepped away. "Please do. I'll, like, miss you so much."

Sam smiled and squeezed her shoulders. "Do all the updates to the building you think are necessary, and keep Sage Advice going for me, okay?"

Then she turned to me.

Have I mentioned how much I hate goodbyes?

My throat closed up as Sam approached. "Take care of yourself, Gina," she whispered, wrapping her arms around me.

I nodded, unable to respond. When I couldn't take it anymore, I pulled away and didn't meet her gaze. "I better get going," I said. "Send me a postcard or something. Do people still do that? Send postcards. If they have them, send one."

I then turned and hurried out the front door. Once inside my car, the dam broke and sobs wracked my body. I should be happy my son was spreading his wings, that he was well-adjusted and had gotten a great scholarship to the university. And I was, but it felt like a piece of my heart had been carved from my body.

And now I had to say goodbye to my friend, and I didn't know when I would see her again as she jaunted all over the world. She said she'd only be gone a month, but who knew? What if she decided to never come back?

After taking a deep breath, I glanced at the back seat. My dog, Daisy, had been uncharacteristically quiet and for a second I worried I'd lost my ability to communicate with her.

"I'm sorry you're so sad," she said, her voice soft and childlike. "I don't like it when you're sad, Gina."

"Me neither," I grumbled. I flipped on my blinker and pulled onto Comfort Road. "But I'm done with the tears. No more. I hate crying."

Daisy remained quiet until my phone rang. "Who is it?" she asked excitedly. "Who is it?"

At the stop sign, I glanced at the screen. My brother, Vic. I wasn't in the mood to talk to the trouble causer, so I let the call go to voicemail.

He phoned again.

With a curse, I pulled over and answered it. "What?"

I loved my brother, but we weren't on the best of terms.

"Gina, I need your help. I'm in trouble."

"What's new?"

He sighed. "This is serious. If I had someone else to call, I would have."

"What happened, Vic?" I asked, my patience gone. I didn't have the mental capacity to deal with him or his self-inflicted issues. "Did you get another drunk and disorderly? Busted someone's jaw in a bar fight? Crashed your motorcycle again? If you're in jail, I'm not bailing you out."

"I'm not in jail. Yet. Remember Phoebe?"

The name rang a distant bell, but then I recalled they used to date. "What about her?"

"She's dead," he grumbled. "And the cops think I killed her."

"Well, did you?" I spat. Frankly, it wouldn't have surprised me.

The line went silent so long, I thought he'd hung up. But then he said, "Gina, I may be a lot of things, and I may do some questionable stuff, but I'm not a killer."

The part of me that knew my brother so well came alive. Yes, he'd been in bar fights, he'd been arrested for drunk and disorderly conduct, and he'd crashed his motorcycle more than once. But he'd never kill anyone.

"Will you help me?" he asked.

"Where are you?"

"At the ranch."

I slammed my hand against the steering wheel and cursed. Daisy barked and began to whine. I didn't want to be involved in any of Vic's drama. Instead, I wanted to go home, cuddle my rescue dogs for a while, and try to forget my loneliness and the feeling that everyone was leaving me.

But, he was my brother and overall, he'd been so good to me. He just didn't treat himself very well. And, maybe a distraction from my own life was just what I needed. "Fine, Vic. I'm on my way."

If you'd like to read more stories taking place in Heywood with Gina and her talking dog, Daisy, then please check out the first book Heywood Hounds Cozy Mysteries, Dog Treats and Death.

ALSO BY CARLY WINTER

The Heywood Hounds Cozy Mysteries

(Small town, talking dog, cozy mysteries)

Gina Dunner and her rescue mutt, Daisy,—a sweet, yet sassy, talking dog—
start sniffing around into murder investigations.

As an amateur sleuth poking her nose where it doesn't belong, what could
possibly go wrong?

The Heywood Herbalist Cozy Mysteries

(Small town contemporary cozies)

From Hollywood, California, to Heywood, Arizona, trouble follows her...

After her husband's brutal killing and her fall from the Hollywood elite, the
disgraced Samantha Rathbone moves to Heywood, Arizona, hoping to forget
her past and live a quiet life of anonymity.

It doesn't go as planned.

Sedona Spirt Mysteries

(Paranormal cozies)

Bernie and the ghost of her dead grandmother find themselves in the middle of
various murder investigations. Danger and hilarity ensues as the crazy duo
follow the clues to discover the killers.

The Tri-Town Murders

(Small town contemporary cozies)

Complete Series

Follow newspaper reporter Tilly and her group of fun, quirky friends as they
solve murders in a fictional, small town in California.

Killer Skies Mysteries

Set in 1965, join Patty Briggs, stewardess extraordinaire, as she flies the skies and solves murders with the help of her friends... and one cute FBI agent!

ABOUT THE AUTHOR

USA Today bestselling author Carly Winter writes fun, small town cozy mysteries, always with a dash of humor and quirky characters. When not writing, you can find her spending time with her family, on a Pilates reformer or enjoying the fantastic Arizona weather (except summer - she doesn't like summer). She does like dogs, wine and chocolate and wishes Christmas happened twice a year.

For more information on her books, please visit: CarlyWinterCozyMysteries.com

Milton Keynes UK
Ingram Content Group UK Ltd.
UKHW040839251023
431306UK00001B/97